Praise for *The Wo*

-- "... a quest of Homeric dim̲ ̲ ̲ ̲ ̲ ̲
a historic saga that gets into the details of wilderness survival and indigenous cultures of centuries gone by, you'll find *The Wolf and The Willow* a riveting reading experience."

Praise for *Windigo Moon*:
The Sequel to *The Wolf and The Willow*

-- "A simply brilliant work of historical fiction"
-- Midwest Book Review

-- First Prize Winner: Cascade Writers Group, 2014 Grand Rapids ArtPrize Competition for the first chapter, "The Raid"

-- Gold Medal, "Best Regional Fiction, Great Lakes Region"
-- Independent Publisher Magazine

-- Honorable Mention, "Best Historical Fiction"
-- Foreword Reviews INDY Books of the Year

-- "We truly enjoyed this beautiful historical novel about the Ojibwa Indians. Essentially a love story, the characters are well-drawn and the landscape lives and breathes. Don't miss this one!"
-- W. Michael Gear and Kathleen O'Neal Gear, *New York Times* bestselling authors of *Moon Hunt*.

-- "Robert Downes's *Windigo Moon* is one of the best novels I've read in a long time." -- Tyler Tichelaar, *Marquette Monthly*

-- "Intricately researched, tightly woven, and vividly imagined, *Windigo Moon* should be on any must-read list."
-- Glen Young, *Petoskey News-Review*

The Wolf
and
The Willow

ROBERT DOWNES

The Wandering

PRESS

TRAVERSE CITY, MI

Published by
The Wandering Press
Traverse City, Michigan

Library of Congress Control Number: Pending

ISBN 978-0-9904670-4-5

The Wolf and The Willow is available at a discount
when purchased in bulk for educational or fundraising use,
or by organizations.

www.robertdownes.com

Cover: Indian Canoe - oil on canvas, circa 1886, Albert Bierstadt

For Jim Moore
my partner in song

Also by Robert Downes:

Planet Backpacker
Biking Northern Michigan
I Promised You Adventure
Windigo Moon: A Novel of Native America
Bicycle Hobo
Sandy Bottom

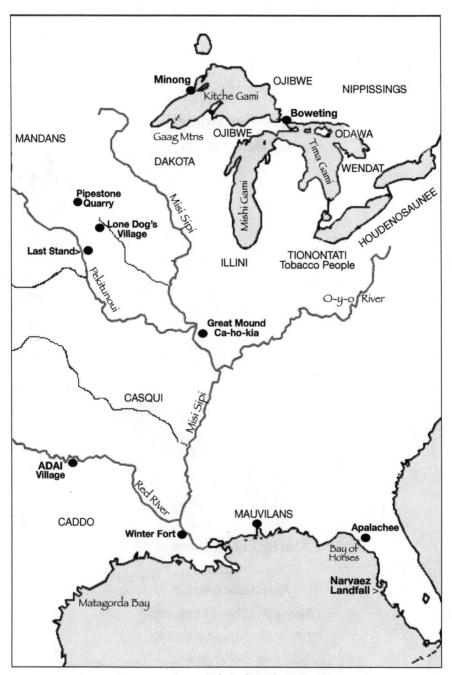

Great Turtle Island - 1528

MANDANS

OJIBWE

NIPPISSINGS

Minong

Kitche Gami

Boweting

ODAWA

Gaag Mtns

OJIBWE

Tima Gami

WENDAT

DAKOTA

Pipestone
Quarry

Lone Dog's
Village

Misi Sipi

Mishi Gami

HOUDENOSAUNEE

Last Stand>

Pekitunoui

TIONONTATI
Tobacco People

ILLINI

O-y-o River

Great Mound
Ca-ho-kia

CASQUI

Misi Sipi

ADAI
Village

Red River

MAUVILANS

Apalachee

CADDO

Winter Fort

Bay of
Horses

Narvaez
Landfall >

Matagorda Bay

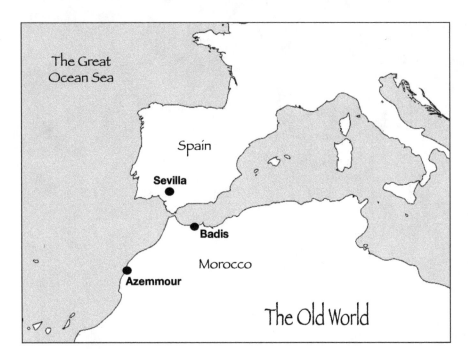

The Great
Ocean Sea

Spain

Sevilla

Badis

Azemmour

Morocco

The Old World

A few words...

Anishinaabemowin: the language of the Anishinaabek.
Ehn: yes, masculine gender
Eya: yes, feminine gender. Also a way of saying, "thus," "and so", etc.
Gaawiin: no
Giimaabi: spy
Kitchi Manito: Great Spirit, the Master of Life
Miigwech: thank you

Places:
Kitchi Gami: Great Lake - Lake Superior
Mishi Gami: Big Lake - Lake Michigan
Tima Gami: Deep Lake - Lake Huron
Misi Sipi: Mississippi River
Pekitunoui: Missouri River

Tribes, then & now:
Adai: a subtribe of the Caddo people
Anishinaabek: The True People, Original People of the Ojibwe, Odawa
and Potawatomi peoples.
Houdenosaunee: Later known as the Iroquoi confederacy
Wendat: Later known as the Huron

"I am here, then I am gone,
        Only the earth and sky
        last forever.
        Now I join them,
        Mother, father,
        Now I join them.
        Now I live forever."

Princess of the Goats

The Coast of Morocco
Spring, 1527

T he girl awoke with dawn's first rooster, shivering beneath her blanket of coarse brown wool. The stone floor was cold beneath her, but as always, she was slow to rise. Trembling, she waited for the bird to crow again, knowing it was old Jahir, the lord of the roost, whose guttural call could wake the dead.

Willow groaned and wrapped her blanket tighter against the desert chill. The brick hearth next to her pallet had gone cold and she feared that its coals had died in the night. It was her job to tend the fire and the cook would be angry, more so the master, if he didn't get his morning tea. And yet, who could rise on a morning as cold as this? The desert, which was so warm by day, had fingers of ice when the sun went down.

Across the gnarled bricks of the kitchen floor, a pair of doves cooed and rustled in their cage by the window as the dawn broke. The sun crept into the new day, setting the doves afire with an edge of red gold. A rosy haze suffused the desert sky beyond the arched window, casting a veil over the distant mountains.

Willow snuggled on her pallet, savoring the last few moments before rising. Her arms were still sore from doing yesterday's wash and now she gave them a cat-stretch, satisfied that they felt strong and tight. She was firm and well-knit, but shorter than she would have liked and barely old enough to be called woman. Swaddled in her blanket, she appeared to be nothing more than a bundle of rags piled on the floor next to the hearth.

Her station in life was low - only that of an *abn*, a house slave. But there were worse fates that could happen to a young woman alone in the world, far from her family and her clan.

"*Wahed, ethnein thalatha, arba-a...*" she counted. As was her custom, she waited to hear which signal would rouse her from her bed: the cry of the *muezzin* from the high tower in the village below, or the third rooster of the morning. This time, the roosters won, yet only a moment behind their crowing came the ululating call to prayer and the summons to bow east to Mecca. She groaned again, pushed herself up on her elbows and dragged her housecoat over her shoulders against the chill. Moments later she un-rolled her prayer rug and stretched forth, mumbling a vow of devotion. But Willow had never been especially devout, and she was on her knees and blowing at the faint embers in the hearth before the end of the prayer had left her lips. The master expected his tea first thing in the morning, and he often awakened even before the roosters in the barnyard. He was a jittery man, nervous, and unable to sleep.

His tea was still steeping in its silver pot when she heard the tinkle of his bell.

"Willow, are you there?" he cried in his rasping voice, barely heard from the far side of the house. *"Willow!"*

"Coming, lord, coming!" she called, cursing under her breath. The old man was worse than any rooster when it came to rising early. Gingerly, she placed a sweet cake, a boiled egg and a dish of brandied prunes on the silver tray that bore his breakfast. The doves thrashed in their cage as she hurried past them, through the great hall and across the small courtyard with its fountain and flowers to the bedchamber of her master, Abu bin Nisar.

The room had the stale smell of an old man, as if the morning breeze had choked and died at the window, yet bin Nisar looked up at her with the hopeful gaze of a child as she entered his chamber. His bedsheet was drawn up to his chin and the tip of his parti-colored nightcap trailed down the side of his gray face, giving him the appearance of a disembodied head amid the swaddle of his blankets. Yet at Willow's approach, he roused himself and sat up, eyeing her like a hungry cat.

"You're *late,* lazy woman!" he cried. "I've been awake an hour now, won-dering if you ran off with a goatherd!"

"Ah sirrah, I could not serve you weak tea, could I?" she replied, sweeping through the doorway. "The tea I've made is fit for a king. Perhaps even the caliph."

Bin Nisar feigned a scowl and shook a bony finger.

"The caliph? A pox on him! It's said he drinks the bath water of virgins, yet it does nothing to cure him. A bad man, I'm told. Misshapen in every way. Come closer... hurry! Come make an old man happy." He puckered his wrinkled lips and with a stoic face she leaned in and accepted his kiss on her cheek, slipping away before his hands could wander.

"A pox, lord? Let us hope the caliph does not hear you," she said, placing his breakfast on the low-slung table beside his bed. "He might order your head on this tray."

"Yes, a pox, and smite his backside with a thorn bush too," he said airily with a fillip of his hand. "We've nothing to fear of him. He's tucked away in the land of the Turks."

"Drinking bathwater, sir?"

"You mock me, woman, but yes, so it's said." He was about to add a jest about Willow's own bathwater but caught himself in time. Instead he said, "It's a long way across the sea from there to here, and the sea is often hungry for caliphs."

"Perhaps he could ride a camel."

Bin Nisar gave her a bemused look. "Perhaps, but that would be a very long and jaunty ride, and I suspect that none would know him by the time he got here."

Abu bin Nisar had the look of an elderly goat, with spidering eyebrows and the yellowing shreds of a gray beard that straggled down his neck. What remained of his teeth were thin, yellow stems and his face tended toward an expression of bewilderment, as if he was uncertain of his whereabouts. His bed robe could not hide the fact that he was thin as a bundle of sticks, as if his bones might snap at the slightest twitch. Yet, despite the gruff way he greeted her each day, he had been kind to Willow during the time that she had served him, always cajoling and inclined to dote on her, though often with a hint of lechery.

He had good reason to look bewildered. There was a long tear in the old man's sleeve, and his dingy bed clothes had been darned in several places, signifying the decline in his fortunes. The tapestries lining his walls dated from the 12th century, yet were mothy with holes, and the rugs lining his villa were worn through in a tatter of threads.

Although Willow thought of her lord's gated home as a palace, to Abu bin Nisar it was a long fall to hard ground from where he had once perched. And now, somehow, she had touched a nerve.

"The caliph," he muttered. "What do you know of the caliph?"

"Why, nothing, lord, it was simply a jest."

"Nay, you know nothing! *Abn!* What could you know of caliphs and kings? And I imagine you know nothing of me. Nothing at all."

Willow grimaced and bit her lip. It was not like the old man to be so peckish.

"I know that thou have been kind to me, sir," she said meekly. "But it is not my place to know more than that."

"Oh, woman, you have never heard my story, have you?" he said bitterly.

"Every man has a story, and I suppose even women have stories, if a man would deign to listen. It is not my place to know, but I have heard that thou were't a scholar."

"Am a scholar."

"Yes, sir."

"Once I was a scholar to the sultan of Granada." A wan smile crossed bin Nisar's face as he nodded in memory. "The keeper of many books. A master of poetry... wisdom..."

Willow ladled a spoonful of honey into his teacup and handed it to him.

"Exalted master, your reputation goes well before you," she said smoothly, calculating her own share of the honey. "Even I have heard of Granada, though much of it is a riddle to me. I have heard that the Moors built a palace there, lording it over all of Spain."

"Well only southern Spain, my dear, but that is the place where my world ended. Come now, sit with me and open your ears. The scales of Allah are tipping toward my death, and I would have someone know of my deeds beyond what is written."

"Me, sir? With your deeds?" She looked down, fidgeting with the hem of her dress. "But what should I do with them?"

"Who else, woman? Art thou a goat? A parrot? Have I not treated you like a daughter? The daughter I never had?" If bin Nisar caught the mirth in her voice, he did not show it. He patted a pillow on the floor alongside his bed, motioning for her to sit. "You will remember. That is all."

"But... sir, I am not worthy."

A stricken look crossed bin Nisar's face. "Who else is there? No one! Someday, surely, you will speak of me."

Willow and the old man stared at one-another, and for a moment she had the strangest feeling that they had become equals.

"As you wish, sirrah. I will consider your story a treasure for safe-keeping," she said half-heartedly, thinking that the old man's deeds were of no more use to her than the chore of washing his soiled under-garments. Surely his prattle would make for a long morning, and her chores at the wash tub would be much delayed. Usually, bin Nisar dismissed her with a grunt shortly after his morning tea, yet now he seemed resolved to spill his secrets into her ears, though why she could not imagine.

Yet, reading her face, a note of bitterness crept into bin Nisar's voice. "Truly? A treasure? I hope that thou art not lying, though I fear it so. It was my plan to reward you, but..."

What else could an *abn* say? That, and Willow's eyes widened at the hint of a reward. "I will swear it on the Quran, sir!" she cried. "You may ask me of your deeds tomorrow and I will remember every word. I will gladly bear witness if you will have me as your confessor."

"Well then, elegantly said!" His face lit up, growing childlike again. Placing his tea cup on the table, he sank back into his pillow and knitted his fingers together. "My memories seem to be slipping away like clouds crossing the sky, but I will tell it, since you have offered to humor an old man. Once, you see, I was a nobleman in the court of Muhammad XI of Granada. I was a learned man entrusted with certain sacred scrolls in his library."

"Such as those at the mosque?"

"Yes," bin Nisar nodded. "Poetry, mostly. Thousands of scrolls and books kept for safe-keeping, to be read only by those who could be trusted with their secrets."

"Ah, and these secrets, did you know them all?" Willow was suddenly at cat ears to hear of what might be in such writings, which were a mystery to the common folk. "Were there spells and summons? Dragons and jinns?"

"Oh, mostly they were quite dull," he gave a wave. "There was much ado about religion and some naughty poems of interest to the sultan. Some bits about strange lands, trade routes and treasure here and there. A bit about jinns, surely. But dragons? I can hardly remember now... but perhaps you will see one, someday."

"Yes, I should hope so."

"Yes," he smiled.

"And sir, you had these writings all to yourself?"

"Oh no, I had a staff of twenty scribes in the palace of the Alhambra, and in those days, I strolled its gardens in silk slippers, fresh from a perfumed bath and attended by eunuchs bearing fans and umbrellas to shield me from the sun. I enjoyed discreet assignations with courtesans as sweet and plump as sugar plums, and gold coins ran from my sleeves in showers."

"Assignations, lord? I do not know this word."

Bin Nisar gazed back at her irritably. "It is not important. But know this: life was good in Granada while it lasted."

Bin Nisar rambled on about the splendors of the Alhambra, its peacocks and fountains. His beard bobbed up and down as he gabbled with shining eyes. He was fond of sharing the joys of Granada to anyone in the household who would listen, yet no one ever seemed to care. He spoke for an hour about the formulas of various inks, both vegetative and those drawn from octopi or squids. And then the properties of parchments woven through with cotton and silk; the blandishments and peccadillos of the sultan; and the times he had been held in high esteem by that same personage; and in a hushed voice, the times he had been upbraided for some palace quibble.

Willow felt her eyelids growing as heavy as the buckets drawn from the courtyard well, but she had vowed to remember her master's deeds. She eyed the sweetened prunes on the table as bin Nisar waxed on, reasoning that the wash could wait another day.

"I imagine that your life was very good indeed, sir," she said, angling toward the table. "Yet why did you leave such an enchanted place?"

"Ah, I was driven from my home like a howling dog! All of us were, even the sultan."

In 1492, he explained, Queen Isabella and King Ferdinand II had driven the Moors from Grenada in their majesties' consolidation of Spain.

"Even the Jews were exiled, for the king and queen decreed that only the *Catolicos* could dwell in their kingdom."

"But why?"

"Why? So there would be no factions to stand against them, of course. It was a terrible time. I was plundered of half my wealth by Isabella's soldiers on the road from Granada. Then I was robbed again by the fishermen of Algeciras, who proved to be nothing more than pirates promising safe passage. Oh, so many of them!"

"As many as fleas on a camel's rump," she repeated the much-worn adage. Indeed, Willow had heard many tales of pirates, both among the corsairs of the Faithful and of the Spanish infidels. The coast on either side of Badis was riddled with their raids and the wreckage of plundered ships.

"Yes, of course, I should have known, but what does a scholar know but of books and silk slippers? All fishermen are pirates, even those villains down in our own harbor, taking whatever they can get their hands on. Know this: I escaped to Morocco with a handful of servants who quickly deserted me. But even worse, I was betrayed by my own brother, who promised me succor, but stole half of my camels and all of their baggage in a raid on my caravan. Even my books! All of my scrolls and books!"

This seemed too much for Willow to believe, for it was said that her master was the richest man in town. But she knew the role the old man expected of her, and so she played her part. "Surely lord, you have been through enough perils to fill a book!" she said. "It's a wonder you're not penniless."

"Oh, yes, that is true. Lucky I'm not a beggar! And now I have only you, the old cook and a one-legged gardener to serve me. So you can see how far I have fallen."

There followed a long pause and then bin Nisar spoke again. "Think of how vulnerable a man is in this world. Think of how easily one is preyed upon. A rose plucked and cast in the gutter. A king reduced to a beggar. Even Hannibal and Alexander, cut down as if they were weeds before a scythe! Such is the fate of man."

"Sirrah, my father told me much the same, but our only hope is to take courage! Death mocks us all, but until it comes, we must trust in the blessings of fate." Willow's eyes glimmered with belief.

Bin Nisar gave her a weary look and his voice dropped to a whisper. "I suppose, but I fear that is a story meant for children."

"But think of your fine home. Think of your furnishings, your sheep, and those who love you."

"Ah, yes, a palace, is it not? A small farmstead with a few sheep and goats outside the bunghole of Badis. Ha! I have thanked Allah for granting me even this and the sixteenth part of my fortune. What you see is no more than a hovel to me, an embarrassment! Yet I endure. What else can an old man do?"

Willow had some thoughts on the matter, having lived in a mud house as a child, yet she kept these to herself.

Indeed, she counted herself lucky. For Abu bin Nisar's house, modest though it was by the standards of the High Moors, was still filled with fine cushions, doves in gilded cages, chandeliers of scintillating glass and the tinkle of silver bells. To Willow, it was a paradise, especially since Abu bin Nisar was in the dotage of his late seventies. He had made a play for her only twice when she was thirteen and each time she had rebuffed him with gentle smiles and giggles as if she did not know what he meant to do with his sad old prick. That, and his gap-toothed wife had taken a liking to her, never dreaming that an illiterate slave girl could be of interest to her learned husband, much less a blackamoor like Willow. Even so, she had led Willow from his clutches with the no nonsense of a grandmother ushering a child to prayers. After that, Abu bin Nisar contented himself with simply hearing Willow sing and play at the brass pipes he had presented with great ceremony on her fourteenth birthday.

Given the much-reduced staff of Abu bin Nisar's fortunes, Willow had been trained as a kitchen wench and also as a lady in waiting, instructed in all of the skills meant to serve the lord of a noble house. How to fold a napkin to make it look like a dove, how to set a table with each bowl and utensil in its proper place, how to lay out her master's clothing each day, how to polish his silver and fill his cup with the proper sense of ceremony... these and a thousand small things were essential to maintaining a nobleman's estate.

One of these small things was singing. Thinking that the old man had fallen asleep in his reverie of the past, she snatched a prune and was about to tip-toe from of his chamber when he jerked upright with a start.

"Sing me a song while I sip my tea," bin Nisar commanded, sitting up at his pillows with his nightcap cocked at a jaunty angle. "I am troubled and in need of soothing."

Just then the cook appeared at the door and shot a glance at Willow before disappearing just as quickly.

"Ah, sadly, I am needed at the washtub and the churn," Willow said, thinking of her chores.

"Oh, the wash, bother it all! A song would help soothe my thoughts."

"Ah, but my throat is raspy today for lack of honey, I..."

"I will grant it," he said with a grimace. "Always stealing my honey! But first sing. Drive these vapors from my head."

"Vapors?"

"Yes, bad news, buzzards, vapors! But sing for me to drive them off! Like an angel if you can or a frog if thou cannot."

Willow poured herself a cup of the master's tea, ignoring his frown as she ladled a spoon of honey and then another. "Which song would thou have?" she asked, bringing the cup to her lips and gazing back innocently.

"The moon," his right hand fluttered. "The moon song will do."

Willow offered a smile and nodded. "As you wish, though I call it the Song of the Red Sea."

"Whatever, but only sing."

She knelt on the carpet with her back to a cushion, feeling for a moment like a courtesan obliged to do an old man's bidding before brushing the thought away. Singing was frowned upon in a home of traditional values, but so too were brandied prunes, yet both had been reprieved. Once, bin Nisar had come across her singing in the kitchen and begged to hear her voice ever since. In song, her voice was soft, hazy, almost smoldering; it was an intoxicant, as heady as the hashish that he hid from his wife.

With downcast eyes and a voice so low that it could barely be heard, Willow began to sing.

> "When the moon comes over the old Red Sea,
> You know I'll be thinking of you.
> You can ride your camel through all of my dreams,
> any old desert will do.
>
> Well I saw the twinkle of stars in your eyes,
> the cool desert wind in your hair.
> And the sand in your toes as we walked a mile
> By the shores of the Red Sea, so fair.
>
> Would you be willing to fly away,
> On a magic carpet with me?

We'll be together and spend all our days,
In a little grass hut by the sea...."

Abruptly, Willow looked up to find the old man gazing at her with lowered eyes, a sheen of drool damping the roots of his beard. His hand moved like that of a small animal beneath the blanket covering his lap, freezing at her glance. She stopped singing and glared at him.

"Does your belly itch, my lord?" she asked with a touch of acid to her voice.

Bin Nisar gave a raspy grunt, followed by a sheepish look. "Ah, yes, so it does. A naughty song, but I like it."

Willow frowned, daring to speak her mind. "It was my father's song and he sang it to me often as a child, but we never thought of it as naughty."

"I misspoke, perhaps," he replied with a fluttering hand. "If only the world was so sweet."

He settled into his nest of pillows and closed his eyes, as if settling into a dream. Then to Willow's surprise, bin Nisar gave a start and sat straight up as if he had been goosed, clutching what little hair remained on each side of his head. He gazed wildly about the room and cursed. "Know this, woman, there is bad news afoot, like a six-legged jackal! I am bedeviled and don't know what to do!"

Willow tucked her pipes into her tunic and studied the old man as she would a frightened child. "Sir, would you tell me your troubles? Did you sleep poorly last night?"

He gave her a cockeyed look and snorted. "I slept like an infant until that cursed rooster woke me. Know this: sleep does not come easy these days. I was relishing my repose, dreaming of old Granada and then came his wretched call. I will have him for dinner! I will have him boiled alive!"

"He is only doing his duty, lord. He is your faithful servant, as am I."

"Yes, truly, he's an old bird like me. But then came evil news."

"Surely, not from Jahir."

"No, dear girl, a disaster," he said, clutching at his beard. "Another calamity piled atop a mountain of troubles. Always more troubles, crushing me under their weight, when I should be as light as an angel at my age. Light as a girl like you! Lord, be happy with your position, that you do not have to face the trials which afflict me!"

Willow raised her cup to her lips and took a sip, eyeing bin Nisar coolly as he fidgeted. Her master was a fussy man, given to fits of drama and inclined to imagine a hurricane in his teaspoon. Light as a girl? Hah! How many maidens in the village of her age were betrothed or married to just such an old billy as Abu bin Nisar? It was only the fact that he was still married to his old woman that she was spared the same fate. He would have her as his concubine if he could. As her father had told her on their parting, her fate was no different than that of an ox at the plow, unless some rich man swept in to claim her. Yet there was no other man in her life, only this querulous old goat whose chatter barely dampened her thoughts.

"Trouble, sir?" she said lightly. "Like that of the Mamluks come to take our heads?" She imagined men on horses with pikes and flailing swords, painting the dusty streets of Badis with blood. "Do you mean for us to flee?"

"No, no, you mock me! It's only Esaak. He's sick at both ends, shitting blood and filling buckets. The rotten boy came down from the hill this morning and had the gardener wake me. Even now he is piled up in the stable, lying half dead."

"Ah."

"Ah yes, he'll pull through, but there's no one to tend the flock, you see, and I will not have one of the vile boys from the village. Thieves, all of them."

"Pirates."

"Yes."

"Can thou not send the gardener?" Willow asked innocently, guessing the old man's thoughts.

"A man with one leg will be of little use gathering the sheep," he scowled. "He can barely handle a shovel."

"Perhaps your sheep will be content to stay in their pasture."

"Nay, they need guidance, as do we all, lest they wander. And what then? The shearing season is upon us and I can't afford to lose a single one. Not one!"

"What will you do then, lord?" She knelt on the carpet at his feet and looked up, summoning a look of concern.

Bin Nisar gave a wild look around, spilling his tea down his chin and drenching his chest. "It seems I shall have to journey up the hill myself, or all will be lost to the wolves!"

Bin Nisar's beard began to bobble again as he squeaked out a flood of tears, wiping them away with a trembling hand. He dabbed at his face with the hem of his bed clothes. "What to do? What to do?"

Willow almost laughed, for she knew what the old man desired. He knew of her skills, learned long ago, south of the desert.

"Nay, lord, have no worries - send me!" she said. "I will be happy to gather your sheep."

"What?"

"Me, lord. I can handle a sheep as well as I can a washtub."

"No, no, that will never do," he muttered. "A woman doing a man's job? Think of the disgrace to my house if you should be found out."

"But lord, I shall dress as Esaak and the meadow is far up the hill. No one will know but you and the sheep. And Allah willing, Esaak will soon be well, with no one wise to our masquerade."

"No, I..."

"I will wear a hood and take your flock to the high pasture," Willow said, kneeling at his side and caressing his wrinkled hand. "No one will know but thee. Rest your mind, our deception will be no more than a day."

"But if you are seen..."

"I will rub mud on my chin to make it appear as if I have a beard."

"Hah! That would only make things worse if thou art caught! And what will we do then?"

"I will take the blame all on myself, lord. I will that say you did not know and are blameless. And yet, you will play the part of a merciful lord and forgive me if I am caught."

"Well..." Bin Nisar cast his eyes around the room, as if someone might be listening. Then, in a voice that was husky with dread, he bent toward her and whispered, "But Allah will know, surely."

Willow smiled. "Don't you think that Allah has greater worries than the sheep of Badis? Surely, God will reward you for your kindness to your flock and your wisdom in sending me to shepherd them. Is it not so?"

"Well..." The old man grimaced and forced a weak smile, relieved that his wish had been granted so willingly. Had he only known that Willow's heart had leapt at the chance to be free of her kitchen chores and house-work.

"Are you sure, child? There are thorns up there and the sheep are not always mindful."

"Thank you lord, I will heed your words."

"But do you not fear the wolves?" he fretted, wringing his hands as if the thought had just occurred to him.

"Nay, lord. I will take Esaak's staff and drive them away."

"Oh, I don't know if..."

"Rest your mind, Allah will protect me. I have no fear of wolves with God at my back." By now the sun had fully risen in the window, silhouetting Willow from behind and setting her dark curls alight with a silver fire. Her hair shimmered with the gleam of a raven's wing, falling past her shoulders and over her milk-coffee skin as she gazed at the old man with her un-nerving eyes. They were jade-green, with a touch of kohl about them, a bit of vanity which bin Nisar and his old wife had allowed without comment. On several occasions the old man had been compelled to turn away from her after gazing too long into those eyes, the pang in his heart being too much to bear.

"Allah? Wolves?" He frowned, thinking that Allah was not always so helpful when it came to protecting young women, but he did not share this with Willow, not wishing to curse himself with blasphemy. Instead he said, "Yes, I suppose that is so."

Catching the doubt in her master's voice, Willow made motions to leave before he could change his mind.

"My lord, the sheep will be waiting and I must hie to them lest they flee to the winds," she said. "Allah willing, I will return before you hardly know I am gone."

His goaty face brightened. "Yes, I suppose that's true, but remember the masquerade. No one must know that thou art not Esaak."

"Yes, lord. Even the sheep will not know, I swear it."

"And take care to shield your face from the sun. I would not have you looking common."

At this Willow gave a bitter snort, for she already had the darkest skin of any in the household. The other servants disdainfully called her a blacka-moor, though she was half Berber Arab.

She turned to go, but the old man called her back.

"Willow!"

"Yes, sir?"

Abu bin Nisar pointed a quavering finger at her and his face took on as grave a mien as if he were speaking before the imams at the mosque. "Remember this, woman! For this will be one of your deeds! Even the humblest among us may have deeds worth noting!"

"Yes, sir, and I hope it will be one of many, enough to fill one of your books," she said, backing from the room and bowing low. Deeds! What did old bin Nisar know of deeds? she scoffed. If she was not tied to him like a cow in his stable, she would show him... what, she did not know, but surely they would be deeds worthy of her own father.

She scurried back to the kitchen, telling the cook of her errand and swearing her to secrecy. The subterfuge, she knew, would be gossiped all over the village by noon, yet the scandal was unlikely to reach the old man's ears.

"But what of the wash?" the cook protested.

"The master volunteered to do it himself if I would tend his sheep. He said to dump the whole basket of it in his chambers."

"Liar!" the cook said with a laugh, "but you won't fool anyone if you go up the hill in your house dress. You must wear Esaak's spare tunic."

Willow made a face, but knew it was so. She made her way to the garden shed where Esaak's rag hung on a peg, its rough brown wool speckled with burrs and bits of straw. It was Esaak's second-best, full of holes and torn at the sleeves, as poorly cared for as the garb of any boy.

"It stinks of him," she said, returning to the kitchen to change her clothes.

"What? You washed it yourself only three days ago and he hasn't worn it since. Thank Allah it bears no nits or crawlies."

Willow frowned, recalling that she had barely given Esaak's rags a rinse instead of a proper wash, and now she rued her negligence.

"I shall look like a beggar in it."

"Thou shalt look like Esaak and none will be the wiser if they see you from afar."

"I suppose." Willow slipped off her house dress and changed, gagging a bit at its odor. "Son of a camel, it stinks!"

Bemused, the cook looked on, grunting her approval, "Stars in the heavens, if I did not know you, I would think you were Esaak himself!"

"Surely, or that of a circus bear," Willow replied, shaking the garment loose around her, "but I suppose Esaak's fleece will keep me warm enough up in the wind at night."

"And his scent will throw off anything skulking around up there. Here, take this pot of tea to the boy and a jug for yourself. And eat before you go, for who knows how long you'll be gone."

Willow did as commanded, downing a bowl of couscous and packing a pot of it for later. Then she was off to the stable, where Esaak lay in the hay alongside a feed pan filled with his vile emissions.

The boy's face was white with sweat and he could barely keep from retching. He nodded his thanks as Willow held a cup of tea to his lips. Taking a sip, he grimaced and croaked, "I fear I have the sweating sickness; see how I tremble! There is death upon me sister; I hear the whisper of angels."

"Shush. You'd be dead by now if it were so. You know as well as I that only the innocent die young and thou have always been a wicked boy. Did you not steal a pie from the kitchen only last year?"

"I might as well be dead!" Esaak cried, his face wet with tears. "The master will beat me, for the sheep have all fled!"

"No, soothe thyself, for I will find them. The master is sending me up the hill to fill your sandals."

If Esaak cared that a woman was trespassing his post, he did not show it. Instead, he brightened a little. He was nine years old, and if anything, the thought of Willow tending his sheep was enchanting.

"But there are wolves up there," he warned. "I saw one once, though it was far away."

"Perhaps it was only a dog," she said, cooling his brow with a wet rag.

"No, a wolf. I waved my staff at it and it ran."

Esaak blanched as if preparing to heave again and Willow knew the time for speaking was over. She also knew that Abu bin Nisar would forgive the boy for deserting his post, for it was well known that he was the lord's bastard.

"Rest yourself and make your thoughts easy, or I will send the wolf down the hill to devour you," she said.

A smile crept over Esaak's pale face. "Now thou art princess of the goats," he said in barely more than a whisper. "The Prophet's sword go with you."

She smiled in return and gathered the boy's staff, leaving him with the cup in his hand, gazing dully atop his bed of hay.

The rose pink of the desert was well away by the time Willow took the long path up the hill, down the gorge and then up the even higher summit to where the sheep were pastured. And though her father had predicted that she would live as if in the yoke of an ox, Willow stepped lightly along, filled with a sense of possibility. Was she not free of the house and its chores? She was practically a warrior, armed with Esaak's staff. She swung at a ragged bit of brush, imagining a battle with wolves. Bold thoughts arose in her mind as she pushed up the hill; anything was possible in this world, anything at all, even for her.

As Esaak had predicted, the sheep had scattered. A pack of feral dogs had wandered up from the village in the night and the boy had been too delirious with fever to drive them away. Two ewes had been slain and their bellies swarmed with flies where they had been gutted. One had its head torn almost the whole way off, dangling from the red chain of its spine.

It was deep into the afternoon before Willow rounded up the sheep and the smattering of goats among them. She drove them to the field where Esaak had constructed a crude lean-to of dead branches for shade from the sun as well as for shelter at night. Then, finishing her couscous, she counted twenty-nine sheep and six goats. They were spread in a half-circle around her, frantically cropping the grass atop the hill. Surveying Esaak's shelter, she wondered how it would be to spend the night in this lonely place, and for a moment the terror of the boy's wolf touched her heart. What if it came for her in the night? She pushed the thought away, thinking instead of her rumbling stomach. The couscous had done little to make up for the day's effort.

That night she went to bed hungry, swaddled beneath Esaak's damp wool blanket and packing herself between two of the fattest ewes. She was warm enough amid their greasy fleece, but deep in the night she awakened and gazed up at the swirl of stars that colored the night and listened a long time for the howl of the wolf. Nothing came to her, and satisfied, she drifted back to sleep.

That morning the cook huffed up the hill with another pot of couscous and peas, a packet of flat bread, and a jug of sweetened tea.

"How goes it shepherd girl?" the cook hailed her, wheezing as she bent and clutched at her knees. She was a big woman, not used to climbing hills.

"I am princess of the goats now," Willow said, making a face.

"Was it cold up here?"

"Not with the sheep for my bed mates."

The old cook grunted. "The master called for you this morning. He'd already forgotten your mission. And his tea was late with the hearth having died."

"Better that than the old man trudging up here himself."

The cook smiled. "Then we would believe in miracles."

They exchanged a few more words and then the cook trundled back down the hill with a promise to return on the morrow. Willow sat on a boulder near the lean-to, gazing upon the sheep which were up and browsing at the grass. By mid-morning her thoughts were as dull as those of the sheep themselves and it came to her that a shepherd's lot was one of endless boredom. She resolved to drive the flock to another meadow that afternoon, if only to give herself something to do.

That afternoon she drove the sheep leaping and baaing to a meadow overlooking the Mediterranean with the goats trotting along behind. It was a field rich with grass, owing to the dew from the sea, and the flock settled in as Willow gazed over the strait. Over the horizon lay Spain, a wicked land that she knew she would never see. For this she was grateful, for she had been told that Spain was a country filled with witch-burning infidels and heartless *Catolicos* who were fond of dining on infants.

She set about composing a tune for her parents, now living hundreds of leagues to the south, with no hope of ever seeing them again. She searched for notes on her pipes, intent on conjuring their faces: her father, golden-skinned with devilish eyebrows, yet always laughing; and her mother, sleek as a cat, dark as midnight.

A soft wind blew up from the sea and the sun was mild under the cool breeze. The wind caught the notes of her pipes and carried the tune south as her song came together. With the notes came fragments of words and a melody, inspired by the wolf that had failed to come in the night.

> "I am a lonely wolf in the forest,
> At night, I sing my lonely song.
> For my lost love,
> The mate that I love.
> Now he's gone,
> And I'm alone.
>
> And I sing oooo, oooo-ooo, oooo-ooo, ooo-oooo...
>
> Each night I sing to the moon,
> Hoping he'll hear my lonely song.
> Now my mate, he is gone,
> I'm left to linger on,
> Calling for my love until dawn."

Willow was quite satisfied with the song and also with the howl of the wolf she had inserted as a bridge. She wondered what her father and mother would think of it. She spent the rest of the morning singing it over and over again, committing the words to memory, for of course she could not read or write; her parents had taught her only the language of numbers. Then too, there was nothing to write on atop the windswept hill.

By afternoon, she was convinced that she had memorized it completely and she sang it one last time, full-throated, with her voice ringing out over the hills.

Behind her, she heard a faint bleat as the last note of the song died on her lips. Too late, she heard a rustle and turned from her pipes to see the swarthy faces of two men rising from the thorns clawing at the hillside. She had been thinking so intently, dreaming so deeply, that she didn't notice the men creeping forward until a lamb started bleating in terror. They were deeply tanned and bare-chested and one had brass hoops in his ears. They had the look of fishermen or sailors.

Willow thought back to Abu bin Nisar's words, that all fishermen were pirates.

One of the men was clutching the lamb by its throat, less than a dozen strides away. The lamb kicked and twisted in his grasp, its eyes wide with fright and its tongue lolling from its open mouth. The men gazed at her with the certainty of wolves, as if she, too, was a lamb for the taking. Slowly, the man holding the lamb twisted its neck until she heard it crack. A smile crossed his face and he nodded.

She gazed back in disbelief, but only for a moment. The men rose from the brush, murmuring with outstretched hands as if they meant no harm, but sure of the intent in their eyes, Willow turned on her heels and ran.

Flinging her staff at them, she scrambled among the bleating goats and sheep, dodging a zig-zag path down the hill toward the house of her lord, raising explosions of dust at her feet. Behind her she could hear the men pounding at her heels, breathing hard. If she could make it to the outer wall, someone would surely hear her! She outran them down the big hill and pounded her way up the next one; ahead lay the steep gorge, beyond which lay safety. She topped the crest of the bleak hill in sight of home and pummeled barefoot down the slope, ignoring the stabbing rocks and thorns. Her lungs were burning and she was gasping for breath, tears of fright springing from her eyes. *Home!* Its white walls were still so far down the path, yet she sensed she was outrunning the men behind her. She plunged down the steep gorge, heedless of the threat of breaking a leg in the sharp descent, then pounded her way back up the last hill to safety.

But then, just as she was on the final slope beyond the gorge, two more men with wolfish grins and dark faces sprang from the brush lining the path and dragged her squirming into their net within sight of her master's villa.

Willow was as thin as her name and not yet fully grown. Yet, she had learned to defend herself in her girlhood with her nails and teeth. Now, she gagged in fright, then choked out a scream and clawed at her captors with her nails, hammering with her fists and seeking to bite. But the men clutching her only laughed and jeered, as if her blows were of no consequence, twisting her tighter in a web of briny hemp. She fell hard into a thicket of thorn bushes alongside the path and cried out in pain. Sprawling there beneath the sun with bleeding feet and a bruise on her knee, Willow knew that all was lost.

The hands of her captors were as rough and hard as horn as they looped a rope over her neck, dragging her across the stony ground over the hill and down to the sea. They tumbled her screaming and begging down to where a shallow-draft galley lay hidden in the shadows of a bluff, lolling in the cove just off the stony shore. There was a line of rowers on either side of the ship, awaiting the signal to flee as her captors dragged her waist-high though the waves. She banged her ribs going over the side of the galley and then they were off with the lash of a knotted quoit laid hard on the backs of the rowers. The boat reared high in the glinting waves, bucking like a dragon in the surf as the rowers winged it forward. It crashed into a trough in the heaving sea, rose up and crashed again, all to the yelling and curses of its commander.

It all happened so quickly that Willow was at a loss to believe it was real, if not for the stabbing pain in her feet and at her ribs. She clutched at the side of the galley and wailed as it sped away from the shore. For a moment she thought of casting herself into the mercy of the waves in the hope that they might push her to the shore, but they grew more menacing with each passing second and Willow could not swim.

Even so, Willow felt as if she would be flung from the boat as if by a giant of the sea as she struggled with the rope around her neck. But before her feet could fly from the deck she was shoved roughly to the spine of the keel among a knot of staring captives. There, cowering in the well of the boat with her arm upturned against the sun she was lashed twice, followed by a kick in her side when she tried to stand.

The galley slipped past the headland, gliding through the swells like a snake and her heart leapt as she heard the cries of the fishermen who bobbed in their boats outside the harbor. *Oh, brave fishermen, for Allah's sake, save me!* she prayed as tears poured down her cheeks.

But it was not to be. Moments later came the heavy thump of a cannon from the fortress on the rocky prominence jutting into the sea before the town. The slavers laid on the whip with cries of *"Mais rapido! Rapido!"* and then came another boom from above, but fainter now, and soon the galley men were laughing and jeering at the distant fishermen as the boat fled deeper into the safety of the sea.

At last the galley gained the rolling swells of the Mediterranean as it sped away from the shores of North Africa. A red lateen sail was raised and the rowers relaxed at their oars as the dusky cliffs of Morocco dwindled away.

Dazzled by the afternoon sun, Willow caught a final glance at the hill where she'd been taken as the galley swayed back and forth over the waves. The livestock of Abu bin Nisar were distant flecks of gray and white by now and had gone back to grazing at the thin patches of alfalfa on the hillside. Ahead, she knew, lay the Pillars of Hercules and what could only be a miserable life as a slave of the *Catolicos*.

Croen of Cork

That was the last time Willow saw her home in Morocco. It was the last time she tasted grilled lamb in saffron, couscous dotted with golden currants, or hibiscus tea sweetened with honey. The last time she teased the peacocks of Abu bin Nisar's garden with tidbits of bread or cooled herself by the fountain in the courtyard of his home. Never again would she pour the master's tea from the exquisite pot of silver, brass and copper that he valued above all his possessions. A mile across the waves, she heard the day's third call to prayer from the *muezzin*, yodeling from the high tower below her master's villa. It was the last time she would hear that, too.

Only the week before, the whole household had celebrated bin Nisar's name-day in a party that drew nobles, merchants and dignitaries from throughout the district. The event had lasted from late morning until long past midnight and had included a horse race on the grounds outside the villa and then a battle between a mongoose and a sand cat. Trapped within a mud-walled pen, the beasts had refused to fight, yet had been cause for much hilarity and betting that ended with neither winners nor losers. Nightfall had brought veiled dancers whirling in silks; an orchestra of Sufi drummers, weaving rhythms on *tam-tams* and earthen *doumbek* drums; and a singer of some renown, who sang praises to Abu bin Nisar as he lay on his divan, nodding with a shy smile. Willow and the household staff had watched it all, peering through the beaded curtain that led to the kitchen. She had admired the slim dancers, weaving like reeds before the mesmerized men at their hookahs. In an odd moment that made her blush in the memory, she had even been introduced to the Sultan of Badis by her master, and the great man had gazed upon her with heavy-lidded eyes and nodded inscrutably before she managed to scuttle backwards with many salaams and bows. To her confusion the Sultan had called out, *"Inshallah!"* - God willing - in a lilting voice after her, which had her puzzling over his intention for days afterward.

Yet, what a day that had been, and once the men had finished with their meal she and the women of the household had feasted on the remnants of chicken *tagine,* tender veal, a tuna fresh from the sea and stews bubbling in iron pots placed in the oven coals. A lamb had been stuffed with rice and raisins, but it was roasted so slowly that it was late for the feast, offering more for the women to share.

But now, there would be no more festivals or name-days. In the days to come, Abu bin Nisar and the shepherd boy Esaak would stand crying on the hillside, looking vainly out to sea for any sign of her and the pirates who were the talk of the town. Though she was no more than a slave in Abu bin Nisar's house, still she had been treated as if she were a daughter, and the lord wept over his tea for days until a new and prettier girl was fetched from the Berbers.

Indeed, Willow had fancied herself a princess in his gabled home, even though her duties included dumping his chamber pot each morning and scrubbing his scrawny back in the bath. Other times she had fancied herself a beautiful courtesan in the palace of a prince, much like the kohl-eyed women from the sultan's harem who floated through the marketplace in town, swathed in silks as bright as flowers. Sometimes, she had practiced their expressions in bin Nisar's mirror when he was off on an errand, posing both demure and haughty by turns while flouncing around his chambers draped in a tasseled tablecloth of fine linen.

But now, huddled in the muck at the bottom of the heaving boat, she felt the ache of a wretched slave, a ward of the damned.

Willow counted sixteen rowers along with eight captives, most of them dressed in the tattered clothing of fishermen, laundresses and livestock tenders; a poor lot destined for hard labor, but a life they knew all too well already. Above them danced a scarecrow of a seaman who waved the long, curve of a scimitar over their heads, screaming incomprehensible demands. His eyes burned as black as an angry monkey from within his skeletal face, which was framed by a ragged thatch of black hair parted in the middle. He wore twists of golden wire in his ear lobes, and the jut of a satanic beard on his narrow chin. Willow glimpsed a heavy golden chain around his neck beneath his shirt of rough cotton, and his breeches were striped tan and maroon above a pair of boots trimmed with spherical bells. He let loose an incomprehensible string of babble, poking his scimitar at each captive's chest as if that would make his meaning clear.

Willow shrank from the gibbering man and drew the hood of her cloak over her head, huddling as best she could atop a heavy coil of rope at the bottom of the galley. She washed her torn feet with seawater sloshing at the bottom of the boat, wincing at its sting. Her feet had been badly bruised by the rocks and pierced by thorns, and now they throbbed with a burning pain.

Above on either side of her, gaunt men flexed at the oars, their ribs as stark as bird cages beneath their blackened skin. The oars moaned like cattle on the backstroke in their leather sleeves, answering with a wooden shriek when they pitched forward as the boat plowed the sea. The galley's prow rose up as if to climb straight out of the sea and then rolled down again, all to the beat of a drum at the stern and the yowl of the oars. Although Willow had lived nearly all of her sixteen years by the sea, she had never once swam in it, and now she quaked in terror, both at the writhing man with the sword and at the tilt and dip of the galley as it crawled through the swells. How, she wondered, could such a frail craft stay afloat amid the endless roll of the waves and wind?

But the galley crawled on and soon they were far out into the strait, fighting with the current that flowed between the Mediterranean and the Great Ocean Sea to the west. The wedge of the lateen sail caught the wind, driving them forward with the aid of a southern zephyr. Only when they were miles from shore did the madman with the scimitar cease his carping. He retired to the shade of a cotton canopy, where Willow deduced from the deference of his fellow sailors that he was the galley's captain.

There was no shade for the captives and the slaves at the oars; they broiled beneath the sun as the boat crawled slowly toward Algeciras on the far shore. Willow and her fellow captives huddled as best they could in the scraps of shade at the bottom of the boat, some of them moaning or crying in despair.

Slowly, the sun crept to the horizon, dipping into the sea in a pudding of cold yellow as a blanket of gray rolled in with a chilly wind from the west. Squinting toward the bleak sky far off over the Atlantic, the crew began muttering and gesturing among themselves and the rowers took to the oars again, plowing on toward the coast of Spain.

That night, as was the fate of all women taken by pirates, the men came for her. Willow had been shivering in the cold wind, seeking shelter beneath a bundle of coiled rope at the bottom of the boat when three sailors came slithering across the deck like apes, shoving the captives aside and leering with lust. Their hands grasped at her in the darkness, rousing her from a half sleep. They tore at her clothes by the light of the stars and a thin moon, some of them with their breeches down around their knees and their horrid things dangling and bobbing in the moonlight. Willow screamed and kicked, hammering with her fists, but the men only grunted and chuckled, at ease with the certainty of raping her in turn. They were rank with salt-sweat and the stench of fish, crowding above her until their bodies hid the sliver of moonlight, blocking out the stars. The three of them closed in around her, smothering her in the darkness at the bottom of the boat. Two men seized her ankles, pulling her legs apart while the third bore down upon her as she whipsawed beneath him.

But then came an attack from above. Over the shoulder of a stinking brute who crushed her to the hull she saw the moonlit shadow of a wiry man with an upraised arm. Down came a barbed whip, slashing at her attacker's back. He screamed in pain and reared back just as Willow twisted sideways and raked his face with her nails, searching for his eyes. The quoit was knotted with barbs of iron and it whipped back and forth in a fury, accompanied by a barrage of screaming, curses and kicks, driving away her attackers.

Willow hid her face from the slashing whip and gasped in choking sobs, pulling her tunic back to her shoulders. Above her, she heard harsh, guttural words and saw the flash of a scimitar as her attackers scrambled to safety. To her surprise, her savior was the wraith-like captain. He gave her a savage look, with his face floating in the faint moonlight like that of a ghost, but said nothing as his men fled cursing and shrieking toward the bow of the boat.

For a moment Willow could have sworn she saw the captain's eyes flicker with a flame, like that of a jinn. The jinns were said to have eyes that blazed with red fire, and although she knew it was only the reflection of a guttering torch, still, her flesh crawled at the thought that her rescuer might be something other than human.

Why had he saved her? The captain had offered no words of kindness or mercy, he had only glared at her as if in contempt. He had the look of the devil himself.

Toward midnight, the temperature took a steep downturn as a cold wind came skipping over the waves from the Atlantic, and with it the stars disappeared one-by-one as if smothered by a blanket drawn over the sky. The captain began shouting above the rising wind, ordering the sail to be taken in and furled against the mast.

Minutes later, Willow heard a sound like the wind whistling through the chambers of a conch shell and looked into the darkness to the west, seeing nothing. But what she heard filled her with terror; a growling, blood-chilling roar gathering in the west, as if from the mouth of the earth itself.

A sheet of rain crept over the water, pelting the sea, driven by the wind. All around her, Willow heard the murmur of prayers, both Muslim and Christian, even from the slavers themselves whose eyes stabbed at the approaching storm in terror. Then, the storm came rushing across the waves and hit them with a hammer blow. Willow heard the shouts of the helmsman bellowing over its fury, ordering the men at the oars to push with all they had, first right, then left, then back again in order to keep the galley pointed into the waves. Every captive was put to work bailing the boat as the sea rushed over the sides in a flood of spray and foam.

The violence of the storm worked at the seams of the galley, threatening to split its narrow planking. One of the sailors worked furiously at chiseling scraps of wool laden with tar into the leaks under a rain of screams from the captain. For hours it seemed that the ship tossed like a chip of wood on the waves. Willow vomited once, twice, and clutched at a rib of the ship, praying to the *Moakkibat* angels of Allah to save her. In the depths of the storm, perhaps those guardians of children heard her pleas, for gradually the storm lessened and crept away to the east like some huge, growling beast.

With the dawn came the news that the galley had been driven almost all the way back to the coast of Morocco. Around her, Willow was surprised to find that every captive and sailor had been saved. Surely, she thought, some would have been swept overboard in such a fury, but the sailors carried on as if the storm had been nothing more than a pea dropped in a puddle. After being served a wooden bowl of grainy porridge the slaves were back at their oars for another long haul to the north.

Of the captives crouching near her, two were camel boys only seven and eight years old. Another was the shepherd, Akmed, a young man from her own town, who was slightly older than herself. Then came a tall, strongly-built woman who had been dyeing cloth in a pot by the sea when she had been seized. A hollow-faced beggar was among them whose ears and nose had been cut off for thieving; he'd been taken by the shore while searching for shellfish. To her right was a haggard man with the look of a grandfather. He was badly sunburned and had a thicket of ginger hair which ranged in tatters over his head, as if he'd been dragged backward through a hedge of thorns. The shreds of his beard had the appearance of a bird's nest, jutting straight out from his chin. He caught Willow's eye and nodded, offering a shy smile through a mouthful of crooked teeth.

No food was forthcoming to the captives that morning, not even the gruel of the galley slaves, nor did Willow imagine there would be any at all on their voyage. Hunger clawed at her belly, yet there seemed nothing to chew on save the ropes on which she huddled. Then, to her delight, she spied something wriggling in the water at the bottom of the boat as her fellow captives dozed in exhaustion. It had flown over the gunwales during the storm. She scrambled after it, seizing a fish that was nearly as long and round as her forearm. Twice it wriggled free before she was able to hammer its head against the bottom of the deck.

Allah be praised, she thought as the fish lay limp in her hands, its blood oozing from its gills across its stricken face. Praise too that her father had given her a small dagger when she had been sent north to Abu bin Nisar, telling her to keep it by her side through every moment of her life, even when bathing.

Being the daughter of a Bedouin wanderer provided an education in survival, if nothing else. Her father had taught her how to survive on many loathsome things when famine struck their home in Azemmour on the southern coast of Morocco, including snakes, rats and things which scuttled in the dust of that dying city. Now, she drew her blade from its sheath beneath her tunic and slit the fish's belly from gills to tail. Then, wide-eyed yet grateful, she sucked at the cool white flesh, seeking access with her teeth. It was slimy and tasted of salt and the sea. Her stomach heaved, but she forced herself to swallow.

"Gimme," whispered a voice over her shoulder. Turning, she found the old man with ginger hair and sea-blue eyes beckoning for a portion of the fish. He was pale beneath his flaming skin and the haunted look in his eyes told her he was starving.

She motioned to the gut pile at her feet, but he made a face and shook his head, no, pleading again, "Please," he begged. "I've had nothin' to eat for three days."

Willow groaned. It was the Prophet's command that she should help him. She tore a final sliver of the slippery flesh with her teeth and handed what was left to him. He devoured it with the ferocity of a starving dog, scarcely bothering to avoid the bones.

"God's mercy on you child," he breathed, stooping to kiss her feet. "By the rood, ye have saved me for another day. I pay you the honor due a queen."

Wiping her mouth with the back of her hand, Willow laughed at the touch of his lips, squirming away. "Thank you grandfather, but from where I sit, a queen's honor is worth no more than these fish guts," she said, gazing at his strange red hair. "You are a man of the north, yes?"

The old man nodded. "Croen of Cork."

"Cork?"

"Mmm. It's a green and homely place awash with rain not far from the end of the world," he said gravely. "I was taken three years ago by your shuttlewit people to slave in hell, and with the help of the Christian souls manning this ship I might see me home again."

"I wish blessings that it will be so," Willow said mildly, though by the look of their captors she doubted Croen would ever find his way free. "The land of Cork, is it far from here?"

Croen gave her a bemused look. "It's just a town, lass. A town in the land of Eire. Have ye heard of it?"

Willow thought a moment and nodded. "The sultan owned slaves of Eire."

"Well may the good Lord stuff him down a rat hole where he belongs," he said primly.

"Thou art a vengeful sprite, though I trust it may be true. My father taught me that all rich men are evil."

"Sure, but that's what all men seek to become, in't it so?"

Willow nodded. "Even my father dreamed of riches, though none called him evil."

"Ah, perhaps the rich need to stew a bit before they're fit to drink with the devil," Croen muttered, "though I would not wish that on yer father."

"The men who hold us are evil enough; they could not be more so if they had the riches of Solomon," Willow said glumly, gazing on their ragged captors.

"A philosopher, are ye? Be that as it may, they managed well enough last night. I thought we'd wake to King Neptune's lullabies after that storm. Only the hand of God saved us. The Med is a fickle sea, either calm as a baby's breath or bucks like a horse with a burr up its arse. There's no in between."

"Is this your king? Neptune?"

Croen gave her a wry look. "I don't expect ye know much of any kings! He's a fellow big as a castle who lives deep in the sea. We call him Lir where I'm from, like your goddess Aishsa. He's a monster who swims about with a pitchfork, making sailors miserable."

Willow had heard of Aishsa, goddess of the waters, but never in connection to the sea, nor had she heard of Neptune or Lir, though she was careful to commit them to memory. "As you wish," she said simply, "though I hope your king has lost the trace of us."

Like herself, Croen had been tending sheep when the slavers took him.

"I was sittin' upright, straight as a brig's mast and sleepin' like the dead in the mid-day sun when they cast their cruel net o'er me an beat me about the head with a club," he said.

"Lucky they did not kill you," Willow replied, noting that Croen's head was fiery enough already with its thicket of flaming hair, but the angry welts on his forehead were even redder.

"Aye, I'm not the pretty lad I once was," Croen said, catching her gaze, "but I'll mend. D'ye think me ravaged?"

Willow hesitated, for Croen seemed very ravaged indeed, but this was no time for truth-telling. "I've seen worse," she lied, "but sir, you must take care to shield your head from the sun."

Croen had also been a slave in the farmstead of a Moorish lord and had learned the common tongue of Castilian Spain. Yet he spoke with a strange inflection and with many unfamiliar words, which she imagined must be Irish. The day wore on slowly as the oars creaked in their stays and the far shore crawled nearer. Seeking to divert her anguish, Willow peppered Croen with questions about Eire, which was apparently a land of miracles and wonders. In Croen's telling, the women of Eire were beauties rivaling the angels and certain beverages eased every pain, including that of existence itself, while the Irish themselves were the most devout in all the world.

"Why then would thou leave such a paradise?" she wondered. "How did you come to live among us?"

"Oh, I'm nay much to look at now, but once I was first mate on a trading vessel out of Dublin."

"Dublin?"

"It's the first city of Eire, you see, a big slave port itself long ago. We were coasting down the shores of Portugal when a storm kicked up. I told 'em it were an evil time of the year to set out, but the captain din' listen. A gale blew us all the way past the gates of the Med and down along the coast of Maroc. We were shipwrecked on a cruel stretch a' desert called the Skeleton Coast."

Croen scratched his back on a rib of the galley, lost in the memory.

"And then?"

"Ah, nay much to tell after that," he shrugged. "We set about becoming skeletons! Most of the men were lost to the sea and the rest of us took to starving to death on the coast. Then there were only three. But the Lord had a plan for us and at last we were rounded up by an evil pack of bandits out roaming the desert wastes. They tied me behind a camel and dragged me along for God knows how many days, giving me only the flesh of a rotted bird to eat while they drank the blood of their camels. They'd slice a vein and lap it like dogs. Din't even bother with a cup, can you imagine?"

"It is a common thing in the desert, though I have never tasted of it," Willow said, knowing that her own father had done the same on his long treks across the Sahara.

At this Croen gave a weak laugh. Oh? A strange dinner, I should think, but I had none of it. Yet I surprised them! They treated me like a goat, and yet I lived."

He had been sold as a slave in Azemmour and then led north along the coast in the hope that he might be ransomed.

"But my people back home have no money, and there was no way to reach them even if they did," he grimaced. "They might as well have pulled on the Pope's cock if they expected to shake a few crowns out for me."

Despairing of gaining a ransom, his new master had threatened to send Croen to the mines. "But I was too old for that kind of work and the mine owners figured I'd be dead within a week with little value in me, so I got turned out as a shepherd instead. Can you imagine? Me, a man of some importance on the wide-ranging sea, chasing after nasty sheep!"

"Ha! No one cares to be a shepherd," Willow said, thinking of her brief stint. "It is dull work and the sheep have little to say."

"Aye, out there with the jackals and the lions growling at night, tending sheep in the chilly wind and the rain, it's not a job for a man like me. I told my master I was a man of the sea, a first mate! But the goose didn't have a clue, nor no ship to sail in. So here's the rub, child. I've been taken by the bloody slavers twice now, you see. They swarmed over me while I was napping, and now this."

"It seems you're lucky that way," she mused.

"Lucky?" He gave her a quizzical look.

"Forgive me, I meant in the way of bad luck."

Croen gave her a sharp look and she blushed. "I meant no insult," she said, "but there are many kinds of luck, and some are stricken with the bad kind."

"Ah, sure, I've known 'em all. Irish luck being the worst of it. But the Lord will see me through."

"Your lord? Do you speak of your master?"

"Nay, not that hogswallow! My lord Jesus Christ, the god man who looks after me." Croen crossed himself, nodding in satisfaction.

"Perhaps he will come walking over the waves," she said dryly.

"Ye know the story?"

"It is in the Quran, the same as your Bible."

"That would be a sight, wn't it?" he chuckled.

Your Jesus has forsaken you, Willow thought, though she kept this to herself.

She had seen the slaves of Eire before, tending the fields around her village or laboring in the mines beyond the hills. Though she had little idea of where Eire might be, she knew that the Barbary corsairs often swept its coast, gathering slaves as they had for a thousand years and selling them to the Moors. The Spanish had traded with the people of Eire for centuries and it was only natural that slavers would follow in their wake.

But the Christians in turn had gathered slaves from among the Moors of the Barbary Coast and black slaves had been traded out of Africa for centuries. Slavery was the way of the world, now, then, and forever. Willow's father had told her of caravans crossing the desert that had 600 or more slaves chained one-on-one, as if a stream of ants, bound for markets as far off as Constantinople and Baghdad.

"If you had converted to the Faith you would have received better treatment," Willow said after a time.

"Hah! Not me!" Croen cried. "I've remained faithful to my savior Jesus Christ and the Virgin mother, and God-willing I'll find believers among these devils who will return me to my people."

"If they are truly devils, then they may not be so kind. Are they Spaniards?"

"Nay, they're Portuguese from the look of their banner, though they might be Spaniards masking themselves for some reason we can't divine. I'd call them Portuguese if I had to bet my life on it."

"But what of the men who pull the oars?" The galley slaves included Arabs, black Africans and pale-skinned men from Europe.

"An unlucky lot from here and there. Someday they'll feed the fishes."

Willow grimaced as she considered the rowers, who were dressed in salt-worn tatters with a miserable cast to their faces. Every man's back bore the scars of the lash. "Do you think they will put us to the oars?"

Croen shook his head, no. "Yer a woman, of no use at the oars, and I fear they'll have worse things in mind, God save ye. As for me, I'm Catholic to my bones, and know the Mass in Latin, most of it anyway. The Portuguese are Catholics too. They'll have to let me go once I say a few Pater Nosters and an Ave Maria."

"Thou might have better luck convincing a camel to give you its cud, for none of them have the look of the pious."

"Aye, think ye so? But know this, lass, a Christian does not forsake a fellow Christian, no more than one of your people forsakes a fellow Mohammedan."

At this Willow rolled her eyes. "A child born to a slave remains a slave in Islam," she said. "The Faithful are no kinder than Christians when it comes to their slaves, for a great many coins are at stake."

"Oh? Well watch this then."

Croen got down on his knees in the wet filth at the bottom of the boat and kneaded his hands together, whispering a prayer. Then he raised his voice to the captain, who stood a few feet away, riding up and down on a low platform as the waves rose and fell.

"*Catolico!*" he cried, pointing to his chest and wringing his hands, "*Cristiano! Catolico! Catolico!*"

The captain looked down and gave him a quizzical look, squinting in the sun. Then he took a sweeping step forward, placed his right foot on Croen's sunburned forehead and gave him a hard shove, slamming him to the deck. Around him the rowers offered a mix of grim laughter, nods and grimaces.

"I too am *Cristiano*," one of the rowers said, a man with dirty blond braids and piercing blue eyes. "Jesus himself wouldn't be freed by these pigs, for they're all sons of the devil."

Croen scuttled away, wary of the captain's boots and wrapped himself into a ball against a rib of the boat. "I'll try the Pater Noster after a bit," he grumbled. "Surely these beasts will bow to our Lord's prayer."

Willow nodded, though she had no idea what Croen meant by a Pater Noster, or an Ave Maria. But if these foul men had no pity on Christians, what would they think of a poor slave of Islam? She had heard of Portugal and tales of its pirates, who were invoked in many a home as a threat to make children behave. *"Be good or the slavers will get you!"* But, beyond that, Portugal was a land that meant nothing to her, no more than Eire or England.

Although Willow knew her numbers well enough, she had never learned to read, not even in the house of Abu bin Nisar. Nor was she privy to talk of faraway places, for what did simple folk know of such things? She had barely expressed an interest of the world beyond her village, as far-off lands were foggy with cutthroats and monsters. And although she had come from a far away place herself, she scarcely remembered it.

Willow was the house slave of a Moorish nobleman but she was not of the Moors, that tawny mix of Berber Arabs and Spaniards. Nor was she a negress out of black Africa, although she had the depth of her mother's dark eyes. She was in truth, a blend of both, black and Berber. Her skin was as smooth and pure as coffee laced with a touch of milk and her hair fell in crisp ringlets past her shoulders, black as ebony and polished with the same radiance.

Her father had been a wandering trader, a Bedouin nomad with Berber roots who sometimes lived on camel's milk on his long journeys through the desert. When that failed, he supped on his camel's blood. He had lost the use of his right leg as a child from the crippling disease, but got around well enough. He had wandered back and forth for years across the faint trails of the desert with his brother and their three camels, trading ivory, nuts, beads and other commodities from the forests of Africa. Willow's mother had been a fruit vendor in Timbuktu, a woman of the Bamara tribe with a wide smile, flashing eyes, and skin like black velvet. They had met at the grand bazaar in that city of mud towers, flies and camel dung and theirs had been a delight at first glance. Willow's mother had been purchased with a dowry of eight camels, two donkeys, six chickens and a monkey. The monkey had been a jest offered by Willow's whimsical father.

Thereafter, Willow's father had given up his wandering ways to settle with his new bride in Azemmour on the Oum er Rbia River by the sea, far down the western coast of Morocco. There, he established himself as a breeder of racing camels. The Arabs to the north were mad for them, willing to pay almost any price. Within two years Willow's mother had been draped in ivory, pearls and gold as the trade prospered, and then came Willow.

How Willow Came by Her Name

Willow had been named Safasaf in the Arabic tongue because of a miracle that had saved her father's life while on the *hadj* to Mecca two years before her birth. It was a long story, worthy of a book, but her father loved to tell it, and on many nights as a child she fell asleep to the sound of his soft voice murmuring the tale in her ear.

As all who follow the Prophet know, every man of the Faithful who has the means must make a pilgrimage to Mecca at least once in his life. For Willow's father, this had been a journey of nearly a year, traveling by camel across the fertile Maghreb region on the Mediterranean coast, a land still friendly to wanderers. Father and his brother journeyed five hundred leagues across the Maghreb without incident, except for fending off the "five nuisances" of crows, kites, rats, scorpions and biting dogs as they traveled east through Libya and Tunisia to Egypt. From Cairo they made their way to the port of Suez, embarking on the Red Sea aboard a sambuk, a half-decked vessel that rocked on the water as if it were a cradle, packed with seasick pilgrims.

"Your uncle and I broiled beneath the sun like goats on a spit as we crossed the perilous sea, begging for shade, of which there was none," Willow remembered her father saying. "Yea, it was the first time either of us had set foot on the waters, and it was a marvel as deep and vast as the Great Desert, yet infinitely more terrifying. For one can step lightly on the sand without harm, but not so those dark waters. And daughter, know this, we were assured that there were horrid creatures lurking beneath the waves, ready to take us at the slightest chance. But such was not our fate."

Homesick for his wife, Willow's father had composed the Red Sea song that he taught her some years later. He had written it while sitting on a beach in the Sinai desert, gazing at the moonrise coming up over the mountains of Arabia.

Arriving at the port of Yambu in Arabia, her father and his brother fell in with a caravan of 200 camels and 300 mules and horses, aiming to make the dash of seven days to El Medinah, the birthplace of Mohammed.

"Joining us was a troop of fifty warriors armed with crossbows, bows and arrows, swords, knives and spears. They bristled like a woman's sewing pad, chocked with needles! The guards were hired at great expense, for it is the custom of brigands to prey on caravans of pilgrims making the *hadj*. Those who prey on the Faithful are heathen idolators, outlawed by Mohammad, yet impossible to root out."

"Oh father, were you not afraid?" Willow would ask, as if on cue.

"Oh, no, not at first," he would reply. "The captain of the guard was a stout Turcoman, as hairy as an ape and round as a wash tub with furious deep-set eyes, mustachios which swept upward in twirling points, and a warlike scowl on his face. He bristled with two swords, a long knife and a heavy lance. Our captain boasted of having murdered a score of brigands with only a club sheathed in iron, and vowed that he had killed lions, too. And never had I met a man more jealous and proud of his courage, for he was sparky as a rooster at the slightest insult."

The captain proved his worth by dangling his sword before the eyes of a quarrelsome band of Maghribis, who had joined the caravan in Yambu, fighting and bickering the whole way along the track to the east.

"The captain had little use for the Maghribis. Although they are considered warriors of some renown in Morocco, he scorned them as cowards. He pledged that he would cut out their tongues if they persisted in troubling the pilgrims, and thereafter they kept their grumbling to themselves."

In a deep voice, Willow's father would imitate the Turcoman captain: "'These Maghribi dogs of a dung heap vow to stand and fight if we are set upon by bandits! But I promise you they will drop their tails and run when it is time to prove their mettle. It is fortunate that you have enlisted my aid, for these mountains crawl with cutthroats who would milk their own mothers to gain a single dinar.'"

Thus, Willow's father and his brother were encouraged to believe that they were as safe as the angels on the path to El Medinah, even though others among the caravan chattered with fear when they ventured into the narrow passes along the way, casting anxious eyes on the cliffs overhead.

Then one night, midway to El Medinah, Willow's father heard the yodeling war cries of a storm of men sweeping down a narrow ravine.

"We were attacked by the Beni Harb, a hill tribe of Bedouins who preyed on caravans of the *hadj*. They flew among us like a swarm of hornets at a cut in the mountains called the Pilgrim's Pass, stabbing and thrusting at all in their way. We thought there were hundreds, though perhaps there were only fifty. Yet many pilgrims died beneath the blades of the hill men, and the rest were taken as slaves or scattered."

"And what happened to the brave captain?" Willow would ask, although she already knew the answer..

"Oh, he and his men scampered like sand rats, back down the way we had come at the first squeak of trouble, taking all of the horses and leaving us at the mercy of the bandits."

As for the Maghribis, those irksome tribesmen of northwest Africa were the only defenders to lift a sword, slashing and brawling to the last man. In the confusion of battle, Father and his brother escaped with a lone camel under cover of the night, bouncing on its back and whipping its flanks until it collapsed from exhaustion and died late the next day.

But that was only the beginning of her father's troubles, for after arriving almost penniless in El Medinah, he and his brother pushed on against all advice for Mecca and the tomb of the Prophet. "We had come so far that we could not dream of going back."

In El Medinah they encountered an Arab named Hassan, who had also escaped the bandits in their luckless caravan. "Hassan begged to join us, having no others with which to travel. He had a sword strapped to his back and vouched that he knew how to use it, so we were grateful to have his company."

"And what did you call yourselves, Father?" Though this, too, Willow knew from many tellings.

"Ah, the name came to us on the breeze. We called our company the Three Swords."

Setting out on the southern trail, the pilgrims entered a skeletal land of rock and thorns inhabited by vultures, ravens and wild men who robbed and killed passersby at will.

Nonetheless, they shaved their heads bare against the cruel sun and trimmed their beards and nails as is the custom of all pilgrims on the *hadj* and pushed on. Yet in a rocky pass choked with thorn trees, they found the way barred by a band of brigands known as the Utajbah, who gathered among the rocks and perched like crows atop the cliffs.

"They demanded treasure to pass, but since we had none to spare, they called for our ears as payment instead. Thus, we Three Swords honored our name and fought like lions against them, backing into a cleft in the rocks before fleeing into the desert."

"And was it a cruel desert, Father?"

"Oh, yes! We were cast into a land as haggard as a corpse, which even the robbers of the Utajbah dared not enter."

That afternoon and for two nights thereafter they stumbled on without water, hoping to circle back to the trail to Mecca and the wells which lay along its length. Yet the way was barred by a wall of stony mountains, upon the slopes of which lived nothing but the heat of the sun along with snakes and scorpions.

"By the third morning we had walked all night and our tongues were as big as gourds, yet as dry as cactus," Father said. "We had sipped our own bitter urine, yet even that was gone and I felt the scythe of death scratching at my throat."

"Oh, but what did you do then, Father?" Willow would ask, though by this time she could barely keep her eyes open.

"Oh, the thing that all must do to survive..." Father talked on in his soft voice as his daughter lulled to sleep. His golden face hovered above her head on her pillow, his eyes darting in remembrance of the trail to Mecca, as if he had never left it.

"There was no other choice but to push on, crawling over the rocks to a pass in the distant peaks. With our heads bared to the merciless sun as is required of every pilgrim, we began dropping in the heat, dragging ourselves to our feet, only to fall again.

"Then, just as we had forsaken all hope and were set to dig our own graves, your uncle caught sight of a patch of green growing in the shadows of a canyon. It was but a single plant, as green as the bush which spoke to the Prophet Moses, nestled in the shadow of a cliff. Yet it stood as high as my waist with many tendrils of delicate fronds. And unlike any other oasis, there were no palms, nor reeds, nor rushes, only this single plant in the devil's land."

The three men dug with their hands; deeper and deeper they dug a full arm's length down beneath the shade of the bush before the moisture of a cool spring began to collect. And then, handfuls of water.

"We were saved, thanks to the providence of Allah! Yet I had never seen this plant before and I asked Hassan of its name. 'It is *safasaf,* a kind of willow, the seed of which has flown here over a vast distance on the wings of the wind, or in the belly of a bird,' Hassan said."

If Willow was still awake by the time her father ended his tale, she would hear the promise that had blessed her with her name.

"I vowed then to the Prophet that my first-born child would be named Willow," her father ended every story with a bobbing head. "And that is how you came by your name."

As a girl, Willow was tasked with helping her mother, first at the fruit stand as a toddler and then at the books of her father's business. She learned the language of numbers, if not words, as she and her mother tallied the sums of camel sales and expenses. Her father, it seemed, had great skill as a breeder of racing camels, yet very little at jiggering the books to avoid the burden of taxes, and thus, he was happy to pass this chore on to his wife and daughter.

But it was the camels themselves that Willow loved and one day she arrived unannounced at the mud walls of her father's livestock pens to cries of consternation and outrage that a girl child of only five had dared to walk the streets of Azemmour alone without a male guardian.

Soon enough, she was wandering between the legs of the camels themselves, getting an instructive kick for her daring. And then as the years crawled by, she took to caring for the rangy beasts, her sandals pounding through the dust of camel shit in the yard as she fetched forage and buckets of water.

Her father took heart that Willow ignored the indignities of those beasts which hawked phlegm from their nostrils, spat in drenching gobs and bit with their snaggling yellow teeth. Willow would give a hard smack on their haunches in return, though more often she worked at their hides for hours with the grooming brush, cooing songs into their ears. She had her favorites among them: Spindly Solomon, Yahya the Impulsive, Mameluke the Overtaker and the dragon bitch, Sitt. A good racing camel could command a price one hundred times that of an ordinary cargo beast and its fame might range for hundreds of miles, from the racing grounds of Fez to those of far-off Tadmekka. In her dreams, Willow imagined that one day she might race the camels she had come to love, albeit in the disguise of a man.

Then one day to her great surprise, her father brought home a lion cub, presenting the squirming beast to his daughter.

"Look, thou, a cub found suckling at its dead mother's teat in the desert with its brothers and sisters lying dead beside it," he said. "I traded Yahya the Impulsive for it, thinking we might train him."

"Am I to be his keeper?" Willow's eyes had filled with disbelief. She was sorry to see Yahya go, but filled with joy at the gift of a lion cub.

Father had nodded. "Even so, but first we must give him a name."

Of course, the only name that would do was Aslan. It meant simply "lion" in Arabic, but to a young Bedouin girl, Aslan sounded just right.

Thereafter Willow became the cub's mother, suckling Aslan on goat's milk dipped in a rag and cuddling together close at night on her sleeping mat. Within a year, Aslan had grown twice the size of his human mother, padding behind Willow as she walked the narrow lanes of Azemmour to the gaping awe of its residents. Her parents' neighbors muttered to themselves when Willow and Aslan strolled by, yet without ever expressing a cross word. For who would challenge a girl whose protector was a young lion? And all were quick to spirit their goats and sheep away when Aslan cast his golden eyes in their direction.

Perhaps it was on those afternoons that Willow learned to walk without fear, a trait which would follow in her footsteps through much of her life.

Yet the city took to Aslan well enough and on a couple of occasions large crowds gathered to watch as the lion chased a chicken released in a square close to the western mosque. Even a lion could not catch a scrambling chicken as Aslan wheeled and slashed in the dust after his dancing prey. Thus, a fresh-killed chicken was always offered as a prize once the exhausted beast gave up the chase, for it would not do to have a frustrated lion walking the city streets, nor a hungry one.

As for herself, Willow could hang on Aslan's neck and tease him at play for hours without fear of reprisal, for the lion loved her and thought of her as one of its own kind. Often, they would walk the hills beyond the city walls, an unheard of pastime for a young girl, but Willow never feared the threat of grasping hands or rapacious men with Aslan padding along beside her, nor even of other lions.

But a young lion is capable of eating a great deal, and a mature lion even more so. Before Aslan was two years old, his fate was sealed by a hunger that swept the city. First came a year without rain, and then another, followed by dust storms that stripped the plains outside the city.

Hard times settled on Azemmour with the famine of 1522 in the wake of the drought, when every crop withered in the field and livestock dropped in their tracks for lack of feed. It was a time when rats ran for their lives in the streets, pursued by the city's starving residents. The drought sucked the city's river dry, taking rich schools of fish along with it. For two years it was as if the plains surrounding the city had surrendered to the Sahara itself as scores of farms turned bleak and brittle for lack of water.

Azemmour was a city-state by the sea in southern Morocco, known for the quality of its fish from the river called the Oum er Rbia. The Portuguese had captured the city in 1513 after the ruler of Azemmour refused to pay a tribute of 10,000 shad per year, a fish prized for its lamp oil and flavor. The wrathful Portuguese soon arrived with 400 ships bearing 8,000 men and a cavalry of 2,500 horses, capturing the city within hours. The Portuguese helped themselves to the fish, wheat, wool and livestock of the city, trading these for gold and slaves in the ports south of the Sahara.

Some said the city was cursed, for after the Portuguese came the drought, stripping both the land and the river of all life. In the wake of the famine many Azemmouris sold themselves into slavery to escape starvation. Portuguese slavers descended on the city, carrying hundreds away into bondage.

"The lion must go," Willow's father said one day over their meal of nothing but flat bread.

Willow gazed down at her empty bowl, her cheeks wet with tears. She needed no explanation, for there were only a few camel bones with scant meat on them to feed Aslan, and they were lucky to have wrested those from the remains of a beast which had fallen dead of old age in father's corral. Two days earlier, Aslan had leapt the mud brick wall of their compound and had seized a neighbor's last surviving goat. Father had been forced to pay triple its price or risk his skin answering to the city's magistrate.

Thus, Willow had been granted an hour to lay with her head on Aslan's ribs as the lion lay panting in the shade of Mother's garden. Then, with Father walking behind her dressed in white cotton and bearing a long staff, they had taken Aslan to the palace gates where he was to join the Sultan's menagerie. Willow led Aslan past the trembling guards beneath the balcony where the Sultan and his family stood watching and then into an iron cage in the shade of the palace garden.

"Now at least, you will not starve," she said, gathering her arms around Aslan's neck and rubbing her cheeks against his mane. Nor kill, she thought, knowing that pressed by hunger, Aslan was only days away from taking a life in the streets of Azemmour. And what would become of her family then?

Willow gave Aslan a final caress and walked home at her father's side. It was the last time she would see the lion, and soon enough, her father as well. This, because Willow now had twin brothers who were only three years of age and in the teeth of the famine, the family was in danger of starving.

Soon enough, Willow's father said it was her own turn to go.

"At least you will not starve," he said as they gathered around their empty table. "I have found a place for you, and it is far from this dread city."

"As you say, Father." Willow said, her eyes cast to the floor. She had been too hungry to argue, having grown thin as a wren. Mother had taken to boiling leather for broth and searching the hills for a few straggling roots, yet it was not enough. All around them, neighbors were dying of hunger and its companion, disease.

Willow's father had too great a stake in the city to flee the famine, along with too many debts, and her mother would not countenance the harsh life of the Sahara. Nor could they bear to sell their daughter as a slave to the Catholic infidels of the Portuguese. So, reluctantly, her father had sold Willow to Abu bin Nisar when she was ten years old to save her from starvation. She had been passed along in north-bound caravans from brother to cousin to uncle all the way north through Khouribga and Fez to her new home on the Mediterranean where her father still had connections.

It had been a journey of four weeks through the dust and heat of the desert and mountains with the specks of vultures and kites circling overhead in the pale yellow sky. Willow had resolved to be stoic in obeying her father's order, but how could she help but be bitter? She could almost taste it as she plodded on in the track of the camels into the furnace of the ceaseless wind. The bitterness twined around her heart and hardened; it made her stronger in its hurtful way, made her feel as if she stood alone against the infinite devils of the world and that she must always hold her breath, be wary, watchful and ready.

At times she wished that she could be swallowed by the desert sands in order to listen underground to the cries of consternation from her relatives until she, too, dissolved into dust. Only her father's parting words, "Be strong! We will meet again!" gave her the will to go on.

She had arrived at the estate of Abu bin Nisar, stricken to her core and shivering like death itself, sure that she was doomed to a life as the lowest of slaves. For what child could feel otherwise after being forsaken?

"You must plow through it, child," her father had told her. "You must plow through your troubles just as the oxen turns the soil."

Plow through it? She had felt just so, like a brute ox, rending the clay of the earth with a rough wooden plow. And where would such a life take her and how could it end? On many nights thereafter she lay awake wondering, which life did her father expect her to live? That of the dull ox, straining its life away at the unforgiving soil, or that of the earth itself, churning beneath the plow's wooden blade?

Only after they had been lost to her forever did Willow realize that she didn't know her parents' names. They had always been simply Baba and Ummi, Momma and Papa.

Her new lord had prized her for the sheen of her wavy hair and her jade eyes, which were a gift of her father, and for the dark beauty of her face, which was a blessing from her mother. To her surprise, Willow had been treated with a measure of deference upon her arrival, and she soon came to realize that she was destined to be more than a field slave, though the vision of a struggling ox never left her. As she progressed through puberty, Willow moved through Abu bin Nisar's house clad in fine white cotton, as incandescent as a candle, bearing his tea cup, couscous, hookah and scrolls. Soon, she had even been granted his name, Safasaf bin Nisar, she being his chattel slave, his *abn*.

Life had been good to Willow as an *abn*, but now, peering over the gun-wales of the galley and hearing the groans of its skeletal slaves, she reflected bitterly that all her skills had come to naught. Willow knew what might be expected of a woman enslaved by the Christians; old bin Nisar had often remarked on her beauty and curves, but unlike him, the infidels could do as they wished. She chewed at her lower lip and gazed out over the sea, dreading to think of what fate held for her.

She felt queasy all through the rest of the day as the galley rolled over the waves. The deck smelled heavily of urine, vomit and worse and her only comfort was the coil of rope which served as her bed. The rest of the captives were spread out along the bottom of the boat, huddled beneath the row of slaves manning the oars. The rowers were manacled to long chains which ran down each side of the ship. From time to time, wind filled the sails giving the rowers a break and then they stowed their oars and either hung their heads or gazed forward with blank stares, reminding Willow of cattle.

"If the ship goes down in a storm or a battle, all of these men will go down with it," Croen told her. "Aye, and we'll go down too," he added, for they had been manacled around their necks with a long chain that bound every captive.

At mid-day, the galley passed a small desert island, which rose from the sea as a low tumble of rocks with a skirt of sand peppered with clumps of cactus. Timidly, Willow peered over the rim of the boat, scanning the island for signs of movement. Her father had been a gifted storyteller, sharing tales he had gathered in his travels through the length of the Caliphate. One of them was of the demon, Delhan, who roams the islands of the world, riding an ostrich and devouring shipwrecked sailors. But if Delhan was lurking amid the rocks, then he and his feathered steed stayed well-hidden. Willow spotted only a lone eagle perching on its shore, which seemed to eye her as the galley sailed past.

The Bad Boy of Badis

That afternoon, Akmed, the young shepherd from a farmstead near her master's villa, began howling his complaints, eyes blazing in the captain's direction. Willow knew of Akmed's reputation as a troublemaker, given to sassing his superiors and stealing their trifles to sell in the market. It was said that he had stolen chickens, too, and he often tried to kiss young women collecting water from the communal well. Once, he had even spoken to Willow, but she had hurried away before he could embrace her. Abu bin Nisar had denounced Akmed as a bad boy who failed to say his prayers each day, as was required of the Faithful. He was the bad boy of Badis.

This, of course, made Akmed irresistible to the young women who gathered to gossip in the market. And Willow had to admit that Akmed was a handsome devil and a courageous one too as he stood before the captain, rubbing his belly in complaint and lambasting him in a string of Arabic. As fierce as a hawk, he had a sweep of well-oiled hair that fell back over his ears, cut blunt at the base of his neck. The beginnings of a thin beard gave him a roguish, devil-may-care look. He was a bold young man, she decided, and yet still a boy with none of a man's caution.

An evil smile crept over the captain's face as Akmed launched into an extended rant, and Willow prayed that their captor did not know Arabic. The captain was as wiry and thin as a snake, and Willow sensed that he was just as quick, and as cruel.

"Thou pig-hearted bastards! Sons of dogs! Swine of the sea! Thou barking, hog-smelling, shit-eating, dong-sucking devils! Your mothers are whores and your fathers are goats! I piss on you! I call down a thousand demons on your bitch mothers and the heathen monkeys who fathered you!" Akmed had worked himself into a frenzy before the disbelieving eyes of the captain, who stood planted on the deck only a few feet away.

"*Que é isso? Que isso?*" the captain wondered, glancing about. But if anyone among the captives and rowers knew what Akmed was saying, they were not inclined to speak.

"Silence, fool!" Willow hissed at him. "Thou art digging your grave in the sea."

"Stay down, ye cocky rooster!" Croen added his voice to hers. "Ye don' know what they can do!"

But Akmed was wound up beyond reason. His mouth frothed with spittle and he began barking and crying, as if in a state of ecstasy.

The captain gave the shepherd a bemused look, then strolled forward on the rolling deck and gave him a hard slap on the face. But to this, Akmed only raised his voice, squawking in protest. He reached out and clutched at the hem of the captain's shirt, tugging him forward. With a look of enraged disbelief the captain pulled free and slapped him even harder, demanding by signs that he huddle on the deck, but this only served to spur Akmed to a series of high shrieks as he raised his hands, begging as if in prayer.

Then, Akmed seemed to go mad. Abruptly, he spat full in the captain's face. He was given a savage kick in the ribs in return and crumpled to the deck, only to leap up again, ranting and screaming. The captain's face went white with rage and disbelief as he wiped away the spittle with his bare arm. He pulled his dagger from his belt and Willow held her breath, expecting him to slash Akmed to pieces. But instead the captain motioned for two men to come forward and gave a single command, casting Akmed's fate. He was lifted kicking and screaming up and over the side of the galley into the pale-green sea.

By now the galley had stalled, turning into the wind with its sail flapping in the breeze. There was a moment of silence on the water and then Akmed emerged sputtering and coughing up salt water with his hair swirling around his face. With a mighty effort, he kicked up clear of the sea and seized the side of the galley with both hands. Akmed lay drifting in the water, struggling to crawl back over the side of the boat.

"Idiota," the captain muttered with a look of disgust. Casually, he turned and rummaged through a pile of rusting tools near where Willow stood, wrenching a long axe from the tangle. The axe head had been forged of black iron, flat as a hammer on one side and with a straight blade on its cutting edge. It looked as if it had been designed more for butchering meat than for cutting wood, and so it was.

With his eyes dancing with mischief, the captain pushed his way up on the rowing bench, shoving a slave to the side. He raised the axe high over his head. Now it was Akmed's turn to gaze in disbelief, with a dawning sense of horror. The upraised axe lingered for a moment against the blue sky before crashing its dull blade down on Akmed's left hand with a hard thunk as it cleaved into the side of the boat. Willow screamed as she saw half the severed hand with three dangling fingers fly up from the gunwale and into the sea. The hand drifted in the waves for several long moments, trailing blood before it slowly sank, its fingers outstretched as if in farewell.

But still Akmed held on with his right hand, his face now horribly contorted with fright. He was begging now as his left arm trailed bleeding in the sea behind him. Willow gagged in horror, choking out a plea, *"No! Please! No!"* she cried, tugging at the captain's shirt tail.

The captain turned and gazed at her with eyes as implacable as a hunting lizard and raised the axe again. But before he could sweep it down, Willow leapt to the gunwale, shielding Akmed with her back and grasping at his arms. The captain wavered, dizzy with anger and now it was the crew's turn to leap to the boy's defense, arguing that he was a prime slave, even with the loss of a hand.

"Ducats, capitao! Muitos ducats!" one of them cried.

The captain dropped the axe with a heavy crash and kicked Willow in her rump, nearly knocking her overboard. But her knees were braced against the side of the boat and now Croen was on his feet, helping to drag Akmed back aboard.

"That were a brave thing ye did girl," Croen muttered. "Ye got some fire in yer veins, that's sure enough; either that or yer as witless as a pig. I thought sure he was going to split ye from neck to tailbone! Rest now, rest. I'll bind up the boy's hand."

Croen tore a strip of cloth from his own tunic and rinsed it in the sea, then bound up Akmed's hand as he rocked and moaned in agony in the bottom of the boat, his eyes glazed over in shock.

"Ah, ye feckin' eejit," Croen muttered as he bound Akmed's ruined hand. "Why'd ye have ta be so stupid? Why'd ye..."

Willow stood staring for a moment, catching the glare of the captain's eyes from where he'd retreated at the far end of the ship. Her stomach wrenched and heaved as she vomited into the sea and then her legs buckled and gave way. She shrank to the deck, shaking in horror and huddled within herself long past sundown, hugging her knees to her chest and breathing prayers to the wind.

At last the galley edged its way back across the strait with the lighthouse and brown pile of Algeciras rising low on the horizon. But instead of making for the harbor, the captain directed the helmsman west along the coast.

"Pirates fearing pirates," Croen muttered. "We're but a minnow and our captain fears bigger fish."

It was true, for from the distant harbor there emerged a huge ship with two lateen sails and two banks of oars, a Catalan ship of war, bound for Barcelona. The ship's 120 oars flashed forward in the sun, clawing at the water as it scuttled like a centipede toward the east. The captain sprang to his feet from where he lay beneath his canopy, casting anxious eyes in its direction, but the brigantine pushed on toward the east and the immense tower of rock that watched over the Mediterranean - one of the Pillars of Hercules.

Half a day's journey on, the galley put into a small harbor and a quick transaction was made with an innkeeper on the dock. A bag of millet and a steaming cauldron of fish stew was brought aboard, and after mixing the grain with the stew, every member of the boat was given a portion. First the rowers, then passing their bowls on to the begging captives.

"I thought they meant to starve us to death," Willow said, scraping the side of her bowl with her finger. The bowl was filthy and caked with grease, but she was beyond caring.

At this Croen gave a grim laugh. "They need us alive when they take us to market and they don't want us so weak that no one will have us."

"To market? To buy food?"

"Why, child, don't you know? We're to be sold like goats. Like," his eyes searched for words, "pigeons."

"Yes, truly, I had forgotten," Willow said numbly. But this was not true, for she had often seen the slave market in Azemmour, and even the small doings of Badis, paying little attention to either of them. "It's just that I did not think of such a fate for myself..."

"'Tis the way of..."

"Hush, I know it well. The way of the world."

That night the galley crept past the harbor at Cadiz, the same golden city of high walls and tall palms that the admiral, Christopho Columbo, had sailed from in his discovery of the New World. Its harbor bristled with the masts of ships under the moonlight, but there was no stopping even though the men at the oars groaned in protest. The galley pushed on, a mile from shore, its helmsman wary of the rocks along the coast.

Willow was sleeping when the galley entered the great Guadalquivir River and pushed its way upstream. She had been kept awake much of the night by anxious thoughts that scrambled through her half-sleep like monkeys. She wakened at mid-morning to find the sea far behind the ship. The river was miles wide, but she could see hills of green on either bank, along with clusters of whitewashed villages.

"I have heard of this river," she said, taking a guess. "My father called it the Nile and told many stories of it. He had seen its crocodiles on his way to Mecca."

Croen harrumphed and spat over the side. "What ye don't know about the world would fill the ocean itself," he said. "The Nile lies five hundred leagues to the east in Egypt. This is the Guadalquivir and a land called Andalusia."

Willow flushed. Andalusia, of course. Even she had heard of that golden kingdom of wine and grain, the breadbasket of Spain. "Then we are going to Sevilla," she said, guessing again in the hope that Croen would not think of her as a fool.

He nodded. "Even so, it's the richest city in the world, I'm told, and a holy place where I hope to be freed by my Christian brothers. It's a port far inland, one of the grandest ports in the whole world, sending scores of galleons across the sea to the end of Africa and west to New Spain."

He paused, as if remembering. "And child, if it's within my power, when I'm free of my chains I'll seek the help of some kind Samaritan to see that you go free as well."

"Well thank you sir, and I will do my best to help you if it is within my power," she replied. But it dawned on her that Croen expected far more from his faith than seemed likely. That, and she resented him calling her a child, she being a woman of sixteen years.

Indeed, she thought, if there was anything left of the child in her, she must kill it off, strangle its weakness and become like her father, a wandering Bedouin of the desert, merciless, doing whatever it took to survive. With her mother and father long gone and Abu bin Nisar beyond any hope of rescue she had only herself and her small dagger to depend on. That, and perhaps Croen, who seemed increasingly childlike in his dream of being released.

Croen had tried a few words of his Latin mass on the four men crewing the galley and they had given him quizzical looks in response, as if he were mad.

But Croen mused on, gazing at the far banks. "A golden city with a great cathedral, I'm told. And there dwells the mercy of our good men of Jesus. Lord knows I've suffered among the bloody Mohammedans long enough. Three years scratching at their bloody fields, Lord forgive me if I curse my old master to hell, though he well deserves it."

But the golden city of Sevilla announced itself with a horrid smell of raw sewage well before Willow glimpsed its high walls, and then came a barrage of small fishing boats and barges, which scuttled to and fro across the river like water beetles. She could see the shit-stained walls of the city rising in the distance, running far out of sight along the riverbank.

For a moment her hopes raised. Perhaps Croen was right, perhaps he would find mercy here, and she would be ransomed with the help of his

Christian brothers. Perhaps he would return her to Abu bin Nisar, or even carry her off to be his wife in far-off Eire. He was an old man, but might not look so bad if he sought out a barber, and he seemed kind enough. Many a young Berber girl had been married off to an old man of means, though surely Croen was as poor as a street beggar.

But then Willow's hopes were crushed by the sight of a line of blackened skeletons with their arms outstretched, chained to a series of pillars beneath the walls of a vast fortress on the riverside. Some of the corpses were picked nearly clean by the birds and rats which swarmed over their tattered limbs.

Willow had seen the bodies of the condemned hung from the sea wall of Badis and on posts outside the gates of Azemmour, but nothing like the sight before her. Skeletons still black with congealed blood dangled in iron chains atop the ancient bronzed bones of many others. She lost count after twenty and turned away, feeling as if she might faint.

"We have come to a place of demons," she whispered, feeling sick.

"It's nothing child," Croen whispered in her ear. "It's just a warning against those who would do evil in the good queen's city. These here are criminals, I imagine. They burn the witches, you know."

Willow gritted her teeth. "For the last time, Croen, in the name of Allah stop calling me a child or I'll cut your throat while you sleep."

Croen's head jerked back as if his locks were tied to a string. "Aye, madame, as ye wish!"

Distantly, they heard the sound of horns and drums and then came a vast crowd marching down a broad lane from the city toward the river. Willow caught sight of banners and poles hoisting golden crosses skyward and a small group of people dressed all in gray jostling along in a knot ahead of the crowd. The crowd crawled forward as would a vast snake beneath the walls along the wharf, which were lit a bright orange by the procession's bobbing torches. Tall shadows danced against the walls as if they were black spirits following the mob. To Willow's eyes, it was a scene from hell.

"*Auto da fae,*" a crewman called out, crossing himself. "*Auto da fae!*"

The other crewmen took up the cry, crossing themselves as well in the way that Willow had observed among the Christians. A black gleam lit up the eyes of the swarthy crewman who had tackled and tied her on the morning she'd been taken prisoner. He had been among those who had tried to rape her and his back was still ripped with scars from the captain's whip.

"What is this?" she asked, glancing back over her shoulder at Croen, who stood transfixed by the crowd. "What is auto da fae?"

Croen gave her an uneasy look. "I have heard of this, but have never seen it," he said. "It means 'act of faith' - a sort of trial."

The crowd made its way across the river by way of a pontoon bridge which swayed and bobbed with the tramp of their feet. Above them, the hulking Castillo de Triana waxed gold in the setting sun. Far up its walls beyond a fringe of cannons, Willow saw men in tilting helmets gazing out over the approaching crowd, with towering pikes held easy in their arms. By now the crowd had reached the walls of the fortress and a masked figure in a flowing red robe with a tall conical hat stood in its shadow, calling out to the gatekeepers. But Willow could see that his request was a mere formality as the massive gates swung open, each door as thick as the length of her forearm. She caught glimpses of the prisoners being pushed along by the crowd, their heads hanging low on their shoulders and their eyes darting like frightened animals. Their faces were smeared with ashes.

"Ah, they are penitents," Croen pointed. "See their tunics all in gray? See their gray faces? They have been humbled before the Lord. They are here to make their penance."

"They are innocent prisoners, humbled by your demon priests," Willow replied. "Look at them! They are just people! Only people!"

Croen's face took on the look of an old turtle as he reeled back, momentarily at a loss for words.

Willow's eyes swept back over the corpses chained beneath the walls of the fortress and then at the knot of prisoners, hustled through the massive gates. They were a mix of groaning men and women of all ages, including some younger than herself. "Nothing good can come of such a trial," she muttered.

"Ah, but this is a trial overseen by the holy fathers of the Church," Croen said, regaining his composure and nodding with assurance. "We mustn't judge them so quickly."

The Test

The roosters were still crowing the next morning when Willow was roused from her sleep atop the coiled rope at the bottom of the galley. She looked up to find the captain snuffling over her like a whiskered rat contemplating a morsel. He seemed a nervous man, given to sudden starts and facial ticks, which made Willow quake under his gaze. She had the sensation of being prodded by a monkey.

By now, Willow knew the captain's name, Bartolomeu Sincid, a pirate out of Lisbon whose specialty was dealing in Moroccan slaves.

"Lavante-se, vamos agora, vamos agora," he murmured quietly, and Willow could see that he was anxious not to be noticed by his sleeping crew.

He freed her from the long chain running the length of the boat; then placing a noose around her neck, he led her across a narrow plank to the wharf. Willow looked back over her shoulder to see Croen glaring red-faced in her direction from the bottom of the galley. He nodded, but said nothing.

Captain Sincid led her along as if she were a goat down a series of narrow lanes and alleys beyond the stone warehouses lining the river. A rooster crowed its dawn song and with a start Willow realized that for the first time in her life she hadn't heard the morning call of the *muezzin,* the wavering cry which summoned the Faithful to prayer five times each day. She had always been careful to bow to Mecca in the east as was commanded, but now that was inconceivable in the hands of the jittering captain.

Soon, they were in the quarter of Santa Maria la Blanca, the haunt of pimps, whores and cutthroats. The alley stank of vomit and the trickle of raw sewage, stretching far ahead in the shadow of ancient buildings constructed from blocks of sandstone. Here and there were patches of blood and hair where drunken sailors had battered one another in the night. A rat peered out from under a step and then darted out before them, scampering between the high stone walls that blotted the sun.

The alley was awash with the filth of night soil and urine, tossed from the upper windows to the pavement below. Midway along the alley, Sincid pulled her into the recess of a doorway as a drove of pigs jostled down the alley, snapping and gobbling at the turds which had been tossed to the street from above. Their squealing was like that of demons as they fought among themselves over the excrement.

"They bite," he muttered in Spanish as the pigs crowded past, driven by a swineherd on his morning rounds.

Willow nodded, grateful now that she was clad in Esaak's rags instead of the long cotton dress which she had worn at her master's house. She stepped gingerly around the urine on the pavement, doing her best to keep an eye on the windows above for anyone late in dumping their chamber pot.

She felt utterly lost in the maze of Sevilla, with no idea of where to flee, even if she could escape. *So now my time has come,* Willow thought as the fretting captain led her along, glancing warily over his shoulder from time to time. Sincid, no doubt, was taking her to some dark place for his pleasure and she shuddered at the thought of being raped by such a gangling ogre. She thought of the dagger beneath her tunic and her father's warning to keep it hidden. She vowed that she would stab Sincid when he least expected it; perhaps she would even cut herself free and run. But where? The captain was quick as a snake, a wiry tough who might think her dagger but a toy, a pinprick. She imagined him laughing at the sight of it and trembled at the thought of trying to stab him; she was sure that her arms would go limp and fail her.

But by and by, they came to a bakery where the captain bought her a loaf of coarse bread. To Willow's surprise, he smoothed her hair back around her ears as if with affection and pinched at her cheeks with a look of concern.

"Eat, eat," he made motions with his hands.

She soon learned the reason for his kindness as they rounded a corner and ducked inside a cul-de-sac. At the end of the narrow way stood a low, iron-bound door framed in thick timbers. Two women with kohl eyes and rouged cheeks not much older than herself sat on the step before the door, smoking their pipes. One had ponderous breasts reaching almost to her navel atop her rolling belly; the other was her frail opposite, thin as a wraith. They eyed Willow up and down before parting, as silky as cats.

Willow had seen a brothel before in the back streets of Badis. The shepherd boy Esaak claimed that old Abu bin Nisar was a frequent guest of that unholy place, wetting his cock with the bawdy women there or smoking opium and hashish. The captain led her down a narrow hallway, dark as the night except for the thin flame of a single lamp, which cast eerie shadows on the sandstone walls. On either side were cubbyholes not much bigger than an animal's crib and in one of them Willow glimpsed a woman lying on a straw pallet on the floor, sleeping off her night's labors. It seemed more a stable than a house of pleasure. It was nothing more than a kennel for slave women, frequented by sailors, paying coppers for the lowest of the low.

But the end of the passage opened into a courtyard under the sun, which seemed an oasis of pleasure and potted plants. A monkey in a velvet cap and an embroidered vest scampered past the broad doorway as they entered, beyond which Willow saw a gilded cage with three doves and a row of potted palms. A long counter ran along the wall to the left, beyond which were shelves filled with ornate bottles in colors of amber, green, red and brown. These, Willow imagined, must be filled with the devilish alcohol of the infidels, forbidden to the Faithful.

Midway through the courtyard an immense fat woman in a silken gown of red and gold sat on an ebony couch, inlaid with sandalwood carvings of exotic birds. The captain hurried over, kissing her on a proffered cheek and babbling his greetings as if they were old friends. She pushed him away with feigned disgust and then offered a sly smile, gazing up through lidded eyes. She had a faint mustache straggling over thick lips painted a stark red, along with tattooed eyebrows that curled in thin scimitars above her kohl-dark eyes. A leather crop lay on a serving table next to her divan and Willow sensed that she was as dangerous as she was gross.

The madame's eyes had bulged at the sight of Willow, as would a hawk spying a mouse, but she quickly lowered her gaze, hoping that Sincid hadn't seen.

"So you have come for the *auto da fae* and stayed for the festival," she said, caressing the captain's back as if he were a cat.

Captain Sincid mumbled something in response and she waved a finger in his face. "In *Espanol*, please."

"As you wish," he said in halting Spanish, searching for words. "Madama Martina, I have brought a rare gift, if the price is right."

The big woman gazed at Willow and frowned. "This *puta* from Morocco?" she said in disbelief. "Where did you fetch her from, the gutters of Tanger? A stable? She's filthy. She has the look of a beggar!"

Indeed this was so, for Willow was still dressed in Esaak's woolen tatters, which had been ragged to begin with, but were now crusted with filth from the sea voyage. Nor had Willow been able to wash herself in anything but sea water.

Willow blushed a hot red, for she understood Castilian Spanish well enough; it was a dialect not far removed from what she'd learned in the house of Abu bin Nisar. Filthy? Yes, in her rough tunic and the cotton sheath of her underclothes. She thought of the cotton dresses and pajama suits lingering in her wooden chest back home. If this creature could see her as she appeared in the house of Abu bin Nisar she would not be so coarse or cruel. And why should she care, anyway?

But then a trill of horror ran through her as she realized that the captain meant to sell her as a whore to this hulking madame.

Martina in turn glared back at her with a scowl. "Wash her!" she commanded.

In a trice, Willow was hustled to a brick tub hidden by a fringe of plants at the back of the hacienda and stripped of Esaak's tunic by the prostitutes who'd ushered her in. A sponge on a handle was produced along with a bar of greasy soap. Willow hesitated for a moment in the shadow along the wall before throwing off the sheath of her cotton underclothes, not caring if anyone watched from behind. The water was cool and clean and she stuck her entire head in the tub before scrubbing every inch of her body with the rough sponge. As an afterthought, she rinsed her clothes, wringing them out as best she could before donning them again.

"Better," Martina said when she returned, dripping on the pavement, "but still nothing more than the trash of Tanger. A shepherd girl by the look of her."

"This trash as you say is a pure one, still almost a child."

"A child? Hah! I think not," Madama Martina sniffed. "I know these brats, they begin pleasuring Arab boys when they're ten, if they're not stroking the donkeys. Why, their own books are filled with tales of women's treachery and lechery. What makes you think I would care for such a wicked one as this? Mohammedans! Arabs!"

At this Sincid gave a merry laugh. "Some say you are Arab yourself! If not for the wicked, where would you be?"

"There are no wicked girls here. We welcome only the doves," Martina said with a squat frown.

Captain Sincid scoffed and rolled his eyes. "Your doves are married to the pox. I would not trust my prick with any of them without a fish skin for a sheath," he said.

"Lies, dirty lies! You dare to defame the flowers of Sevilla?"

This was too outrageous even to provoke a laugh and Sincid responded with a dry look of pity. "The only flower in this cesspit is the one before you," he said.

"Pish! She would be of no interest to the gentlemen we serve."

Sincid smiled, raised his nose, and gave a rat-like sniff. "Did you fart, madame? I think something stinks here."

"Watch yourself, captain."

"Come and see then, come and see," Sincid beckoned, smiling at the bluff.

Even Willow knew that the madame was trying to negotiate her value down. Yet, her insults couldn't conceal the hungry gleam in her eyes, for given the test, Willow might be worth a great many doubloons.

Martina studied Willow closely. She noted that her eyes were the color of jade, quite out of character with her cocoa skin. They were so beautiful that she almost gasped with the thought of how much gold the woman would bring, for what man could resist such eyes?

But this is not what she told the fidgeting Sincid.

"Look at her eyes; it is a sign of the pox! She will be dead within the year."

"And how comes a virgin by the pox?" Sincid replied smoothly.

The madame saw her error, but rebounded just as smoothly. "Perhaps there is a hex upon her then," she said dismissively. "She has eyes like a snake. Ugly, frightening even! No man will want her."

"Liar. Her eyes are a treasure. They make her a queen."

"No, I think not," she said, making a face. "I know men. I know what they are willing to pay for a woman, and they will shun her. Who would want such a woman with such frightening eyes? I can barely stand to look at her."

"I will take her elsewhere then!" Sincid said with a sneer. "Do you think I am the toy of a fool? I have honored you as a woman of good sense, bringing this treasure straight to your house! Yet now I see that you have wasted my morning."

"Wait, wait. Let me consider..."

Sighing, the madame waved to the women who stood watching from the doorway. They came forth and led Willow to the counter along the wall. Then, one on each side, they grasped her legs, cradled her back, and hoisted her wriggling and protesting atop the bar. One of them caressed her forehead as she lay quivering, while the other held her hand.

The madame strolled forward with a grave look on her face and lifted the hem of Willow's tunic, gazing within. She motioned a boy forward and twisting to the side, Willow could see that he bore a small dish of fragrant oil. Madama Martina swished her fingers through the oil and then with a grunt and a careless look, no different than that of a woman washing dishes, she reached under Willow's dress and slid a long finger within that place which no man or woman had ever touched. She probed deep within, searching for the unbroken hymen.

Willow gave out a scream of outrage and kicked back, squirming free in a fury.

"Be still, hell cat!" the madame cried, motioning for her servants to seize Willow's arms. "The test is older than the pyramids and all who enter here must endure it!"

Martina's arm fell heavy on Willow's left leg, pinning her down as the women on either side of her tightened their grip. Willow twisted harder this time, straining to bite the women who held her, but all to no avail. Beaten, she quivered like a bird caught in a snare, tears streaming down her cheeks as she was violated again.

"I will kill you for this," she hissed through clenched teeth. "I swear it!"

But Martina only grunted, searching again as Willow growled through clenched teeth.

Then, the ordeal was over. Wiping her fingers on a proffered scarf, Martina huffed in feigned resignation. "She's as soiled as the sewers, abused by camels," she said, scowling. "She's as wide as the rain spouts of the cathedral. Surely she's been violated by a donkey, at least."

"No!" Captain Sincid's eyes flared wide in disbelief.

"Even so. I'll give you a tenth of what you ask, no more."

But Sincid's patience was at an end. "Bueno, we go then," he said brusquely, tugging at Willow's arm. He made to hurry her out the door.

"No, captain, hold a moment..."

"We're done. No more insults!" Sincid kept pushing for the door, hustling Willow before him.

But before the slaver could reach the shadow of the hallway, Martina sighed and raised a hand in defeat. "Attend, attend," she said wearily.

"Why should I attend?"

"Let me consider..."

"Fah!" He spat over his shoulder. Turning, his face was filled with wrath, his black eyes aflame. "Whoremaster! Snake! There's another house, and another. A hundred houses in Sevilla will rejoice to have my dove!"

Martina quailed. "Hold!" she cried, the hope of an easy score dying in her eyes as her jowls drooped in resignation. "She's a pure one, as you say, a virgin."

"And?" Sincid leaned in, leering in triumph.

"And? Name your price and make it sweet to my ears."

The captain bent to her ear and whispered a figure, to which Martina's tattooed eyebrows arched in disbelief.

"Never!"

Then began an hour of haggling interrupted by orange and ginger tea as Willow huddled against the wall, smoldering at her violation. Another hour passed with a serving of sugared dates and more tea as the captain and the madame bargained on. At the end of it, neither Sincid or the madame seemed satisfied as each gave their final offer, swearing it was as inviolable as a prayer etched in stone.

And little did Willow know that her own kindly master, Abu bin Nisar, had conducted similar negotiations with the Sultan who ruled the lands around Badis. Anxious of his looming poverty and dripping with greed, he had described his serving girl as being as pure and beautiful as the *houri* virgins who cavorted in Paradise for the pleasure of those who died in the service of Allah. Indeed, she had been spied upon by the Sultan's vizier in the town's marketplace, and then by the Sultan himself, who had stalked her while draped and cowled in the disguise of a woman. Abu bin Nisar had been only a week away from confirming his bargain when the slavers had spirited Willow away, depriving the Sultan's harem of another morsel.

In the end, there was no agreement on the price of Willow's maidenhead.

"I will see what the market will bring," Captain Sincid said upon taking his leave.

"To hell with you, bung-licker," Martina said good-naturedly. "You'll get half of what I've offered in the market. You'll be back, and then my offer will be lessened with each hour you're away."

"We'll see," Sincid said, his lips tightening to a slit. He threw his noose over Willow's head again and gave her a rough yank toward the door.

By now the streets of the port were filled with knots of sailors, merchants and women hurrying to and from the markets. But off in the distance, Willow could hear the sound of trumpets - the same ones she had heard the night before - and dimly, the roar of a crowd. The captain plowed on, muttering to himself in anger at being denied the jingle of gold, and perhaps at the prospect of explaining his disappearance to his crew.

"*Auto da fae, auto da fae,*" he grumbled at the sound of the crowd ahead, speaking now in Spanish. "Yes, I should give you to them instead of that fat witch. Hah! I should give her to them, I think! Maybe I will slip a word in the priests' ears. It would do her good."

Somehow Willow knew that the captain would never do anything of the sort, for the masked priests she had seen leading the crowd in their conical hats and gowns of black and red projected a demonic power of the sort which would likely send her captor scampering like a frightened cat.

"Yes, and I will speak to your priests about you," she said defiantly, ripping the tether of her noose from his hands.

He quickly leaned in to grasp it back and looked in her eyes as if for the first time, offering a thin smile. "Oh my dear, that would not be wise."

Soon enough, Willow learned that the captain's words rang true, for as they rounded the last warehouse to the square fronting the wharf her eyes followed the jeering crowd to the fortress across the river. There, just beyond the gates, stood ten stakes with a flaming human being chained to each one, burning like candles in the sun. A billowing cloud of greasy black smoke rose from the line of twisted corpses, accompanied by the pop and crackle of fat consumed by the fire. Even at a distance, Willow could see the blackened faces of the damned grimacing in the agony of death.

The captain's eyes narrowed to cat-like slits and he frowned at the murderous ritual across the river, crossing himself before pushing Willow back across the narrow plank to the galley. She scrambled to the bottom of the boat to where Croen lay huddled, grasping his legs in his arms and rocking back and forth.

"What in the name of the angels is this?" she cried in disbelief.

Croen looked over at her, pale beneath his sunburn. "The judgment of the Lord's servants, child. The penitents, they..."

Willow was still in a fury over her treatment at Madama Martina's, and now she snapped, striking Croen in the chest with her fists. "I knew this would happen! I warned you of this!" she cried.

Croen reared back, startled. "Ah, yes, I remember now. My apologies."

"Who are those people and what did they do to deserve such a fate?"

"Jews," he answered. "Pretenders to God's truth. They had to be rooted out. It's a thing called the Inquisition, presided over by the priests under the blessing of Rome."

"Jews? The lowly Jews? How can they be here? All know that they were driven from Spain." Willow had heard the tale of the Jews in the home of Abu bin Nisar.

"Aye, they left while I was still a young man, in 1492 it was," Croen replied. "Old Queen Isabella and King Ferdinand showed 'em the door along with the Mohammedans. Wanted the whole country to be Catholic, ye see; din't want any traitors rising up against 'em."

"So how can they be here now?" Willow's eyes swept the far wharf where feral dogs and clusters of rats were swarming beneath the damned, licking at the puddled blood. A crow sat atop the blackened head of a tall corpse, pecking at its eyes.

"Ah, some stayed behind, ye see. Those who left were plundered as clean as chicken bones on Sunday. But some were allowed to stay if they promised to give up their faith. The king and queen decided they were too valuable to lose, for they were the traders, the shop owners, and bankers who lent money to the royals in times of need. They could nae afford to let 'em all go, so they offered to make them Christian, don't you see? Those who wished to stay in Spain were baptized as Catholics."

"So where's the sin in that?" Willow wondered, grateful that the roar of the crowd had dwindled as the spectators drifted away in knots along the wharf.

"Well, don't ye see? The churchmen suspected that those who took the vow were only pretending. So there've been trials, don't ye see, the trials of the Inquisition to root out the unfaithful.

"But here's the thing," he leaned in close. "It's with the help of the rack, the thumbscrew and bright red iron that the unfaithful tend to confess, and there's not much hope for the innocent. Dear no. I expect it will all be sorted out by the angels at yet another trial."

He nodded toward the opposite shore. "If these people were innocent and truly Catholic, they'll be granted a measure of grace in our Lord's heaven.

"But then, of course, no Jew is permitted in heaven," Croen said as an afterthought. "No, it's off to hell with that lot, or wherever God cares to put them."

Groaning, Willow collapsed on her rough bedding, numb with the day's events.

"At least you were spared the screaming," Croen offered. "Ah, it was terrible loud and a misery to my ears, but a mercy that most of them died in the smoke, choking on it before they got the worst of their licking. Most... Still, a terrible thing to behold, even if their judgment was just.

"And where were you, love?" he added, as if it had just occurred to him. "I was terrible worried for ye."

"Being fitted for a whore's collar," she said miserably. Ah, but then a thought struck her: the dagger. Father said that should she ever need it, the blade would ease her into the next world, free of all cares. She had tested the knife's edge with her thumb many times, finding it wickedly sharp. She vowed to cheat both the captain and the madam if it came to it. Neither had thought to search her.

"Well that explains it then," Croen interrupted her thoughts.

"What?"

"I wondered that they hadn't raped ye," he nodded to the captain and his crew. "Thou art worth something dear to these lizards."

To Market

As it happened, the quarter of Santa Maria la Blanca was the haunt of many who slaved in Sevilla, which, along with Lisbon, boasted more souls in bondage than any city in Europe. Slaves made up the seventh part of the city, with a mix of blacks from the kingdoms of Africa and the so-called white slaves of the Moors. In what little time they had to spare, many of Sevilla's slaves loitered in the quarter, rubbing elbows with the hoodlums, whores and cut-purses of the city. It was here that Willow was brought to market in a square fronting a small church.

It had been a good haul for Captain Bartolomeu Sincid, and he strolled along with his black eyes burning with purpose at the head of twelve captives, who were strung neck-to-neck with iron collars and a thin chain. Two of his crew brought up the rear, armed with staves and a whip, though these were used more to keep mischief-makers at bay than to hurry along the captives.

Willow had never felt so miserable, even more than when her father had sold her north from Azemmour. She had been badly shaken by the violation of her body the day before and had spent the night in a sleepless rage, plotting revenge, with murderous scenarios flying through her head like the *jinns* and *rocs* of old Arabia.

"I will kill them, I swear by Allah I will," she murmured as she straggled through the twisting streets.

"Ah, lamb, say it is not so, for they will kill thee long before you hoist a blade to their throats," the woman chained ahead of her muttered.

"I have made my vow and I will live to fulfill it," Willow answered, but her words fell flat, empty of menace, and if anything, she felt shrunken, collapsed, incapable of action. She had passed from one life of bondage to another and the thought of it made her feel as if she had become a stumbling ghost, blown by the winds of fate. What horrors might await her? She gagged at the thought of it as they trudged along.

All along the route through the twisting alleys and filthy streets, Willow and her companions were subjected to jeers and catcalls as they trudged through the dust. She was bound between two other women, and the three were the targets of crude comments and gestures. One drunken seaman with long black mustachios and the look of a dark beast dragged down the front of his breeches and flogged his penis at them as they passed by, waggling his tongue in tandem. A tall woman of the Moors chained behind Willow hawked up a great ball of phlegm and spat in his face, uttering the ululating cry of her people in triumph. The drunkard cursed and made claws of his hands to seize her, but was clubbed hard across the face by one of Sincid's sailors. Willow looked back to see him lying on the paving stones with his face awash in blood and his ruined nose smashed sideways. His tongue lolled and his left eye rolled askew, showing as white as that of a butchered cow.

"Vai! Vai!" the seaman cried, pushing the line forward. He paused for a moment to give the drunkard a hurried kick back to the pavement as he struggled to rise.

At last they pushed through a crowd to a low platform in front of the church, from which a priest in a black robe stepped forth to bless them, waving a brass censer of incense strung on three chains. He stood behind the platform, ringing the air with thin clouds of fragrant smoke.

"Dominus vobiscum, et cum spiritu tuo!" Willow heard Croen cry out to the

priest in Latin from several places back in the line. *"Soy Cristiano, padre!"* he cried. *"Yo soy Catolico!"*

Croen's quote from the Catholic Mass was clear to every bystander in the crowd, including the priest. But if the priest knew or cared that Croen was baptized a Catholic, he didn't show it. He gave a somber nod and a bow before retreating backward one slow step at a time to the church doors, closing them behind him.

Captain Sincid had observed Croen's plea with a bemused grin. "Irish rat," he said in heavily accented Spanish, prodding him in the chest. "Priest no care for you."

This elicited laughter from those standing nearby, for all knew that a man from five hundred leagues to the north was fair game in the slave markets of Sevilla, especially those drawn from the savages who dwelt in Eire, who were considered barely a step above the beasts of the field. Croen stared at the shuttered doors of the church in disbelief and then at the uncaring crowd.

Captain Sincid gave him three pats on the cheek and then a hard slap to bring him back in line. "There!" he gestured, beckoning to the auction block.

Willow noticed that many in the crowd were well-dressed men swathed in parti-colored velvet and silks, adorned with great flopping hats and carrying silver-tipped canes. More than a few gazed at her with hungry, appraising eyes. Of these, most were lustful and goaty in their looks, by turns fat or spindly, old and ugly, speckled with warts, pock marks and goiters. There were also richly-dressed women in the crowd; the madams of Sevilla's storied brothels, looking for fresh blood. A shiver ran through Willow's thin frame as she looked away from those who caught her eye. At the back of the crowd she glimpsed Madama Martina pushing her way forward; a shark come to claim its fish if she could.

Captain Sincid's captives were the only slaves on the block that day and the bidding began with the lowest among them. The two camel boys, ages seven and eight, fetched 11 and 14 silver ducats, the value of a small flock of chickens, a case of table wine and a few loaves of bread. The hog-faced beggar was sold as a galley slave for much the same. Sincid scowled at the price, lambasting the auctioneer, who shrugged, assuring him that better things were yet to come.

And indeed, he proved to be a prognosticator, for the tall woman who had spat in the drunkard's face fetched 18 golden ducats, a value far greater than that of mere silver. Although she was no beauty, she had a sensual quality and had read the crowd well, waggling her hips in a slow dance and drawing two fingers across her smoky eyes and then down across her chest to caress her belly in a slow, silky manner. She cupped her heavy breasts in her hands and raised them up and down, staring into the eyes of the mesmerized merchants of the town. The auctioneer had touted her as being skilled at dyeing and weaving fabrics, but her smoldering display had driven the price up from eight to ten and finally 18 ducats as lust spread like a house fire among the bidders. She was fetched from the dock by a toothless old cloth merchant who stood a foot shorter than her, grinning like a crocodile. She turned with a grimace and shrugged at Willow. "Good hunting to you, sister," she said. "Our fate is in the hands of Allah, and He hath delivered me to this toad. May you fare better."

Willow nodded gravely as the old gnome led his prize away. How much would she fetch when her time came? she wondered. Not so much as her bold sister, she imagined.

Then came Akmed, clutching his ruined hand before him by his wrist, pale as death and sick with pain. His clothes were streaked brown with blood, as was the bandage fashioned from Croen's tunic. The auctioneer touted him as a strongly-built prize, almost a man and capable of doing great service despite his cloven hand. But he got few takers, and those who bid would agree to no more than 10 silver ducats, less even than that fetched by the young camel boys. It was whispered in the crowd that Akmed was a trouble-maker, and had thus earned the mutilation of his hand. And who would want such a slave, and one that was crippled to boot? In the end, Sincid declined to sell him.

"He'll man the slaver's galley, that one," Croen whispered in Willow's ear. "He can still pull an oar, even if his hand is a stub."

"God's mercy on him," Willow whispered back, imagining the captain's cruel lash applied with zest on Akmed's back.

Then came the other woman among the captives, a meek yarn-carder who bore a resemblance to the sheep she curried. Unlike the tall woman before her, she was no temptress and Sincid glumly accepted five golden ducats as her price.

Then came the older men, with Croen being the second among them to be auctioned. But before the auctioneer could begin his spiel there came the sound of trumpets down the way and the beating of a drum. Long down a narrow side street came a troop of men in steel breastplates and plumed helmets, all of them bearing tall pikes. The tips of the pikes had been honed to a razor edge, flashing like mirrors in the sun.

"Hold on there!" a loud voice commanded. "Hold in the name of the King's men!"

Into the square marched Captain Martin de Cabeza, a soldier of fortune at the head of twenty men clad in leather and steel. He strutted through the square, a sword of blue-gray steel upheld before him like a torch. His breeches were striped black and red and a scarlet plume crowned the half-moon helmet atop his head. A red dragon crossed his breastplate, which was burnished as black as his matching chain mail. Like every man in Sevilla, he wore a beard and a mustache, though his was cropped short with considerable care, giving him a rakish look. At a shouted command, the long pikes of his men lowered to chest level, then waved up again in a choreographed sweep before stamping their butt ends down to the pavement with a resounding clash.

"I need men - men who are ready for the sea and treasure!" he announced in a loud voice. "I need men for New Spain!"

Laughter rippled through the crowd and from the rear came a voice, "Go back to Tabernas, captain! The men here are more at ease waving a drumstick than a sword!"

And at a glance, one could see it was so, for Willow imagined that a troop of monkeys could conquer the dissolute, pot-bellied men of the square.

But the captain was not dissuaded. "If there are no men among you, then I will look to the slaves," he growled, motioning for his men to clear the way.

"New Spain - hah! The devil's den! The end of the world!" From the clamor of voices Willow gathered that New Spain had the scent of horror among those gathered in the square. Even she had heard of its perils: Abu bin Nisar had told her it was a land of immeasurable wealth, yet guarded by monsters and one-eyed ogres, far beyond the heartless ocean. Many who journeyed there never returned.

Captain Cabeza strolled up to the auction block and appraised the three men standing there. He ignored Croen, directing his attention to a couple of solidly built teamsters who had been caught leading their camels along a coastal road. Neither proved suitable, and the captain turned to go with a dissatisfied look on his face.

"I'm ready for the sea and treasure, captain!" Croen spoke in a loud voice as the captain turned away.

Cabeza turned and snorted in amusement. "That may be, grandfather, but thou art too old for my purposes."

"Aye, but old means wisdom, captain, and knowledge of the sea."

"And have you this knowledge?"

"More than most, sir. More than most."

"Speak of it then."

Croen's face grew animated, gazing earnestly into the captain's eyes as he filled Cabeza's ears with promises.

"I pledge meself a seaman of the first rank, captain! I know the waters all the way from the Hebrides to Alexandria and have chivvied ships as a mate on the Great Ocean Sea itself before being cruelly taken by the Mohammedans. I have sailed down the coast of Africa, a place which few sailors know! I have even sailed to Iceland, sir, at the far end of the world! Not many men can claim that."

These boasts, Willow thought, must surely be bald lies. Croen had told her that he was the first mate on a trading ship, but she had not believed him, suspecting that he was only a simple fisherman given to tale-telling. Yet Croen was clearly desperate to escape the fate of slaving in Sevilla, and she had seen his eyes light up at Cabeza's promise of treasure. Envy washed over her as she imagined Croen bound for the New World, for surely it could not be a place as wicked as Sevilla.

"Would'st thou lie to me, grandfather?" Captain Cabeza said, stroking the bristle of his chin.

"Nay, captain," Croen said with a knowing chuckle. "I pledge an arm and a leg and my body to the fishes if it is not true! For I can read the sea like no other man, be it cold waters or warm. Think on it, captain. Ye say you're bound for the New World? In truth, I have not been there, but I've spent many nights poring over charts and exchanging tales with those who have. And I am a good, Christian man, devoted to our savior Jesus and can work as hard as ten mules put together. I could be of good value to you, captain, very good value."

Croen nodded in assurance, gazing into the captain's eyes, which twinkled with amusement.

"Ten mules? This would be a feat worthy of a ballad," Cabeza said with a laugh, summoning his treasurer. It was true that Croen was an old man, but his hair was still ginger-red, absent of any gray, and the captain decided that he would be capable of a few years of service, at least.

Cabeza bargained absently for Croen as Captain Sincid gaped at his good fortune. For, as it turned out, Captain Cabeza seemed to have little acquaintance with the value of Irish slaves on the block. Croen was sold for twelve golden ducats, a wild stroke of good fortune for the slaver.

"Friend, I don't mean to doubt you, but I wonder if you can find your way from one end of a ship to the other, much less across the seas of the world," Willow said quietly, just before Croen was led from the platform.

"Hah! I've been hoisting sheets since long before ye were born, child," he answered, casting a wild look of exhilaration around the square. "And though it's true I was only a seaman instead of a first mate, I've kept me eyes open all these years and know the seas of which I speak, if only in the tales told round the pickle barrel! I'll learn the rest soon enough or feed the fishes if I nay."

"Well, may your luck be kinder this time," she said, with her heart rising in her throat.

"And to thee," he answered gravely.

The teamsters were each sold for a palm of silver and then there were none left on the dock save Willow. Yet how was she to know that she was the treasure reserved for last? Her maidenhood was expected to fetch a high price from the lecherous men and gimlet-eyed madams who surged forward to where the auctioneer and Captain Sincid stood.

Captain Cabeza and his troop had lingered for some refreshment among the merchants selling wine to the spectators. But now they heeled around and made ready to leave the square. Willow searched for a last glance at Croen, who had disappeared in the crush at the back of the conquistadors. A tear trickled down her cheek as she heard the opening bid called aloud by the auctioneer.

"Gentlemen, ladies, the bidding starts at one hundred golden ducats!"

A monstrous gasp of dismay arose from the crowd and the merchants and madams pressed forward, their eyes stabbing at her as she stood alone on the slave dock. One hundred ducats! Even for such an unspoiled beauty it seemed excessive, and virtually every madam in the crowd scoffed and turned away, cursing. Yet Willow saw that there were wealthy men exchanging knowing looks and muttering among themselves. Off to the side, Captain Sincid looked on with glee.

"Strip her!" a voice rang out. "Strip her that we might see!"

"No!" Willow shook her head, clutching her tunic to her body and backing away in alarm. But the auctioneer cupped an ear to the crowd, egging on the assembled men and grinning in agreement as more voices rose among them. "Aye! Strip her! *Strip her!* Let us see!"

With a grandiloquent gesture and an outstretched arm, the auctioneer bowed to the crowd and motioned for his men to disrobe Willow so that all might see her worth.

But just as she was twisting away from their grasping hands, she heard a booming voice as it rose above the tumult. *"My lord, give a thought to her, for she is a princess who might serve you well!"*

It was Croen who made the thundering plea and even to Willow's ears it seemed insanely impudent and worthy of a whipping. But Captain Cabeza hesitated a moment in mid-step and then turned on his heel, as if humoring an idiot.

"A princess, you say?" He motioned for Croen and the Irishman was dragged forward with a soldier grasping each arm.

"Aye, sir, she was a serving girl to the great Sultan of Persia, the high Poobah himself, and was named a princess of Maroc for her troubles!" Croen sputtered, staring wide-eyed into Cabeza's face.

It was such an outrageous lie that Willow feared that the captain would sweep forth his sword and filet Croen's pale flesh. But the captain gave a hearty laugh, as if he was in on the joke, and he strolled up to the low platform where Willow stood quivering at her fate.

"Are you truly a princess, girl?" he teased, raising her chin with an outstretched finger. "Are you worth one hundred golden ducats?"

"No, m'lord, merely a serving wench, though my father was held in high regard. He was considered a prince of the desert by those who knew him," she replied miserably, twisting her chin from his touch and gazing down.

Captain Cabeza snorted at this. "I can easily imagine," he said acidly, turning to leave.

It was then that the auctioneer rushed forward with Captain Sincid close behind. "But m'lord, this girl is unblemished, a virgin! A mango! Think of how she might serve thee! Think of the nights of pleasure, knowing that she is a dove of unequalled worth, and yours alone!"

To this Cabeza answered with a cold stare. "I have no use for virgins."

Who knows then what made Croen speak the words, which seemed so foolish and unwise, he being a newly-conscripted slave of a proud captain. At the very least, he should have been lashed, if not deprived of an ear for his impudence, but he piped up with Irish vigor, "She's a right-lively shepherd girl too, sire! Aye! And she is handy with goats, and... and sheep!" as if this might be of especial value to a captain of conquistadors.

Captain Cabeza gaped at Croen and laughed in disbelief. Shaking his head, he turned to go.

Yet Willow's voice rose in a last desperate plea.

"And camels, too, captain!" she cried. "I have great knowledge and experience with camels!"

Cabeza waved in dismissal. "Camel tenders are as common as drunkards, even in Sevilla."

It was Willow's last chance.

"And a lion, captain!" she cried. "I was mother to a lion!"

Turning, Captain Martin Cabeza looked at her as if with new eyes.

"A lion?"

He Who Outruns the Wolves

Spring, 1526
Lake Superior, Upper Michigan

It is no easy matter, standing upright in the middle of a canoe as it tilts up and down in the waves, yet the fisherman known as Wolf had done so many times. Now, he stood braced above the waters of the vast lake, Kitchi Gami, peering into its pale green waves with a spear in his upraised arm.

A pearly shadow passed beneath the canoe, almost too deep to be seen, much less speared. It was an impossible cast, but he attempted it anyway, aiming just ahead of the passing fish and thrusting his spear with all of his strength.

But the extra effort and a rising wave on the other side of his canoe took him a whisper past the brink of balance and his body followed the spear into the water.

"Faugh!" He tumbled upside down in the green haze of the lake and its sunlit flecks of algae before clawing his way back to the surface, coughing up water. He'd taken a spout of lake water up his nose and the space between his eyes throbbed with the pain of it. For a moment he lingered in the waves, coughing and sneezing. Another wave lapped over his head, pushing him down again before he flailed back to the surface.

He sputtered and snorted, bobbing amid the waves. Most of his brothers and sisters could not swim, yet Wolf was at ease in the water and his arms were the best part of his physique, strong and supple. He swam back to his drifting canoe and couldn't help laughing as he clung to its side; laughing even more so when the end of his spear bobbed up with a lake trout as long as his arm still wriggling at its tip of a barbed antler.

With a grunt, he hoisted the trout into his canoe and kicked for the shore, pushing the craft as he clung to it. It was his fourth catch of the day and all of the fish were long and fat. His uncles among the shamans would be pleased.

Reaching shallow water, Wolf dug his toes into the sand and climbed back into his canoe, shaking off the chill as he paddled east for the river that led to Boweting. During the fishing season Boweting was home for hundreds of the Ojibwe and their kin the Odawa. The river along the settlement fed into a strait that connected three immense lakes: Kitchi Gami to the north, Tima Gami to the southeast and Mishi Gami to the southwest. The lakes were the sweetwater seas of the Great Turtle Island, a vast continent bounded by two oceans and covered with endless plains, forests, mountains and rivers.

In those days, there were tribes beyond count ranging across the Great Turtle Island, but the great lakes and their forests served as the heartland of the Anishinaabek - the True People of the Three Fires: the Ojibwe, Odawa and Potawatomi.

Wolf had been born among the Odawa, but now counted the Ojibwe as his people. In truth, there was little difference between the people of the Three Fires, with many ties of kinship and clans, and only slight differences in the manner of speaking. But these were good times for the Ojibwe in particular; the lakes were filled with fish, the forests rich with game, and their enemies were far away.

Aside from its wealth as a fishery, Boweting was the home of the lodge of the Mide-wi-win, where Wolf had studied the ways of the shamans these last five years. Sadly, in his uncles' eyes, Wolf was more inclined to go fishing than to sit by their sides, learning the ways of magic and medicine. His uncles were grateful to have the fish he provided, but still, there had been grumblings, which often had Wolf slinking away like his namesake.

Reaching the banks of the Great Lodge, he dragged his canoe up from the shore, turned it over, and covered it with wet leaves to keep its birch skin damp and supple. He threaded a leather thong through the gills of his fish and slung them over his shoulder, hobbling up the lane toward the lodge with the trout dangling over his back as if they were a cloak.

"Ah, look at the fish hunter!" A trio of women stood smiling as he passed. "What did you bring us, Wolf?"

It was Singing Tree who had called out in a teasing way, and he gazed back at her with shining eyes. Once, they had been lovers, but that was several summers ago and now she was pledged to another. Still, Singing Tree loved to flirt and Wolf warmed to her voice and the knowledge that she still burned for him, if only in a small way.

"Would you like a fish?" he called. "I will give you one if you will roast it for me. Then we might share a pipe."

But she was not inclined to take the bait.

"Oh, I've had my fish for the day," she said, sauntering alongside him. "Too many fish and not enough meat. Fetch me a partridge or a slice of elk if you wish to make me happy."

The lane on which they walked passed through a row of bark lodges, some of them round and built for only a family or two, while others were domed longhouses that could house four families or more. Women hurried by, bearing firewood on their backs, and a group of men gossiped beneath a nearby tree. It was a small village, one of many that made up Boweting, but it was a place of some importance owing to the shamans who gathered there.

Singing Tree jingled as she walked, with a scrim of copper bells lining the edge of her skirt. Her long braids fell past her breasts, which Wolf noted were fuller now than he had remembered. She caught his gaze and smiled. "Not for you, brother," she said, guessing his thoughts.

"I would rather be your man than your brother," he said, gazing at her hopefully. "You know I still long for you."

"All men are brothers, as we are all sisters," she replied with a wan smile, "but we are not to be lovers again."

"Sister, you bring me tears."

"Then you must find the pelt of a skunk to dry them. It will give you something else to think about."

"Ahhh... I do not see your bow, but you have filled my chest with arrows!"

"Then savor your pain, brother, for I am sure you will find another woman soon enough."

"But none like you..."

"Hush!"

On an impulse, Wolf pulled the thigh bone of an eagle from his braided hair and said, "Then would you care for this to remember me when you are wed to another?"

Days before, he had found the eagle's carcass floating by the shore of Kit-chi Gami, picked clean by scavengers. He had taken the bird's thighs and polished them, expecting to turn them into whistles. But for a woman such as Singing Tree, one would do just as well as an ornament.

Her eyes lit up as he handed it to her. "Truly, you are a magician! I can use this, *miigwech*," she said.

"Meet me tonight," he said, gazing into her eyes. She was his own age, barely twenty summers and irresistible. He thought again of their time together, so long ago now, it seemed, and dared to forget that she was betrothed.

But Singing Tree eyed him coolly. "Ah, you are too bold, Wolf, and bad birds will be singing if we meet alone. I have another man now and their voices will reach his ears. Besides, grandfather is looking for you."

"Wabeno?"

"*Eya*. He has been asking all around for you."

They made plans to share a pipe by the river later on, accompanied by Singing Tree's elderly aunt to vouch for her chastity, and Wolf hurried up the way as fast as his crippled foot would allow. At the top of the hill he reached the lodge of his uncles, known to all as the Good Hearts for their kindness and healing ways.

It was a rambling shelter, empty except at times of ceremony. Bowed over and covered with a roof of elm bark, the lodge was one hundred paces long and twenty wide. It could accommodate three hundred of the Anishinaabek, but most stood outside and observed the shamans performing their rituals within on days of ceremony. At those times, a screen of balsam firs covering the sides of the lodge was removed to allow viewing.

"Where were you?" Wabeno demanded when Wolf reached the old man's dwelling alongside the lodge.

"Out fishing, grandfather," Wolf stammered. It was unlike Wabeno-inini, Man of the Dawn Sky, to be short with him. "I've been fishing along the north coast."

"Long time gone!"

"Three days, grandfather. Only three days."

"Your uncles complain that you have neglected their teachings," Wabeno said as a wave of disapproval passed over his face. "Again."

Wolf squirmed under Wabeno's stern gaze. "Even shamans must eat," he replied, "and I've brought these for their evening meal."

Wolf was an apprentice of the shamans, but his heart was more in fishing and spinning tales than in sitting through the lessons of the elders, which often made him drowsy, causing his thoughts to wander.

Wabeno softened. "Meal? My son, you were gone so long that I thought perhaps the fish had eaten you. We have need of you."

"Me, grandfather?"

He nodded. "*Ehn*."

"What can you need of me?"

"You will learn tomorrow. We will meet in the sweat lodge at mid-day. Prepare yourself. Eat well tonight, it will be a long day."

With that, Wabeno accepted a fish for his old wife to roast over the coals and left Wolf standing there, mystified.

Wabeno-inini was the great elder of the shamans, wizened and wrinkled with age, with a face as pugnacious as that of a snapping turtle. It was said that he was older than the stoutest oaks of the forest, and that his mind was deep with knowledge dating back to the time when the Anishinaabek had migrated west from the Great Salt Water, Zhewitakanibi. Thus came his name, Wabeno-inini, Man of the Dawn Sky. He had taken Wolf into his lodge as an apprentice five years ago, honoring him as a son, and had imparted all he knew of the Ojibwe and their cousins among the Odawa and the Potawatomi.

On many nights through the years Wolf had sat with Wabeno before the lodge fire, drinking in his stories of the True People. Some of the tales wandered back to the time of the Old Ones when gigantic beasts roamed the earth amid rivers of ice that towered above the land as tall as mountains. Stories, too, of spirits that stalked the night and flew through the sky, catching men unaware in their nets. Wabeno had told him how men, filled with desire and wonder, had climbed down from their hole in the sky amid the stars after discovering women walking the earth. Thereafter, they had married the animals, becoming one with all the creatures of the earth.

Wolf in turn had regaled Wabeno with his own clutch of stories, the sum of which could fill a hundred quivers with arrows. On many winter nights they had talked almost until dawn with the north wind, Biboon, howling outside their lodge.

Wolf had been inducted by acclaim into the Society of Shamans at the age of fifteen summers by virtue of his ability as a story-teller with a gifted memory. He had served five years now as an apprentice, but a poor one at best. The lessons would not stick! Instead, he begged to hear his teachers' stories and with little prodding, his uncles' eyes would brighten at some long-lost memory. Their teachings would fall by the wayside as they told of the strange things they had seen and heard in their own youth. Thus, Wolf absorbed every story his uncles told, winding back to the days of their grandfathers' grandfathers, yet learning little of the ways of a shaman beyond some skill with herbs.

Although his left leg was cursed with a club foot that had never healed, Wolf was quick to skulk off into the forest like his namesake when it came time for his lessons. Often, his uncles cried out for him in vain as he paddled his canoe far down the coast of Kitchi Gami, entranced by the far horizon.

"Wolf! Where are you? Come to us! Wolf!" Yes, sometimes he could hear their voices calling on the wind or sounding from the waves as he paddled along, yet still he would slink away in the hope that a fish or two would ease his uncles' wrath.

The next morning, Wolf arose from his sleeping robe in the longhouse that served as the abode of the apprentices. He ate the cold remains of a fish grilled the night before and gathered his spear with the intention of going fishing again. It was then that he remembered Wabeno's summons. What could the elders want of him? They had summoned him to their sweat lodge only once before, when he was an in-between man in the ceremony of acceptance.

"It is no small thing to be summoned," muttered Whisperer, who shared the same sleeping platform in their lodge.

"It can only mean ill," Wolf said.

"Perhaps they mean to make you their headman," Whisperer said in jest.

"I would sooner carry their dump buckets."

"We have done enough of that, brother. Leave it to the younger ones," Whisperer replied in the low voice that gave him his name. Part of a shaman's apprenticeship was performing chores for the old men, and these could be odious, such as collecting their birch buckets each morning to be washed out on the banks of the river.

"Perhaps they plan to make me chief of the dump buckets."

"Perhaps. Perhaps they are angry that you are so often away when you should be chewing at their wisdom. Old men are peevish about such things."

"Ah, brother, you have speared it." Of course, a rebuke was in the wind.

A thrashing was just what Wolf expected when he entered the sweat house at mid-day.

The elders' sweat house was at the end of a short trail leading uphill from the Great Lodge. From the top of the hill one could see the many wigiwams and longhouses scattered far down the river. Some had been stripped of their bark covering or were bent over in ruins, awaiting the fall gathering when thousands of the Anishinaabek would travel to the river for the running of the whitefish. It was a time for catching and drying the wide-eyed fish for the coming winter. Yet, it was also a time of festivals, races, dancing, drumming and more, eagerly awaited throughout the year. Young men and women, especially, came to size up those to wed from other clans, while visitors from friendly tribes came to trade.

Wolf thought of the coming festival as he gazed down the river to the east. Already, a number of families were gathering along the banks, some of them with pretty daughters. It was this season that he hoped to find a woman who would have a reluctant shaman for a mate.

Midway up the hill, a gaunt dog crossed his path, pursued by four others. Its ribs were stark against its sides and one ear had been torn halfway from its head. The gray dog whirled in Wolf's path to snap at its pursuers, receiving a nip on its hind leg for its valor. For a moment its frightened eyes locked on Wolf's and then with a yip it dashed off over the side of the hill as the pack scrambled along behind it.

"An omen," Wolf muttered, wishing he had cast a stone at the snarling pack.

The sweat lodge was larger than most, nearly five strides in diameter and sheathed with thick panels of elm bark. Its entrance was covered with a leather flap and Wolf could hear a faint drumming within, like the beating wings of a grouse. Two thick-set women stood outside, heating stones over a bed of coals, to be carried inside and doused with birch containers of water. They nodded to Wolf, but neither spoke. He stripped off his leather breeches and laid them alongside the walls of the lodge, hoping the women would take care that some passing dog did not seize them. Then, standing naked, he looked out over the hill and took a deep breath, exhaling hard to cleanse any bad spirits that might be lurking within him that morning. Three times he completed the breathing ritual, and then, feeling renewed, he turned to greet his uncles.

Creeping within a short passageway on his hands and knees, Wolf's eyes strained in the darkness. The lodge was nearly as dark as a moonless night and the air within was close and heavy with steam scented with sassafras. Wolf made out the finger-tap of a drum and the vague shapes of his twelve uncles, who appeared as black shadows lining the wall.

Wabeno called to him. "Wolf, your place is beside me."

The council began cordially enough. A pipe carved with a raven's head was passed to the six directions, with each of the shamans tasting its smoke, including Wolf. He sat cross-legged beside Wabeno, listening to the tap of the drum and a song delivered in a musing voice by one of the elders.

> "Father, the birds are leaving
> Mother, the wind is sighing
> Sister, the snows are coming
> Brother, the fish are gathering
> Bring them,
> Bring them all
> To us, bring them all."

Despite the omen of the running dog and his fear of a thrashing, Wolf began to wonder if he had been summoned for some honor, possibly even an induction into the inner circle of the shamans who guided all others. Even in the darkness he sensed that his uncles seemed easy in his presence;

there was no taint of anger that he could detect. On the far wall, one of the shamans ripped a loud fart, which was greeted by good-natured groans and laughter.

The elder's song ended and the tapping of the drum faded away. A moment was taken for the women outside to enter and replenish the stones and their cleansing steam. Then, the pipe was passed around again, but this time in silence. Wolf began to fidget in suspense. What was coming? When would they speak?

But it was he whose words were summoned.

"Tell us a story," Wabeno's disembodied voice called out. "Tell us the story that none of us have heard."

"The story?"

"*Ehn.*"

"You have heard them all in my time with you, father," Wolf replied after a moment, his voice low and uncertain in the darkness. "I have emptied my quiver, I have cast every arrow."

"Not all. Tell us."

Not all? Wolf ran through his memory of countless nights by the fire, offering every tale he'd ever heard. He had spoken of demons, animals, heroes, monsters, spirits, shape-shifters and more. Great journeys, courageous deeds, lost lovers, star-struck maidens, night-walking dandies... grim warriors, far-off tribes, the miracles of the shamans, tales of the Old Ones and the Great Flood... What story had he not shared or collected?

Wolf was renowned as a tale-teller all along the coast of Kitchi Gami and beyond. Crippled from birth, the role of a story-teller had been one of the few ways forward and he had been blessed with a prodigious memory. Beginning as a child, he had gathered hundreds of stories, sharing them in the winter lodges and around the summer camp fires of many families. He had shared every story he knew, except...

There was only one. It was the story he had never told anyone, not even Wabeno-inini, the shaman he called grandfather. He was uneasy with it; the story rode his back like a demon, whispering that he should never speak of it, and yet his uncles somehow knew of it. Now, they demanded that he speak.

"There is only one story you have not heard, but it is a small thing and I do not wish to tell it," he said, feeling low and miserable. "It is a story of a man who matters very little. Grandfather, uncles... it is not worth telling."

"Tell it," Wabeno commanded.

"I cannot. I..."

"Tell it!"

Wolf squirmed in the darkness of the lodge with all eyes and ears upon him. It was all he could do to summon the words.

"Not so many years ago there was a village on the shores of Manitowaaling, the big island to the east," he began. "And into this village was born a crippled babe.

"To the horror of all who saw him, the babe had gray eyes rimmed in fire, just as clouds are rimmed by the sun. His eyes were those of a wolf, and his father held him up in anguish when he crawled from his mother's womb, for the babe's left foot was cruelly twisted to one side. It was clear to see that he was a clubfoot, of no use to anyone if he could not be healed.

"But uncles, as you know, such a deformity is easily made right while one is yet a babe, though there is a sharp pain in the healing. Yet the pain is soon forgotten, and today many walk among the Anishinaabek who were treated just so as infants, not knowing they ever had such a curse upon their limbs."

Here, Wolf heard the rumble of agreement from several of the shamans, who had healed just such infants themselves.

"But it was not so for the babe with wolfish eyes," he continued. "A shaman was summoned who was the greatest healer on the island. His fame was known even to the Wendats and the Haudenosaunee to the south. So great was his power that he could send his spirit flying at night to distant places to rest like an owl in the branches of a tree. It was said that he had lain with ghosts in their graves, yet did not fear them, and had even raised the dead a time or two. He was dressed as fine as any man you can imagine, wearing the antlers of a stag atop his head and a cloak of eagle feathers with his face painted black as death. He came to the village at the head of a long parade of followers, chanting and drumming, promising all who gathered that the child with strange eyes would soon be set right.

"As you can imagine, the shaman was an old man who had seen many lifetimes come and go; he had witnessed many infants raised to men and women and then laid in their graves, yet still he lived on. The babe before him was just one more. He told all in the village that healing the babe would be a matter of small consequence. Then, he called out to the spirits in a loud voice and fanned healing smoke over the babe's head, breathing spells into its ears.

"Oh uncles, can you imagine what came next? As all in the village stood watching, the shaman gripped the babe's left foot and gave it a hard twist into its proper place, expecting a scream that would freeze the blood of a warrior. And what a sound it made! Uncles, it was like the snap of a breaking bone! But the babe only cooed and gazed upon him in delight. And when his parents unwrapped his swaddle of rabbit furs the next morning they found that the babe's foot had gone crooked again, cruelly twisted back to one side.

"Again the shaman was called and again the harsh treatment was delivered with a sickening snap, and again the babe only cooed and smiled. Yet again the next morning the crippled foot had returned to its bad position. For seven days the shaman worked his treatment, all in vain."

Wolf paused in his story, expecting some murmur or exclamation, yet the shamans sat as quiet as stones in the darkness. It was as if he was speaking to the dead.

"At the end of seven days and seven nights the shaman declared that the babe was filled with an evil spirit," Wolf went on. "The proof was there for all to see in the babe's eyes, which seemed merry enough, yet were those of a wolf. His mother and father were filled with terror, demanding that a council of elders be held to decide his fate.

"Know this, uncles. It had been a bad year for fishing and a bad year for hunting, too, and there were many mouths to feed in the village. The elders of the village reasoned that the child would be of no use as a hunter when he was grown, as he would not be able to run after game. Then too, he would be useless as a warrior, for a raider must be able to run to his enemy and then run for his life. And they feared that he would frighten the fish of Tima Gami with his eyes. "Nothing good will come of him," the eldest among them said, and all agreed.

"So a decision was made to a place the babe on a refuse pile a short way from the village, a place which was well known as the haunt of wolves and coyotes. 'They will decide the babe's fate,' the eldest among them said."

Here, Wolf paused, motioning for the pipe to be passed again. Pausing was a trick he had learned to make his listeners as anxious as a pack of coyotes, waiting to devour the guts at the skinning of a deer. One-by-one, the pipe glowed red in the darkness of the lodge as each of the shamans took a draught and passed it on.

"Surely, the story is not done yet," one of the shamans spoke from the darkness after the pipe had gone around twice. Around him, Wolf could feel his uncles fidgeting.

"The story? Ah, yes," he said, as if he had forgotten.

"As it happened, there was a woman in the village, Waabigwan - Cornflower, who had never given birth to a child of her own. Some said she had been driven mad by her empty womb and had even practiced the ways of a witch with no result. Shamans and midwives had labored over her in vain, casting spells of fertility and providing her with magical potions to produce a child, yet nothing came of their efforts. It was whispered that she had spread her legs for any man who would have her, yet no babe ever came. The failure of each lover filled her with a hunger beyond reason, a hunger that nothing but a babe could fill.

"Her hunger was like those starving to death in the heart of the cruelest winter, forced to eat leather and the bark of trees. Like a starving soul, shriven of the last taste of life, she had lost the last glimmer of hope for a child."

Again Wolf paused, letting his words sink in. He had spoken low, aiming to send a shiver through the spines of his listeners, who held their breaths in the darkness.

"Can you imagine her, uncles? Can you imagine her hunger? Some said she was a mad woman who would do anything to fill her lust for a child. If she was not a witch, then she soon would be!

"So it was that Cornflower crept behind the elders as they bore the infant gurgling and cooing to the haunt of the wolves. And hiding behind a shield of spruce trees, she watched as they placed it atop the pile of bones, broken pots and rotted leathers beyond the village. The old men made signs over the babe, begging its forgiveness, and a gift of tobacco was placed at its feet in the hope of soothing its spirit upon its death. Then the elders pushed back down the trail with fearful glances back to where the infant lay chuckling as if it couldn't be happier with its fate. Surely, it would be devoured by wolves with not a bone left to give trace of it! Yet it was then that Cornflower dashed from her hiding place and seized the infant, raising it to the sky in her arms, swearing to Kitchi Manito and all the spirits of the world that no harm would come to him.

"For two days she kept it hidden in a box of spruce adorned with porcupine quills, suckling the babe on the milk of a bitch that had recently had puppies. But such a thing cannot remain hidden for long in a village of many eyes and straining ears and all heard a new babe crying at night, which could not be accounted for.

"The old men of the village were not pleased and they came in force to carry the possessed child away. But Cornflower barred their path, hissing and clawing, screaming and spitting. Have you ever seen a raccoon fight, uncles? Whirling and twisting and raking with its claws? It was just so with Cornflower, who threatened to rain down curses and claw the eyes out of any man who dared touch the babe that she swore was her own!

"As it happened, Cornflower was the niece of Makade-gookooko'oo, Black Owl, who was considered the wise uncle of the village, always quick with a kind word and a smile, and well-loved by all. His chest ached at

Cornflower's anguish, and it was he who offered a solution. He gathered the whole village to witness Cornflower's fate, and that of the babe.

"'Stay brothers and sisters, for who knows the ways of the spirits?' he said. 'There may be some use for this clubfoot that we cannot know. He has endured great pain, and yet he laughs. He has the eyes of a wolf, and yet they shine with good intentions. Who are we to judge him when his creator made him so?'

"Just as Makade-gookooko'oo spoke, the crack of a thunderbird's wing was heard from the white shield of the clouded sky, echoing off the distant cliffs, and the people of the village leapt in terror. Know this, uncles, it was only the wind splitting the heart of an old tree beyond the lodges, but all swore that it was thunder on a clear day and they took it as a sign.

"So it was that the elders gabbled in fear, vouching that the babe was blessed by the spirits and filled with a powerful magic that would reveal its mystery in time. Their eyes had been opened! It was Makade-gookooko'oo who gave the babe its name in a sly jest that put all at ease. 'We will call him Animi-ma'lingan, He Who Outruns the Wolves, for he has eluded those who would devour him in the forest,' he said.

"And it is true, that night a chorus of wolves was heard howling in the forest, as if to say the right decision had been made. Or possibly, their sorrow at being denied a meal."

At this, there came a murmur of soft laughter from the shamans gathered in the darkness.

"Ah, how strange it is that a people can turn so quickly from good to ill and then back again," Wolf went on, "for now Animi-ma'lingan was regarded as blessed and had a powerful companion spirit who must not be angered. Soon, women who still had milk in their breasts begged to suckle the babe, hoping to gain a touch of his magic through their teats.

"And yet, uncles, one can be blessed and still not be happy, for as the boy grew he found he could not play as other children did. He could not run as boys do, nor play in their war games, spearing the hoop or thrashing rackets at baggatiway. Instead, he could only watch in the company of girls playing with their dolls. The boys of the village paid him respect, not out of any kindness, but because his mother was said to have the evil eye and would curse anyone who taunted him. They blessed him with the common name, Wolf, but they pitied him, knowing he would never be a hunter, nor a warrior.

"In time, the elders of the village took notice of the wretched boy sitting with the girls and invited him into their company as they knapped at arrowheads and smoked their pipes. Buried in their gossip of village tales, Wolf discovered stories that the elders remembered from long ago. Stories of heroes, animals, spirits and monsters tumbled from their lips, and these Wolf would tell the boys of the village as they sat with their own pipes. Thus, Wolf spent many days in the elders' halting footsteps and many nights by their fires, gathering their tales. Soon he knew the legends of every elder in the band, and then those of every woman too. Uncles, the women told him secrets which no man could ever begin to suspect! And though his gimp leg made him a turtle on the forest paths, he proved to be an otter at paddling, strong enough to race with the waves of Kitchi Gami."

Here, Wolf paused again, as if deep in a reverie. The old men of the sweat lodge leaned closer, wondering...

"Ah, but he never felt that he truly belonged in the company of those who raised him, and what is a man who is alone in the world without a clan?" Wolf began again. "He is nothing! So the clubfoot decided that he would turn his back on his village and seek out every clan on Kitchi Gami in the hope of finding a new home. Even before he was an in-between man he began paddling to villages along the Spirit Island's coast, collecting stories and sharing those he had learned. In time the mystery of his birth and his purpose was revealed, for his memory was firmer than any snare fashioned by men, never forgetting, always grasping for more, always hungry. Some claimed he had a memory as deep as Kitchi Gami. He had been cursed by the spirits, yet they had also given him a blessing.

"Soon, he was hailed at the gatherings of the Anishinaabek from one end of Kitchi Gami to the other, speaking by the evening fires with a voice that grew stronger as he came to his manhood. And uncles, as you know, there is a skill to telling a story, and Animi-ma'lingan for all his failings as a hunter and a warrior had learned the ways of an orator from the best.

"His words drew ancient warriors and chieftains, eager to share their own deeds that they might be remembered. In time, even the headmen of distant bands came calling, borne on litters or wrapped in furs and paddled in canoes by their sons, hoping to share their stories so that they might live beyond the time of their deaths through the memories of He Who Outruns the Wolves."

A long silence followed the end of Wolf's story, for it was true that the twelve shamans within the lodge had themselves hoped to live beyond death by sharing their legends with him. Such tales would be passed down through many lifetimes, especially if they had been crafted by a storyteller as gifted as Wolf.

"Thank you Animi-ma'lingan," Wabeno said at last. "*Chi miigwech.*"

Wolf was grateful that the shamans could not see the heat on his cheeks, for he was embarrassed in the telling of his birth. "Uncles, you have made a braggart of me," he said, feeling small.

But there were kind words and murmurs of approval in the darkness of the lodge, and the women were called in to replenish the stones and their steam. Soon, Wolf found himself drenched in a cleansing sweat that washed away his chagrin.

Yet he was mystified as to why the shamans had called for him. Did they simply wish to hear his story? No.

"We have reached a decision that concerns you," Wabeno said, his face limned in a crescent of sunlight shining through the edge of the door flap.

"Grandfather?"

The Man of the Dawn Sky swept the dense air of the sweat lodge with a hawk wing fan. "Hear our judgment."

He could feel their eyes searching for him in the darkness and see the outline of their faces, shadowed dim as ghosts in the pale light rimming the door flap. Those who had spoken of him tenderly when he was barely beyond his boyhood were hawk-faced and stern now. Wolf's thoughts flashed on the time he had watched a trio of coyotes devouring a still-breathing rabbit. It was not the same, and yet it felt as much.

One by one, his teachers complained of his incompetence.

"He has picked up a small twig of herb craft, but not enough to serve as a proper *nenan dawiiwed* to heal the sick," one complained, speaking as if Wolf was not even present.

"He has failed completely as a juggler of spirits," said another, this being a *djasakid* who healed by working on the patient's mind. A *djasakid* might use masks to frighten away evil manitos and also hollow bones to suck demons from the patient's flesh.

"He remembers the rituals well enough, but he will not perform," said one of the oldest among them, who had tried in vain to teach Wolf the bone technique.

And when it came to speaking with the dead on behalf of the living, Wolf was accused of being a coward. He had communed with the dead only once since he had been with the Mide-wi-win and had returned shaking with fright and drenched in sweat, refusing to speak of the horrors he had seen. He would never willingly take that path again.

"Yes uncles, it is true, I do not care to speak with the dead, nor to see the spirits that surround them," Wolf said miserably.

This raised a clamor, for above all, the shamans prided themselves on communing with the dead.

Wolf sat silently through his condemnation, knowing it was unwise to offer a rebuke. Those who incurred the wrath of the shamans could find themselves pursued by hexes, unpleasant spirits and dark creatures of the underworld.

It was no surprise. He knew the rebuke of the elders was long in coming, yet little did he care, for he had spent five years in the company of old men, studying their birch scrolls and listening to their windy prescriptions and was heartily sick of it. That, and at the end of five years of instruction, Wolf suspected that many of their rituals held no power. The masks, the sucking-bone and the objects concealed in a shaman's mouth to be produced as evidence of healing had all come to him as a sham one day as he lay dreaming in the sun on a sandy beach. He had found healing properties in certain herbs and mushrooms and knew the value of wafting smoke, but had no desire to make herb craft his calling.

But it would not do to insult his teachers with such revelations.

"Wise teachers, have mercy," he spoke when the last complaint was aired. "You have been as fathers to me and I share your disappointment. You have called me your son, yet I am still a babe to your teachings for reasons known only to the spirits. I have failed you and now my heart bleeds with a wound I cannot bear. If you wish to banish me, I will bow to your judgment."

The Good Hearts sat silent at this, too disquieted to speak, for though they had condemned Wolf as a student, still, they loved him as a son. Countless times he had sat at their feet, listening to their tales of long ago and entertaining them through five winter nights with tales of his own. Wolf seemed to have more stories within him than in all of the birch bark scrolls piled high on the shelves of the great lodge.

"We have a purpose for you," Wabeno said at last. "I myself have traveled among the spirits to see what they wish for you, as has every man among us. You have troubled us, Wolf. You have been a mystery to us."

Wolf craned forward, his eyes stinging from the sweat running down his face.

"The spirits told us nothing!" Wabeno said irritably. "Yet we believe they hold you close. Your eyes shine like those of the wolves, your foot that cannot be healed... these are signs we cannot forsake."

Wolf shifted his crippled foot unconsciously. It was a burden that was long past any hope of healing. He could walk well enough with a hobbling gait, but he would never run.

"Of what use could the spirits have for my lame foot?" he asked.

"That is not for us to know, but they gave it to you for a reason. The proof lies in the story of your birth. Seven times you were healed and seven times broken again. We cannot know what the spirits intend. As you know, every man has a gift, yet is also blessed with a curse so that he does not grow too big in his moccasins."

"What would you have me do?" Wolf said in a quiet voice, feeling their judgment bearing down on him. "Do you wish me to leave?"

"In a way, yes."

The red light of the pipe lingered and a wry smile crept over the lines of Wabeno's face. "The only thing the spirits told me is that you were named Outruns the Wolves, for a reason," he said. "We have a purpose for you that will be known only to this council."

Purpose? Leave? Wolf's thoughts scrambled like a squirrel in a basket, for how could he be one of the Good Hearts without mastery of their craft? They had already dismissed him.

Wabeno leaned forward in the darkness, his voice dropping to a murmur. "Your purpose is revealed in your name, for you will outrun the wolves on behalf of our people. From this day on you will present yourself as a simple trader known only by your common name, Wolf, making your way quietly through the world."

"A trader?"

"*Ehn.*"

"I do not understand..."

"You will learn."

Wolf was mystified, and, it must be said, somewhat insulted. "Grandfather, I know nothing of trading beyond a few stories," he protested, "and how could I serve you as a trader? All that I know of trading is that of crafty men traveling from village to village with canoes full of furs, maize, copper and... and gifts for women!"

"A trader nonetheless," Wabeno nodded. "As Wolf you will be our eyes and ears in the world far beyond this lodge. You will be cloaked as a wandering trader, taking copper, honey and furs to the four directions in exchange for corn, tobacco and fine things for our women. But most of all, you will return with stories of those living far beyond our shores. You will serve us with your memory, if not our medicine. We honor you now to serve as our *giimaabi*."

A *giimaabi*... A sick feeling filtered through Wolf like ice water tricking through a vein of stone. Here at last was the revelation; here was the judgment of his uncles among the shamans. It seemed more a punishment than an honor.

"A spy, grandfather?" he protested. "A *giimaabi* is dishonored among all peoples as a back-stabber and a false friend. To be discovered means death, and not a quick one."

Wabeno frowned. "We do not ask this lightly," he replied. "No man among the Ojibwe can tell another man what to do, not even the war chief of a band facing certain death, not even a shaman. We will accept your will if you refuse us."

This, Wolf knew all too well. A headman used the wisdom of his tongue and the support of those in his band to persuade, cajole, reproach and harangue. Charisma, oration and consensus were the tools that moved men and women to action, yet often as not, those who failed to act faced dishonor and condemnation.

So, it took only a moment for him to realize there was no other choice. Wolf knew that he could refuse Wabeno, yet not without enduring the censure of the Good Hearts. Still, his head reeled with questions.

"Grandfather, am I to forsake even my name? How?..."

But Wabeno shushed him. "You will always be Animi-ma'lingan to us, but you would be wise to go forth by your common name, since your fame as a storyteller is well known even to the birds, and they might chatter to our enemies. Better you should go forth as simply Wolf, a small man, little noticed. You will appear to others as a trader with a gift for telling stories.

"As for what we ask, do you not think that we have had other spies roaming the earth?" he went on. "They protect our people, they direct our warriors, yet they remain hidden to all. They are the secret warriors of our people. We need eyes and ears among our enemies; without them we are as blind and deaf as the rocks by the shore. Without the *giimaabis*, who would know that our enemies are gathering against us? Who would know when it is time to flee and when to strike?'

The stone in Wolf's chest lifted a little at Wabeno's words.

"There are others?"

"There have been."

"May I meet them? I would learn their ways, hear their stories..."

An uneasy expression crept over the old man's face. "Someday, when you walk among the stars, perhaps then you will meet them."

"Then they live with the dead."

Wabeno nodded, his face growing somber. "This is why we need you, now more than ever. All others have taken the path to the West."

"Tell me how they died."

"Painfully. I will not spare you this. They died because they were not as wise as Animi-ma'lingan. Not as clever, nor as favored by the spirits. I see within you our best hope. I see the defeat of our enemies lying at your feet."

Wolf grimaced at Wabeno's praise; nonetheless, the flattering words found their mark. His thoughts churned in the darkness... distant journeys... strange peoples... dodging death in the guise of a trader... All appealed to a young man's vanity and his head swelled with the thought of what he might become. Best of all, the path of a *giimaabi* would offer an escape from the drear life of the Good Hearts, who were kind enough as uncles, yet ancient as the oaks.

"Tell me what I have that the others did not?" he said at last. "What weapon? What charm? What spell will protect me?"

At this Wabeno gave a dry chuckle, placing his hand on Wolf's knee and shaking it. "You have your stories," he said. "The one thing all people crave. Your stories will protect you."

"Stories," Wolf snorted. "Every storyteller knows that sometimes the arrows fly before a word can be spoken."

"Ah, but who would kill a trader? But we will not toss you in the fire just yet. First you must prove yourself. You will hone your skills, just as a man sharpens his knife."

Mission to Minong

Thus, Wolf was given the first of many missions, little knowing that the shamans considered it little more than a romp - a practice mission which even an in-between man might undertake.

He had set out in the company of six Odawa traders who had grumbled at being tasked with sharing the burden of their canoe with a clubfoot. But their irritation quickly turned to delight as Wolf's powerful arms, shoulders and chest propelled them through the water like the whipping tail of a trout.

Even shamans must provide for themselves, so Wolf had spent countless mornings over the past five years paddling his canoe over the gray-green waters of Kitchi Gami, questing for fish to feed his uncles. Thus, his upper body grew as strong as a bear as he cast his nets into the grey wash below, drawing up lake trout, walleye, whitefish and perch. Shame over the infirmity of his left foot made him paddle with far more determination than most. That, and Wolf had little fear of the boundless waters of

Kitchi Gami, sometimes going out of sight of the shore to the place where monsters dwelled. As all knew, the deep reaches of the lake were the haunt of Misshephzhu, the lynx-headed dragon of the depths, whose serrated tail generated the storms of Kitchi Gami. That, and of monstrous serpents which streamed through the waters, sometimes devouring fishermen, even those coasting near the shore. Wolf had seen them himself when the lake roiled with the anger of a storm, or at least thought that he had.

But given his strength and his knowledge of endless paddling songs, his Odawa brothers soon came to love him, sharing many tales of the trading life by their fires each night. They loved him all the more when he opened his large leather packet of fine tobacco given to him by Wabeno to use as trade goods. The tobacco was of great value, traded for many furs to a tribe of planters living at the southern end of Tima Gami, the lake of the Wendats. Rich and smooth, it was far more satisfying than kinnikiinick, the blend of coarse tobacco and willow bark that the Ojibwe and Odawa were used to smoking.

Wolf had been born among the Odawa on the north shore of Manitowaa-ling, yet he had left home barely out of his boyhood and there were many things he did not know about the people whose name means "trader."

One night as they made their way along the coast, the Odawa boasted of the times they had paddled beyond sight of the shore in their canoes, which could be as long as five men laid end-to-end and as wide as a man lying with outstretched arms.

"Why then do we not cross Kitchi Gami to make our trip shorter?" Wolf asked. "It is a long way along the coast."

"That would be foolish," the eldest among them replied. "My young brothers have neglected to tell you that the crossing is a dangerous thing. Kitchi Gami is alive with storms and waves two or three times as high as any man, and so we keep to its coast. The spirits of many of our brothers walk the sands beneath these waters and we do not wish to walk among them."

He paused, gazing out on the waves, which thundered ceaselessly on the shore. "Brother, these waters took my own second son just two summers ago, and he was only a bow shot from the shore," he said.

Wolf nodded, but the next morning he found himself alone on the shore while the others were breaking camp. The northern horizon was limned with a black band of clouds that throbbed purple with every lick of light-ning, yet the sky was blue and bright under the sun where Wolf stood watching. Although there was no shore to be seen on the northern hori-zon, he could see flights of hawks, eagles and other birds making their fall migration to the south.

The birds spoke to him of clear skies ahead and on an impulse he threw his swag into the small scouting canoe and set out north into the void of Kitchi Gami until he was only a speck on the horizon, far beyond the cries of his Odawa brothers.

The elder of the Odawa cursed him as a fool and fretted on the shore as Wolf disappeared on the horizon, bidding his men not to follow. Yet, around him, the young braves urged a chase, declaring that their honor was at stake. And though it was true that not even a headman of the Anishinaabek could order another man to do his bidding, it was also true that few men could resist a dare if they wished to continue being considered as men. Who could resist such a challenge? With a nod, their leader gave his consent and they ran their long trading canoe into the waves. Digging with their paddles, they set off with the ferocity of wolves at the chase.

Even so, it took them most of the day to catch Wolf amid the chop of the waves, and still there was no sight of the northern shore, only the flight of raptors overhead to show that it must be somewhere beyond the thickening mist.

Curses rained down on Wolf as he sat grinning in his canoe, but also yells of admiration as he bobbed on the waves before them.

"Brothers, I did not mean for you to follow!" he cried above the wind, "but now that you are here, I am joyful of your company."

"Joyful? Hah! There are many bad things out here," a paddler named Lame Moose called out. "Have you seen them, fool?"

"*Ehn*, I strangled a water snake and ate it already," Wolf called back. "It was longer than three of you put together."

"Is this true?" The youngest of the Odawa spoke in earnest, looking wildly about. He was an in-between man of fourteen summers, on his first trip as a trader.

"Yes, young brother, but don't worry, I have saved two for you."

At this, even the hard men among the Odawa laughed and relaxed, for the lake began to calm, with the chop of its waves waning to a placid surface.

What Wolf had not shared with the Odawa was that he had a gift for reading the weather that surpassed even the wisest shamans of the Mide-wi-win. That morning he had sniffed the air, knowing it would be a mild day on the lake, despite the fearsome clouds to the north. Then a passing hawk had told him it was a narrow stretch of Kitchi Gami, and thus the path of migration. Wolf was well aware that Kitchi Gami can awaken and roar at any moment, but the sky was at peace and the lake was smooth and shining blue-green. If the birds could traverse it, so could he.

Even so, it was a journey of a day and a night.

That night they paddled by star light, following the great white band of the Spirit Trail which glimmered overhead. Silent and faint with exhaustion, they paused beneath the knife's edge of a tender moon to eat a meal of dried fish before pushing on, guided by the North Star. Every man among them, save Wolf, had a hank of fear lodged in his throat, for all knew that these black waters were the haunts of many unspeakable things, trolling beneath their frail craft.

So there were no idlers, nor any complaints, just an urgent push forward with their aching backs and arms. The elder, White Tree, had cautioned them not to sing the rhythm songs which normally drove their efforts. "We must take care not to awaken what lives below," he said in a murmur.

And brothers, sisters, it is true, sometime deep in the night a great vast shape slithered beneath their canoes, only the length of two paddles below the surface of the water. Its vast body was silver and speckled as if with stars. Gazing into the water, Wolf and the Odawa could see its body dimly reflected in the glow of the Spirit Trail of stars far above.

"Misshipeshu," came a hushed voice over the water.

"Be still, lest it hears you," came another.

Every man froze at his paddle and held his breath as the creature passed, even Wolf. This, all knew, was the terror of the lake - the water dragon which lashed forth great waves in a storm, dragging men to their deaths.

Wolf could not help but think that he had been a fool to make the crossing, and that soon, he might be residing in Misshipeshu's gut. But then the creature spoke to him and he knew it was only a passing school of *nahme*, the sturgeon, eight big ones moving in a cluster, each a long as a man; they passed by in the guise of a slithering monster below the surface of the lake. He gave a small laugh, yet held his tongue, not wishing to spoil the horror afflicting his brothers. They would share their brush with the monster over their home fires for the rest of their lives and Wolf was not one to deny them that pleasure.

Long after the apparition passed, the Odawa dipped their paddles timidly into the water and pushed on. In the gray dawn a faint green sliver of land rose from the mist, and by mid-day they touched the rocky shores of the place called Agawa.

The people of a village on the shore rushed to meet them, singing and laughing, astounded by their crossing. That evening, around a feast of venison and turtle, White Tree vouched that they had seen Misshipeshu amid the waters and had only narrowly escaped being devoured. "We saw its horns, like the ears of a lynx, and its serpent tail," he said. Then, the in-between man, Leaf, had recounted Wolf's tale of strangling a serpent, swearing that it was true.

Wolf gave credit for the crossing to White Tree who had assented to following him across Kitchi Gami, and the elder was honored in turn as a hero worthy of a star when his time came to walk the Spirit Trail. The tale grew in the telling until the crossing was painted in red ochre on a rock by the shore, there to stand testimony to the heroic deed for many lifetimes.

Thereafter, Wolf was captured with a young man's zeal to see the Great Salt Water far to the east. Surely, his uncles among the shamans would be impressed by such a feat. But young men are apt to abandon such plans almost as soon as they conceive them, and so it was with Wolf. He left the Odawa and paddled alone to the northeast up a river whose current drained him to his bones as he pushed against it. The river required so many portages around its rapids that he soon lost heart at ever reaching the ocean. Instead, he wintered among the Nippissings on the inland lake that the tribe called home. The Nippissings were cousins of the Odawa and Ojibwe; yet they were a lonely people who were happy to greet a wandering trader.

They were more than kind, granting Wolf a suit of caribou hides to warm him through the coming winter and lodging him in a village of several hundred along the lakeshore. He spent much of the winter fishing for pike through holes chopped through the ice. Often, the wind howled at his back, chilling him to the bone, yet the fishing was good and not a soul among the Nippissings starved that winter.

Once, he was invited along on a hunt for the caribou of the forest, which wandered in small herds, seeking the shelter of the trees for protection from wolves. The hunters hiked for two days through the forest on snowshoes, pulling sledges in the expectation of returning with them piled with meat. Another day was spent repairing a v-shaped thicket of branches and brush near a path used by the deer.

Wolf considered its long tangle of branches a fine trap, much like those used by the Ojibwe to herd moose to their deaths. The next day, he waited with his spear at the end of the thicket as the frightened caribou were driven into the trap by a team of boys beating sticks together. Thrusting his spear at the bucking mass, he took a bull caribou through its throat, narrowly losing an eye to a prong of its antlers.

"Blood in the snow, brother. Blood in the snow," one of the hunters spoke to him as they butchered the meat. Beyond the thicket, a pack of eight wolves sat hunched in the bright winter sun, waiting their turn as the entrails were tossed in a pile. Six caribou were taken in the hunt and there was good eating that night, with much of the meat packed in snow to last until spring.

His nights were spent snug in their lodges, wrapped in furs and trading stories around a low fire. The language of the Nippissings was ancient to Wolf's ears, but he understood them well enough and they had many curious tales, especially about the Cree, who lived to the north in the barren lands where the tree line faded into tundra.

"They spend much of the winter in their wretched lodges, dozing in a half-death to avoid the cold," said Crow Foot, a chieftain of the Nippissings, who hosted Wolf in his lodge for the winter. "But they are seldom hungry, for in their land are herds of caribou beyond count and the Cree take just as many each fall.

"Of course, if the caribou fail to come, the Cree eat only bones and leather," he added, "and then they turn to bones and leather themselves."

Crow Foot spoke of Paija, a she-monster of the Cree who had a single leg which grew out of her vast belly. "She comes at night amid the roaring blizzards, stalking those who have broken certain taboos."

"And this thing has only one leg?"

"Yes."

"How can it walk?"

"She is like a snail, dragging herself along. Her footprint is as long as your forearm. She is a slobbering giant with teeth like knives, covered in thick black hair."

"Ugly."

"Yes."

"I would like to see this one-legged thing."

"Ah."

"Perhaps it is only a bear."

Crow Foot gave a bitter chuckle. "Then you would die, young brother, for she is no bear! She is a soul-eater. A man who gazes upon Paija has his spirit torn from his body through a great hole in his chest. One look at her is death."

Wolf wondered how those who saw Paija were able to survive long enough to describe her, but this he kept to himself.

Crow Foot said that beyond the Cree lived an even stranger people at the end of the world, who traveled the Great Salt Water in skin boats, hunting white bears and creatures that appeared as giant otters.

"The Cree have fought them over caribou since the beginning of time," Crow Foot said. "They live in lodges of snow and go about clad in furs as if they were bears. They are little men with narrow eyes, yet they hunt great beasts of the sea amid mountains of ice that float on the water. Brother, I have heard that a man can walk on the back of the fish they hunt. These fish are *kitchi manameg.*"

"I have heard of them," Wolf replied politely, for the Ojibwe had long known of the presence of whales, which dwelled at a distance of several moons to the east. Traders told of a great river that opened onto Zhewita-kanibi, with whales cavorting where the fresh water met the salt.

But Wolf had doubts about the rest of Crow Foot's story, for what man could live in a lodge of snow?

Wolf had gifted half of his tobacco to the Nippissings in exchange for a cargo of caribou hides. While traveling with the Odawa traders he had learned much of the gift-giving ceremony involved in trading.

"Never give away too much, nor too little," the wisest among them had said, "and always keep some of your goods for the next village you meet, for a trader who arrives with empty hands may end up trading his own life."

As winter turned to spring, the melting snow revealed the pit mines that the Nippissings worked to dig for copper. These were simply holes dug down to where copper-bearing rock could be found. Along with the copper was a strange metal that Wolf had never seen before. Hammered into the shape of an arrowhead, it shimmered the same color as the surface of a lake when it is mirrored by sunlit clouds.

"It is a rare thing of little use," said Crow Foot. "An ornament at best."

"I have heard of this, but its color is strange." Wolf turned the arrowhead amulet in his hand, eyeing it curiously. "Is it the cousin of copper?"

"*Ehn*, it is a thing called silver and it lives side-by-side with copper, though only in small amounts," Crow Foot said. "We have found small streams of copper here in the rock, but nothing like the rivers of copper found at Minong."

All knew that Minong was the large misty island on the north shore of Kitchi Gami far to the west. But it was a chilly, wet place, visited only by miners.

"Is there much silver there too?" Wolf asked.

"Who can say?" Crow Foot shrugged. "But I think not, for we have found very little in our own pits. You must go and see for yourself if you wish to know, though only a fool would paddle all the way to Minong!"

"Brother, I think I have no choice but to be a fool now," Wolf said, "for if it is as wet and cold as you say then surely the miners will need my hides."

"But what of your people?" Crow Foot gave him a questioning look. "Have you no family to return to?"

No, Wolf thought. Nor any woman. At best, his clan was among the old men of the Mide-wi-win. The shamans had given him little direction, telling him only to bring them new stories when he returned.

"Perhaps I will meet my kin at Minong," he replied in a lie that died on his lips. Crow Foot scoffed in response. "You are a strange man, brother," he said, "for if your kin lived on the isles of Minong, you would surely know it."

That spring as the ice of the vast lake slowly melted, Wolf paddled with a new company of the Odawa along the north shore of Kitchi Gami to the copper islands. His canoe was filled with caribou pelts intended for trade with the miners, who were often soaked to their bones by the endless rains. It was here that men had stabbed at the earth since the time of the Old Ones, harvesting the copper ore lining the rock below. But the islands were relentlessly damp and whipped by rain, and all knew that there is nothing better than the well-insulated cloak of a caribou pelt to ward off the chill.

It was a long paddle to the copper islands, but at last Wolf and the Odawa crossed a wide bay to behold the figure of a sleeping giant lying on a narrow peninsula. Its face and body were carved from a series of plateaus rising high above the lakeshore. The giant's body was a long, rambling mountain, and its dark face of stone gazed straight up into the sky.

"Does it live?" Wolf asked, for the stone giant looked as if it might rise from the earth and stretch its limbs at any moment.

"*Ehn*, but only when it is hungry for a passing fool," replied one of his brothers who was sweeping a paddle behind him. "Take care you do not appear too tasty."

Wolf gave a quiet laugh at this, but something about the mountain giant filled him with unease. "Why does he sleep?"

"He guards an isle of silver, which lies ahead. Someday perhaps he will awaken to defend it. Some say it is Manabozho who sleeps there."

All knew of Manabozho, the demigod who worked his magic on behalf of the humble and the needy. A shape-shifter and trickster, Manabozho walked among the people of the earth in many guises, including that of animals. Gazing at the reclining giant whose head and chest rose far above the pines along the shore, Wolf could not help but wonder if someday he would meet him walking the earth in the guise of a man. A *giimaabi*, like himself, perhaps.

Not far ahead, the silver island was very small, rising less than a man's height above the lake. Its shore was black with dark pines, hidden in fog. Wolf pleaded to stop and examine a pit mine there, but his brothers hurried on, anxious to reach the big island of Minong - the "good place" of much copper and many moose drawn to its swampy terrain.

When at last they touched the shores of Minong they found a small village in a quiet bay where racks of fish and strips of moose flesh stood drying in the sun. Or at least the hope of drying, for Minong was a wet place, forever given to fog and rain off Kitchi Gami. Wolf stumbled up the shore, pale with exhaustion from paddling for days against the wind and fell asleep at the base of a tree. Feeling utterly drained and blue around his lips, he rested for a day in the village before walking the pathway to the copper mines. These were long trenches dug by the hands of many generations of long-dead men.

But now the mines were alive with men digging at the earth. Eager to see the veins of copper, Wolf clambered down a ladder made from a shattered tree into a pit twice as deep as that of a tall man. It was dark and wet down below, with mud sucking at his moccasins, and for a moment, Wolf felt as if the earth itself had swallowed him whole.

"Look here, brother," a miner named Winter Mink, pointed as they wandered through one of the trenches in a drizzling rain. "This is the prey we seek."

To Wolf's eyes there was only a thin streak of green limning the rock, but Winter Mink attacked the wall with his digging stick, revealing more of the brittle shale. The streak of green grew to a finger's-width as it trailed on through the shale, growing as wide as Wolf's hand before dwindling again to nothing. Then, Winter Mink raised a stone hammerhead and gave the shelf of rock a terrific blow. A chunk of shale fell away to reveal a broad swath of brilliant green, as bright as the first leaves of spring, almost as if the rock itself was ablaze with an unearthly green fire.

A cry went up from the mud-streaked miners, who clasped each others' shoulders, jigging with delight.

"How do we take it, brother?" Wolf asked. "It is still bound by the rock."

"You will see, but first we give thanks," Winter Mink said. "We do not wish to anger the earth, nor the things which lie below."

Wolf nodded, for it was only fitting to sacrifice to Grandmother Earth for what she had provided. A hole was dug and a palmful of Wolf's tobacco was placed in the ground, accompanied by words of thanks.

That afternoon, the miners built a fire against the stone and kept it burning until dusk. Then, with buckets of birch bark sealed with pitch, they hurled torrents of water against the heated rock. With a crack it split open, delivering its treasure.

On the following day Winter Mink revealed the art of the miners. The ragged pieces of copper were heated again and pounded into arrowheads, spear points, amulets, pipe bowls, needles and many other useful tools. Hammer stones were used to shape the metal.

"Brother, you are a magician," Wolf said in admiration as Winter Mink spread his work before him on a wolf pelt.

"No, only a miner, and not for long," Winter Mink replied. "By the Ricing Moon I will return to my woman and my people. I have this to give her."

He raised a copper necklace which had been polished to a high sheen, with the metal interspersed with purple and white shells traded from the Great Salt Water.

"Your woman will smile on such a treasure," Wolf mused.

"You could do the same, brother. Take my place in the mines if you wish."

Wolf stifled a smile, thinking that the miners could practice their craft for no more than five moons before the winds of winter swept the island and drove them to misery.

"Sadly, that is not to be," he said. "A trader has only one trail in life and that is to travel on."

"I think you are something more than a trader," Winter Mink replied with a shrewd look. "Your grandfather, Wabeno-inini, sent word to us that you were to be treated kindly, and we only hear from him on matters of great importance."

"Ah, but it is because of my damaged leg," Wolf said. "He treats me like a child."

Winter Mink snorted. "I have never known Wabeno to treat anyone like a child, not even children. You are favored by him in some way that cannot be known."

"It is a mystery to me too, brother," Wolf said lightly, guessing that eluding prying questions was part of Wabeno's test of his abilities. "But what have you there?"

He pointed to an amulet in the shape of a fish dangling from a leather thong around Winter Mink's neck. It was enough to distract the miner. Wolf recognized it as the silver he had seen among the Nippissings; it was the color of sunlit clouds when they were gathering for rain.

Winter Mink fingered the amulet and pulled it from around his neck, handing it to Wolf. "It is married to the copper, but in small amounts, just as a flea rides the back of a moose," he said. "It is silver."

The fish amulet was well-crafted and burnished to a high shine. "I have seen it among the Nippissings," Wolf said, handing it back. "It is a fine thing, though they said it was of little use."

But Winter Mink refused its return. "It is yours now," he said. "I had a dream in which I handed it to you and the spirits of the earth spoke their thanks. I cannot take it back."

"I am not worthy of such a gift..."

"The earth believes it to be so, and I can find more of it. Take it!"

"But what can I give in return?"

"Hah! All who dig here crave your tobacco. There is nothing but willow bark to smoke on the island and it is nothing but shit. There are many who would be happy to trade with you."

Wolf weighed the amulet in his hand and offered a practiced frown. "I would give all of my tobacco and half of my pelts for this and your copper."

And so after a day of bargaining over the relative worth of copper, tobacco and caribou pelts, an exchange was made between Wolf and the island's miners. When they heard of what he had traded away, his Odawa brothers scoffed at his generosity, saying they would have bargained much harder.

Thus, Wolf reasoned that he still had much to learn about the flinty ways of a trader if he wished to maintain his disguise. Yet he was pleased with how the trading had gone, and with the silver pendant, for although the miner found little to value in the metal, the sky-shining fish struck his fancy as a good luck charm. He draped the thong around his neck along with the cowrie shell necklace that Wabeno had given him as a badge of his service.

So it was with high spirits that he set east into the sunrise for home, bearing a canoe of copper and the last of his caribou pelts. He paddled along the north shore of Kitchi Gami, bobbing amid the waves all the way to Boweting, more than half a moon to the east. The days rolled by with Wolf hammering with his paddle from dawn to dusk, until his body felt part of the canoe itself, like an otter, whipping through the waves.

The Tobacco People

Late that summer, Wolf rushed up the pathway to the great lodge of the shamans nearly ten moons after he had set out on his first mission. His heart brimmed with pride at the wonders he seen and the tales he'd gathered. Again, he met in council with the twelve Good Hearts, recounting everything he had seen and heard. He spoke of the crossing of Kitchi Gami, the hospitality of the Nippissing and the miners of the north shore. The shamans had listened to him politely, asking few questions, some drowsing off as he spoke.

By the end of the day, Wolf began to suspect that his uncles had heard most of his stories long before and were as sleepy as turtles lolling in the sun, anxious to get back to their pipes, their wives, and the day's meal. When his last story had been told - that of hunting eagles on the painted cliffs near Kitchi Minissing - eleven of the twelve had stood and filed out of the sweat lodge without a single question, pausing only to nod to Wabeno, each one touching Wolf's shoulder as they departed.

"Grandfather, have I done wrong?" Wolf asked, utterly bewildered.

Wabeno smiled, his wizened face crinkling. "No, Wolf, we are well pleased. Great deeds lie before you."

"Great deeds?" For a moment Wolf felt as if he was a brother of the caribou, being driven to some fatal end.

Guessing his thoughts, Wabeno said, "Your uncles sent you on this journey as a test, and they are pleased with your answers. You are a chosen man now."

"My uncles have a strange way of showing it."

"Hah! They would chatter like birds if they had complaints. Rest your thoughts; you are the eyes and ears of our people."

"Ah."

Then Wabeno asked him a strange question.

"Tell me, are there beauties among the Nippissing women? You did not speak of them."

"Beauties?"

"Yes, good women. Women to suit a man."

What did Wabeno care of women? Wolf wondered. It was an unseemly question.

"Yes, some."

"Are they strong? Craft-wise? Do they care for their men and their children?"

"Oh yes, very strong, and very skilled."

"Young and frisky?"

Wolf's head reeled, for he had never known the old man to have a craving for women. Yet what did he know? Wabeno was a secretive man, rarely sharing anything of himself, as if his heart was locked within a walnut shell.

"Yes, there are many good women there, grandfather," he said gravely, "but I do not think that any would suit you, and surely your wife would not welcome another." In fact he was sure that Wabeno's old woman would bury a hatchet in the head of any young wife that her old man brought home. What could he be thinking?

Wabeno gave him a mild look, saying nothing more on the matter and Wolf had the feeling that something else was expected of him, but what he did not know.

But the moment passed. Wabeno drew forth his pipe along with a coal nestled in a clay pot.

"Come, follow the smoke," he said, drawing on the stem and passing it on. "This is where you are going."

Wolf took the pipe and inhaled; the tobacco was smooth and intoxicating, the same as that which Wabeno had given him for trading.

"The smoke does not go far," he said, watching it fade away.

"No, but your path is to the south where the tobacco grows, far down the coast of Tima Gami."

"To the land of the Wendats?" The eastern shore of Tima Gami was home to a confederation of six tribes whose fields of maize, beans, sunflowers and squash spread as far as a man could walk in a day.

"Even further, to the Tionontati, who call themselves the Tobacco People," Wabeno said. "They can be a prickly folk, but you will bring them a canoe full of furs, which they much desire. You will become as a brother to them, sharing their fires for the winter as you did with the Nippissing. You will gather their stories and enchant them with your own."

"But grandfather, I have only just returned." Wolf was about to add, "and the fall festival is coming," but held his tongue.

Wabeno ignored him, pausing to draw on his pipe. It was a handsome thing, carved as a raven out of the red pipestone of the Dakota, who lived far to the west. The pipe had a stem fashioned from the leg bone of an eagle. A wan smile crept over his face as he savored the tobacco.

"It is good, yes? The smoke is like a story that whispers good things."

"Yes," Wolf replied, though he scarcely knew what Wabeno meant.

"Yes, stories. You will inhale them as if they were smoke and bring them home to us, breathing out what you have learned."

Stories? Wolf was mystified, for how could tales of the Tionontati help the Anishinaabek?

"Am I to know my purpose?"

Wabeno settled back against the wall of the sweat lodge and blew a smoke ring. "Only to listen and to make them laugh with your own stories," he said, "but always with an ear toward the plans of our enemies, the Haudenosaunee. The Tionontati know them well; they are neighbors who speak the same language and share the same hunting grounds far to the south. They know their pathways, their villages, and often even their plans when they take the raiding trail. These are things we wish to know."

Wabeno hesitated and Wolf could tell there was something more.

"For five summers now the Haudenosaunee have plagued the eastern villages of the Anishinaabek, raiding our people among the Odawa and Ojibwe," he said. "All who survived were carried away to serve as slaves in their fields."

"How many, grandfather?"

"Many," he answered with a wave of his hand. "Last summer the Haudenosaunee raided a village on Miniswiigob, bringing many tears to the eyes of our people. While you were gone, many of our headmen met in council on the Turtle Island, Mishi Mackinakong, plotting a raid to free our people in the coming spring. But first our warriors need to know where to strike. We are as blind men, groping in the darkness in a land we do not know. You will be our eyes and ears."

Again the talk of eyes and ears. Wolf nodded in a daze tinged with fear. Over countless winter fires he had heard stories of the invincible five tribes of the Haudenosaunee, who considered themselves the Older Brothers of all the tribes from the Great Salt Water to the Misi Sipi. Those who did not submit could find themselves overwhelmed by hundreds of warriors, carried off to slavery, and worse.

"Will I travel again as a trader?" he asked, though he knew the answer.

"*Ehn*, with a canoe of furs."

"I fear that I am as poor a trader as I am a shaman," Wolf said with a downcast face. "My brothers among the Odawa said I often pulled the smallest piece of meat from the pot."

Wabeno shrugged. "The Tionontati will love you all the more if you bargain in their favor."

"What will I ask of them?"

"You will trade your furs for a canoe full of maize and tobacco. But it is their stories that you will seek, and they must not suspect."

"They will distrust me..."

"No! They will fall under your spell, for you can weave a story as fine as any woman can weave a basket. To the Tionontati you will appear as a simple trader with great knowledge of the world and they will grow to love you for it."

"Love me?"

"Yes. For what do people need to pull them through the winter once their bellies are full and they are swaddled in fur? They need stories above all else."

"Stories." Wolf scoffed. "I have never considered their worth."

"No?" The old shaman raised an eyebrow. "Without stories, many of us would crush each others' brains out while enduring the bitter nights of winter. We hunger for stories as much as we hunger for meat. Where would we be without stories?"

"Even you, old man?"

Wabeno nodded. "Even me."

Wolf poked at the fire in silence and Wabeno guessed what he was thinking. He tapped out the ashes of his pipe, which had gone cold.

"If they discover that you are a spy you will suffer a horrible death, longer and more painful than you can possibly imagine. But you will be honored for your sacrifice, I can promise you that."

"A comfort to me, grandfather," Wolf said wryly.

"But you will not get caught, Animi-ma'lingan," Wabeno said, leaning in and speaking low in his ear. "You are called He Who Outruns the Wolves for a reason."

Again these hollow words... they did little to cheer Wolf or give him courage, for clearly he could not outrun the schemes of the old man and the shamans. He had planned to remain in Boweting through the winter in the hope of entrancing the village lovelies with tales of his recent adventure. He had even hoped that Singing Tree might not be wed.

But it seemed his fate was already borne on the clouds floating to the south.

"When must I leave?" he asked, barely concealing his misery.

Wabeno cocked his head and considered. "As soon as your arms are rested. And plan on a pleasant winter, for the land of the Tionontati is much milder than here and they have plenty to eat."

"And what else would have me do, grandfather?" Wolf growled. Now it was his turn to read the old man's thoughts.

Wabeno's eyes sparkled and he blew another smoke ring.

"Yes, that too," he said. "Bring me more of their best tobacco."

Thus, Wolf was introduced to Hawk Tail the following day, who believed him to be nothing more than a simple trader like himself on a mission to ferry a load of furs to the Tionontati in exchange for a canoe brimming with maize and tobacco. The Anishinaabek would be in need of the Tionontati's maize come spring, a time when the meat of animals is thin and bitter from the long winter. The Tionontati, in turn, had long since hunted every fur-bearing creature from their farmlands and were happy to see traders from the north.

For half a moon they paddled south from Mishimackinong into Tima Gami, the lake of the Wendats, without incident.

"Why do we travel all the way to the Tionontati?" Hawk Tail asked one evening as they sat before their fire on a small island. "The Wendats are close by and they have enough maize to fill every bowl among the Anishinaabek for a lifetime. And are they not our friends?"

To this Wolf grunted and shook his head, no. "The corn is finer among the Tionontati, as is their tobacco," he said, "and they are well known for their kindness to strangers. The Wendat are known more for treating strangers as sport."

"Sport?"

"Torture."

"Is this true?"

Wolf shrugged. "We do not care to find out. But it is also well known that the women of the Tionontati are beauties beyond compare who fancy wandering traders for the gifts they bring."

At this Hawk Tail scoffed, but it served to dissuade him from any further questions. "I will judge these beauties and their tobacco for myself," he said. "You are welcome to pass judgment on their corn."

"I'm sure it will be as sweet as honey," Wolf said dryly, reflecting that he had asked the same question of Wabeno, who told him that a stay among the Wendats would do them little good. The Wendats and the Haudenosaunees were cousins of a sort, yet they had been fierce enemies for many lifetimes and were careful to hide their movements and intentions from one-another. Only the Tionontati could provide the information sought by Wabeno and the Mide-wi-win.

It was only a day later that Wolf and Hawk Tail encountered a party of the Haudenosaunee themselves, scouting in a long dugout off the shores the Wendat homeland. Their craft emerged from the lee of the island and an excited shout went up when they spied the Ojibwe canoe.

There were four hard-muscled men in the craft, all of them tattooed in rivers of black and red, the tendrils of which crept across their faces, making them seem as hideous as demons. They had shaven their gleaming heads nearly bald, except for scalp locks no bigger than a chipmunk's tail at the back of their skulls. Clearly they were warriors, but they waved a friendly greeting across the water, beckoning Wolf and Hawk to a meeting.

"Brother, I think it's time we put our backs to it," Hawk Tail muttered as the Haudenosounees' dugout paddled in their direction. "They mean to seize us."

"*Eya*, no doubt of it," Wolf replied. "But let us show them their folly."

To this Hawk Tail gave him a quizzical look and began paddling frantically from the front of their canoe, but Wolf called for him to desist. "Hold, brother. We are heavy with trade goods and even in their wretched dugout they might catch us. I have a plan to save our skins and we will add to our fame with it."

The dugout coasted nearer with the Haudenosaunee paddling with urgency now, still proclaiming their friendly intentions. Wolf smiled and nodded in their direction, as if greeting the brothers of his clan.

"Come closer, come closer," he called in their language, for his tutoring had included three long days speaking with a captured Haudenosaunee boy back on the isle of Michilimackinong.

Wolf and Hawk Tail balanced in their canoe, bobbing on the water as they waited. *Eya*, it was the canoe itself which served as their weapon, for only those tribes which lived in the far north were gifted with the kind of birch which makes a fine canoe. The tribes of the south relied on cumbersome dugouts, hacked from the trunks of large trees with tools of stone and hollowed out with coals. Their boats were treacherously slow and tippy. Wolf had noted a flaw in the dugout from afar; it was sleeker than most but had an odd knot in the middle that kept the helmsmen busy correcting its path through the water.

When they were only a canoe length away, the Haudenosaunee revealed their intentions, reaching out with grasping hands and screaming their delight as Hawk Tail raised his paddle to beat them away. One of them raised a war club, seeking to strike a stunning blow.

Wolf knew that the Haudenosaunee valued slaves above men killed in battle and that in another instant they would be in the clutches of a dismal fate. But with a flick of his paddle and the power of his mighty shoulders he wheeled his canoe in a semi-circle backwards, ramming the Haudenosaunees' dugout broadside. Their canoe bowed and flexed, bouncing against the dugout, which veered sideways, almost halfway over. One of the men grappled at Wolf's back, but with a thrust of his paddle he stabbed the warrior in the chest, using his body as a lever to tip the dugout and its men into deep water. With another flick of his paddle, quick as a brook trout,

Wolf was a canoe-length away from the men in the lake, who grasped in vain for their overturned craft, which rolled like a log in the water. For good measure, Wolf paddled over to the upside down dugout and pushed it beyond the reach of the floundering warriors.

"Walk with the fish, brothers," he called to the drowning men. "Walk with the fish."

He lit a pipe from a coal they had carried in a clay pot and they watched as the choking Haudenosaunee sank beneath the waves of Tima Gami, one by one.

A silence settled on the water, though it felt as if the shouts of the drowning men still lingered in the air. Somberly, Wolf gazed at the place where the warriors had disappeared. He had never killed a man before, much less four, and now he was uncertain as to how he felt. But he was a *giimaabi* now; was that not the same as a warrior? He had been given no choice...

"That was a good trick," Hawk Tail said at last, "though I thought you were delivering us to our death."

"No, brother. Our enemies are like the fox which lives all its life on land and can easily catch a rabbit," Wolf said as the dugout floated in the distance. "But we Ojibwe are like the otters, living on the water. We make our homes on islands and spits of land to guard against raiders. We play in the water all our lives and hunt its fish in our canoes. The water is the friend of the Ojibwe. But for the foxes among the Haudenosaunee..." here he paused to take a pull on his pipe, "that is not so."

Hawk Tail gazed into the depths, catching the eyes of a dead warrior floating just beneath the surface. Gingerly, he grasped his paddle and pushed the dead man deeper, until the corpse floated out of sight, arms uplifted in the dull green gloom. "If only we had their hair," he muttered, "though there was not much of it."

As traders, Wolf and Hawk Tail spent the winter before the fires of the Tobacco People, offering tales of the Ojibwe, far to the north. Wolf held the Tionontati spellbound through many long winter nights with his stories of animals, spirits and the monsters of the underworld. He even wove stories of the Old Ones and a time when the earth itself was covered beneath vast sheets of ice. The Old Ones, it was said, were two or three times the size of men who walked the earth today, and they hunted wondrous beasts that were so big that a bull moose was like a squirrel by comparison.

"Indeed, we have found the skeletons of these creatures, buried in the bogs," Wolf said. "Some have tusks as long as a tall man and they stood as tall as the trees."

Or so Wolf said. And then he would lean back on a bed of furs in the Tionontati's longhouses, drawing on his pipe and listening to their stories in turn. He had to admit, it was a pleasant way to spend the winter, which was far milder than what the Ojibwe knew in the north.

At times the Tionontati would talk about the Haudenosaunee to the east, with whom they had an uneasy truce, paying tribute to save their skins. Wolf would feign a mild interest, careful not to ask too many questions. He learned that the Haudenosaunee were forever at war with the Wendat people to the north and often with the Illini of the west, crossing the Tionontati's territory to get at their enemies. Thus, the Tobacco People were considered neutral, yet were well aware of the Haudenosaunee's movements.

One chieftain, in particular, liked to wax on about the Haudenosaunee, for he had been a slave in one of their villages as a child and had many bad things to say about them. Wolf spent many evenings in his lodge, telling stories long into the night, and listening in return. Sometimes, Wolf asked for his advice. "Brother, tell me which rivers I should avoid so that I might not fall into the hands of such foul people."

The chieftain, in turn, was eager to fill Wolf's ears with all of the paths and rivers down which the Haudenosaunee traveled. And more than that, their plans for a spring raid to the west.

By winter's end, Wolf knew more of the Haudenosaunee's habits than even the chieftain, for he built upon his knowledge by telling his tales from lodge to lodge, gleaning small bits of information in each one.

No one ever suspected that Wolf was a *giimaabi* for the shamans of the Mide-wi-in. A backstabber, a spy, a false friend, whose discovery would ensure a long and painful death.

As for Hawk Tail, he was a simpler man than most, and had never wondered why his uncle, a shaman of the Good Hearts, had asked him to accompany Wolf far to the south on a trading mission. Nor did he consider that there might be some sinister purpose to their journey. He did not know that Wolf was a shaman of sorts, as well as a trader, for this was sworn to secrecy. Instead, he busied himself trying to discover if the maidens of the Tionontati did indeed prefer the company of wandering traders. In this, he was disappointed.

Yet the winter had passed pleasantly enough, and their bellies were filled with cornmeal mush every night, wretched though it was. That spring, Wolf and Hawk Tail set out on the long journey home with their canoe riding low in the water, packed to its rim with maize and tobacco. Only Wolf knew that they had a rendezvous with a council of war chiefs on an island far to the north. It was the same island where he had been born.

To Find a Woman

The maidens of Manitowaaling stood knee-deep and naked in the waters of Tima Gami with their skin glistening in the sun as they waved farewell to the warriors paddling south in a fleet of canoes.

The women, young, lush and lovely, waded along the shoreline, as naked as the day they were born, the tresses of their hair streaming in the waves, doing little to cover their charms. They had been up all night singing and dancing to the drums with their lovers, and now came the culmination of their farewell. It was a teasing tradition: a woman stood waving her good-byes, naked, lascivious and tantalizing in the shallow water in the hope that her man would take care, infinite care, on the raider's path in order to return to her and all of the pleasures that she promised.

The young men in their canoes hooted and offered lusty yells in appreciation, promising to return with captives and trophies after crushing the warriors of their age-old enemies, the Haudenosaunee.

Up from the shore ranged the village and its palisade of notched pines where the elders and small children stood, smiling and nodding at the spectacle. And beyond the palisade loomed a wall of spruce, black and silent in the mist, save for the distant cawing of crows.

A dun-colored dog limped alongside the village wall, oblivious to the laughter wafting up from the shore. It paused to scratch behind its ears before moving on, snuffling at the tall grass beneath the palisade. A cloud of mosquitoes floated up from the grass, dispersing at the touch of the sun as it filtered through the trees to the east.

Some of the elders stood grinning on the shore, savoring memories of their own departures on some long-ago morning. Others stood silent with puckered lips and haunted eyes, recalling times which had not turned out so well.

But all expected some sliver of hilarity as the ancient ritual played out on the water.

"Red Doe!" One of the young braves called out to his lover, rising to his feet in the middle of his canoe amid cries of alarm from his brothers. He was nearly as naked as his sister-cousins by the shore, clad only in a narrow thong and a swirl of tattoos. He waved his club, clowning with both hands over his head, and the canoe swayed sideways in response. Too late, he clutched in desperation at the air before plunging over backwards, crashing beneath the black surface of the bay. He was dragged back over the side of the canoe and given a slap on the head with a paddle along with a mix of insults and laughter. Almost in answer by the shore, one of the maidens slipped on the slime of a submerged rock and fell backwards into the water, raising a tinkle of laughter from her sisters as the flotilla crept away. Two of the warriors cast a final backward look over their shoulders, laughing their goodbyes over the waves, but gradually the calls of farewell fell to a whisper as the warriors paddled south on the gray expanse of Tima Gami. Soon they were around the rim of the bay and lost to sight.

Watching at a distance, Wolf knew that some would not return, and others would come back broken forever by their wounds. Those captured by the Haudenosaunee could expect far worse.

But this, he mused, was a fate he would never come close to enduring.

Wolf held no hope of ever being a warrior and all that it meant in the eyes of his brothers, who tended to smile, good-natured but grim at his affliction before dismissing him as a man of little consequence. When the young men sat around the fire at night, weaving their tales before the shining eyes of others, Wolf knew that he had little chance of ever receiving the same admiration. He was well-liked, and had some acclaim as a wrestler owing to the strength of his powerful arms and shoulders, but muscle and sinew was not enough on the raider's path; a warrior had to be able not only to strike a blow, but also to run fast and long to save his skin after the blow was struck, and at best with his lame foot, Wolf could only hobble.

Thus, the contradiction of his name, Animi-ma'lingan, He Who Outruns the Wolves, had filled his heart with pain on more occasions than he could remember. He had outrun the wolves at his cruel birth, but for all that, he could never manage to catch what a man desires most. He knew that somehow his affliction was a gift of the Great Spirit, Kitchi Manito, yet how or why he had yet to discover.

He felt a presence at his shoulder and knew by scent that it was Hawk Tail. They had lain close together for warmth throughout the winter nights in the drafty longhouses of their hosts. They had eaten the Tionontati's wretched corn mush from the same bowl and had paddled for more than a moon each way there and back, their voices rising in the paddling songs. *Eya*, he knew Hawk Tail's scent well enough.

"Why the bad face, brother?" Hawk Tail asked, prodding him in the ribs.

Wolf squirmed, shrugging off the cloud of his thoughts. "A man always wants what he cannot have," he said.

Hawk Tail gave a quiet laugh. "And what could you want, brother? Did you not eat today? There was meat in our bowl. Something for our bellies to chew on."

Wolf nodded toward the shore. "What could I want? Only that."

Hawk Tail's face grew somber with reflection as he watched the departing warriors. "Then you are not alone. I, too, wish to join them. Indeed, when I was younger than you, I went raiding, not once but twice."

Hawk Tail launched into a story of his exploits against a rival clan of the Nippissings far to the north and how he and his father had crept up on a camp of caribou hunters, only to be routed by the call of a snooping raven. But Wolf lost the trace of the story as his eyes lingered on the women striding in the shallows, wringing their hair now and wading toward the shore to where their tunics lay.

One of the them, a lank beauty with ribbons of wet hair past her knees and the sharp eyes of fox, glanced at him and their eyes caught and held for three beats of a bird's wing before she looked away, feigning a laugh with her sisters as she hurried past. Wolf knew it was only right for a man to yearn for battle and a place in the raiding party, and that is what he wished Hawk Tail to believe. But it was the women he wanted above all. The reward due a warrior. One woman would do.

"... and, brother, it is because of us that the warriors will succeed," Hawk Tail's voice drifted back into his thoughts. "Where would they be without the gift we brought them?"

Gift? Wolf knew that Hawk Tail spoke of the canoe full of cornmeal they had traded from the Tionontati, which would sustain the warriors on their raid. But Hawk Tail and the warriors would never know that, he, Wolf, had brought forth a far greater gift - one that would surely spare their lives. No one would ever know, except for his uncles among the shamans who had sent him far to the south. In a secret council of the shamans and war chiefs at Manitowaaling, Wolf had shared what he had learned of their enemy's plans for the spring. It was on the basis of his findings that the raid had been launched.

That had meant a good deal of innocent prying among the Tionontati, and also many meals of their bland corn mush.

"May our warriors savor their maize more than we did," Wolf replied with a grim smile. Turning, he whistled to the dun-colored dog, which had been a parting gift from the warriors in thanks for the maize. The dog limped their way with a gimp leg and Wolf noted that it was also blind in one eye. Had his brothers been mocking him? The idea was too ignoble to contemplate.

"Let us prepare for tomorrow," he said. "We must patch our canoe or end up feeding the fish with our bodies."

That night, Wolf lay on his bear hide, unable to sleep, with his hands still sticky from the pine pitch they had used to repair their leaky canoe. He thought of the woman with the eyes of a fox, knowing that she would never be his. Although Wolf was in the prime of his manhood at twenty-one summers of age, only one woman had ever offered to be his mate, and she had seemed a poor fit. Nor would any father consent to giving his daughter to a clubfoot. The young women of the villages he passed through liked him well enough and considered him handsome. Some had even shared the pleasure of their bodies in the solitude of the forest, but all knew at a glance that he could never provide as a hunter. His gray-gold eyes drew women to him like fish to a torch at night, yet just as quickly they were apt to dart away. Some of it, he knew, was the fear of getting too close to a man who, it was said, spoke with the spirits and had the eyes of a wolf.

So, although he could mark himself as a trader, a shaman and a storyteller of wide acclaim, Wolf could not say that he had ever been a warrior, nor any sort of hunter. And so, not a husband either. He was, at best, a mystery, even to himself.

But it was no mystery that he was at war with his desires. He desired a woman and a place in her lodge, but he also loved to wander. Before he left Boweting, Wabeno had told him that he was cursed with the wandering sickness and would never know a home. And it was true, even as a boy he had felt an irresistible impulse to journey far beyond the distant hills that marked the boundaries of his people.

"You walk a restless path," Wabeno had said. "You cannot lie in one place too long."

The curse meant he would never feel easy in a lodge for more than a season, nor learn the settled life of planting corn like the Wendats, the Haudenosaunee or the Tionontati. Within days of arriving at a new place he felt the itch to leave. What woman would stand for a man who could not grow roots?

Glumly, he mused that it would take a woman in great need to accept a cripple with the eyes of a wolf as a mate, someone who would settle for him as no other choice.

There had been a meek woman among the Tionontati whose eyes never rose to meet his own. Her people called her Sideways Woman because she was a person of few words whose habit was to look off to the side on the few times that she spoke.

As it happened, Sideways Woman had saved his life when he first arrived among her people.

Wolf and Hawk Tail had been welcomed by the Tionontati, who were pleased to receive their gift of furs, promising to gift them with maize and tobacco in return. Wolf had begged to stay among them for the winter, claiming that it was too deep into the fall to return north. The chieftain among the Tionontati had given him a puzzled look, for the leaves had barely turned color at the southern end of Tima Gami, but had agreed after Wolf told him there was already ice on the northern lakes. This was a bald lie, but what could a southerner such as these tobacco farmers know? Wolf assured him that the snow would be as deep as a man's waist within a matter of days in Boweting.

Like the Haudenosaunees and the Wendats, the Tionontati lived in long-houses constructed of supple trees, stripped of their branches and bent in a half circle, then covered with bark. These could be fifty paces long and ten paces wide, housing as many as ten families.

Seeking his place in a longhouse, Wolf had resolved to climb to a high shelf at the top of the lodge, up where legs of venison, ducks, fish and other meats were cured amid the smoke which gathered there before billowing out one of the five holes in the roof. He thought it would be warmer there at night.

"You will never awaken if you sleep there," a voice came from below as he rummaged for a place in the darkness. "The smoke lives there and it kills."

It was his first meeting with Sideways Woman, who quickly scuttled from the longhouse when he made his way down the ladder. To his surprise, he was covered in soot from the many years of smoke which had blackened the shelf upon which he had hoped to make his bed. The Tionontati had mocked him when he strolled from the longhouse, blackened from head to toe, and shared his tale of seeking a pallet amid the deadly smoke. But this of course, only endeared him to them - they considered him a harmless fool. Unwittingly, this was just the guise that Wolf wished for all to see.

A day later, Sideways Woman had offered a wan smile upon meeting Wolf while gathering firewood in the forest and soon took to huddling close beside him as he wove his tales of spirits, animals and heroes for the Tionontati around their fires at night.

Wolf had found her pleasant company, yet felt no burning in his breast for her, nor even in his stones. Yet, by the end of his stay that spring, she had presented him to her father as the man who would share her lodge, and in a moment of despair Wolf had reluctantly gone along with it. He had ventured to her family's lodge with a string of fish as a gift. Although he was no hunter, fish swarmed to his net like birds to a fruit tree. But her father had glanced at his cruelly twisted foot and grunted his refusal, not even deigning to speak a word with him.

Now, as sleep settled over him, Wolf thought of Sideways Woman and the disappointment in her eyes as he and Hawk Tail had loaded their canoe for the long trip north. "Take me with you," she had said as they stood on the muddy shore on the morning of his departure. And though she could not bring herself to meet his eyes, he could feel her chest aching.

But Wolf had felt no ache in return and no wish to hold out the branch of hope. "I am not for you, nor for your father," he said. "I am a trader with no home, no clan, and where I go you cannot follow."

"Take me," she had insisted, turning to gaze fully upon him for the first time. "I will wait by the shore tonight and flee with you to wherever you wander. I will cook for you and warm your bed. I will give you children..."

For a moment Wolf had been tempted to place her in his canoe and paddle away. But by then the whole village had turned out to see him and Hawk Tail off. Among them was the family of Sideways Woman and her stern father who stood glaring in their direction.

Indecision tore at him, for no other woman had ever been so bold. But just then he heard the call of a loon overhead and looked up to see it flying north. It seemed an omen, breaking the spell.

"You have honored me, and I am grateful," he said, not unkindly, "but we are not meant to be."

Behind her in the crowd he espied a young man who stood frowning in their direction, backed by two friends who stood glaring and talking heatedly amongst themselves.

"There is your man," he whispered, "the tall one with the claws of a lynx around his neck. He is a shy man, but he has asked me about you and I was a fool not to see you in his eyes. Go to him and be happy."

Those had been his last words to the only woman who had ever longed to be his wife, and now as sleep crept over him Wolf reflected on how strange it was that the one thing he desired above all else should seem so elusive.

He woke up late the next morning feeling a pang of regret for Sideways Woman, who lingered in his thoughts, even though it had been half a moon since their parting. She had wanted him, even though he had not wanted her, but still, that was something to consider. Confusion circled in his thoughts like a dog chasing its tail. Perhaps he should have crept back in the night and stolen her away from her father. But what then? He had a secret life, known to only a handful of old men, and she could never have a place in it.

"Are you ready, brother? Or will you sleep until the full moon?"

Hawk Tail had shouldered his pack and was heading down the low hill where they had made camp. Wolf groaned and scrambled for his things, trailing down to the lakeshore where their canoe lay waiting. The parting gift of the dog limped along behind him and took its place in the middle of the canoe.

It was an uneventful day on the pearly waters of Tima Gami and they made good time with a southern breeze at their backs. Home was only three days away and they put their backs to their paddles, threshing at the waves as their canoe sped along the shore.

The dun-colored dog made a fine meal that evening, with its meat so tender that it fell from the bone. Wolf reflected that even if the warriors had been mocking him with their gift, still, he and Hawk Tail were well-satisfied with the outcome. Ahead lay Boweting, from which they had departed last fall, and his reunion with the shamans of the Mide-wi-win. Paddling through the waves with the muscles of his back straining, Wolf wondered if Singing Tree had a sister.

Setting Sail

Captain Martin Cabeza owed his commission to the influence of his uncle, Alvar Nunez Cabeza de Vaca, who served as treasurer for a grand expedition to the New World in search of gold.

Uncle de Vaca was second in command under the one-eyed, red-bearded ogre, Pánfilo de Narváez, a man noted chiefly for his incompetence and cruelty. Yet, as a big man in Cuba, Narváez had enough clout to mount an expedition to the new-found land of La Florida. A minor noble with few prospects, Martin Cabeza felt lucky to join him.

A man who possessed more luck than skill with a sword, Cabeza had done his uncle the favor of standing in for him in a duel over the seduction of another man's wife. He had skewered her cuckolded husband in a kidney, yet not so deep as to kill the man, which might have made for a court inquiry with unpleasant consequences.

Grateful, yet eager to place his nephew as far from wagging tongues as possible, Uncle de Vaca had lauded Martin as a golden warrior and superb commander of men, who would no doubt help chivvy the cascade of riches expected to be discovered in La Florida. And though he knew nothing about sailing, Captain Cabeza had been rewarded with the command of a ship in the coming expedition. Narváez intended to sail with six ships and 600 men, along with a handful of women, 50 horses and more than a dozen dogs of war.

Captain Cabeza was of a threadbare nobility, nearly penniless and of such slight importance that he earned barely a nod at the Spanish court. His sandy holdings lay along the desert of the Tabernas in southeastern Spain where the farming was tragic at best. The estate had few tenants, and most of them were generations behind in rent. His vineyards were periodically strangled by drought, and only half of the old *castillo* on the property was habitable; the rest had been a tumbledown ruin since the time of the Moors. Cabeza had sold his ancestral birthright and everything he owned to fund his portion of the expedition, with all of it going to pay for horses, weapons, slaves and men.

In that regard, he was a desperate man, wagering all he owned, along with his life, on the chance to make good in the New World. Outwardly, he was confident and commanding, but the rat of poverty gnawed at the inner man. He had staked his life on the belief that Florida would produce the same cascade of riches as Pizarro found in the Incan empire of Peru.

As for Pánfilo de Narváez, he was that same commander who had been ordered to the land of the Mexicas in 1520 with orders to arrest Hernan Cortez, who had flouted the authority of the governor of Cuba. The attempt had been a disaster.

Cortez had sailed for Mexico in 1518 with 11 ships and 500 men. He had burned all but one of his ships on the shore at Veracruz, sending the last ship back to Spain. With no possible means of escape, it was a do or die situation for his conquistadors.

Yet they were hardly alone. Cortez had marched over the lush mountains to Tenochtitlan, the capital city of the Aztecs, in the company of tens of thousands of warriors from vassal states who were bent on overthrowing their overlords. In time, hundreds of thousands of Indians flocked to his standard, never realizing that they, too, had sealed their fate.

Narváez had pursued Cortez to Veracruz, where despite overwhelming numbers, he failed to overcome a small garrison that Cortez had left behind. Frustrated, he withdrew to a native city known as Cempoala.

In response, Cortez gathered a force of 250 men and attacked Narváez in a pounding rain, capturing his horses and artillery. He then set fire to a temple where Narváez had retreated with a handful of musketeers and crossbowmen. Driven from the temple, Narváez was stabbed in his right eye with the point of a pike. He spent the next two years as a prisoner in Veracruz, while his men joined Cortez in the conquest of Tenochtitlan.

As it happened, one of the black slaves in Cortez's expedition was infected with smallpox, which quickly spread to the Aztecs. It was the horror of the pox, as much as anything, which led to the fall of Tenochtitlan, for the skin of its victims bubbled with pustules and boils, followed by a rapid death.

But as for Cortez, he seized mountains of gold and jewels, going on to conquer all of Mexico. Word burned throughout Spain that there were cities in the New World which glittered with gold, silver and precious gems; riches that were so common that they were of little value to the Indians.

More than that, there were miracles to be had in New Spain. In 1513, the explorer Ponce de Leon had discovered La Florida over the course of Easter Sunday. Legend had it that within the wilds of Florida was hidden a spring that promised eternal youth to all who drank of it. That, and Leon returned with rumors of gold further inland, perhaps even surpassing the stupendous treasures of the Aztecs. And then, of course, came Pizarro's conquest of the Incas and dozens of galleons carrying immense wealth back to Spain...

What a mad, swirling time for Spain! Anything seemed possible, even a golden ladder to the moon! Men everywhere were talking about treasures beyond comprehension, slaves beyond count, and women - beautiful women - who could be gathered by the score in the New World.

All that was required to seize these riches was a company of bold men wielding Spanish steel with a capacity of violence, and as it happened, the dukedoms of Iberia were filled with such men. From the forests and hills of Extremadura to the ghettos and docks of Barcelona, hard men with nothing to lose flocked to the standard of Pánfilo de Narváez and the hope of finding seven cities of gold in the land of La Florida.

And so it was that Captain Martin Cabeza strolled the slave market of Sevilla one bright morning in 1527 in search of men with skills above the common riffraff. The agents of Pánfilo de Narváez had beaten the recruiting drums in taverns and towns across Spain, hoping to enlist soldiers of fortune, but Cabeza had suffered the loss of a key man and still hadn't found exactly what he was looking for.

Cabeza had smiled at Croen's claim that he was a Catholic, for these were as common as sand in Spain. Indeed, what other faith could any man admit to? Yet he had listened intently when Croen vouched that he had sailed as far as Iceland as a young man, and also to the Canary Islands and along the African coast, where there were few safe harbors and accordingly, a continent from which few sailors returned. Such a man might be useful on an expedition into the unknown.

The girl was of no use, and he was irritated that she dared to stare so insolently at him amid the line of slaves on the dock. Her bearing was as haughty as any of the women he had glimpsed at Court. Yet, she had piqued his interest with a single word. Lion.

"I was mother to a lion," Willow had called out as he was turning away.

"A lion?"

"Yes, sire. His name was Aslan and I raised him from a cub. I gentled him even though he was far bigger than me. He grew quickly, he..."

"How came you by a lion?" Cabeza interrupted. He did not believe that the slight blackamoor girl standing on the slave block had raised a lion, but his head was still giddy with wine and he was willing to be entertained.

"My father bought him from a wandering trader who found him nursing at his dead mother in the desert," Willow said quickly, as if her words depended on their speed. "My father traded in camels and purchased the cub, hoping to sell him to the sultan for his zoo. I was given the task of raising him. My father often charged me with caring for his beasts."

Willow's story of Aslan tumbled from her lips and the captain was soon bound by her spell. Indeed, the whole square had gathered to hear her tale and Cabeza's conquistadors were compelled to force the crush of the crowd back with their pikes.

"Hmm, hmm, hmm," Captain Cabeza hummed to himself as Willow concluded her story. She could tell that a thought had hatched behind his eyes.

"And you say you have experience of camels as well?"

"Yes sire, from the time I was only five."

"Five? What do you mean, five?"

"Five years of age," she replied. "Yea, I could walk beneath their bellies and not even touch my head."

The captain snorted at this boast, but he was captured now. Off to the side, Croen made as if to speak, but Willow motioned him to be silent. It was her game to win or lose.

"These camels, it is said that they are vicious beasts. Is that so?" he asked.

"They can be, my lord. They can bite and spit and kick. Once I saw a camel bite a man's hand off in payment for his cruelty."

Captain Cabeza nodded. "And you, such a meager woman, thin as a wren, how did the camels treat you?"

"As I treated them my lord, with kind words and sugary dates. It was the same with the lion, though with gifts of meat."

"But surely these were very old and feeble camels, or very young," the captain mused.

"Nay, my lord, they were racing camels, the most high-spirited in all the

Sahara. They were all proud beasts and some were very whimsical and difficult to handle." She hurried on with descriptions of Yahya the Impulsive, Spindly Solomon, Mameluke the Overtaker and the finicky bitch, Sitt, among other camels she had known.

"Why, Solomon could run three leagues in only..."

"Enough of that!" the captain raised a hand. "Let me think."

He set to pacing back and forth, squinting up at the sky now and then and the tall captain's interest gave Willow hope. She straightened up from her bonds and lifted her chin, the sheen of her dark curls glistening in the sun.

"Hast thou never ridden a camel, sire?" she asked in a mild voice.

Cabeza stiffened. "A commander rides horseback," he replied. "But I have heard that camels can be treacherous."

Then, bending her way and speaking in a low voice he added, "Pray you do not address me as sire again. It is an insult to the king."

By now the pirate Sincid was fidgeting at the captain's elbow, gaping in disbelief at the talk of camels and livestock.

"She is a virgin, sire, a sugar plum, a mango, ripe for your staff!"

"Still your tongue or lose it!" Cabeza roared, irritated at being interrupted. Sincid slunk back, confusion written on his face. He jerked as two of the captain's men seized him by his arms.

"Call him sire again and I'll stick this knife up your ass," one of his captors whispered, fingering a short sword that seemed anything but a knife.

Cabeza returned his gaze to Willow, who stood smiling now at Sincid's discomfort. "And have you any experience with dogs?"

Dogs? Willow hesitated, for among her people dogs were considered vicious scavengers, fit for only sounding alarms in the night and consuming the offal thrown from windows after the day's meal. They roamed the lanes of the Arab towns in packs, driven barking from place to place with sticks and a hail of stones. Dogs were one of the "five nuisances," along with scorpions and ravens. Indeed, there had been times when she and Aslan had gone hunting dogs in the streets of Azemmour before the famine sent the last of them to the stew pots. Dogs? Filthy, barking dogs? Yet she sensed that her fate depended on her answer.

"My lord, a dog is no different than a small camel to me, or perhaps a goat," she lied. "We had many dogs in my town."

"And you did not fear them?"

"No, lord, of course not. For what have they to fear of me? Why, when this wretched pirate took me, I was guarding my master's sheep from wolves. Surely, wolves are more to be feared than dogs."

Cabeza fingered his slim goatee and gazed upon her with appraising eyes.

"And what is your name?"

"Safasaf - Willow."

"Sometimes, perhaps, the willow is of more use than the whip," he mused.

In that instant, Willow knew her fate had been decided.

"This one," the captain said, pointing at her chest. He nodded to a shrewd-looking man bearing a sack of coins at his waist.

Then the haggling began and Sincid jerked free of his handlers, gesticulating with many squawks of protest and a mixture of hope and disbelief. Down came the bargaining from Willow's price of one hundred golden ducats to only ten with Sincid's voice rising steadily higher in outrage, protesting over and over again that the girl was chaste and a virgin fit for a lord with a bounty on her maidenhead that must be paid. "It is a sin! An insult!"

But still Cabeza's treasurer shook his head no until the captain himself reared around and glared.

Another ducat was offered, bringing the price to eleven, and with it Sincid exploded.

"No!" he cried. "She is worthy of the king himself! She is worthy of the king's harem!"

There came a gasp from the crowd of well-dressed merchants and nobles as well as from the commoners and slaves. Too late, Sincid realized his fatal error as all gaped in his direction with expressions of disbelief, crossing themselves at the blasphemy.

"A harem?" Cabeza said, feigning outrage. "A Muslim dog's harem? You dare to compare his Catholic Majesty King Charles to a degenerate sultan dog of the Moors? God help you the Queen should hear of this!"

"No! I did not mean..." Sincid flustered, sweeping his arms and circling in his place. Behind his back, Cabeza's treasurer smiled.

As is said among the Arabs that three things are irretrievable: the released arrow, the spoken word and the broken vow. So it was that Sincid's insult could not be safely tucked back into his mouth unheard. All twenty men under the captain's direction placed their hands on their swords, some with knowing grins on their faces, and for a few moments it seemed as if Sincid's head was in danger of parting from his shoulders.

But the pirate Bartolemeu Sincid had survived greater storms than this. "A gift, my lord!" he cried, falling to his knees and clutching at Willow's tunic. "A gift of this precious woman to you with blessings on your house and adventures! I ask nothing but your forgiveness, nay, not even your favor, but only your forgiveness and mercy!"

Hurriedly, Sincid crossed himself and then crossed himself again, groveling and sniveling in an outrageous manner.

"Watch your lips then, that they do not flee your face at the point of a knife," Cabeza said in disdain. Then, giving a grunt and a nod, he turned to go, his company forming a line of two abreast behind him.

Seeing that the captain was no longer looking, Willow placed her sandal on Sincid's shoulder where he still lay kneeling and gave a hard shove, sending him tumbling to the paving stones.

Sincid's face crashed to the pavement, and when he rose up it was with a long, bloody scrape on the right side of his face, alongside his eyes blazing with hatred.

But for once he was speechless as Willow and Croen straggled behind the conquistadors, still tethered by a chain. The muttering crowd parted, gaping at the ragged-haired old man of Eire and the dusky beauty of the blackamoors, wondering why such an odd pair had been chosen.

The company marched down a narrow alley back to the docks. Up ahead, Willow glimpsed a forest of masts and spars, then as they emerged onto a broad wharf she beheld a row of three stubby galleons and several brigantines bobbing in the river. They marched straight down the wharf and up a studded gangplank to the deck of a mid-sized ship. A brilliant macaw, as red as a sunlit ruby, squawked a greeting from an overhead spar, releasing a stream of excrement to the deck. The ship stank with the sharp reek of men used to bathing in seawater along with the filth drifting up from the hold and the stench of the harbor itself, which served as a toilet for thousands.

The name of the ship was emblazoned across its stern, and though neither Willow nor Croen could read, they learned soon enough that their new home was *El Tigre - The Tiger.*

There at last the bonds of Willow and Croen were loosened under the sun. A light breeze blew up the river, wafting the stink of the wharf away and offering a hint of the far-off sea. A weathered sailor with a face burned olive-gold by years at sea greeted Captain Cabeza on deck. While Cabeza was captain of the troops, it was Francisco Mendaña who was captain of the ship. He preferred to be called Capitão Mendaña in his native Portuguese.

"I know why she is here, but what of him?" he gestured to Croen. "He's doddering old for the sea."

"I have a purpose for the woman, and it's not what you think," Cabeza replied. "As for the Irishman, he has vouched a knowledge of the western sea from the shores of Africa to those where the Northmen dwell and may be useful. If not, you can use him for bait."

Capitão Mendaña scrutinized Croen with a frown, as if he were an oddly-striped animal of a peculiar color, grilling him on the isles of the Canaries, the coast of Africa and the perils of sailing the North Atlantic. Soon they were in an animated discussion and when the captain learned that Croen had sailed a lateen-rigged nao as far south as Port Gentil in Gabon he was convinced of his worth, for he, too, had sailed to that odd land, halfway to the edge of the world, and even along a stretch of the Ogooue River, "a place that killed a third of my crew with the fever."

"He'll do," he said, slapping Croen on the back and ordering him forward with a nod to where the first mate stood standing. "Orders at the helm for this one," he called out.

But as for Willow, Captain Cabeza himself led her down a hatchway and into the darkness of the ship's belly. Climbing hand over hand down the ladder, she suddenly felt very small and vulnerable in the half-light filtering from above. The heavy smell of excrement and urine hit her like a blow to the face, and below her feet she noticed a scattering of straw leading to a dark chamber beneath the low-hanging upper deck.

"You understand that you are to prove your worth, yes?" Cabeza said in a low voice, his eyes obscured in the darkness below decks. "What lies before you has the devil within him."

Willow nodded, too frightened to speak. Was Cabeza the devil of which he spoke? Had he led her below for some evil purpose? But then came a roaring and stomping from the darkness ahead and Willow discerned the scent of animals. That, and the smell of their fear.

Suddenly, it was all clear to her - the talk of lions, camels and dogs. She gave a little laugh as Cabeza gaped at her in surprise.

"I'm ready, lord," she said. "Show me to your devil."

Dragón

The dog leapt out of the darkness like a black thing from a nightmare. In the space of a gunshot it hit the limit of its chain and slammed back into the nook from which it sprang.

Willow's eyes were still getting used to the darkness, so she perceived it as nothing more than a black shadow against the darkness, feeling the whisper of its claws passing inches from her face.

But Captain Cabeza had seen it well enough. "Back, demon!" he cried out in fright, shoving her backward to safety.

Again the dog lunged forward, barking furiously this time, its teeth slashing at the air as it reared on its hind legs, its forelegs scrambling in an eye-level dance. Yet by now Willow could see the iron collar around its neck and the thick chain binding it to the darkness within. Spotting an errant bone at her feet, she kicked the bloody limb back into the beast's chamber and it seized it in its jaws, backing into the darkness with a long growl, its yellow eyes trained on her.

Willow's blood ran fast, driven by her pounding heart as Captain Cabeza regained his composure. A wave of vertigo swept through her, and for a moment she feared that she would faint.

"Did you not see it woman?" he asked, "It nearly took out your eyes."

"I saw him well enough, Lord," Willow forced herself to speak, feeling almost strangled.

"Mother of lions, you're a brave one," he muttered, shaking his head, not realizing that Willow had not seen the leaping dog in the transition from bright sunlight to the darkness of the deck.

"He is yours now," the captain added. "He is called Dragón."

"Mine, Lord?"

"Yes, it is time to pay for your freedom. His master died the cholera while whoring in port, and we could not afford to lose him! You must gentle this beast, train him to obey as you did your lion. And woe to you if you fail me, for I see Dragón already wishes to taste your neck."

"Yes, my lord," Willow said meekly, with her thoughts flying around like a haystack in a hurricane. Gentle this beast? This devil was her fate? She heard the beast roaring and snapping at its bone from the darkness ahead. Aslan had been a kitten by comparison.

"But sir, what is he?" she said after a moment as the dog growled from its den.

"What do you mean?"

"Our dogs... they are not like this. They are low, thin creatures, yet he is so big, I should think him part horse."

Cabeza snorted. "He's a Rottweil, bred in a place called Swabia. The Swiss call them butchers' dogs because they herd their cattle and haul their meat wagons. I believe he's also part Dane; it's said they've bred a very large dog there and he certainly fits the bill."

Meat wagons? Swabia? Willow nodded gravely, though she had no clue.

"His handler was a Prussian, a heretic as ill-tempered as his dog. It was he that made the dog so cruel and I'm not sorry to see him go, though he taught the brute well enough. He's a dog of war, trained to kill. Do you know the Prussian tongue?"

"No sir, but I can learn." In fact, Willow had never heard of Prussia, nor any of the kingdoms of Germany.

"A pity, for those are the only words he understands. But you must teach him to understand Castilian Spanish."

"Certainly, sir. It will be far easier, I'm sure."

"And see that you do not turn him gentle."

"Yes, sir, if he does not eat me first."

"Pray that does not happen."

"I will sir, truly."

But of this, she was not quite certain. Willow had never heard of the Europeans' dogs of war, which were trained to go for a victim's throat. Unleashed, they would dash ahead of a line of infantrymen, leaping into the enemy's ranks to bite and slash in a fury, ripping at a victim's abdomen with their legs, sowing confusion and terror. The dogs of Morocco had been thin, starving curs; yet this thing had a head as large as a bucket, and its mouth bristled with fangs. She gazed into the darkness where the dog was still slobbering at its bone, pausing now and then for a menacing growl.

"Well?"

"My lord?

"Are you satisfied? Can you do it? Or would you go back to your master?"

Back to the loathsome Sincid and his wicked men? "Oh yes, my lord," she answered, nodding rapidly.

"Yes, what?"

"I will train the beast, sir. He is a lesser demon."

Captain Cabeza gave her a thin smile. "Go to it then."

He hoisted himself back up the ladder leaving her alone with the dog.

Watching him depart, Willow wondered, did the captain expect miracles of her? Surely, he could not expect her to teach the dog Spanish. At best, the dogs of Morocco had been taught to understand the word, no, as they were driven with curses from one lane to the next.

With her eyes now adjusted to the darkness, Willow examined her surroundings. The dog had disappeared within a cubby built into the curve of the hull. It was utterly black within with no trace of Dragón. Yet she could hear him well enough, crunching and slavering at the bone she had kicked his way. An empty water bowl stood at the entrance to the nook. How long had it been empty? she wondered.

Glancing about, Willow discovered the tools of her new trade: a rake, a shovel, a bucket, and a barrel of water. Surely, the dog needed water. Any child of the desert knew of such a need. She found a dipper pegged to the hull with a leather thong and as quietly as she could, she filled it and crept toward the nook's entrance and its empty bowl.

Abruptly, the slobbering noise within ceased, replaced by a long, low growl. Willow held the dipper out at arm's length, she was only the length of her forearm from the dog's bowl when it sprang once again from its cave, raging and tearing at the air with its claws and teeth. The ladle fell from her hand as she sprang back to safety.

"Stupid beast!" she cried. "How am I to water thee?"

As if in answer, the dog licked at the water spilled on the deck. Then, instead of retreating, it stood panting in the heat before her with his tongue lolling sideways from its mouth.

Dragón stood as stout and squat as a king's table. He was nearly as tall as Willow's shoulder and his broad chest and legs were thick with muscle. His coat had the sheen of black velvet, yet to Willow's eyes it seemed as thin as that of a mouse, revealing the sleek muscle and bone working below. A ragged scar ran from his split eyebrow in a crescent halfway down his face and he had several more scars on his back and torso. Abruptly, the dog gave two thundering barks and turned, kicking some of its filthy straw in her direction before slinking back into its nook.

"He's a warrior, that one."

Turning, Willow found herself face-to-face with a lank man hanging on the ladder with his limbs spread like a monkey. In her fascination with Dragón she hadn't heard him creeping down the rungs. He had a broad face with wide-set eyes and a thatch of hair the color of straw that fell about his head like a tumbled-down haystack. He was dressed in the same rough woolens as the other seaman she'd seen when coming aboard the ship and stank like rotten chicken. But the most striking thing about him was his size; he seemed as large as two men, a giant.

"Hello sweetie," he said, reaching out as if he meant to pull her head to his. Willow sprang back, though not so far as the entrance to Dragón's lair.

"Oh, shy are we?" he smiled, revealing a gap where two upper teeth were missing. "Ah, we'll get to know each other soon enough, for its a long passage to the far side of the world. A long way..."

"Yes, sir, I believe it so," Willow said politely, concealing her fright. There was something disturbing in the manner of the seaman. He gazed upon her in the same manner as the slavers, as if she were his toy.

"He's been there before, you know," he nodded to the darkness where the dog had begun growling again, "He was with Cortez when he marched on Tenochtitlan in the land of the Mexicas. Tore the throats out of women, children and warriors alike, he did. Disemboweled them with his claws. That's a devil dog you've got there."

The seaman lay draped on the ladder, gazing into the darkness where Dragón sat growling. "Aye, they'd never seen the like of him, and they never will again, poor bastards," he said after a moment.

By now the hairs had raised on Willow's forearms, for the sailor seemed in no hurry to leave and it had grown quiet up on the deck. He was pillowy, with long arms and lips so thick they seemed almost lewd. She'd dodged the embrace of creepy men in the corrals of Azemmour and among Sincid's crew. The seaman was clearly of the same tribe, and the spread of his body barred any passage, as if he were a gargantuan spider, draped over the web of the ladder.

Abruptly, he scratched his crotch and gave his genitals a tug beneath the folds of his breeches. "How much?" he asked.

"My lor... what?" she replied, thinking he was speaking of the dog.

"For your charms, lovely. For your charms. For what's between your legs. How much?"

Willow felt her head swirling. First the dog and now this loathsome pig? How much must she endure?

"You are mistaken," she said coldly. "I have nothing for you. Get away from me!" She crept towards the rake leaning against the hull; it wasn't much of a weapon, but it was all she had.

A sly look crossed the broad face of the seaman as he slid down the ladder to the deck, only two steps away. He was almost in her face now, close enough for her to feel his breath, and his body was so big that it crowded out the scant light from above. He took a lazy step forward, reaching for her with a broad arm as if she was already his. The rake was within her reach, but he'd have no trouble seizing it from her.

"No!" She pushed back against the wall, utterly trapped.

"Come, sweetie, I have a doubloon and there's time enough for it." His eyes were hot on hers, moist with intent. Behind her, the dog began a long, low growl from the darkness of its kennel.

But before Willow could answer there came the thump of boots directly above and a voice. "Garon? You buggering sea snake, get up here!"

A face glared down from the hatch above and Willow could see it was that of the ship's captain, Mendaña. "Come on now!" he called. "Leave off that woman; we need you at the hoist."

Philip Garon touched a finger to his forehead and began climbing the ladder. "Right along captain, right along," he said. But at the top of the ladder he pursed the slab of his lips in a kiss. "It's a long way to the New World, sweetie, a long way," he said, with his eyes shining with mirth. "There's plenty of time for it."

He left Willow shaking in the shadow of the lower deck. She cursed an oath worthy of her father's camel tenders; one that would have earned her a whipping back home. Caught between two devils and Allah knows what! she raged. Teach a dog to understand Spanish - insane! The unspeakable insult of the toad-faced sailor! She would speak to Captain Cabeza and have him whipped! But that thought died almost as soon as it was conjured, for who was she to demand anything at all? For a moment despair almost overwhelmed her and she steeled herself, remembering that the captain had held out her only chance.

As for Dragón, she wondered at the seaman's words. Cortez? Tenochtitlan? The Mexicas? She had heard of none of these in Morocco, yet perhaps they lay ahead. And the horrid dog, with the body of a bull and rearing like a demon... had it really done such cruel things? What might it do to her?

Nor did she know where she would sleep. Captain Cabeza had left no instructions and there was nothing but a pile of straw outside what served as the dog's kennel. It was meant, no doubt, for Dragón.

"Ah, well, I must make do for myself," she said, resolving to probe deeper into the ship in search of a blanket. At the least, she could make a nest of the dog's straw. It wouldn't do to bother Captain Cabeza, for by now she felt that the less she dealt with men, the better.

Skirting Dragón's hutch, she learned that there were other dogs concealed in the darkness of the lower deck. There were six of them, with some in pitiful condition and not nearly as fierce as Dragón. Am I to care for all of these? she wondered. The answer was clear enough, and quickly she turned to the water barrel, fetching ladles for each dog's bowl. The killers lapped and whined, wagging their tails, yet Willow was careful to stay out of reach of their jaws. Garon's tale of savaged throats and her own peoples' distaste for dogs were warning enough.

As for Dragón, she took the rake and pulled his water bowl toward her, filling it and pushing it back again. Grudgingly, the brute appeared from the shadows and lapped at the bowl, then stood staring at her with his long tongue lolling from his mouth.

"*Perro bravo, es bueno, si?*" she addressed him. But Dragón offered no glint of understanding; instead he gave a thundering bark and retreated once again to the shadows.

The dogs appeared to be starving, so Willow climbed back up the ladder in search of food. A sudden breeze swept through the harbor and all around her men were shouting, scrambling, and hoisting bales of cargo beneath the sun amid the freshened wind. Suddenly, she was filled with exhilaration. Despite all its dangers, she was going to the New World! What would father think? What would mother think, and scrawny old Abu bin Nisar? New Spain was said to be a horrid place, filled with monsters of every description and savage one-eyed men who ate people alive. Even she had heard of it in Morocco, though the tale-tellers scarcely believed it. But she was going, and now she was keeper of the dogs. Dogs! Filthy dogs, of all things! What idiocy! How stupid! Dogs? Who in Morocco could imagine such a thing?

"You. What are you doing up here?" It was Captain Cabeza, pausing as he ordered a troop of men hurrying past with sacks of grain on their backs.

"My lord, the dogs are hungry! What should I feed them?"

Cabeza paused as if he had never considered it.

"They look like they haven't been fed in days," she pushed on.

"Yes, yes, the fools of this ship wouldn't know their mothers from a monkey," he said, "but let them eat the same shit as the men. Aye? The cook's down by the bow. Fetch whatever's handy."

"Yes, my lord."

"It wouldn't do for the dogs to starve. Not where we're going."

"My lord?" she said, intending to bring up the seaman Garon. It seemed a trivial thing to bother Captain Cabeza with, yet still...

"Yes, surely, get off with you now," he said, irritated. "Bring what the cook has to spare and God help us all, from what they tell me."

Willow made her way to the shelter of the foredeck, finding the galley and its bemused cook who gave her one of his delicious biscuits, fresh from the oven, and then another. "I once had a daughter like you," he said, smiling at the memory. "You must come and tell me your story, for it's lonely here with only the cook fire for company and I could use some help stirring the pot."

Willow smiled and repressed a giggle, for the cook had tufts of hair growing out of his ears, and though he was bald on top, great tangles of his gray hair extended like wings from either side of his head. He had a red face and an impish smile. There was no trace of lechery in the old cook's manner, and Willow said she would gladly visit. She left with a bucket of mush, the contents of which she could scarcely imagine, and the cook had given her a blanket to boot, though it stank of horse.

She struggled back through the darkness below decks with the bucket carried before her in both hands and then ladled its contents into the bowl of each dog in her care. All except that of Dragón, for he still growled in the blackness of his den and she dared not creep within his reach. Instead, she scoured the remnants of the bucket with her hands, fashioning a ball of mush that she tossed as gently as she could to the entrance of the dog's cubby. To her relief, the dog's great head emerged from the darkness to seize the offering in its jaws, its head turning sideways and its long tongue lapping every kernel of the gruel from the floor.

"Eat well, beast, for it's a long way to the New World," she muttered.

That night, Willow huddled in her blanket atop a gathering of straw just beyond the reach of Dragón's lair. Her sleep was uneasy, clutching at the dagger her father had given her in case the cow-headed seaman Garon came for her in the night. But she heard only the restless stirrings and nightmare yips of the dogs, and in the morning she watered them once again and made her way up on deck. But first, she knelt atop her blanket and made obeisance to where she assumed that Mecca might lie. She had fallen off the custom of bowing five times daily to the resting place of the Prophet due to the trials she'd been through, and now she resolved to begin her prayers anew.

She climbed the ladder to the poop deck and to her surprise, the caravel was heading down the broad river. Surrounding it were several lateen-sailed brigantines of the sort that had been captained by the pirate Sincid. The river was apparently shallow and treacherous, for its pilot charted a meandering course around numerous wrecks, some rising from sandbars in mid-stream.

Turning, she saw that there were also horses on board, and an even greater number of pigs. To her relief, there were also several women lounging about or threading their way through the livestock and men.

"Sister, what is this?" she called to a woman who looked to be her own age, perhaps fifteen, a bit younger.

"What?"

"The horses! Where did they come from?"

"Did you not hear them? They were hoisting them aboard all night, stamping and snorting."

"Ah, I have barely slept in days," Willow replied. "The sons of Baal could have clattered on the deck all night and I would not have heard them."

The young woman scrutinized her. She had a golden complexion, sensuous lips and eyebrows as thin as scimitars.

"You are of Islam," she said, not as a question, but a statement.

"Yes, sister, and you?"

"*Catolico*, of course. From Genoa. You would do well to accept the sacrament if you wish any peace on this ship. There are priests aboard, and they will hound you."

"I in turn will pray for you, and for them," Willow replied with a small laugh.

"I'll have need of your prayers with this crew," she said, grimacing.

"Sister, what do they call you?"

"Serena. And you?"

"Safasaf - Willow."

"Ah, the horse-keeper. And the dogs, too, I hear."

"Horse-keeper?"

"Surely you did not think you would be caring for only a few dogs. I hope you like shoveling shit." She made to hurry off to an errand at the bow of the ship.

"The angels grant we meet again," Willow called after her.

"We should scarcely miss each other," Serena called over her shoulder with a smile. "It's a small ship."

Indeed it was. Capitão Mendaña's caravel was seventy-two feet long and twenty-three feet wide, with a mainmast bearing two sails, a mizzen mast outfitted with two lateen sails and a square-rigged foremast. A half deck covered the bow of the ship and a similar deck covered the stern. Every inch of the *Tiger* was crammed with seamen and soldiers who struggled to manhandle a cargo of barrels, bales and timber into its bowels. Amid the hubbub were the horses, hanging in slings from a bridge of timber that spanned the deck. There were six of them swaying with the back-and-forth motion of a pendulum as the ship eased down the river.

Willow was conscious of the catcalls and whispered advances of the seamen around her as she walked the deck; it was something that would become as familiar as the wind and the waves in the months ahead, yet already she managed to push them away with a haughty face. Striding toward her from the bow came Captain Cabeza.

"So you've awakened princess," he said. "Three times I looked for you and here the sun is high."

"I've barely slept in days, captain, but I am no layabout," she replied, neglecting to point out that the sun was barely above the eastern horizon. "Sir, am I also the keeper of the horses?"

"Indeed," he said, nodding. "Consider them as valuable as your father's camels, and God help you if you lose one."

"Lose one, my lord?"

"Even men are lost on a long sea voyage," he said glumly. "But these are worth more to me than men, especially that one," he pointed to a horse hanging in the nearest sling. "Montoya."

It was the captain's horse, a well-built stallion of medium size, but well-muscled.

Montoya was dappled in cloud shapes of white and brown and possessed with eyes rimmed in a milky blue. At the sound of his name, he twisted his head in their direction and flicked his ears forward, showing his long teeth.

"His eyes, they are like those of a beautiful woman, are they not?" Cabeza said.

"Indeed they are, sir," she replied, though she had never seen eyes so blue, certainly not in any woman of Morocco.

Willow stood spellbound as the captain rhapsodized about his horse. It was almost as if he was speaking of a lover. She had to bite her tongue to keep from giggling.

"Montoya was born in the marshlands outside Cadiz, that splendid seaport of tall palms and golden walls," he said dramatically, as if speaking in a play. "He took his name from his father, who had been raised among the Basques, far to the north of Spain. His mother was a dusky beauty from Catalonia, introduced by a noble family on their journey to the Court's summer festival in Zaragosa. They coupled in a glen before an audience of royals, and then came Montoya, a stallion with eyes like blue pearls."

Willow could scarcely imagine a royal audience observing two horses rutting as a summer entertainment, but then, the Spaniards were a strange people. Who could say what sort of perversions occupied those born to royalty?

"Is that what makes him special, captain? His eyes? They are very fine. We had dishes of that color in my master's palace."

Captain Cabeza cocked his head and grimaced at the absurdity of her question.

"No, daughter, not simply his eyes. This horse is a destrier, a war horse trained for battle at the country estate of an Andalusian gentleman. By the age of four he was taught to face the sound of gunfire, the crash of steel and the whir of wooden swords. A horse like this will charge through the crack and blast of cannons and through their billows of black smoke on command."

"Truly, he's a wonder. Are there many horses like him?"

"Sadly, no, and many of such quality die in battle, for they make fine targets." Cabeza explained that Montoya's father had been conscripted in the armies of Charles V, who had unified Spain, and had fought in the king's wars on the Italian peninsula, bearing up under a sheath of heavy armor.

"Montoya's sire died in the battle for Milan four years ago. He was impaled by three bolts as he charged a line of crossbows, struck in the chest after his armor fell awry."

"A sad way to go for what must have been a fine horse," she said, imagining a similar fate for Montoya.

"Yes, but even sadder if my horse dies of the flux at sea. So treat him well."

"I will, lord," Willow said, already imagining a daily brushing for every horse, along with toting their forage and water. Their leavings would be collected and dried for the cook fire. Between the dogs and the horses she would have plenty to do and was grateful for her training in her father's corral in far-off Azemmour. No one would have to tell her how to care for her beasts. Already, she thought of them as her own.

The Great Ocean Sea

At last the ship reached the mouth of the river and the port of San Lucar de Barrameda where it was joined by four other caravels. Several more days were spent provisioning the ships and hauling more horses and livestock aboard. To Willow's eyes it seemed that an immense number of men were coming aboard, what she imagined to be an army.

"It's said we'll be sailing with six hundred men, and all of them horny as goats when they're not buggering each other," Serena said as they watched a line of men streaming up the gangplank and down into the hold, loaded with supplies.

"Buggering themselves? What do you mean?"

Serena made a face. "Pray you do not find out. The sailors are the worst of them - the marineros. Watch out for them."

"Have we no protection?"

"Aye, rape is punished by death, and not a pleasant one, but that's not much protection if you're caught in the dark or have a bag tossed over your head, is it? We all sleep together."

Serena said that she and four other women slept in a tangle below the foredeck near the bow, ready to rise as one and shriek if they were disturbed. That, and every woman slept with a knife at her side. But Willow had resolved to stay toward the back of the ship with the dogs, where the seaman seemed hesitant to tread. Just beyond was where Captains Cabeza and Mendaña had their own small cabins, and she reasoned that their presence would provide her with a measure of safety. Then too, she had her father's dagger, which she had sharpened to a razor's sheen in the galley.

One morning Willow awoke to the sound of trumpets and the crash of cannons as the flotilla of five ships hauled their anchors from the stinking muck of the harbor. It was a sunny day with a steady wind blowing to the west, and Willow and Serena held hands at the rail and grinned with the optimism of youth as the sails of the *Tiger* unfurled with a thunderclap. Locking arms with their long hair streaming, they danced in a circle to the cheers of the men aboard, and clearing the harbor and its jetty, it seemed as if the spirits of all aboard were high enough to fill the billowing sails. The sailors began stamping a rhythm and clapping their hands, cheering the girls on. Then they too joined in the dance, and soon the decks of every ship were alive with whirling men and the few women among them, dancing for the joy of leaving. Reaching the middle of the strait, Willow glimpsed the low shore of Morocco far to the south. She gave her homeland a final look, biting her lip, yet with no thought of tears, and turned her eyes to the west and the New World.

A pleasant surprise was a new dress from the cook, who had instructed her to call him Uncle Luis. He had sewed it from scraps of cast-off sails. The canvas was comfortably weathered and a dingy off-white, yet presentable enough, and Willow was happy to discover that it was capable of shedding a light rain. More than that, she was grateful to be free of her rough tunic, for which she found a new use as a pillow.

Uncle Luis had been scandalized to find her sleeping on the deck amid a scattering of straw and had fetched a hammock woven of hemp. "Most of the men sleep on deck in good weather," he explained, "but some swing in these nets down in the hold, as tight as bats hanging in a cave. Admiral Christopho Colombo found these among the Indios of New Spain and made a gift of them to sailors everywhere. For that he should be the patron saint of sailors. Before the hammock, all men slept on the deck in all weather."

He'd brought a hammer and two spikes, nailing the hammock up just outside Dragón's hutch. "Colombo was a man of Genoa like me, you know," he added, ignoring the growling at his back.

"And like Serena," Willow said. She had never heard of Christopho Colombo, but Serena had spoken of Genoa.

"Just so," Uncle Luis nodded, crossing himself. "She's a pure one yet, but her mother's a whore and the favorite of every man on the ship. She'll be richer than King Charles by the time we reach Hispaniola with all the doings at the foredeck. It's sad that her daughter is so pretty."

Willow did not know what the old cook meant by this last comment, except perhaps that Serena might find herself schooled in her mother's profession. For now, at least, her new friend was employed as a seamstress and there seemed to be no end to the mending required for the ship's sails.

Uncle Luis claimed to have cooked for Colombo himself along with other admirals of Spain. Willow was happy enough with his meals, for she had eaten much worse in the famine of Azemmour. She was allotted two pints of water each day and one pint of wine. Otherwise, Luis told her she could expect hardtack biscuit along with beans or chickpeas and salted fish four days a week. Tuesdays offered a bit of rice and salted pork or bacon. Salted beef or mutton and a bit of cheese would be served on Thursdays and Sundays.

"Sir, apologies, but my faith does not allow me to eat pork," she said, "nor to drink wine."

"Ah, where we're going such rules can be disregarded, for your god cannot see you out on the open sea," he said, waving a hand dismissively. "A greater concern is that of hunger, and you may be dreaming of pork by the time we cross the ocean. The food is not so good as we go along. It spoils, and the water turns to piss. That's why we drink wine, and pray for a rapid crossing."

For some on board, the quality of the food hardly mattered, for with the roll and sway of the ship on the open sea, many of the soldiers, priests and even seamen turned green and vomited their scant meals over the side. Some lay about like dead men, clutching at the railing, rising only to heave again until the side of the ship was painted with their vomit. Even the horses, pigs and dogs grew seasick and Willow seemed to be forever cleaning their mess with a bucket of seawater lifted from the pitching waves by a long rope. She was thankful that the seasickness did not bother her, reasoning that it was much the same as riding the undulating back of a camel.

Between the vomit and the stench of the unwashed men, the ship smelled like an open sewer; its deck ran with streams of filth along with lice, cockroaches and rats. Even when a passing shower washed the deck clean, the ship and its masts stank of rotting caulk, not to mention the horrors of the bilge.

As for herself, Willow had fallen into a routine of feeding and watering the dogs each morning and then climbing the ladder to tend to the horses. It was no more of a circuit than twenty feet, but she was fearful of walking any further unless she was accompanied by Serena and the other women. There were more than eighty conquistadors aboard the ship, along with a crew of twenty-seven marineros and that made the deck very crowded indeed. Inevitably there were whistles, doffed hats and buttery compliments from any man standing nearby when she climbed the ladder to care for the horses. Yet she didn't feel particularly threatened, and Serena had told her that Captain Cabeza had gathered all of the men at their departure, spelling out the rules and promising cruel justice to anyone who molested the women on board.

Yet on her fifth morning aboard the ship, the cow-faced seaman Garon had brushed up behind her as she bent over collecting hay for the horses. She had straightened with a start, hissing at him, but he replied with a gap-toothed smile and a devilish glee in his eyes.

"Ah, I see you have not forgotten me," he said, speaking in a low voice with his piggish eyes darting. "In your dreams, am I?"

"Do you think I dream of rats and snakes?" she replied. "Not them, nor thee."

Garon chuckled. "As I have said, it's a long way to the New World, princess, months at sea sometimes. Aye, a long way, and I mean to make you mine long before we land. I pray thee, accept my coin so we might be wed for as long as the journey lasts. I dreamt of thee last night and could not sleep for desire of you. If it's more coins you need, then I will suffer to grant it. Accept it, darling, or I'll have you for free."

"Pig!"

"Nay, sweet, there's something here for you to raise your skirts." He pursed his lips as if to kiss her. In his palm lay a small brown coin bearing the likeness of a king, whose face had been worn to nothing at the edges. "Take it."

Around her, several men looked on at the unfolding drama, some chuckling among themselves, others eyeing the scene with speculation. Willow flushed beneath their gaze and in a blind rage swept her pitchfork at Garon's hand, striking the underside of his palm with the flat side of its tines. The coin leapt from his hand, flying over the rail into the sea.

"God's balls!" Garon cried, gazing at his empty hand, which bore a long scrape seeping blood, and then back at Willow, who stood shaking with rage.

It had been too much for her. The abduction, the ordeal on Sincid's ship, the Jews burning on the wharf, the brothel and the slave market... Enough! The fighting spirit Willow's father had bequeathed her rose in her throat like a shot of hot bile. "Pig!" she cried again. "Keep away from me, filthy dog!" She jabbed her pitchfork at him, quaking with anger.

But the tines stopped an inch short of his belly and the brute stared dumbly back at her as if she were simply flirting.

"Call me a pig, will you?" he said, showing his missing upper teeth in a ghastly smile. "Well you'll have a pig's cock to savor as soon as I bend you over, and you owe me double now for what I've paid you. I've made you my whore now, lass, instead of my sea-bride, and any man here will attest to that. You'll grant me what's owed or follow my coin into the sea!"

With that he turned and climbed atop the ship's rail, hauling his way up the rigging. Despite his bulk, he scrambled as quick as a monkey up the shrouds.

Across the way, she caught the eye of Croen. They hadn't spoken for several days now, he being busy with duties below deck. He sauntered over and gazed up at Garon's bulky form, weaving in the wind just a few hands below the crow's nest.

Joining the ship's crew had done nothing to improve Croen's appearance. If anything, the thicket of his ginger beard and flaming red hair had the look of a squirrel's nest.

"Stay well clear of that one," he said. "He's the ship's bully and even the captain fears him. A Frenchman, that's him, with all of their bad traits and none of their good."

"Captain Cabeza? Surely..."

"Surely, indeed," Croen said. "Captain Cabeza is a gentleman, used to dealing with peasants of the meekest sort in his country home, along with prissies in silk hose and petticoats at Court. He's not used to this rough bunch of dung beetles, and they know it. They know how to play him, aye they do. Oh, he pretends to have steel in his backbone, and perhaps that will yet prove true. But he's just a boy playin' soldier in their eyes. He'll have to dole out some rough punishment when these feckin' gobshites feel it's time to cross him. Otherwise," he drew a finger across his neck, "he'll be their kitten.

"He's a bit of a gobdaw, you know," he added as an afterthought, pursing his lips and nodding.

"A gobdaw?"

"Gullible, a milk goat, easily led. I spied it in him at the market in Sevilla," he chuckled. "Why else would he take us on?"

"Why, he took us on because we have value!" Willow exclaimed. "It was, as my father would say, a transaction, and you proved our worth."

"Aye, I spun a tale around a kernel of truth and thank God, he swallowed it."

"And you must not forget, he has promised his men the riches of kings," Willow added. "None would kill a goose if it means losing its eggs."

"True enough, but we're bound for an unknown shore, some say a paradise and some say a hell. We'll likely need an eagle instead of a goose."

Croen had been given the odious job of keeping the hull caulked with scraps of wool and hot pitch; it was no easy task since the endless twist and pull of the ship's hull meant that a crew of black slaves were kept ceaselessly pumping the bilge free of water that seeped in at a frightening rate.

"We might as well be sailing in a sieve for all the water we're taking on," he muttered.

"You make it sound as if we might sink."

He cocked a pale red eyebrow at her and snorted. "I can see you're a child of the desert," he said. "Of course we might sink! The bottom of the ship is filled with stones for ballast, and a line is chiseled in the hull just above the rocks. If the water in the hold rises above that line, then this nag and all of us aboard will get a trip to the bottom of the sea. Ah, we'll dine at King Neptune's table then, or his fish will dine on us."

"Then all of our problems will be solved," Willow said dryly.

"And we also have the wretched tournedos to deal with," Croen carried on, warming to his tale. "They're devilish sea worms that bore into the hull, rotting ships to ruin."

"I have not seen them," Willow said, gazing at her feet, as if the wretched tournedos might be crawling there.

"Ah, it's only old ships that they favor, but there are other things in the sea, too, which might take a ship to her grave; things like the kracken with tentacles as long as the masts and a beak large enough to crack a ship's hull. Ah, and armies of mermen that swarm over ships in the night, and the mermaids that dine on smitten sailors. But worst of all are the hurricanes, aye, the big storms at sea. And the scurvy that rots yer teeth from yer head, and limp sails in a windless..."

"For the love of Allah, stop!" Willow cried. "I've enough trouble with these dogs without fearing for monsters and mermen and we have an army of men to withstand them. Worry about keeping us afloat! Worry about the cracks in the hold!"

Croen offered a grave face. "Oh, I promise you we'll stay afloat despite all the perils of the sea. I'm beseeching our Savior day and night and urging every man to do the same. There's plenty of scoffers amongst them, and heathens such as yerself, but we'll pull through. In the meantime..."

Croen paused as the seaman Garon landed with a heavy thump only two footsteps away. The two glared at each other. "You're the slave man who came aboard with her highness," the seaman said at last. "Bought in the market like a chicken, I hear."

"Get yer feckin' face clear of us and don't go botherin' her again," Croen replied with a growl and an ugly note to his voice.

"Who are you to tell me anything, old man?"

"She's my daughter and I won't see her disturbed."

Garon responded with the look of a hunting toad, his thick lips drawn grim and wide across his face. "Surely, and thou a red-headed monkey from Eire and she a blackamoor from the dregs of Morocco? I think not, uncle. She belongs to any man who'll have her and I know she fancies me."

"Keep away or..."

"Or what?"

Croen searched his thoughts for some threat that might be of use for an old man facing a hulk half again his size, coming up with only one. "Or by the rood, I'll speak with the captain of you and yer jinks, ye cocky rooster" he said, "and he'll be pleased to pluck yer feathers."

"Wot? Like a boy telling his mother? Hiding behind the captain's skirts?"

"Leer if ye like, fool, but the captain seeks to make his reputation with the men, and taking down a pig such as yerself would do him a service. Think on it."

Garon gazed at him in cold contempt. "That'll be the last time you speak to anyone."

"But speak I will, remember that, and I'll recommend the stocks and the lash, along with a gelding," Croen said as the big man turned away, lumbering to where a knot of rough-looking seamen stood looking on. To Willow's eyes they seemed as watchful as jackals and a trill of mirth ran through them as Garon reached their company. He mimicked Croen's threat, mincing before the grinning men. A chill ran through Willow's body, thinking that nothing Croen could do or say would stop Garon from coming for her.

"Pray that the devil makes a ladder of his spine," Croen muttered. "Ignore those bastards and keep close by the captain." He pushed his way to where they stood lounging at the railing and flung his arms up in the air, uttering an un-Christian-like curse.

But the marineros only laughed, gazing back at Willow as if she was raw meat.

Willow stowed her pitchfork and retreated into the darkness of the half deck, pondering her situation. She had a more immediate problem with what to do about Dragón. The war dog continued to lunge at her with gnashing teeth, dancing on its hind legs and slashing with its claws. The more she saw of the beast, the more frightening it appeared with its huge black head and heavy jaws. She shuddered to think of the dog's jaws closing on her, and one night had even dreamt that she had slipped and lost an arm to Dragón's teeth. Each day she was compelled to mold its food into a ball to toss within its reach. For water she kept on sliding its bowl back and forth with the rake, having to fight with the beast as it gripped the handle in its jaws. Serena had told her that Dragón had been much attached to his former master who'd died in Sevilla. "Perhaps he is waiting for his master's return and thinks you are a usurper," she had said.

"I was told that he was a cruel man."

"Perhaps cruelty what your devil dog needs. If fills something within him."

"Then he will go unfilled."

By now the other six dogs in her care had taken to her, even allowing her to rub the nape of their necks and brush their coats as they stood panting in the heat. Each day their handlers stopped by to exercise them on deck, sometimes engaging in war games that involved an attack on a leather dummy. But Dragón seemed a long way from having his neck rubbed, with no question of being exercised on deck; he seemed to have nothing within him but a whirlwind of violence.

Yet one thing seemed to calm him. Willow still had the pipes she'd been playing to her flock on the day she'd been taken by Sincid's men. They were tethered to a leather thong, which she had hidden beneath her tunic. The pipes, her dagger and her dress were the only possessions she owned. Even her sandals had been lost, though Croen promised to obtain her new ones once they reached the port of Hispaniola on the far side of the ocean.

Dragón had crept from his dark hutch and cocked an ear the first time she had played a simple tune taught by her father. It was called "The Bird and the Monkey."

> "Bird and monkey
> fight for fruit,
> Bird and monkey,
> hear them toot."

It wasn't much of a song, offering a handful of notes, but to her surprise, Dragón thumped his tail and sang along in a low, tuneless "Oooooh..." gazing at her as if seeking approval.

"Ah, perhaps your master was a singer?" she said as the dog gave her a quizzical look.

Thereafter, she spent an hour each day singing and piping just out of Dragón's reach after she had finished her chores with the horses. The dog handlers had shared a few commands with her in Spanish, and these she repeated, pantomiming "hold!" and "attack!"

But Dragón only looked at her stupidly, growling his disapproval.

Within days, Capitão Mendaña's ship was far out on the ocean. One morning, Willow went on deck to tend to the horses and found that the last shadow of land to the east had vanished. The *Tiger* rolled forward on the swells with the ocean stretching to the slit of the far horizon.

"It's like riding the back of a giant bird of the sea," she said to Serena, who joined her each morning, helping to groom the horses with a stiff brush. "The sails are like wings. See how they spread?"

Above her, every sail on the caravel was billowing tight against the wind and Capitão Mendaña had even set the studding sails at the bow of the ship. All five caravels of the fleet were ranged in a line heading west, with several brigantines coursing behind. Their own ship was at the southern end of the line.

"Would that we could fly like a bird," Serena replied, "For I fear it will be weeks before we cross these waters, maybe months."

"It's no different than crossing the desert," Willow said. "You just keep going."

"Yes, until you hit a rock and sink."

"There are rocks out here?" Willow gazed at the endless expanse of ocean, seeing nothing of the sort.

"They ring the islands along with reefs that cut ships in two as if they were knives; but fear not, we're more likely to die of dullness long before we strike a reef."

"Ah, reefs - one more thing to fear along with sea worms. Do you know which is the commander's ship?"

"What? Narváez?" Serena made a face. "His ship is that one, in the middle. We're lucky to avoid him. If ever Satan lived in a man, it's him."

The words were barely out of her mouth when Serena crossed herself and looked around, a sudden fright settling on her face. "But never say that I spoke of him thus," she said. "Bad things would come of it."

"Sister, I would not betray you even if hot coals were laid on me. But whisper why it is so."

Serena held Willow's hand, moving so close that their shoulders rubbed. "Have you ever heard tell of a person being thrown to the dogs?"

"We have a saying like it in my own land," Willow replied, thinking of the hyenas that prowled the outskirts of Azemmour.

"Then know this. The devil dogs in your care will dine on the Indios when we reach New Spain, for Narváez is unspeakably cruel and has been a student of other captains of the conquistadors who are just as bad."

"What?"

"Yes. My mother told me of women and children butchered to feed the dogs, and babies, too. That, and a thing called *la Monteria infernal*, in which the Indios are hunted for sport."

"How could your mother know of such things?" Willow asked. Serena's story of dogs dining on human flesh seemed beyond belief.

"The men who lie in her arms each night told her as much, and there have been many men," Serena replied. "They say we're going to a place called La Florida - land of the flowers - to follow in the footsteps of a captain named Ponce in search of the Indio's treasure. He, too, was a cruel man who used dogs to terrorize the Indios. He had a dog named Becerrillo, a beast who was infamous for slaughtering the people of that land."

"I have not found Captain Cabeza to be evil," Willow said. "He dotes on his horse and is afraid of dogs, though he would never admit it."

"No, he is no Narváez, nor a Ponce de Leon, but do not count on him to be kind, sister, for he will have his orders and all of these conquistadors are hard men. It takes a hard man to command them."

"Do you think that the captain is a hard man?" Willow asked, remembering Croen's claim that Cabeza had little experience with the sort of villains who packed the ship.

"He will have to be if he wishes to keep his head," Serena replied. "Oh, the stories my mother has told me..."

But before she could speak further, Captain Cabeza threaded his way through the throng of men on deck and bade them good morning. Cabeza had abandoned the metal breastplate that he'd worn on the day of the slave auction, but Willow noticed that despite the growing heat of the morning he wore a sleeveless sheath of chain mail over a tunic of heavy cotton covered with metal plates. He also bore his sword at his side on every occasion. Croen had told her that mutinies were common on the Great Ocean Sea, both among the conquistadors and the marineros. "Even a king has to watch his back in court," he had said, "and this is a far cry from a kingdom."

"You've done well to care for the horses," Cabeza said, stroking Montoya's back. "See how he glistens."

"The brushing calms them, my lord," Willow replied.

"Mmm... And how go the dogs?"

"None have bitten me," she said, looking up with hopeful eyes. Serena smirked at this, and making her excuses, she hustled back to her place at the bow.

But Captain Cabeza accepted her statement as if it were an achievement. "And Dragón? How goes he? Have you gentled him yet?"

"He is singing to me, my lord," she replied. "He misses his master and perhaps his heart is broken for his loss, but I play at my pipes and he sings along in his own rough way. I would not step in on him yet, but soon I hope to have him as gentle as a lamb."

To this, Cabeza gave a good-natured grimace, knitting his eyebrows. "We have no need of a lamb; simply make him manageable."

Willow was anxious to know if Dragón had tasted human flesh, but there was no way to ask without betraying Serena's confidence. Instead she asked, "Sir, do you think Dragón is an evil dog? Is he cruel?"

Cabeza paused for a moment to consider. "He is simply a dog, no different than the wind or the clouds," he mused. "Only men are evil, only men know the difference between good and evil and only men make such choices. Satan gave us the knowledge of good and evil and the temptation of choosing between them when Adam and Eve tasted the fruit of it in God's garden."

"I would think thee a priest with such talk."

"I know the difference between good and evil," Cabeza said, crossing himself.

"But the dog, sir, if he is not evil, then can he be cruel?"

"Oh yes, I imagine those he slaughtered thought he was quite cruel. But why do you ask? Would you convert him to Islam? I should find it quite humorous to find him bowing to Mecca."

"No, sir, for such would be blasphemy. I... I only hope that he is no sinner."

"Then pray for him, woman, but be careful not to make him your lamb, though I can scarce imagine it."

"Yes, lord," she said, curtsying.

Cabeza hesitated a moment. "Have you had any trouble with the men?"

"Trouble?"

"Advances."

Willow thought of the seaman, Garon, and his threatening ways, but rousing the captain against him might cause the seaman to seek revenge, so she said nothing.

"No, sir. None have troubled me."

The captain studied her with skeptical eyes. "Well then, I guess our company holds more pious Christians than I might have imagined," he said, turning to leave. "Let me know how you fare with Dragón."

Willow pursed her lips and blew a sigh of relief as the captain walked away. How easy it would be for him to command her to his bed, she thought. He had even allowed her to use his seat of ease so she didn't have to risk the dangers of the privy above the waves at the front of the boat, where there was peril both from the sea and the men who lurked there. The captain could seize her at her ablutions at any time, if he wished. But Serena had told her that Cabeza preferred the company of boys and young men to women, and each night after he retired to his quarters a handsome, curly-headed blond conquistador no older than herself came creeping down the passageway to tap at his door. Dragón growled in his cubby as the lover passed by, but never barked or lunged, seeming content to keep the captain's secret.

Willow carried on brushing the horses until long past midday and then turned her attention to the dogs. The feeding, watering and cleaning kept her busy until sundown and after that she joined Serena and the other women at the front of the ship for the day's gossip and tales of far-off countries and strange customs. Serena's mother, Luticia, had many bawdy tales of the men she had known, and beyond the knot of women sat a dense ring of men who laughed and muttered over every story, often sharing stories of their own.

Yet one story put them in a somber mood.

"I met an old witch in Hornachos before we sailed," Luticia said. "I was traveling with the soldiers as they collected men and we were far from the sea, though she spoke of it well enough. She was an old hag, a Moorish woman with a face as dry as a clay pot who claimed to have the second sight. When I told her that we were bound for New Spain she became very grave, as if overcome by a vision. She warned me not to leave the ship, saying that very few who wandered ashore would live. 'You must not go into the forest,' she said, 'for it is a land of dark magic and spirits. Only those blessed by God will survive.'"

"That is true of any man or woman," a deep voice sounded from the circle beyond where the women gathered. "Only those blessed by God survive."

"Yes," Luticia agreed. "Perhaps it was only an evil woman's foolish tease, yet she shook me to my bones. Take care not to march into the forest, she said, or you will never come back."

Willow couldn't help but shiver at the prophecy, though perhaps it was only the cool breeze of the oncoming night. Was she bound for this magical forest? She had never seen a forest, yet she had heard tales of ferocious animals, snakes and monsters. She prayed that the captain would not compel her to go.

Each evening, often as not, the sun burned its way beneath the western horizon in a radiant ball of crimson fire as the evening star of Venus rose to greet the night. The caravel rose and fell with the dark swells as its neighbors dwindled to shadows, with only a single light at the stern of each ship to ensure that none were lost beneath the stars. Willow gazed at the tendrils of purple clouds ribboning the blood red sky to the west and was thankful that the New World and its prophecy was still far away.

A Soldier of Spain

The fleet stopped briefly in the Azores to take on more water and feed for the livestock, with many on board the ships gazing wistfully at the shore, rethinking their decision to float west in what might well be their coffins. Some slipped over the side of the ship in the night and dog-paddled to shore, taking their chances with the local authorities. All who weren't busy hauling cargo and barrels of water were confined to the ship under the eyes of a sword-bearing guard.

"We are prisoners now," Willow said to Croen as they stood at the *Tiger's* railing, watching the unloading of a hay wagon on the stony dock.

"We are all prisoners in this life until our time comes to meet our savior Jesus Christ," Croen replied, crossing himself. "I hope someday you'll convert and will meet Him with me."

"Thou art kind but old, Croen, and I hope to pass this life long after you're gone," she said tartly. "I hope to meet the archangel Gabriel, who has my fate written in his book. It's said that he sits outside the gates of Paradise, writing with a long quill. Perhaps he will introduce me to your Jesus."

"Hmph!"

"But forget your heavenly spheres and think on our fate today," Willow went on. "Will we ever be thus? Prisoners?"

"I think not," Croen said with enthusiasm. "There's talk all 'round the ship of the New World and its cities. Some are larger than even Napoli and paved with gold, which to the Indios is as common as clay. It's said that there are many towns of good size and fields of a yellow grain that run far out of sight."

"Hah! If gold is as common as clay, it will soon be worth nothing in Spain," Willow replied. "I kept my father's books and when there is too much of anything, even camels, it soon dwindles in value."

"True enough, child..."

"Don't," she warned.

"Daughter, then. And I think the ships of these greedy bastids will sink soon enough with all of the gold they'll be loading. But Lord knows, it's likely there will be a place for us among the Indios. Such towns may have need of our skills."

"Perhaps, but I have heard tales too," Willow said, thinking of the stories told by Serena's mother. "It's said that the Indios are not always friendly. Some say they can turn the skies black with their arrows and that whole armies have disappeared among them, never to return."

"What armies?"

"That of a captain named Ponce, who discovered La Florida fifteen years ago."

"Ah, I've heard of 'im. He were an ill-fated bastid. He made a mess of Puerto Rico."

"Truly? I do not know of this place, but it's said that he returned to Florida a few years ago with hundreds of men and women..."

"To start a colony." Croen nodded.

"Yes. But the Indios made a pincushion of him for his cruelty. Serena's mother said he died of his wounds."

"Aye, that's so, in a place called Cuba. But he had far fewer men than we, and our armor will protect us."

"Oh? And have you been issued armor?"

"No," Croen said glumly.

"Nor have I, nor will we. And what of the prophecy? Death in the forest, she said."

"That of the old witch? All the more reason to pray. We must pray for our Savior's intervention."

Willow had no response to this, not wishing to encourage Croen any further, for the old man could blow like a wind with endless talk of his faith, and as far as she could tell, his devotion had done little to serve him.

"I hope you are right, uncle," she said. "I hope the Indios will receive us with grace and that our own men will treat them kindly. But uncle, if six hundred men bearing swords and pikes landed at your town in Eire, would you think they came with good intentions? Would you receive them kindly?"

"Ah, but who's to say we'll be with these men when we land?" he gave a smile and a wink.

"What?"

"The New World is a big place and all eyes will be trained on its wonders and not on us. If we wish, we can slip away."

Slip away? Willow had never thought of fleeing, and as her father had once said, better the devil by your side than the one over the next hill. She was happy enough tending the dogs and horses, and Captain Cabeza had treated her kindly. But still...

"Escape? To the land of the Indios? Perhaps," she replied uncertainly.

"Aye, if they have fine cities and well-mannered folk, then surely there will be a place for us. We'll tell them we're potentates of a far-off land, come to do them a service."

"Poten...?

"Royalty, m'lady! Poobahs! The duke and duchess of... uh..."

"Swabia, perhaps?"

"Aye! Swabia will do nicely."

"And what royal gifts will we bring them? They will expect great things of us if we are truly royalty."

"Why, wisdom, of course! Knowledge of the wide world. And I will take it upon myself to share the words of our lord and savior, Jesus Christ. What greater gift than that?"

Willow rolled her eyes. "I'm sure they will be delighted. Thou should have been a parson, Croen."

Croen's ginger beard fluttered in the wind as he bobbed his head in agreement. "Perhaps I shall be yet, princess. A parson in the New World with a tidy parsonage to keep me in me old age."

A gentle wind blew them steadily west for two weeks. The New World had barely been discovered, yet already the mariners of Spain and Portugal had identified those particular trade winds calculated to send a ship far across the Great Ocean Sea and back again.

But at the end of two weeks the fleet found itself becalmed under a suffocating blanket of heat and humidity. Men, women and animals alike agonized in the stillness, roasting beneath the glowering sun. The water ration was cut in half after a conference between Cabeza and Mendaña, which only added to the misery. And as Uncle Luis had promised, the meals grew wretched. One night, they dined on a soup of boiled pig bones, stripped of their marrow, with only shreds of tendons and gristle to gnaw on.

Time stopped. Standing at the railing on the second morning, Willow saw the puffball of a cloud, far up in the sky of piercing blue. By midday, it hadn't moved a whisper and the ocean seemed as thick as syrup.

Boats strung with tow lines were launched, with men straining at the oars to drag the ships west through the sluggish sea. They scuttled like beetles, crawling over the lank ocean.

The lower decks of the ship were hellishly hot and stinking all the more for lack of any breeze, so all on board took to sleeping on deck. Yet that was agony, too, for there was no respite from the heat and after a week of dead calm they were snapping at each other like a pack of feral dogs. Military discipline was enforced as much by common consent as brute force; the conquistadors were freebooters to their bones, willing to obey only if compelled by a combination of steel and gold. Thus, Willow imagined that Captain Cabeza was growing fearful of the mutiny Croen had spoken of. His face was impassive, grim, yet even from across the deck she detected his eyes flaring with alarm at moments when turmoil erupted among the men. There were fights over gambling, insults traded between seamen and conquistadors, and shoving matches over seemingly nothing. There were too many men, too crowded together, and Cabeza kept two sweating, steel-clad guards by his side at all times.

With the calm came disease. It had lingered within the men all the way from Spain, but now, driven forth by the heat and the abominable filth of the ship, sickness in the way of dysentery and its bloody flux began taking their toll. There was a dead man or two on deck each morning, tossed with little ceremony into the sea, and by day the ill huddled in the shade as best they could, gasping for water with their trousers soaked in blood and excrement.

A mix of evil looks and fear settled on the faces of those who were yet unaffected, and with the sails hanging limp there was little to do. The idleness was a danger unto itself as the men began whispering amongst themselves.

"He'll have to do something soon to show the men who's master," Croen said as they watched the tow boats slapping futilely at the sullen sea.

"Master? It would do them no good to oppose him," Willow replied. "It makes no difference to the wind and the sun if they throw him overboard."

"True, but most folks like someone to blame for their troubles, and often it's the head man. When there's a drought, it's the king who gets the blame. When a ship's becalmed, it's the captain or some poor bastid they choose as a Jonah. Sometimes even a woman."

"Bad things happen to those who disobey their masters in my country."

"Here, too, very bad things. But the men are going mad. Watch yourself."

That night, long past the witching hour, Willow lay in her hammock with her underclothes soaked in sweat from the awful heat. She had tied one end of her hammock to the ladder leading up to the deck in the hope of catching some cooler night air. Despite the heat, she was sleeping as if among the dead and didn't heard the footpads creeping down the ladder's rungs, inches from her head. A broad hand hovered a moment and then clamped hard over her mouth.

Willow shot awake and tried to scream but her attacker slapped her hard across the face and she went limp as a trail of stars trickled behind her eyes. Dimly, she was aware that she was being lifted out of her hammock as if she was as light as a pillow. She heard a purr of satisfaction as the man who held her stepped deeper into the darkness beneath the half deck. She was too stunned to struggle against the arms that clamped her in their vise. She felt herself being lowered to the deck. It was as black as the bottom of the sea where she lay and Willow could see nothing at all, not even the hand clamping her mouth.

"Shh... shh... there's a knife to your neck, pretty one," came a thick voice in her ear. "Would you like to feel it? Would you like to swallow its blade? Then keep quiet now and..."

From the blackness beyond the ladder came a rustling and a sound like great wings flapping. And then a deep-throated scream resounded in her ears as she was slammed to the deck. Thereafter came a violent rending and snarling mixed with screaming and curses as she scrambled back for the safety of the ladder. In his ignorance, her would-be rapist had blundered to the entry of Dragón's hutch in the darkness, and though the dog was on a short chain, it was long enough for him to seize the man's leg. He writhed on the floor, kicking and screaming as the dog sawed at his leg with its terrible fangs, dragging his body closer to its claws. Willow scuttled away on her hands and feet, her eyes flaring in horror into the darkness. The screaming seemed to go on for a long time, as did the dog's horrible growls as it twisted and tore. Then, Captain Cabeza burst naked from his quarters with a lamp in one hand and a short sword in the other while half a dozen men stormed down the ladder from above. Willow backed into a corner beneath the ladder while the men wrestled her attacker from the dog's jaws in a spreading pool of blood. The dog was clubbed once, twice, before it yelped and let go. By the light of the captain's lantern she made out the wide eyes and thick head of the French seaman, Philip Garon.

"Up! Get him up!" Cabeza roared, and Garon was dragged and pushed back up the ladder where he was tied to the mizzenmast with a length of rope passed a dozen times around his chest. By the light of the moon it was clear that his left leg was ragged in its ruin, with chunks of flesh hanging loose and a stretch of bone gleaming white against the blackness of Garon's blood. The ship's barber - who also served as surgeon - came forth with spirits and a needle, stitching the wounds as best he could by moonlight. The Frenchman cursed and screamed as the stitching continued until a plug of twisted rawhide was stuffed in his jaws. All who looked on agreed that the dog had done a fine job of destroying the leg with its rending fangs. A leather strap was required to hold the torn flesh together. A pint of brandy was poured down Garon's throat, yet for the rest of the night he sat upright and groaning, tied to the mast with his bandage seeping blood.

But that was not the end of Garon's ordeal, for Captain Cabeza had promised death to anyone who raped any of the women aboard. And now he had a chance to prove that he was a hard man - harder than any aboard, should there be any doubters. Lying in his bed of corded rope later that night, he smiled at the generous turn of fate.

All night Garon lay sobbing and groaning in pain before the mizzen mast and when the dawn came it revealed the angry red slashes across his left leg with pieces of flesh missing. The stitching of the barber's needle had been haphazard under the light of a half moon and it looked more like the black tangles of a fishing net stretched over a ghastly ravine in Garon's flesh. Willow rose from her hammock and climbed the ladder to the deck, lifting her eyes just above the hatchway to peer at her attacker. She felt nothing for him, neither remorse for his agony, nor exultation; it was enough to know that he was no longer a threat.

But not so for Captain Cabeza, who mounted the half deck after the morning meal and called every man on the ship to assembly.

"The King has set rules regarding the women who serve on his ships and Garon has violated his Majesty's trust," he began stiffly, backed by his sergeant and a half-dozen chosen men armed with swords. "In the name of the King, the penalty for violating a woman is death."

The captain let this sink in as more than one hundred men stared back at him in an eerie silence, made all the more so by the placid sea in which the ship sat becalmed. With the sun only two hours above the horizon, it looked to be another scorching day with no wind in the caravel's sails.

"There has been no violation, so there will be no sentence of death," Cabeza went on, "But there will be punishment for the attempt."

This time there was a murmur from the crowd, not of complaint, but approval, for Garon had far more enemies than friends. Some claimed he was a cut-purse who had stolen what little belongings they owned, either through the force of threats or from beatings. He had a habit of ripping golden rings out of the earlobes of sailors, the proceeds of which were meant to be used for a proper burial upon the death of a seaman. Yet none could oppose him, for Garon was a giant compared to most on the ship, and he had a sixth sense for guarding his back. A popular boy who had resisted him had disappeared in the night, and though no one could prove it, many thought that Garon had raped the lad and tossed him overboard.

Thus, the assembled men listened carefully when Cabeza cried out in a loud voice, his eyes betrayed by a touch of glee. "I put it before you now as to what punishment is fitting for Philip Garon? Would you give him the lash or set him to cleaning the hull?"

A choice? The men gave sidelong looks at one-another and shuffled with a murmur passing among them. No commander had ever requested an opinion on a matter as grave as martial punishment. But the answer came quick enough from a young seaman who'd been blindsided by Garon with a blow to the face and robbed of some coins sewn into the hem of his breeches.

"The hull!"

Aye, the hull. The verdict rippled through the crowd like a wave, and at the mast, Garon squeezed his eyes tight at the thought of it. "The lash, lord, the lash, I pray you!" he called out, his voice thick with fright.

Croen had pushed his way to the hatch where Willow looked on and now he squatted beside her.

"Look what you've done, woman," he said, mocking her. "You've made him your rag doll."

"Me? It was the dog, not I."

"Aye. You'd likely be lying dead in the hold with a broken neck this morning if not for your demon dog. No witnesses and nothing to tell. But now the bastid will serve as entertainment for the men."

"By cleaning the hull?" she scoffed. "It's a punishment not much worse than soap-stoning the deck."

Croen gave her a curious look. "Ye don't know, do ye?"

"What, sir?"

"He's to be dragged under a ship from one side to the other. There are barnacles under the hull, hundreds of them as sharp as knives. Have you seen barnacles before?"

"Yes," she nodded, "on the dock in my town." There had been thousands of them beneath the waterline, black razors draped in the slime of the sea wall.

"Then imagine being dragged over them - they rip a man to shreds. It's a bad way to die, but often worse if you live. The English call it keelhauling. The hull was scraped clean in Sevilla, but by now I warrant there are enough barnies to shear him like a sheep."

Willow gazed from Croen back to where Garon lay bound to the mast. He was weeping now, one arm raised, seeking mercy. "I don't care," she said.

"Nay, I doubt his own mother would care. Still, there's good sport in it. Sometimes a man's head lops off his shoulders when his skull bangs away at the keel, but many simply drown."

Though she had no pity for Garon, Willow felt sickened by Croen's description. She'd seen hangings before, even crucifixions. They served as public entertainment as well as punishment, yet she was not one to gawk at another's suffering.

But now she saw Capitão Mendaña speaking to Cabeza on the half deck, and though they weren't arguing, it seemed close to it.

"We need this man," Mendaña spoke low into Cabeza's ear. "He's the only man aboard who's been to La Florida. He was with Ponce only six years ago."

"What of it?"

"He was there when a people known as the Calusa attacked the colony and drove it into the sea. He's a bad man, but he knows the land ahead. He's fought the Indios; he can guide us."

"It's late for that now," Cabeza replied, fidgeting. "The men have decided his fate and we will handle the Indios when their time comes, rest on it."

"You were foolish to offer them the decision," Mendaña replied, his eyes blazing. "Need I remind you that we are the captains and they are the mob? They will not respect you for giving them a say. They will think you are weak. They will say this is a *democracia.*"

"I will deal with anyone foolish enough to think so, but for now the dice is thrown and there is no going back."

Cabeza made a stern face to Mendaña, yet he was stricken by the captain's words; perhaps he had been foolish, as if the ship were indeed a democracy and prey to the mob. Yet he knew that the men would consider him even weaker if he changed the punishment. By now they were in a celebratory mood at the coming spectacle.

"Tell them we need Garon to save our skins," Mendaña urged.

But the patrician in Cabeza could see no other way forward and he raised his hands in resignation. "I cannot do that."

"Then ease the punishment. There is a way."

And so it was that a rope was passed under the bow of the ship and strung midship from one side to the other. Garon was lifted by four seamen and a sack bearing three cannonballs was tied to his good leg, along with the rope to be used for dragging him under the ship. Another rope was tied around his waist to lower him into the water.

But it was Capitão Mendaña who supervised the punishment, and only the most experienced sailors knew that he had rigged the affair to cause little harm to Garon, providing he did not drown.

Garon screamed for mercy as he was lowered over the side to the cheers and mocking yells of the marineros and conquistadors. He screamed and cursed all the way down to the waterline, waving his arms over his head as he went under. Gazing over the railing, Willow could see his stricken face fleeting into the depths of the quiet sea.

"Drag him slow," Mendaña commanded five conquistadors holding the rope on the other side of the ship. "Slow so that he suffers all the more."

And so the giant Frenchman Philip Garon, veteran of the docks of Marseilles, the slave fields of Hispaniola and the swamps of La Florida was dragged slowly under the hull of the *Tiger*. On deck, every soul held their breath, imaging the man's agonizing drag, down in the sea beneath the ragged hull. The seconds ticked by, stretched to the point of horror. What man could survive such a fate? Yet the yellow mop of Garon's hair floated up from the depths, as if an errant jellyfish, and then the man himself emerged from the waterline as pale as death at the end of the rope, yet with only a few cuts on his back and a bleeding head.

"Bring him up," Mendaña called out, beckoning Serena forward.

Garon was hauled up the side of the hull by five stout men and dragged over the railing, flopping face-down on the deck as if he were a tuna fished from the sea.

"Sit on him," Mendaña demanded.

"Sir?" Serena looked about in confusion.

"Quickly now." He seized her by her arms and shoved her. Serena could not have weighed more than one hundred pounds, but her buttocks landed full force on Garon's back.

It had the desired effect. A torrent of sea water belched from the Frenchman's mouth, followed by a furious coughing and puking. Garon writhed on the deck with the entire ship looking on. Then he lay face-down, moaning and cursing, fearing to raise his head.

"Why, he's barely been scratched!" said the seaman who had called for the keelhauling in the first place. "Please, sir, let's do him again."

Yes, again. Despite the suspense of the long pull underwater, it had been a poor outcome and the men expected - demanded - blood. Often, a proper keelhauling meant three passes under the hull of a ship, and a death sentence would mean being pulled the full length of a ship's keel. "Again! Again!" a chant went up.

Yet just then the angels intervened with a trace of wind tickling the sails. Those on deck felt the caress of a breeze on their faces and all eyes lifted as the shadow of a cloud drifted over the sun.

"God save us!" a call rose up. "We're moving!" The breeze grew steadily until the lank sails began to billow.

Captain Cabeza had been brooding in the background over Mendaña's handling of the punishment, but now he seized his chance to make good. "Who are we to revoke the will of God?" he called out in a loud voice. "We have a heavenly decree!"

Mendaña gave him a quizzical glance, and muttered something obscene in a low voice before calling out, "See to the sails, all of you! And bring in the tow boat!"

His punishment served, Garon was untied and left to lie on the deck in a welter of blood and puke. The ship's barber stooped to look him over, but seeing that he was only badly scraped, gave a satisfied nod and left him gasping in the sun.

Looking on, Croen scoffed at Garon's punishment. "A disgrace. Mendaña let Garon cheat the barnies," he said.

"Do you think so, uncle?" Willow replied. "They dragged him along so slowly that I thought he would surely die."

"Ah, but it's getting pulled fast underwater that kills a man because that draws him close to the hull where the barnacles live," Croen explained. "The Capitão risked drowning him, but you notice he weighted him down with three cannonballs instead of one, which is proper. He made sure that he sank well under the ship and only earned a scrape or two instead of being skinned alive. Then, when Garon was back on board, t'was your friend's rump that brought him back to life. And though we thought they dragged him slow, it only seemed that way. A man can hold his breath for twice that long if he keeps his wits."

Willow gazed at Garon with a grim set to her face. By now he had crawled into the shadow of the railing and was making the attempt to rise, collapsing back on deck.

"Ah, you won' have to worry about him nay more," Croen said, guessing her thoughts. "He's going to have trouble enough with that leg after what the dog served him. You can spit on him and he won' lift a finger to ye."

Croen gave her a knowing look and a smile, but Willow was not so sure.

A week later they reached the port of Santo Domingo on Hispaniola, the island known as "Little Spain," where conquistadors had indeed fed living human beings to their dogs as they scraped the island from one end to the other for Indian slaves. When Cristopho Colombo landed in 1492, it was said that millions of the Taino people lived on the island in five chiefdoms. But the Spanish had enslaved tens of thousands to work in their gold mines and sugar plantations, massacring thousands more. Within twenty-five years less than 30,000 Tainos survived, and then a smallpox epidemic wiped out almost all who remained. Now, they were being replaced by black slaves out of Africa.

Garon was hauled to shore in a stretcher, nearly dead and unable to stand. His festering leg had gone black where Dragón had ripped him. He did not come back.

But as with the Azores, Willow and Croen were not allowed to leave the ship as it lay anchored in the harbor and they spent a dreary week on board as the seamen and soldiers flocked to the port's taverns and brothels. Across the way, they could see the tower of the Fortaleza Ozama, the tallest building in the New World and a prison for pirates as well as a fortress. From the deck of the ship they heard singing, shouts and occasionally, the discharge of the town's cannon, signaling the muster of the port's guard.

Willow spent her time singing and playing to Dragón as before, murmuring thanks for his protection. The remaining dogs and horses had been taken ashore for exercise, so it was left to her to give their pens a good cleaning. Yet, Dragón was still too agitated to approach.

"You will get fat and lazy if you won't move," she said to him in reproach. "You must learn to trust me or they will run you through and serve you for dinner."

Dragón cocked his head at this, snarling softly. Yet after six weeks at sea the menace had gone out of his snarls and he no longer danced on his hind legs or lunged at Willow when she went to clean his straw with her long rake.

By the fourth day of her imprisonment aboard the ship, Willow had had enough, knowing that it might be weeks before they sailed.

One of the horses had died while the ship was becalmed and had been butchered for its meat, both for the men and the dogs. That morning, Willow came to Dragón's hutch bearing a wooden platter of meat. Taking a breath, she held the platter out before her, singing a soft tune that she sensed the dog liked. Slowly, she crept within the killing space of the dog's chain, placing the meat on the deck before him. To her surprise, Dragón looked up as if in gratitude and waved his tail.

"You are no different than my Aslan, though he was a golden beast and thou art black," she said softly as the dog wolfed down its meat. She was only inches away now and on an impulse, she reached out and stroked the dog's vast head. It showed a fang and its tail ceased wagging for a moment, but then it carried on eating again as if she wasn't there. Emboldened, Willow stroked Dragón's head, daring to do nothing more.

But that afternoon she sat on the floor and inched slowly into Dragón's space, playing low on her pipes. The dog crept low out of its hutch, growling as it came and Willow nearly choked in fright, poised to scramble to safety. But instead of lunging, the dog gave a sigh and laid its head on her lap, flopping sideways to the deck and panting in the heat of the day. Again Willow reached down to stroke the dog's head, caressing the ruff around its neck. Its body was huge - it seemed bigger than her own - and far more powerful. The weeks of captivity on a chain seemed to have had little effect on its muscles, which rippled beneath its skin.

Dragón seemed happy to see her the next day, wagging his tail in anticipation, and she stepped into his space as if they had been lifelong companions.

"Today we will work on our lessons," she said. She had memorized all of the commands of the other dog handlers and now she ran through them, sit, lie, hold. To her surprise, Dragón quickly followed her commands.

"Ah, beast - thou have learned the Spanish tongue, I see. Or perhaps you knew it all along and were only pretending.'

On an impulse, she brought forth the leather training dummy and placed it where Dragón could reach it.

"Attack!"

The dog lunged as if on wings and caught the dummy by the throat, ripping and twisting with a ferocity that stood the hairs up on Willow's arms, sending ripples down her back.

"Hold!"

The dog dropped the dummy from its jaws in an instant, obeying the next command, "Sit!"

"*Bueno,*" Willow said, tossing the dog a biscuit. For the rest of the day they ran through the lessons again and again until Willow was satisfied that Dragón would obey her every command.

But there was one more test that would put her own life at stake.

The next morning on their sixth day in port, Willow ran through Dragón's lessons and fed him an extra helping of the butchered horse. Then, she loosened the iron clasp on his collar, holding her breath as she slipped the chain from his neck.

"Come."

The dog looked around warily as if fearful of leaving the entry to its hutch, but then stepped forward as commanded to where Willow stood with a leash at the foot of the ladder.

"Now you are my lion," she said, clipping the leash to Dragón's collar. "Obey me or..." She could not finish the words, but satisfied, she scrambled up the ladder with the dog climbing behind her as if it were a monkey.

There were only two guards left aboard along with Croen and a handful of slaves. One of the guards gave a shout of alarm at the sight of Willow standing beside the huge beast whose head rose to her shoulders.

"Jesus!" Croen cried, crossing himself and gaping at Dragón's size.

"Come," she said, "we're going ashore. But let me and the dog go first."

The guards made to block her with their axe-headed pikes, but Dragón strained forward, nearly dragging Willow off her feet. The guards scrambled for safety as she cried, "Hold!"

"Sirs, I beg you, do not provoke him!" she called out.

"Aye, he'll rip yer throats out, black devil that he is!" Croen added.

The guards - both of them barely sixteen years old - needed no more encouragement, almost tripping over each other as they retreated toward the bow.

"Advance," she said, and Dragón stepped out on the gangplank, looking uncertainly at the water below before dashing along its length. Again, Willow nearly fell into the harbor in her haste to keep up, but once ashore, she commanded Dragón to sit as they took their bearings.

They stood on the quay and watched as a long line of slaves walked along its length bearing rocks on their shoulders in an ant-like procession that wandered far down the malecon bordering the harbor. The slaves were a mix of black Africans and Tainos, worn down from their ceaseless toil and barely covered by their rags. One-by-one the rocks were deposited in the water at the end of the quay and then the line circled back, with hundreds of men shuffling under the eyes of a single guard.

At the base of the quay stood the walls of Santa Domingo, beyond which stood the stone tower of the fortress. A market of many stalls was piled up before the walls, packed with fruits and vegetables, pigs, chickens and exotic offerings such as parrots and monkeys. The market was crowded with customers and some of them turned to gaze at Willow, commenting on the size of the dog. A lunatic among them began to babble and dance herky-jerky in their direction, but fortunately, was held back before he could approach.

Dragón growled at the onlookers, showing his teeth through curling lips and suddenly Willow realized her mistake. The dog was only half-tamed, and in an instant it could attack, dragging her along by its leash as if she were a rag doll. It was trained to go for the throat, to tear and kill and kill again. If it dashed toward the market, it would have the same impact as the blast of a cannon.

"We need to go back to the ship," she said, trying to wheel Dragón around. But the dog was intent on the crowd now and could not be moved. She might as well have tried moving a statue of iron.

Then she spied Captain Cabeza hurrying her way along the wall with four soldiers at his heels and her heart fell.

"What is this?" he cried, his face clouded with disbelief. "Why are you off the ship?" Behind him, his soldiers held their swords pointed low to the ground, their eyes upon the dog, which gave two thundering barks of warning.

But Cabeza had come one step too far and Dragón wheeled and growled with bared teeth, ready to lunge.

"Sit," Willow said in a low voice as the captain stepped back in alarm. To her surprise, Dragón obeyed, planting his haunches in the dust. "He... he is... he needs exercising, lord," she stuttered, almost overcome by fear of what the dog might do. "He has been idle too long. He will be of no use to you otherwise."

"You have gentled him?" Cabeza said in amazement.

"Yes, sir, I think so, with the help of the horse meat. He listens to me, though I beg you not to come too close just yet. He is yet half wild, and though he knows you well enough, it would be best not to tempt him just yet."

"Ah, the horse meat," Cabeza said, as if this were a magical remedy. "And you, what are you doing ashore?" he demanded of Croen.

"Ah... I came to see that the dog is protected, sir," Croen said. "I know he is dear to you."

"Protecting this creature?" Cabeza scoffed. "He could take off your arm with one tug of his jaws."

But the captain said this with a smile, and he was clearly pleased that Willow had reined in Dragón.

"I thought we were going to have to feed him to the sea," he said, looking down at the dog's huge head. Dragón had settled himself and now sat panting, with his tongue hanging sideways out of his huge jaws.

Yet there was one more test of Willow's command, for as they stood talking a handsome carriage rolled up behind Captain Cabeza and his men. It was drawn by four horses and was clearly an expensive conveyance with inlays of gold leaf emblazoning its ebony sides. From its door burst an excited child of no more than six years old.

"Alonso!" his mother cried from the shelter of the carriage.

But Alonso had spied the dog and would not be stopped. He came running alongside the line of slaves, beaming with delight. Dragón perked up his ears and scrambled to his feet at the sight of him, his lips drawn back in a growl to reveal the scimitars of his fangs.

"Look out!" Croen cried, leaping in front of the child's path. But Alonso was agile as a chicken and he easily dodged the Irishman's grasp, running headlong toward the dog of war, which was growling now in warning.

Too late, Cabeza and his men realized there was trouble of some sort just behind their backs. Croen cried, *Sweet Jesus, no!* just as Alonso rounded the men as fast as his legs would carry him. He was only steps away from Dragón's jaws when a single word rang out.

"Hold!"

Cabeza seized the boy by his collar just as his hand brushed the side of Dragón's face, but Willow's command had worked its magic and what might have been the death of the governor's youngest son was delayed for another day.

Alonso's mother ran across the cobblestones of the malecon with her long skirts flouncing and the boy's governess close behind. Madame Zuazo's face was as pallid as a ghost beneath her rouged cheeks and she jerked the boy from Cabeza's grasp, shrinking away from Dragón in the same moment. For his part, Alonso burst into tears and was hustled back to the carriage by his governess, wailing all the way.

"Captain, my thanks to you," she said, flustered. "The boy, he..."

"No harm was done, senora," Cabeza said with a low bow; all of his men followed suit, as did Croen. Willow spread the folds of her dingy dress in either hand and curtsied, still clutching at Dragón's leash.

"This dog," she gestured, "he's as big as a tiger! A pony... an elephant!"

"Yes, my lady, but pray stand back, for he is a dog of war, a soldier of Spain. And fierce as a lion to our enemies."

"He would have made a meal of poor Alonso," she said with a frown. "A dessert."

"Ah, no, he's quite gentle with children," Cabeza lied. Behind him, his men suppressed a smile.

"And your blackie? Such a pretty girl." Madame Zuazo turned her attention to Willow, still speaking to Captain Cabeza. "Is she an octoroon?"

Blackie? Octoroon? Willow stood wide-eyed before the richly dressed woman who spoke of her as if she was of no more consequence than the passing slaves.

"Nay, lady, she is a blackamoor out of Morocco," Cabeza said smoothly. "Her father was an Arab of sorts, I believe a camel merchant, and her mother a negress of far-off Timbuktu."

"She's a princess of the great Sahara desert," Croen piped up, earning a black look from the captain.

"Really? How droll." Madame Zuazo eyed Willow up and down. "I could use such a pretty girl in my household. A princess at that! Would you be willing to part with her? There would be gold in it for you."

Willow looked from the lady to the captain and back again as Dragón mirrored her movements. At this, Captain Cabeza couldn't help but smile.

"Apologies, lady, but I must say no. For the princess is master of this dog, and he will have no other. She is a soldier of Spain. We will have need of her where we're going, and of him."

Landfall

"We might as well be searching for Prester John," Croen grumbled as he and Willow stood at the railing of the *Tiger*, gazing at the fleeting shores of Cuba.

"Prester John? I have not heard of him," Willow said, gazing at the palms on the fleeting shore. Dragón lay dozing by her side on the deck.

"Ah, nay. No one knows him. He's a will-o-the-wisp. He's a Christian king said to be living in Asia or among the Ethiopes. The kings of Europe went searching for him long ago in hopes that he'd help them fight the Mohammedans with his vast army. Pack of eejits, they were."

"And, do these eejits think this king lies before us?"

Croen squinted into the blank sea to the north where they'd been told that Florida lay and spat. "Truly, we may see his kingdom yet if Asia lies ahead, though I have no faith in it."

"Asia? Hah! Foolish man. My father told me that Asia lies beyond Mecca, and we've gone far in the wrong direction."

"Foolish woman," Croen replied with a thin smile. "Ye don't know, do ye? The world is round, and we've come to Asia from the backside of it. La Florida is said to be a large island and beyond it lie Nippon and Cathay. Perhaps it's only a short way there! If so, ye may soon be wearing silk robes, satin slippers and a crown of jewels on yer curly head."

"I should like that quite well," she replied, thinking of what her father would say to see her adorned as a real princess. Still, she put more faith in her father's knowledge than that of Croen. After all, Father had wandered over half the world on a camel, whereas Croen was an ignorant seaman from Eire.

It had been seven perilous months since they had landed in Hispaniola and by now the expedition of Pánfilo de Narváez had been battered and diminished before it had hardly begun.

The expedition had spent forty-five days in Santo Domingo, where more than one hundred and forty men had deserted, either scared off by tales of monsters and the terrifying Indians of Florida, or seduced by the promise of easy riches for those who remained on Hispaniola.

Then, two ships and more than sixty men had been lost in a hurricane at the port of Trinidad in Cuba. The hurricane had been presaged by a cold wind and heavy rain, and rather than seeking shelter ashore, most of the men had chosen to ride out the storm. But the port was a poor landfall and many ships had been lost there through the years. The city-dwellers warned them to flee, but they paid no heed. The storm shattered the town, blowing the roofs off of houses, tumbling down walls and snapping trees like kindling. The two caravels and all hands were blown to splinters. The only sign of them was a rowboat found lodged in a tree when the storm lifted, along with the bodies of two seamen blown far ashore and smashed beyond recognition.

Fortunately, Narváez had taken the remaining ships, including the *Tiger*, to a safer harbor. But there had been more storms along the southern coast of Cuba and at times Willow felt as if the ship was a wine cork bobbing in a rolling barrel of salt water. When she wasn't heaving her guts or clutching at a railing in blind terror she was on deck in the wall of rain, seeking to calm the horses, which threatened to crush her as they reared and stamped in fright.

At times Willow felt that Allah himself was against them. They had gathered more men and a brigantine at their last port in Cuba, bringing their company to 480 conquistadors and 80 horses. The burdened ships had become a floating hell, with the horses and men crowding every inch of their decks, accompanied by a swarm of biting flies and the stench of urine and excrement. Sometimes the smell was so thick that Willow felt she could hardly breathe.

Alas, the horses did not fare well on the crossing to Florida. Thirty-two of them died in the passage, which took seven long weeks amid the winter gales of early 1528. Some suffered broken legs despite the slings that held them; others died of sheer misery. Only Montoya, the captain's steed, seemed to fare well, for he was safe in his sling and given special attention by Willow. Often, she marveled at his milky blue eyes, sometimes braiding his mane and singing to him. The horse was gaunt from weeks at sea, yet still well-muscled; Cabeza had exercised him daily on their stops in Cuba and Hispaniola.

"Now thou art the king of horses," Willow murmured as she brushed him. "As handsome as the king of Spain, perhaps even Prester John."

The passage had taken its toll on Willow, too, yet she no longer had any fear of the men aboard; some might leer at a distance, but none dared to come close with Dragón by her side.

Despite the misery of the close-quartered ship, she felt optimistic. Captain Cabeza now esteemed her as the handler of Dragón, since several of the other dog men had tried to take charge of him without any luck. Dragón would answer only to Willow. Soon they would be in Florida and perhaps emissaries from China would be there to greet them on the beach.

Once, in a rare moment, Captain Cabeza had confided that they were sure to find treasure in the New World, a land which had already been claimed by Spain.

"Sir, if I may ask, how do you know you will find gold there?" Willow asked while brushing Montoya's coat. "How can you be certain?"

"The story is well-known by learned men, scholars of great education and piety," the captain replied. "The way to riches was inscribed in a number of sacred books, hand-written by monks centuries ago. These texts are closely guarded in monasteries spread throughout Portugal and Spain, yet I have seen one with my own eyes and have no doubt of its truth."

"And do these books offer a map?"

"Sadly, no."

"Would'st thou tell me the story, sir?" she said as her brush swept over Montoya's back.

The captain shrugged. "It is no secret, and there is no harm in your knowing. It is known that eight hundred years ago there were seven bishops in Portugal who commanded a vast treasure. But then the Moors crossed over from Africa, sweeping all in their path. The bishops gathered their treasure and set out west with their followers across the Great Ocean Sea to an island called Antilia. They established a kingdom dedicated to the Holy Catholic Church and Antilia became known as the Isle of the Seven Cities of Cibola."

"Sir, how great was their treasure?"

"It is said that the streets of their cities are paved with gold."

"Ah, then sailors must have returned to report on it, else no one would have known the fate of the bishops."

"Certainly."

"And are we bound for Antilia?"

Cabeza hesitated. "This we can only hope. Perhaps Florida is Antilia. Perhaps it lies just beyond."

"Or perhaps Asia?"

"Perhaps. But that is why we are here, you see. To find the bishops, and hopefully share their gold. Their cobblestones alone will be enough to fill our ships."

The captain caught the grimace on Willow's face and added, "They will see us as ambassadors, sharing news of their cities with their cousins in Spain. Perhaps they will even sail home with us."

Willow nodded thoughtfully. "Yes, sir, that would make them very generous indeed."

"That is our hope."

"But I wonder, does anyone know how the bishops came by their gold before they set sail?"

This seemed to catch the captain by surprise. "Why... I suppose it was gathered from the fall of Rome, or perhaps the sack of Constantinople."

"Ah."

Abruptly, Captain Cabeza reminded himself that he was jawing with a slave, far beneath his station, and that some of his men were looking on. He patted Montoya on the rump. "Carry on," he said, turning his heel toward the bow.

Cibola, Antilia, Asia, and even talk of a miraculous spring that could give one the gift of eternal life. The wonder of it all made Willow dizzy. How lucky she was to live in such a time of miracles! Allah had elevated her to the station of a warrior and surely there would be riches waiting for her in the New World. She had shushed Croen when he spoke again of escaping, for why escape when they were of value to such a large expedition? Cortez had conquered the empire of the Aztecs with a force not much larger than their own. Like the savage men around her, Willow thought there was little to fear and much to be gained.

Yet Florida hardly seemed a land of riches when at last they sighted its low coastline of mangrove swamps, dunes and underbrush as thick as any jungle. If anything, it was a gray and dreary shore and Willow strained to catch sight of any towers which might mark a city, perhaps even one of Cibola. But for days the features of the shoreline remained flat and uninviting, until at last they came to a wide bay, at the end of which was a small village of Indians.

That night there was much talk on the *Tiger* as the ship lay anchored offshore. Narváez had sent a man to an island in the bay, where he had endeavored to speak with the natives. The meeting had gone well, with each party communicating as best they could with sign language. The Indians had granted the emissary a gift of fish and venison before departing. It was a good sign and the news rippled through the fleet.

Gone now was the Moorish woman's prophecy of doom, for the next morning, hundreds of men were piled into dinghies and paddled to shore with flags fluttering from the bow of each boat. Willow was among them with Dragón, serving as part of the personal guard of Captain Cabeza.

Their boat reared and crashed through the surf until its prow bit the shore.

Then, after seven weeks at sea, Willow gasped to feel solid earth beneath her feet, her toes wriggling in the cool sand. It was Good Friday, a religious holiday of the Christians. "That's a good omen," Croen told her, "even though it's the day our savior Jesus was tortured to death on the cross."

"An omen indeed," she replied, casting her eyes up and down the shore.

Willow followed a stream of men up to the village with Dragón at her side. The houses were small and roughly made of palm leaves and thatch, though one lodge in the center of town was large enough to accommodate several hundred villagers. Yet the village was eerily empty, without a soul to welcome them.

Dejected, Willow walked back down the sand path to the sea, wondering if the tales of Asia and Cibola were nothing more than stories told to children. And where had the people gone? Perhaps even now they were gathering their forces.

Ahead she saw a brigantine gliding toward the shore; it was a small ship with a mainmast and a lateen mizzen that had joined them in Cuba. With its shallow draft, it was coasting right up onto the beach.

But before she could look closer, she stumbled on a fishing net lying half buried in the sand, entangling her foot. Drawing the net free, she found a small trinket of a dull yellow metal. Entranced, she studied it closely, failing to notice Dragón growling at her side. She shook it and it gave a metallic tinkle. It looked to be some kind of rattle or bell. Her eyes widened as she realized what she held. It was gold, pure gold, a golden rattle, she was sure of it.

"Give me that," a voice commanded as Dragón began barking at the intruder. At the same moment, the hairs stood up on the back of Willow's neck in recognition.

Looking up, she was startled to see the pirate, Bartolomeu Sincid, gazing down at her against the gray sky of the morning, backed by half a dozen men. And hobbling over the side of the brigantine with half of his leg stuffed into a wooden bucket at the end of a long peg was the cow-faced Frenchman, Philip Garon.

Wabeno's Dream

Boweting was not a town in the same sense as those of the Wendats or the Haudenosaunee, which were made up of longhouses surrounded by palisades. Rather, it was a ramble of small villages and huts scattered for miles down the river that linked the big lakes, Kitchi Gami and Tima Gami. Only the great lodge of the shamans was protected with a palisade of sharpened pines, to which people might gather for safety in times of trouble.

Otherwise, it was only the constant stream of fish from one lake to the other that brought hundreds of the Ojibwe and Odawa to live for part of the year along the river.

That, and they came for the great festivals held during the running of the whitefish each year, when thousands of the Anishinaabek gathered to catch and dry the fish in preparation for the coming winter. Often, those from other tribes such as the Wendats, the Nippissings and the Cree made the journey to Boweting to fish, trade and join in the celebration. Then the air would reverberate with the pounding of hundreds of drums and the stamp of dancing feet. There would be foot races staking hefty wagers and games of baggatiway with hundreds of men on each side, flailing their rackets in a wild melee. Concerts, plays, jugglers, magicians, comedians, poets and more rounded out the fun, which was especially dear because all knew that soon, the cruel wind of Biboon would be blowing from the north, bringing winter in its teeth.

For once, however, Wolf was not among the storytellers at the festival. Since his days as an in-between man he had been accustomed to speaking by firelight to crowds in the hundreds. But Wabeno-inini, Man of the Dawn Sky, had asked him to be mindful of his new role as a trader and his secret life as a *giimaabi*, the eyes and ears of the twelve shamans of the Great Lodge.

"We know this will pain you, but we ask you not to speak," Wabeno had told him.

"What! How can I not speak when so many wish to hear me?" Wolf cried, outraged at Wabeno's request.

"You must put your old life to rest, so that you will survive your new life," Wabeno said dryly. "Remember that now you must appear as a man of no importance."

"But what must I say when I am called upon?"

"Say that you have forgotten for now. Say that your throat is sore. Say what you will, but remain silent and let your legend fade for a time."

Wolf understood him well enough, for a well-loved man is soon recognized, and that would prove unhealthy for a spy. There were times among the Tionontati when he feared that some wanderer who had seen him telling tales far to the north might point him out as something more than a trader.

But words were the only thing he had to offer when it came to making his way through the world, and without them he truly was "a man of no importance." And this was a stinging blow to his pride.

"You must bear it," Wabeno said, guessing his thoughts.

Thus, reluctantly, he had agreed to remain silent during the biggest festival of the year. Reluctant, because in the past, many young women had been entranced by the stories he had shared with hundreds. Wolf had been much in demand. Now, he was asked many times by friends and admirers why he had chosen not to speak. There were frequent requests for his best stories, told with an actor's skill that could summon shivers of horror or gales of laughter, depending.

"Tomorrow I will speak, brother. Tomorrow, sister," he replied, though tomorrow never came.

But Wolf seldom lacked for things to do, for he could stand for half a day in his canoe amid the rapids, catching the fat whitefish that streamed into his net or within a thrust of his spear. He had an inexplicable ability to call to the fish; indeed, some said he knew the thoughts of animals themselves, and his canoe never returned empty. The shamans of the Good Hearts ate well, thanks to Wolf, and often there was much to share with the villagers living down the hill from their lodge.

Then too, he enjoyed drumming at the festival, carousing with friends and flirting with the many nubile young women gathered there from distant clans. It was the season of love-making, and Wolf was ever hopeful, especially since it turned out that Singing Tree had been wed while he was away and had no sister. At night, he attended the story-telling, sitting far back from the fire in the shadows so that no one would recognize him and call out his name.

Yet even with the good fishing and the merriment of the gathered tribes, Wolf soon grew restless.

"The fire of the festival has died for me. I am not good at being idle," he complained to Wabeno one afternoon after dropping off several sleek whitefish.

"Nor are your uncles," Wabeno replied, and by this Wolf suspected that the shamans of the Great Lodge were anxious, fretting over the massive raid which had departed from Manitowaaling more than a full moon ago. No one had heard a single word as to the fate of the warriors, not even from those shamans who claimed to speak with the birds, which might bring news from the south.

Yet a day later a runner came dashing along the banks of the river from where his exhausted companions had left their canoe.

"We have won!" he cried all along the way. "We have dealt the enemy a great blow! Our people are free!"

Reaching the palisade of the shamans, the runner was lifted onto the backs of a tremendous crowd as he called out his good news. The old men of the Good Hearts flocked down the hill from their homes and joined the dance of celebration with hundreds, singing and crying for joy along the riverbank.

That night, Wolf joined Wabeno for a meal of elk loins and roasted maize at the old man's lodge near the top of the hill. Then they shared a pipe, savoring the fine tobacco which Wolf had been gifted by the Tionontati. From the perch of Wabeno's lodge they could see hundreds of fires lit far down the river, along with the sound of singing and drumming which had continued unabated since the runner's arrival.

"It is thanks to you that our warriors succeeded," Wabeno said, passing the pipe. "As you learned, the Senecas who enslaved our people mounted a raid on the Illini, far to the west. They were far off on the war trail when our warriors swept down on their towns and freed many of our people who were enslaved. To this we owe you great honor."

"Father, it was nothing," Wolf replied, though his cheeks burned with the praise. The Senecas, he knew, were one of the six tribes that made up the league of the Haudenosaunee. They lorded it over the Illini and other tribes to the west, insisting that they were the Older Brothers of the lesser tribes, who were required to give tribute or risk slavery or death.

For a change, Wabeno seemed almost jolly.

"Ah, Wolf, it is a great deed that you have done," he said, "and if we could, we would parade you through the festival and sing loudly of your courage, for we could not have defeated our enemies without your knowledge. Their towns are well fortified and they have warriors beyond number. They would have beaten us even if we had surprised them.

"No," he continued, "we had to strike when their warriors departed, and only you could tell us when to attack."

"Perhaps we should send a gift to the head man of the Tionontati," Wolf said with a grim smile. "It is thanks to his hatred of the Haudenosaunee that he sang like a robin."

Wabeno nodded. "Yes, perhaps, though I think it likely we will need to seek him out again."

"Again?"

"*Ehn*, the Haudenosaunee will seek revenge, for we have kicked up a nest of snakes. Our warriors burned three of their towns and captured many of their women and children, mocking the old ones left behind. Even now, at a great distance, I can hear their chieftains crying for vengeance. Such is the way of all men in all lands - to be struck and then to strike back."

"Will they come soon?"

"No. We have heard that things did not go well in their raid on the Illini and it will take many moons to mend their wounds and rebuild their towns. Our friends among the Wendat will keep a watchful eye for them, and our own people will be watching, too."

Wolf's heart fell at this news, for he imagined that the shamans might dispatch him back to the Tionontati or to some lonely post far down the southern lake, watching for the Haudenosaunee in their clumsy dugouts. It could be a year before their enemies responded.

Guessing his thoughts, Wabeno patted his knee and said, "Have no worry, for we have need of you elsewhere."

Then, as he had done once before, Wabeno asked a strange question.

"Tell me, what did you think of the women of the Tionontati?"

"The women?"

"Yes."

"Grandfather, you speak in riddles."

"Are they good women?"

Had the old man gone mad? Wolf had never known Wabeno to prattle on about women as did some men, nor had he ever succumbed to lechery. No one knew Wabeno's age, but he was said to have lived two or even three lifetimes. He was no young buck, and he had never been known to stray from his old wife. What did he care of women?

"They are like women anywhere," Wolf said with a shrug.

"Strong women. Skilled."

"Yes."

"Beauties among them."

"Some, yes."

"But none caught you."

Wolf grimaced, thinking of Sideways Woman. "Almost, but she was not for me."

Wabeno gave him a curious look and grunted, saying no more on the matter.

As for himself, Wolf had never spoken of his longing for a woman to any man - least of all his uncles among the shamans - for such would lack dignity. He doubted that even Wabeno could tell that he was burning inside. Perhaps the old man thought that he was attracted only to men.

Even so, he resented Wabeno's prying words, for what could it matter to him?

"Will I be traveling again, grandfather?" he asked, anxious to speak of other things. "An arrow is not meant to be idle."

"Oh yes, traveling far," Wabeno replied, with his eyes glinting. "Perhaps further south than any of the Ojibwe have ever traveled. Soon, your uncles will come begging this favor of you. I will come begging."

Wolf could only guess where that might be, for in the time he'd spent with the Tionontati, they had seldom spoken of the lands to the south, other than the hunting grounds south of a river called the O-y-o, which were shared by a number of tribes.

"Is it beyond the O-y-o?" he guessed.

"Perhaps," Wabeno shrugged. "But first to the west."

"Now you have mystified me, but I will go where my uncles ask," Wolf said, taking a deep draw on the pipe and then coughing violently.

"You draw too deep!" Wabeno said, laughing, "and you speak too soon. A *giimaabi* must be careful not to agree too quickly. You do not know what we will ask of you."

"Tell me then," Wolf choked out the words, feeling his stomach go green with the heavy draught.

"Ah, later, later," Wabeno said lazily. "Let us smoke for now and think peaceful thoughts, for who knows what will come tomorrow?"

Tomorrow brought a chill rain and Wolf spent the day standing in his canoe amid the rapids, stabbing at fish with his barbed spear. He walked along the riverbank in the rain that evening, entering a lodge here and there to greet and be greeted. The fires outside the lodges had been doused by the storm and most everyone was indoors, huddling against the chill. Wolf reflected that he had no lodge to call his own, for without a woman, what did a man need of a home? It made him feel glum and he slept that night among strangers, whose squalling child kept him awake almost until dawn.

At daybreak he wandered up to the Great Lodge of the shamans, hoping that they would speak to him of his new mission. But they were busy preparing for a ceremony involving a number of magical rites to be witnessed by hundreds. They shooed him away, forgetting to invite him to a meal.

Now I have become a hungry dog without a home, he thought, slinking away. He glanced about, wondering where he would sleep that night and wishing he was gone.

At last the festival began to dwindle as the fish finished drying on the racks by the river and the Anishinaabek began departing to their villages along the coast. It was then that Wolf was called once again to the sweat lodge for a council. Once again he stripped off his clothing and entered the lodge, which was filled with fragrant steam. But this time a small opening in the roof allowed the morning sun to filter into the lodge, and he could see all twelve of the elders gathered in a circle around the outer edges, with most looking grave, yet agreeable.

"Brothers, we have Wolf to thank for our victory over our enemies, and for this gift of tobacco," Wabeno began. A chorus of approval arose from his uncles with nodding heads and smiles all around. Then came a lengthy time of bluster and praise in which Wolf was hailed as the Ojibwe's son of the morning and many other fine things until his head began to swim.

Abruptly, Wabeno called for the chatter to cease and the shamans fell as silent as owls, awaiting the true reason for the gathering.

"Animi-ma'lingan, we bring you here to beg a new mission," Wabeno began, addressing him by his formal name.

Wolf said nothing, remembering Wabeno's caution not to be too quick to agree, nor to speak too soon. He composed a pleasant expression, as if he were the most patient man in all of the Great Turtle Island, even though he was bursting to shout out that he would gladly don his moccasins and leave in an instant.

"I have told you it is far south, yet not how far," Wabeno said. "I fear it is a long way..."

"Where, grandfather? And why?"

"Ah, perhaps it is only an old man's confusion, but I have had a dream," Wabeno said with a drawn face. "It was of a strange animal, like none we have ever seen before, running over a land with no trees that stretched far beyond sight. At first I paid it no heed, but then I had the dream again. Three times I dreamed of this animal, yet three times I set it aside, not knowing its meaning.

"Then this spring as winter broke, a group of our kinsmen wandered beyond the Gaag Mountains far to the west to the place where rice grows on the water. One day they found the body of a man who had been beaten to death, with a scuffle of many feet surrounding his body. They took great care for their safety after that, turning east toward home and creeping as silently as they could through the forest, for none knew what enemy might be lurking there. But days later they came upon a youth who was starving and near death, and taking pity, they made a litter and carried him home to us, nursing him as they went."

"A lucky man."

"Yes, but he could tell them nothing, for he was of the Dakota and none of our men could speak his language. At best he signed that his party had been attacked while hunting and he was lost. Our hunters brought him to me, and though I do not speak much of his tongue, I know a few words. Over many nights by the fire I have learned that his name is Anokasan-Duta. To us, his name is Red Eagle."

Wolf nodded. It was a slight tale, but something he could share around a lodge fire once he had learned more of the captured hunter.

But then before the eyes of the gathered shamans he learned that he was to become part of the lost hunter's story.

"Anokasan-Duta has been adopted by one of those who found him, but we have begged for his return. We wish for you to take him home."

"To the Dakota?" Wolf almost choked. "Grandfather, uncles, you know me as a story-teller, and I tell you true, I have heard many stories of the Dakota, and they will surely kill me."

Many times, Wolf had gathered tales of the Dakota Sioux, who lived in the woodlands to the west and were sworn enemies of the Ojibwe. They were not as fierce as the Haudenosaunee, but there had been skirmishes with them for many lifetimes and no one wished to fall into their hands. Long ago, the Ojibwe had driven the woodland Dakota from the shores of Kitchi Gami and they had never forgiven the newcomers.

Wabeno raised a hand. "There are two things to know," he said. "There is a peace between our peoples now and Red Eagle is the son of a powerful headman who lives beyond the Misi Sipi. He will be your protector as you travel to the west, and all will welcome his return."

"But won't they seek vengeance for the dead man? They will think it was our people who killed him."

Wabeno shrugged. "Perhaps."

He took a pull on the pipe, which had been passed around the circle as he spoke. It was the same pipe with the handsomely-carved raven head that they had smoked more than a year ago when Wolf had been informed of his new life as a spy.

"Do you see this pipe, Wolf?" Wabeno went on. "Do you see its fine carving of red stone? Then you must know it comes from the quarry of the Pipestone People, far to the west, beyond the Misi Sipi."

"*Ehn*, I know it, grandfather. Its place is sacred."

"Yes, it is a quarry where all are welcome to come and dig for the red stone. Every tribe, every people."

"I know the story well. It is a place where all are welcome, or so it is said."

"Then you understand. All who seek the pipestone are granted protection to pass through the lands of the Dakota. Once again, you will travel in the guise of a trader, offering gifts of copper to all you meet. You will say that you are on a peaceful mission to dig for the pipestone and to show your goodwill, you are returning Anokasan-Duta to his people."

"It is a good path grandfather, as long as the Dakota's eyes are not too sharp."

"They will not see through you. The boy will be your proof."

"If you say it, grandfather."

"Do you accept?"

There came a long pause as Wolf recalled the old man's admonition never to agree too hastily. He dug at the space between his toes with a twig as if mulling the matter over, knowing there was no other choice. He could feel the eyes of the shamans upon him, as a rabbit feels the gaze of an owl.

"I will do as you wish," he replied at last, though his thoughts churned, for despite Wabeno's reasoning, it sounded like a fool's quest.

He suspected that many among the Dakota would not respect the fragile peace with the Ojibwe. Many would not even know of it, and the world was full of rash young warriors, eager for glory, who would yearn for his scalp. And how many would have heard of Red Eagle, or care about his reunion with his people?

Wabeno stared at him, guessing his thoughts.

"I would not send you to your death," the old man said. "The Dakota are a witless people, with their thoughts as dull as mud. You will dazzle them with your stories and your guise as a trader."

Stories? Wolf suppressed a smile, for the lesson of many stories was that one should never assume that an enemy was witless or dull.

But he did not say as much to Wabeno. Instead he said, "It is good to know that our enemies are so easily fooled. But what of the dream animal of which you spoke?"

"Ah! Here is vision and magic! Red Eagle told me of the same animal," Wabeno said, his face lighting up. "It is a living thing and not a spirit. He spoke of a people living far down the Misi Sipi who had captured a creature they called the sunktanka. It means great dog in their language, sacred dog, though I do not think it is a dog. They described the animal as I had found it in my dreams."

"Tell him!" A voice carried from across the half-dark lodge. "Tell him what you saw!"

"He spoke of a creature that is as big as a she-elk, with the same face," Wabeno said. "It has a long tail, flowing almost to the ground in many strands, like the hair of a woman, and also a fringe of hair running down its neck like that of a warrior. It can run faster than a whitetail and it can speak! Yes, speak, though no one understands its language. Some say it can fly, as fast as any bird."

"Does it have wings?"

"Who can say? But I saw none in my dreams."

"Who are these people?"

Wabeno held out his palms in the sign of unknowing. "To the boy it is only a legend told by his grandfather. He knows only that the people of the sunktanka live near the end of the great river, the Misi Sipi."

Visions of the beast and the river to the end of the world swirled in Wolf's thoughts. "Truly, grandfather, I would like to see this creature. How far off is its home?"

Wabeno shrugged. "Who can say? It is far."

"Someday, perhaps it will come to us."

Wabeno nodded. "Yes."

The pipe went around the circle again as the shamans shared their thoughts on the meaning of Wabeno's dreams and the sunktanka. Wolf sat mystified among them, barely hearing their voices. What did Wabeno-inini need of him when Red Eagle might easily be turned loose at the borders of the Dakota's territory? And why journey to the far-off pipestone quarry? And the mysterious animal... what of it?

As Wabeno-inini was fond of repeating, who can say?

"We have many questions," Wabeno said, interrupting his thoughts. "We do not have the answers, but all will be revealed on your journey."

"I understand, grandfather," Wolf said gravely. "I will deliver Red Eagle to his father's lodge and bring you the pipestone."

At this, Wabeno gave a dry chuckle.

"*Gaawiin,* Wolf, no. Your journey to the land of the pipestone is merely a ruse to help send you down the Misi Sipi."

"The Misi Sipi?"

"It is the animal we want," Wabeno said quietly. "We want you to bring us the sunktanka if you can, or at least its scalp. My dreams demand it. The spirits demand it."

Wolf gaped, almost laughing. Old man Wabeno had gone crazy!

"But grandfather, even if I can find the sunktanka after many moons of traveling down rivers I have never seen, how will I catch an animal that is fleeter than a deer? I can walk, yet I cannot run! I cannot fly!"

"This, I do not know," Wabeno said mildly. "Who can say?"

"And grandfather, how will I know this animal when there may be other creatures which are just as strange far down the river?"

The pipe had gone around the circle once again and Wabeno accepted it with a thin smile, holding it aloft before his glittering eyes, then taking a long pull and exhaling toward the weak light filtering from the smoke hole in the roof.

"Oh you will know it well enough, for in my dream I saw its eyes, and they were as blue as robin eggs."

What a King Desires

La Florida at last. Willow felt like weeping for joy, for although the weather was gray, wet and dreary, the terror of the great, heaving ocean was finally behind her. She curled her toes, enjoying the scrub of wet sand, filling her lungs with air that no longer stank of foul men, excrement and rot.

The golden rattle she had found caused a sensation among the men and was quickly brought to the attention of Pánfilo de Narváez. The one-eyed commander had even spoken with Willow, dismissing her as soon as she showed him where the rattle had been found. None knew its meaning, nor why it should be attached to a common fishing net half buried in the sand, but all agreed that it was a sign of great riches, which must surely lie inland. Outside the circle of Narváez's men, Willow heard mutterings of Asia, Cibola, and treasures worthy of Cortez lying inland.

The men aboard the five ships were as eager to reach land as Willow, and soon the beach was milling with more than five-hundred men, horses and a smattering of women. Only skeleton crews of seamen had been left aboard the ships, which sat as serene as gulls on the placid waters of the bay.

Willow joined a handful of youths in tending to the horses. Only forty-two had survived the crossing from Cuba, and these were pushed over-board to swim to shore. Reaching land, they galloped up the beach as if starving to feed on the grass at the top of the bluffs. By now, Dragón was completely in Willow's control and had even lost his air of menace around strangers. He scampered up and down the beach, running and nipping at the other dogs of war, splashing in and out of the water. As the day went on, the sun began to make its appearance, brightening the mood of all ashore.

Narváez had chosen the abandoned village to make his camp, but it was a habit of the Indians to flee to the forest whenever raiders were nearby, and the heavily armed conquistadors gave every appearance of trouble. That afternoon, two villagers emerged from the forest and made angry demands for the invaders to leave.

Willow was shocked by their appearance; they were tattooed in undulating black lines from head to toe, wearing only breechclouts of rough cotton. Both had shaved heads, save for a plug of long, carefully braided hair at the apex of their skulls. They wore elaborate shell necklaces, which Willow imagined were signs of their embassy, with thick plugs of bone piercing their ear lobes. And in a world that was already filled with hard-muscled men, they were so wiry that every tendon and strand of their muscles stood out in sharp relief. Such men would not be easily conquered, she thought.

While in Cuba, Narváez had purchased an Arawak slave to serve as an interpreter, and there was also a Taino seaman from Hispaniola aboard one of the ships. Yet neither could understand the language of the Indians who had appeared from the forest. Even so, their message was clear enough, expressed by signs and gestures. Leave.

Of course, Narváez did nothing of the sort and the messengers were lucky to escape with their lives as his men began pilfering the meager supplies left in the village. It was April - a long time since the harvest of the prior fall - and the people of the abandoned village had almost exhausted their winter store of maize, which was discovered in a pit filled with clay pots.

"The Indios will have nothing to eat when they return," Croen muttered as they eyed the strange, yellow grain. It was furred with mold and fungus from months of storage. "Though I imagine they'll feel lucky to save their skins, and I warrant we'll soon be gone."

"They will attack us," Willow said with certainty. "That is what my father's people would do."

"Aye, but look around ye. These people have never seen a horse before, nor armor, nor men with weapons that can shear off an arm with a single blow. They'll learn to fear us soon enough."

"Or perhaps we'll learn to fear them," Willow said, thinking of the hag's prophecy.

Captain Sincid had all but ignored her after she'd surrendered the golden rattle on the beach. In fact, he had leapt back in alarm, gibbering like a monkey when Dragón lunged at him. He was the same skeletal figure with burning black eyes that Willow remembered, though now he wore a swath of purple satin wrapped around his mop of crinkled hair.

"Little sparrow, you have come back to me," he said to her in a low voice, though his eyes were fixed on the golden trinket in the palm of his hand.

Willow gave a husky laugh. "I'm hardly your sparrow now, pirate. I am the master of this dog and he will be happy to eat you at my command."

Sincid gave a long pause before speaking, pursing his lips and turning the golden rattle over and over as if trying to guess its secret.

"Yes, just as he ate poor Garon's leg. But never forget that I saved you from the filthy cocks of my men," he said at last. "Were it not for my whip, they would have ravaged you until you were as raw as a penny whore. I excuse you from the disgrace in the market at Sevilla, for that is a matter I will take up with Captain Cabeza, but you still owe me, my dear, and someday you will pay."

At this Sincid gave a knowing smile, though his eyes were as cold as those of a reptile.

Willow said nothing in reply, though she was tempted to release Dragón. It would be so easy - the slaver Sincid and then her tormenter Philip Garon, who braced himself on his wooden peg a few steps back, gazing sullenly at her and the dog that had prompted the removal of his leg. Dragón's fangs had proved deep, and it was the filth of the dog's mouth that had infected Garon's leg on the night he had attacked Willow. He had suffered a hideous operation in Hispaniola with the removal of his leg at the knee joint. Even though Garon had been blind drunk on a bottle of rum at his leg's departure, still he felt the bite of the ragged saw and the burn and stink of the cauterizing iron, filling him with a horror that shook him to his bones. That, and although he was a habitual rapist, Garon suffered the conceit that he was a lady's man, expert at seduction. But that usually meant wrapping two of his huge hands around a pretty neck, squeezing with all his strength until a frightened woman would do anything he asked to keep from being choked to death. But now... now he was something entirely different - a vengeful ruin.

He glared at Willow with his widespread eyes and the expression of a toad and it was plain that Garon blamed her for the bucket strapped to his thigh and the long peg that bit the sand. A wave of blind rage welled up within her; she was on the brink of releasing the dog and hell be paid for it when commander Narváez bulled his way to the beach and seized the golden rattle from Sincid's hand.

Instead, she fingered a lower eyelid, pulling it down to give Garon the evil eye. Then she spat on the sand and cursed him. "Next time, my beast will devour your balls."

Narváez gave her a quizzical look. "Who is this woman?" he demanded.

"She found the treasure, guv'ner," Croen spoke up, for he had been following Willow when she stooped to examine the gold shining in the sand. "She's a princess of Araby, ye know, and likely to find much more treasure. She's got a nose fer it."

"Get this fool out of here," Narváez ordered. And after he had posed his question to Willow, she too was happy to leave, for Narváez, Sincid and Garon seemed a trinity of monsters in human form. Demons, jinns, evil spirits. She intended to stay as far away from them as possible.

Willow saw little of Captain Cabeza over the next few days, save for his daily ride on the beach astride Montoya. She marveled to watch them as the horse thundered far down the beach, almost out of sight before wheeling around and pounding back alongside the bubbling surf. It was the only time she saw Cabeza looking happy, for mostly she spied him coming and going to the command post of Narváez with a grim set to his face, or preparing his men for departure.

"We canna' stay in this wretched village," Croen said as they sat on a log on their third afternoon ashore. "It's gold this lot is after, and there's sure to be plenty of it inland. Whole cities of it. Your trinket proves it!"

"But perhaps it was only from the wreck of a ship sailing from Mexico," Willow said.

"Nay, they'd not sail this far north. It's certain there's the wealth of Peru here, perhaps just a little way inland." Croen pointed to the woods beyond the beach. "The men all have the fever now. They can smell it."

"Gold, I'm sick of their fever for gold. Why do men care for gold when all that matters is what they put in their bellies?"

Croen snickered. "I would answer that with a question. How often did ye taste meat back in Morocco?"

"Only when there were scraps from my master's table," she said, remembering the feast on Abu bin Nisar's name-day before her capture.

"Aye, and that's because only the rich enjoy meat at their tables, while we dine on flat bread and lentils, if we're lucky. But often, their meat has gone bad by the time it reaches their plates, eh? Yet with gold, the rich can dine on finer things. D'ye know why men sail all the way round the world and risk their lives to fetch spices from Asia? It's so rich men can hide the taste of bad meat, which soon goes rotten and foul-smelling. Only that! They crave pepper, and that takes gold. This lot - every man among them - hopes to gain enough treasure to buy a farm with a fine villa in Spain, or even in Hispaniola, and then sit down to a table that doesn't stink of rotten mutton."

"Well, I should think they would be more intent on raising lambs than robbing the Indios of their gold," Willow said with a sniff. "Then they could have fresh meat each day to chew on."

"Aye, but even so, a rich man is never satisfied; he wants to be even richer! He wants to be a governor, and a governor wants to be a prince, and he desires to be king, and that means he must have spices for his table to suit his majesty, paid for in gold."

"Then what does a king desire?"

Croen squinted toward the horizon and spat. "Why, he wants an empire of course, with elephants, armies and conquests, like Hannibal or Alexander."

"Hah! Then I will be pleased to remain with the ships and the women while the men go searching for their empires."

"Truly, I'm happy for ye, but I've a fortune to seek. I nay have need for spices or a vineyard, but I'm an old man now and a small taste of the Indio's lucre would set me up like a prince in Dublin."

"Dublin? What of it?"

"It's a place where whiskey flows in canals and pretty girls wait on men of good fortune," Croen said with a hopeful smile and a light in his eyes, as if he were already there.

"I will come to see you then, great prince, if I am granted a measure of gold," Willow said solemnly.

Croen cocked his head and made a face. "I'm sure you will."

Then came startling news. Narváez and a company of men had journeyed north along the coast, coming across four Indians, who showed them the wreck of a Spanish ship. No one in Narváez's party could understand the Indians, whose language remained a mystery. Yet, Narváez had showed them samples of gold, gesturing as to where it might be found. Making signs with their hands, the natives had told them that a great deal of gold, silver and pearls could be found in a rich province called Apalachee, far to the north. At least, that is what the Spaniards thought they meant.

Returning to the camp by the bay, Narváez decreed that the expedition would be divided into two parties, with most of the men bound for the interior of Florida, while the marineros and a small company of conquistadors would sail north to where a pilot believed there was another bay.

Not everyone was happy with this decision. Captain Cabeza's Uncle de Vaca had argued that the ships' pilots had gotten lost along this coast on a previous trip, and were not even sure that the promised bay existed. That, and what would happen to the men on land if they could not find the ships?

But, perhaps seeking to emulate the great Cortez, who had burned his ships and left his men no choice but to do or die, Narváez insisted that the ships head north along the coast while he searched for Apalachee.

"I'm thankful that we shall remain with the ships," Willow told Serena as they watched the men prepare for departure.

"Ah, but I wish to join them," Serena replied.

"Do you not fear the prophecy told by your mother? I believe it so. None will return from the forest."

"That was only the ramblings of an old gypsy woman trying to frighten foolish people. Those who remain on the ships will have no chance at the gold, if any is to be found. Don't you desire your share of the riches?"

"I value my skin more than riches," Willow said, leaving off that she had never seen a forest before and found the darkness beneath the distant trees frightening.

"Well as for myself, I am sick of these stinking ships."

"Sister, you are not alone in that, but at least we will be safe."

Willow slept well that night, believing that she would remain with the women aboard the *Tiger*. But that morning, Captain Cabeza formed up his company of men in a long line, two abreast, and to her shock and surprise ordered her to join the expedition. More than 300 men and 42 horses were bound for the interior of Florida while Capitão Mendaña sailed north along the coast.

"But lord, should I not stay with the women aboard the ships?" Willow asked, quailing at the thought of being the only woman to march with the men.

"You are the only one that the dog will obey, and we need him," Captain Cabeza replied curtly. "He is a soldier of Spain, and strange as it seems, so art thou. But be thankful, for the dog will carry your possessions."

So it was that Willow wrapped Dragón's neck in his collar of iron spikes, draping his chest and torso in thick leather armor that was spangled with protective metal discs. She placed her tattered blanket in the dog's panniers along with a wooden bowl, a knife and a spoon. Rounding out her possessions were her dagger, her pipes, her sailcloth dress and a pair of sandals which Cabeza had purchased in Cuba. She owned nothing more.

"So you're to join us now," Croen said when he heard the news. "Be happy, for that snake Sincid is remaining with the ships along with Garon, and they'd work their evil if ye stayed behind."

"It seems there is evil both ahead and behind," she replied glumly.

"Not so, have faith! We've an army here as great as the one Cortez took to Mexico, and Narváez plans to follow in his footsteps with the same strategy. We're heading to the heart of this island where its cities must surely lie. Lord, I've been praying on it."

Somehow, Croen had weaseled his way into joining the expedition and had armed himself with the short sword of a soldier who had died of dysentery at sea. He had no metal armor, nor even chain mail, for that was expensive, but the dead man had surrendered his *cuerra* of protective leather, which now covered Croen's torso. It was an improvement on the quilted cotton gambesons that most of the men wore. And while every man in the expedition was outfitted with a cheap kettle helmet fashioned in Cuba, only a very few, such as captains Narváez and Cabeza, could afford the full plate of armor and chain mail. As for Willow, she had no protection at all if an arrow came winging her way.

"Thou art a gladiator now," she said, admiring Croen's trappings, though truthfully, he looked more like a foolish old man than a warrior.

"Aye, but I hope the Indios will treat us kindly when we find them, for I've nay wish to lock swords."

"The Indios we saw did not look friendly, nor did they look rich," Willow said. "If they have cities of gold, why are they as naked as beggars?"

"Ah, ye know, even the richest cities in the world are surrounded by paupers. All we can do is go and see for ourselves, eh?"

"Truly."

Late that morning, the serpent of three-hundred men and their cavalry of horses crawled up from the beach. The war dogs ran barking and yipping back and forth on either side of the column as it headed for the forest down a well-trodden path. Soon there were within its cool shade and the trees grew ever larger as they left the beach behind; their branches were filled with strange birds and draped with long beards of gray vegetation.

Willow's eyes darted back and forth as she cringed beneath the overhanging limbs, expecting to be seized by some monstrous forest creature at any moment. So many trees! Walls of vegetation, twisting vines and thorns clutching at every step. To one born in the desert the jungles of Florida were as frightening as had been the sea. But the long line of men ahead of her gave no inkling of fear, and gradually she grew more confident.

Cabeza's company brought up the rear of the expedition, with the captain looking resplendent astride the warhorse Montoya, a jaunty red plume dancing on his helmet. Willow and Dragón brought up the end of the column and once, when she lagged a few feet behind, a long blue snake darted out of the underbrush, whipcracking across her path before disappearing into the foliage as she leapt back in alarm.

It was surely an omen, she thought, gazing at the wall of trees and brush on either side of the path. Anything might be hidden from sight here, only an arm's-length away. Anything at all.

Apalachee

To the men of Spain the forest beyond the beach seemed a vision of Eden, filled with immense trees dripping with gray-green moss, along with cascades of flowers and flights of songbirds in colors beyond the scope of rainbows. No one had seen trees such as these in Europe for hundreds of years, and some were so large that it took six men with arms outstretched to girdle them.

Yet these same trees and the tangled brush and vegetation at their feet offered cover for hidden foes, and as the days went by the men began falling one-by-one to the Indians. Without warning, an arrow would come zipping from the brush, piercing a man through his throat, chest or leg. The conquistadors' faint armor of cotton or leather sometimes deflected the shafts, but even a scratch could bring death in the days to come, for the barbed head of every arrow was poisoned, or smeared with excrement.

Only once during the first two weeks of the march did anyone spy an attacker, appearing as a dark shape flitting for a moment in the brush before disappearing.

Villages came and went, all empty, all barren of supplies. Narváez had intended to live off the land as the great Cortez had done, yet Florida was not the same rich and welcoming country that Mexico had been. The villages were all small, some with less than a dozen huts, and though they were surrounded by crops, these were still seedlings, months away from being harvested.

"Where have all the people gone?" Willow wondered as they huddled around a fire one night. "It's as if they've been taken by the spirits."

"Ah, they're all hiding in the forest, I suppose," Croen replied. "They mark us for warriors and go running. And who's to blame them? The Frenchman Garon might have told us something of them, for he was here only a few years ago with Ponce de Leon, but the captain left him behind. No sense dragging a cripple along, though I imagine he might have told us something of value."

Indeed, Garon might have told them of the horrors inflicted on the natives by Ponce, a litany of torture, rape and enslavement as he probed the coast of Florida. That, and for the past decade, Spanish slavers had prowled the coast, raiding villages and seizing captives for their mines and plantations. Word of the Spaniards' evil ways had raced through every tribe, and now as the Moorish hag had prophesied, the men of Pánfilo de Narváez were walking deeper into their doom.

Yet it wasn't only arrows to be feared, for there seemed to be endless swamps and rivers to cross as the expedition made its way north, along with great tangles of fallen trees, impenetrable brush and fields of cane which stretched for miles. Wading chest-deep through the swamps, men found themselves covered with leeches, bitten by water moccasins and pestered by clouds of mosquitoes the like of which no man from Spain had ever seen. Where the swamps ended, often the men found themselves mired in dunes of deep sand, which made walking difficult, draining them of what little strength they had left.

Willow suffered as much as the men, grasping at Dragón's collar as she struggled waist-deep through swamp water. Once, an arrow had clattered off Dragón's armor, spinning past her, with its barbed head narrowly missing her arm.

Days later, Croen handed her a shield taken from a soldier who had died in the night in the wake of a high fever.

"Ye may need this," he said, "Strap it on yer back like so and it will protect you from the rain as well as arrows."

"It will make a turtle of me," she said with a laugh.

"Aye, a great turtle warrior!"

The shield was of a sturdy leather the color of ox blood and at its center was a gleaming, four-pointed star of polished steel. It was comfortably light, and though Willow doubted that it would be much protection against a swordsman, she reckoned it would shelter her from arrows. Around her, the men joked that she needed only a sword to play the part of an amazon warrior.

That afternoon, she had crept down to a river to wash herself and a ferocious creature had leapt from the water. She darted sideways with the snap of its jaws at her heels, but the monster pursued her, running incredibly fast on its short legs. Only the distraction of Dragón had saved her; the dog had leapt on the creature's back, biting and clawing at its eyes before taking a hammering blow from its tail. Her screams had brought several crossbowmen running and they had filled it with their bolts. It was the first of many times that she would see an alligator, and this one was nearly twelve feet long.

That night, the beast was roasted on a spit, with a leg tossed to Dragón for his heroism. All agreed that the reptile tasted like chicken, and thereafter, a point was made to search the shoreline of every river and swamp for more to fill the bellies of men and dogs alike.

But the occasional deer or alligator did little to stem the hunger of 300 men, and they had scant supplies of moldy hardtack and rotting salt pork from the ships. They raided the granaries of every village they passed, but often the corn was spoiled, or squirreled away by the fleeing natives. Weakened by hunger, more men began to die as the clouds of mosquitoes delivered malaria and yellow fever with their sting.

On and on they pressed, with Narváez and his captains astride their horses, always urging that the riches of Apalachee lay just ahead. At Apalachee all expected to find the lost city of the Catholic bishops at last, and perhaps even a way off this horrid island to the delights of Asia beyond.

Yet, over the next two months of wandering from one deserted village to another, the expedition began to disintegrate as hunger, disease and fading hopes took their toll. Many of the men had open sores from carrying their weapons on their shoulders, and some had worn their boots to tatters. The men began to whisper and grumble that they might never reach the safety of the ships; for who knew where they were bound and where they might land? Even so, there wasn't any hope of desertion, for beyond the safety of the armed column lay sure death at the hands of the Indians.

Narváez did little to help their cause, for sometimes he offered the trade goods of beads, red cloth and iron pots at the villages they passed through, but just as often he commanded his men to seize whatever they could, including the native women and whatever slaves they could press into carrying the expedition's supplies. Native runners ran before his march, spreading the word to beware.

By now, Willow had come to think of Dragón as being almost tame. The dog ran freely among the company of men without any sign of threat, and at times was even playful. But those thoughts were dispelled upon their first battle with the Indians.

They had come to a wide, fast-running river, which took a full day to cross by way of a roughly-fashioned raft. A nobleman had tried swimming the river with his horse, and both had drowned in the attempt.

Reassembling wet and exhausted on the other side of the river, they were startled to find a force of more than 200 warriors melting from the trees at the far side of a muddy field. A single arrow fell among their ranks, as if testing for the range, followed by desultory volleys unleashed from a distance.

Willow had witnessed a camel charge of Berber tribesmen at a festival in Azemmour and also a parade of Mamluk warriors at an exposition in Morocco, but she'd never seen anything like the native warriors gathered on the far side of the field. They were all heavily tattooed and wearing nothing but breechclouts of cotton or leather. Some wore nothing at all, but were painted head to toe in black and red with fearsome designs drawn across their faces. Their scalps were plucked bare except for bristling crests of stiffened hair or a single braid cascading from a topknot. Many had longbows, the arrows of which easily reached the line of conquistadors, while others carried spears, shields and clubs.

Willow's knees went weak at the sight of the churning warriors. "They mean to scare us to death," she said to no one in particular, gasping as her heart began to race.

Adding to their menace, the Indians uttered terrifying cries and screams, shaking their weapons and leaping in place as if they were madmen. They began unleashing flights of arrows in greater numbers, like the rain-pocks of a gathering storm. Here and there an arrow found its mark, piercing a soldier's inadequate armor of quilted cotton and leather.

"Give them a taste of the matchlocks," Captain Cabeza ordered, striding before the flights of arrows without a care in his armor. "And make it hot! A dash of hell fire will make them dance."

But the captain of the musketeers came forward looking crestfallen. "Captain, all of our matches were drenched in the crossing," he said. "Our guns are useless."

"Can you do nothing?"

The answer was no, for the smoldering match fuses served to light a small amount of gunpowder in a matchlock's priming pan, igniting the charge within the bulky guns.

"Apologies, but..."

"What of the arquebus?" Cabeza demanded. It was a heavy matchlock of a higher caliber, mounted on a staff.

"It too is soaked clean through, lord."

"Mother of God! The crossbows then." And so began a duel of arrows as a blizzard of crossbow bolts answered the missiles beyond the field. The sky zipped with a black rain of arrows and bolts and Willow cowered as best she could beneath her shield with Dragón by her side.

Here and there a crossbow bolt found its mark, but the Indians beyond the field soon grasped the need to seek the safety of the trees at their backs. Sheltered by the trees, they could pick the Spaniards off one-by-one with no danger to themselves.

Within minutes, the ground where the conquistadors stood had blossomed in a thicket of arrows, with several men and horses hit, and the storm was growing in intensity. With their backs to the river, there was no place to hide and no chance for a retreat. Even worse, within the space of a few steps the field before them was revealed to be a marsh, calf-deep with mud. The Indians had planned their attack well, for they could melt back into the forest long before the conquistadors might reach them with their swords and pikes.

Yet there was one thing they could not have known.

"Set free the dogs on my command!" Captain Cabeza cried, rallying the handlers to his side. "You, too, mother of lions," he commanded, when Willow gave him a questioning look. Shaking violently and holding her shield before her, she joined the line of dog handlers at the front of the troops as they gave the command as one: "*Attack!*"

Twelve dogs shot forward, racing toward the warriors gathered a long bowshot away. The dogs easily danced on the flattened debris of the marsh, appearing as ripples in the low grass, rushing closer and closer to the warriors, whose arrows were futile amid the vegetation.

Suddenly, more than one hundred yards across the marsh, Willow saw Dragón's black form leaping from the brush as if he had wings, seizing a tall warrior by the throat. Her stomach flipped as she saw the dog twisting and tearing amid a fountain of blood as the horrified warriors at either side recoiled in fright. None had ever seen a dog the like of Dragón, who was covered in his battle armor of metal discs and leather. An arrow banged off one of the iron discs fastened to his leather *cuerra* and he turned with flashing teeth and tore into a knot of men who scattered and ran. One raised a club, lined and serrated with the teeth of a shark, but the blow never fell as Dragón barreled into his chest, driving the warrior to the ground.

Around him, more of the war dogs were leaping, seizing and tearing, their terrible spiked collars doing almost as much damage as their teeth. But that was not all, for as the dogs bit, they also dug with their claws at the abdomens of their prey, ripping at the flesh of all who stood in their way. Dragón seized another warrior, whose neck spouted a beard of blood as he fell thrashing beneath the dog's teeth and claws. Elsewhere, she saw a warrior stab at a dog with a stone-tipped spear, but the shaft glanced harmlessly off the dog's sheath of boiled leather and metal plates.

Hot on the heels of the dogs a horn blared and with a full-throated roar the conquistadors charged behind the cavalry of nearly forty horsemen, lurching and slogging up to their knees through the swamp of black, grasping mud. Like the Indian warriors, they too, screamed their war cries, brandishing their swords and pikes as they clawed their way slowly across the marsh, yet by the time the panting men reached the place where the warriors had stood jeering and hooting, the Indians had melted into the forest. Only a few remained, firing arrows into the oncoming mass of men, yet they too had disappeared by the time Narváez's men reached the tree line.

Yet off to the side, Willow saw Dragón dashing toward another target with his long fangs bared. It was a woman not much older than herself, wearing only a grass skirt and clutching at the hands of two small children. The dog was closing on them with frightening speed as they emerged from their hiding place behind some low-lying trees and ran for their lives.

"Hold, Dragón! Hold!" Willow screamed until it felt as if her throat would rip with the effort, but it was useless amid the tumult and war cries of the battle. The dog was too far away to hear her, racing toward the woman and her children and their certain death.

Almost, for just as Dragón reached the thicket of trees where the woman and her children had fled, Croen leapt from the brush, waving his arms. Puzzled, Dragón braked at his feet, and this time he heard Willow's command as she stumbled toward him through the tall grass.

"Oh, you horrid beast. Thou art truly a monster," she said, but softly as she came level with Croen and the dog.

"I thought he was going to make a dinner of me!" Croen said. "But I saw the wee ones and could'na let him by."

"What were you doing hiding in the brush?" Willow cried, grimacing as she inspected the gore covering Dragón's jaws.

"Ye dinna' take me for a soldier, did ye? I run off to the side and hid meself as soon as the order was given to charge. I've no mind to become the Indios' pin cushion. The lady and I was hiding together with her children and by signs I made her to understand that I meant no harm."

Willow didn't know what to think, for Captain Cabeza had ordered her to loose the dog on anyone who stood in their way, and by that she knew he meant women, children and the old ones too. One evening, he had sat with her and talked of the battle of Tenochtitlan, and how Cortez had loosed his dogs on the thousands of terrified citizens of that city of causeways and canals. The dogs had been used to instill terror in the Aztecs, and Cabeza had made it clear that he expected as much of Willow and Dragón.

She looked across the field of battle with apprehension, fearing that the captain would be angry if he'd seen Dragón denied of his prey. To her relief, Cabeza was mounted on Montoya on the far side of the marsh, sitting idly among several other horsemen in the wake of the battle.

A week later there came another battle after a chieftain offered to lead the expedition to Apalachee. Instead, he led them into an ambush when they were chest-high in swamp water, weighed down by their armor and unable to use their weapons. They struggled for solid ground amid a wild melee zipping with arrows and bloodcurdling screams. Willow hid beneath her shield with one arm, clinging to Dragón's collar in water that was almost over her head.

Once again, Narváez's men survived, clawing their way free of the swamp's black water and driving the attackers away, but this time with bloody losses, and more died in the days ahead from the poisoned arrows, which also claimed several horses. The battle for Florida was nothing like the conquest of Mexico, where there had been great cities to lay siege, helpful allies, and city-dwelling natives who were easy prey, both at the tip of a sword and at the touch of smallpox. In Florida, there was only a succession of empty villages and jungles filled with death-dealing warriors.

For Willow the nights were filled with terror as she huddled beneath her blanket and shield, nestled against Dragón for safety. A curtain of frightening sound swept over the expedition's camp each night - the screams of panthers intermixed with those of lurking warriors; the deep-belled hoot of owls and the flap of their wings as they swooped close above; the cries of night birds and small animals, killing or being killed; and always the chorus of millions of frogs, chirping until she thought she would go mad.

Weeks later, sick and starving with a trail of dead men buried in their wake, the soldiers of Pánfilo de Narváez stumbled at last into fabled Apalachee, finding only a village of forty grass huts, sagging low to the ground to withstand the winter storms. Almost hidden in a gray drizzle of rain, a line of sullen villagers gazed out from the safety of the woods beyond, and their half-naked appearance made it clear that this was no Cuzco or Tenochtitlan with muraled rooms full of gold and emperors to hold for ransom. With stabbing eyes, the bedraggled men of Spain took in the scene, knowing in an instant that there was nothing in the way of gold, silver or pearls in Apalachee. At best, there were only some mortars for grinding corn.

By now, any man among them would have traded a handful of gold for a handful of golden corn, yet only a few kernels were found in the town's granaries. In a panic, runners were sent to the coast, returning days later with the news: the coast was empty and their five ships were nowhere to be found.

The Bay of Horses

One-by-one, the horses were killed for their stringy meat to feed the starving men stranded on the beach, with a new horse facing the butcher's blade every three days.

It wasn't enough. Many of the men had grown so weak that they'd been unable to bear any burdens, tossing aside helmets, shields, matchlocks, crossbows and armor on the long trail to the sea. There were fewer than 250 of them now, a little over half the number that Narváez had started with from Cuba. Half naked in their ragged clothes, they scanned the horizon for any sign of a sail, but none ever appeared.

Again and again the Indians attacked, coming in waves at a village named Aute, which Narváez had plundered for its maize. The conquistadors had fought their way free, but had been harassed all the way to the vacant sea.

Captain Cabeza had grown increasingly strange during the three months that they had wandered the interior. He seldom spoke to Willow now, and when he did, it was only to utter some curt command, calling her princess and sniggering as if at some private joke. Mostly, he sat astride Montoya, muttering at the stupidity and incompetence of Narváez, who had sent the five ships and their only means of rescue to a vague rendezvous that could be anywhere along a thousand miles of coastline.

Cabeza had threatened to kill any man who threw away his sword or pike, and thus, many who were sick and weak from hunger had dragged their rusting weapons along behind them, rendering them all but useless. Some of these men were flogged, and some were not; there seemed to be no telling who or what would inspire Cabeza's wrath, but as the march to the sea wove on, some took to calling him *La Serpiente* - the serpent.

There was no doubt now that Captain Cabeza had become a hard man, ruthless with his commands and pushing his men past the brink of their endurance.

And by now, all agreed that Florida was no island, and certainly not the Isle of the Seven Cities of Cibola. It was as if they had wandered into the precincts of hell.

"If the bishops of Portugal landed here long ago, then they were most likely roasted by the Indios," Croen said as he and Willow gnawed at the heart of a cactus they'd found growing on the beach.

"Little good your bishops would do us, and if your legends are true, they would be more than eight hundred years old by now."

"Saints can live that long, it's well known," Croen said with certainty. "They could pray for our souls. I fear we'll soon have need of their prayers."

"Yes, though I would rather they offered me dinner," Willow said, spitting out a dry mouthful of cactus; it was woody, inedible.

"Ah, don't lose hope, chi... my lady. We'll soon be free of this place... I have prayed for it, ye know."

Free to go where? Willow wondered. She caught the eye of Captain Cabeza, glaring at her from the beach. Abruptly, he turned on his heel and walked in the other direction, his sword swinging at his heels like a tail.

"We must return to work," she said. "The captain looked our way, and not kindly."

"Aye, he's an angry man now, for he gave up all he owned in Spain and he din't have much to begin with. Now he canna' go back, nor forward unless he finds the gold, and it gnaws at him."

"But does it not also gnaw at Narváez?"

"Nay, not like our captain. Narváez is governor in Cuba and can return unblemished, taking up his post with barely a care. As for the rest, none of these men ever had so much as a doubloon in their pockets to begin with. It's our captain who's in a fret. He dreams of owning a palace, yet now he's lucky to find a grass hut to sleep in. See how he clutches at his horse? It will never be eaten, for it's all he has left."

She and Croen had fared better than most of the men, since as a girl living by the sea in Morocco she had learned how to hunt for mussels, oysters and other mollusks. Croen had the same skill, having lived on the southern coast of Eire. They collected their share of horse meat, finding it rank and almost impossible to chew, but it was the slugs of the sea that gave them strength.

They had been bivouacked in a rough fort on the beach for the past month, raiding Aute to plunder its corn. Weeks earlier, a decision had been made to construct five barges in an attempt to reach the Spanish outpost of Pánuco on the east coast of Mexico. But building boats big enough to carry nearly 250 men seemed an impossible task. They had no nails, sailcloth or rope. Nor did they have a forge or tools. There was no oakum to be had - the fibers of tarred rope used for caulking. Above all, no one had any knowledge of ship-building.

Yet they had a carpenter, and a bellows was constructed from some wooden tubes and a deerskin in order to smelt metal. Soon, stirrups, spurs, breastplates and other bits of iron were being hammered into nails, saws and axes to construct the boats. Men set to work felling pine trees and planing them into boards with their swords. The tails and manes of horses were braided into rigging, and men gave up their shirts to be sewn together for sails.

Four attacks were made on the village of Aute to seize the Indians' corn, and the natives had responded in kind, peppering the raiders with their arrows. Once, they pursued Narváez's men to the beach, killing ten of them who were collecting shellfish within sight of the camp.

Forever after, Willow remembered those days as if in a dream from which she never expected to awaken. All around her the rank, shuffling, starving men worked at the rafts by the sea in the desperate hope that they would bear them away to Mexico, which might well be a thousand leagues to the west for all anyone knew. At times the sea rose to mock them, sending towering waves crashing against the shore. How could their flimsy rafts survive the battering waves? she wondered.

The expedition had been a chronicle of woe. Sunburned backs and fever, bad water and too little to eat amid the endless torment of mosquitoes and biting flies. The burial details and the mournful services... All that and the ever-present danger of the Indians and their arrows, winging from the forest day and night to fall among the men, protected only by the walls of their rough fort. Some talked of surrendering to the Indians in the hope that they might become slaves; the alternative was starvation or death at sea.

It was as if the Great Spirit of this land had set his hand against them, ensnaring them in the blackness of mangrove swamps and jungles filled with mosquitoes and snakes. It was as if their own gods no longer knew or cared of their fate, deepening their despair.

"Jesus has abandoned us," Croen said glumly as they sat on a log after mucking around for hours in search of shellfish.

"Your Jesus loves you, but cannot find us here," Willow replied. "Perhaps he hears your prayers, but does not know where to look."

"Perhaps."

"You must keep to your prayers."

Croen chuckled and spread his palms to the sky. "Prayers? I suppose I'll see Jesus soon enough and will ask him then."

Willow wondered if Croen even prayed at all now, for hope seemed to be withering within him. He had always been as thin as a walking stick, yet he was skeletal now, with a faraway light in his eyes. She had no doubt that Allah was as unheeding as Croen's Jesus, for what deity could find them in this godless land?

Yet at last, the final log was lashed to the rafts and the sails sewn from the mens' cotton shirts were raised on the knotted pine masts. With their place of departure dubbed *Bahia de los Caballos* - the Bay of Horses - for all of the steeds that had been eaten there, the men pushed off, heading west along the beaches lining the coast.

It had taken nearly two months to build the rafts and the rains of fall had drawn on by the time they were finished. On the day of their departure, 242 men crowded aboard the makeshift barges, nearly 50 men to a raft. Every horse and dog had been eaten by then, save two, Captain Cabeza's favorites: the warhorse Montoya and the devil-dog, Dragón. These crowded aboard Cabeza's barge along with Willow and Croen.

"What ships! Not fit to sail across a pond!" Croen exclaimed, shaking his head at the ramshackle fleet. The barges were a little over thirty feet long, and sank so low in the water that the gunwales were only six inches above the waves

"Will our craft handle the sea?" Willow asked nervously as the men raised the patchwork sail. The raft bobbed uneasily in the waves, sometimes cartwheeling in a circle as its helmsman struggled futilely to keep it on course.

"Ah sure," Croen said, "until it doesn't, and then we'll either swim for it or feed the fishes. Can ye swim, m'lady?"

"No."

"Nor can I, but your dog will do. If we capsize ye must seize his collar and hold on for dear life. He'll make it to shore, that one."

"But what of you?"

"Ah, you'll find me holdin' onto the horse's tail."

Captain Cabeza told the men of his barge that his horse was being held in reserve so that it might be eaten when all else failed, while the dog would serve as protection from the Indians, should they land. But Willow felt that this was the last grasp of the captain's feverish mind, knowing that he had lost all, including his dream of a dukedom in the New World or a return to glory in Spain.

"The horse and the dog are all he has left," she confided to Croen. "He'll never let them go. He'll die first."

"Aye, and the men know it, and will be happy to help him along."

And what then? she wondered. Dragón had been by her side since they had left Spain, threatening to tear any man's throat out who came near her. But he was not invincible, and one thrust of a sword would send him to his death. And what then?

For the next three months, Narváez's ramshackle flotilla made its way along the vast gulf in the hope of reaching Panuco, the northernmost out-post of Spain in Mexico. Narváez had told his men that Panuco might be only one hundred leagues - 300 miles - possibly even less. But in fact it was more than 1,000 miles away, far down the coast of Mexico on the chopping, twisting sea.

Keeping close to the shore and begging for food from any Indian vil-lages or fishermen they could find, the men were almost naked as the fall dragged on into the cold, cruel gales of November. Fresh water was an even greater concern, for the containers they had made of horse hide quickly rotted, dispensing undrinkable filth. Over and over again they landed on beaches lined with long-leafed pines in the hope of finding a stream or a spring, yet finding nothing. Driven by thirst, some men drank sea water and were soon convulsed in agony as the salt tormented them from within. Men flung themselves into the sea, seeking release from the torture of drinking the brine, or died writhing at the bottom of the rafts. The thin flesh of these were cut into strips and roasted on the beaches by the starv-ing men, all to the horror of the Indians who found them washed up on their shores.

Once, they passed by the marshy delta of a vast river, its freshwater cur-rent pushing them far out to sea, requiring days to paddle their way back to the coast. Starving and with their clothes in tatters against the growing cold, the men lost the strength to paddle on, letting the wind push their thin sails where it would.

One night, a storm arose, heaving the rafts like chips of wood in a wash bucket and Narváez called out to them in the darkness as the flotilla drift-ed apart. He had taken the best raft and the strongest crew for himself, but the one-eyed, red-bearded butcher and his men disappeared into the night amid towering waves, never to be seen again.

Less than one hundred men struggled on, seeking the safety of Mexico, yet once again a storm arose and they were washed up naked and freezing in a place that came to be known as Matagorda. Here they were greeted by Indians who first took pity and then turned on them in a rage once their feasting on human flesh was discovered, for that was an intolerable taboo among the natives of the coastline. Many of the Spaniards were slaugh-tered, others enslaved, never to be heard from again.

The *Chronicles of New Spain* report that only four men survived the expe-dition of Pánfilo de Narváez after eight years of wandering among the In-dians across the deserts, mountains and plains of northern Mexico. Among them were Captain Cabeza's uncle, Alvar Nunez Cabeza de Vaca, and Es-tebanico, a black slave from Azemmour, the same famine-stricken city of Willow's childhood.

But such was not the fate of Captain Cabeza, nor of Willow and Croen, Dragón and Montoya. For long before their raft reached the marshy delta that had driven the others out to sea, the gusting winds sent them spinning into a long bay that was miles wide. All night the wind blew them north, deeper into the bay, with the morning revealing a low coast of longleaf pines. And there to their surprise they found the wreck of a Spanish caravel piled up on the beach and a man with one hand waving desperately from the shore.

Red Eagle

To Wolf's dismay, the captive named Anokasan-Duta, Red Eagle, was a boy of only twelve summers. Old man Wabeno had said that he was a youth, but this seemed beyond reason. Wolf had little experience of children and the thought of taking the boy on a journey for the length of what might be two moons to the west through dangerous country was madness. The boy was not even a proper in-between man!

For his part, the boy gave Wolf a surly look when Wabeno introduced them at the lodge of the hunter who had found him starving in the forest.

"This is your new elder brother," Wabeno addressed the boy in the Siouian language, a few words of which he had learned in his youth. "He will teach you something of our ways, and you him." He nodded to Wolf, who gazed at the boy as if struck dumb.

The boy nodded gravely at Wolf. "He has a bad leg and looks like a fool," he replied.

Wabeno nodded and smiled. "*Ehn*, you have divined it. He is indeed a fool. He is a simple trader, hoping to exchange gifts with your people. Perhaps you can help him."

At this Anokasan-Duta brightened a bit, for as Wabeno suspected, the boy would be happy to feel he was of some use among his captors. And when the boy was returned to his father, he would vouch that Wolf was a simpleton, for an elder of the Ojibwe shamans had said as much.

The hunter who had rescued Red Eagle had adopted the boy into his family, as was the custom with many captives. But he reluctantly agreed to give him up after Wabeno and a delegation of shamans had approached him with their plan to return the boy to his people.

"The boy's return will help keep the peace with our enemies," Wabeno had said, omitting the true purpose behind the mission, which was to allow Wolf to travel through the homeland of the Dakotas.

The hunter and his family had begun calling the boy Migizi, which means Eagle in Anishinaabemowin. But Wabeno explained that the boy chaffed at this, so Wolf resolved to use his Siouian name, Anokasan-Duta.

But of course it was rude to use a stranger's name or to ask for it until both parties had grown quite familiar, and this could sometimes take several cycles of the moon. Thus, Wolf did not call Red Eagle by his name at all for some time. Instead, he took him fishing.

"Waugh!" the boy screamed in fright from the front of Wolf's canoe as he paddled away from the shore into the green waves of Kitchi Gami. He was of a tribe where the forest meets the plains, and though he had paddled on rivers and small lakes before, the vast expanse of Kitchi Gami filled him with terror, especially since Wolf had taken them far from shore. He dropped his paddle and clutched at the sides of the canoe with both hands. Turning, his face was a mask of fear.

At this Wolf gave a small laugh and a reassuring look, offering to return the boy's paddle, which he had retrieved as it floated past. But Red Eagle shook his head, unable or unwilling to loosen his grip on the rim of the canoe. The boy's terror grew even stronger when Wolf rose to stand in the middle of the bobbing canoe, scanning the water with his upraised spear.

"There!" he cried, thrusting the barbed spear at a brown shadow just beneath the water. With a cry of triumph, he lifted the wriggling fish from the surface of the lake and brained its head with his club.

"You try now," he said, signing the words with his hands as he spoke. But as he expected, the boy refused to relinquish his grip on the canoe. Yet he watched Wolf intently as he speared a second fish, and by the third fish his fear had evaporated. It was a gentle day with no breeze and the sun was pleasantly warm on the water.

"You try," Wolf said, once again making signs with his hands. This time the boy turned and climbed shakily to his feet as Wolf settled into the stern of the canoe, holding it steady with his paddle. He made a couple of half-hearted stabs at the water, and once Wolf leaned forth to seize his ankle to prevent him from tumbling overboard. Although the boy failed to spear a fish that day, it had been a good start and they shared a meal of whitefish on the shore that evening, trading a few words back and forth: fish, water, canoe, knife, fire...

Thereafter, Wolf took Red Eagle fishing each day with the intention of learning his people's language. Wolf had a memory as deep as Kitchi Gami and rarely forgot a word as they spoke, first in the language of hand signs and then by pointing and repeating. The boy quickly forgot his fear of the lake, and with that came the loosening of his tongue.

In time, Wolf coaxed the boy's story from his lips as they sat before their cook fire on the beach at night.

"How did you come to us?" he asked, using a stick to prod a fish as it roasted in a sheath of wet leaves atop a bank of coals.

"I was lost and your people found me."

"This we know, but how?"

"We were hunting. My father and his brother," the boy searched for words.

"Your uncle."

"Yes. We came upon a herd of elk and followed it east along a river. It was only my father, my uncle and me and we had been many days on the hunting trail."

Wolf gathered that Red Eagle had begged to be taken on the long trip to the eastern forest to prepare himself for manhood. It was the sort of dream a boy fancies, and Wolf could not help but think that he, too, had yearned to wander when he was the boy's age.

"We came upon the elk at a bend in the river, but as we crept forward we saw a band of men hidden in the trees. They fell upon us, beating my uncle with clubs. There were six of them, maybe more, and they had us in their snare."

"Who were these men? Of what tribe?"

The boy gazed up at him and it was clear he didn't know. "Bad men," he replied.

"My uncle was crying in pain beneath their blows, but there was nothing we could do. There were too many! My father seized me and we ran down a gully and over the next hill."

"And your uncle?"

"He lay at their feet when we ran," he said, with his cheeks wet with tears. "There was no hope of saving him. My father thought only to save me."

They ran all day through the forest, yet soon they heard the men behind them, hooting and yelling in the distance. In a panic, they stumbled into a small lake, where his father hid him in a thicket of cattails, promising to return when he eluded their pursuers.

"That was the last I saw of my father."

Red Eagle had hidden amid the reeds for two days and two nights, pestered by flies, with only roots to eat. Thereafter he had fled to the east away from the pursuers. The Ojibwe hunters had found him days later, lying at the base of a tree and near death.

"You have done your father great honor by living," Wolf said. "He would be proud of you. Surely, your clan longs for you."

"Yes, elder brother, but they are lost to me now and I do not know if my father lives. What is my life if he has died because of me?"

"He calls to you. I can feel it."

Red Eagle gave him a cold stare. "You are kind, but a fool to think so, for if my father still lives then he is far beyond your mountains, beyond even the Wakpa."

"Wakpa?" It was a word that Wolf did not yet know.

"The great river."

Ah, the Misi Sipi, the grandfather of rivers, which ran to the end of the earth. Wolf had collected many stories of it from wanderers and traders through the years and longed to see it. Wabeno said he must follow it part of the way if he wished to reach the pipestone quarry of the Dakota.

For the first time he did not feel uneasy with the idea of taking Red Eagle home, for what man did not wish to gaze upon the great river?

After half a moon of fishing off the shores of Kitchi Gami, Wolf declared himself ready to depart on his mission, while for his part, Red Eagle had speared almost ten fish.

"I have learned the Dakotas' language and am ready to leave," he told Wabeno-inini one evening.

The old man's pipe nearly fell from his mouth in surprise. "You speak their tongue already?"

"Enough. The boy is a good teacher, and I will learn more as we travel."

"He barely spoke a word before you met."

"Ah, but the fish taught him to speak. They gave their lives so that he might teach me."

Wabeno gave him an uncertain look and fingered his necklace of cowrie shells. "If only the fish were as willing to teach the rest of us."

Instead of fishing the next day, Wolf asked Red Eagle to help him load the canoe with bars of hammered copper and packets of the Tionontati's tobacco.

"What is this?" The boy held up an ingot that had been polished to the gloss of a sundown.

"It is a gift for your father," Wolf replied.

"A gift?"

"As Wabeno told you, I am a trader and these are my gifts."

"My father?" the boy said bitterly. "Trader, your gifts are bones and ashes. My father lives with the spirits now."

"Did you see him die when you were lost?"

"No, but that was the fate of my uncle."

"Your uncle died so that you and your father could live."

"Yes."

"Honor him. Be strong! Believe! Is your father a weak man? A coward?"

Now the snare had been set and Red Eagle bristled with anger. "No!" he cried.

"Then know this. Surely your father still lives, and he and your mother must be crying out for you. The wise men who live atop the hill have asked me to return you to your people."

"And what will you gain by this?" The boy's eyes narrowed with suspicion.

Wolf held out his palms. "Small things. The friendship of your people. A gift of their pipestone for a gift of our copper. Your return will show our good feelings."

"That is all?"

"What more could there be?"

At this Red Eagle's solemn face broke as if he had been struck. "Elder brother, your people have been kind to me and have honored me as a son, but this is beyond my dreams! I ache for my people, and never thought to see them again, but this..." he choked off.

Wolf looked at him gravely and gave a low chuckle. "We are not always so kind, young brother, but the spirits have moved the elders on your behalf. Thank them, if you will, and pray that we make it to your home, for it is a long way and I don't have a turtle's idea of how we will find it."

"It is to the west, brother!" Red Eagle pointed with a boy's naïveté. "We need only go west!"

Yes, to where the sun lay in its bed each night. But how to prepare for such a journey? Wolf only knew that the Misi Sipi ran somewhere to the west of Kitchi Gami, and the boy would be of little help. Wolf spent a day in consultation with traders who had traveled to the west, and then searched among the many birch scrolls of the Great Lodge for the pictographs that might guide him. The way seemed simple enough, though he would need help if he were to carry a cargo of copper.

So it was that days later Wolf and Red Eagle joined a party of Ojibwe warriors who were making the long trip home from their attack on the Haudenosaunee.

"They know of the portage that will take you to the Misi Sipi," Wabeno said. "It is a small stream, only a day's walk from the lake, yet it joins the great river and all of the rivers beyond. One of those rivers will take you to the boy's people."

"One thing I do not understand," Wolf replied. "Why must I return the boy to his home if my mission is to find the animal of your dreams? It will be a long way from my path down the Misi Sipi."

Wabeno gave him a bland look. "The boy knows little of the sunktanka, yet perhaps his people can tell you more. This, and there are many dangers along the river. It is our hope that his people will help you."

Wolf was careful to keep his own face as smooth as a polished beach stone, yet his thoughts were anything but smooth. Help me? he wondered. That was a thin hope. He would be alone among his enemies, and what if the boy's father was dead? Perhaps the Dakota would demand his adoption to replace the men they had lost. Perhaps they would demand his death.

"But that is all far off and undecided by the spirits," Wabeno said, guessing his thoughts. "Tell them your stories; seduce them with your words."

Wolf scowled. The old man could read the thoughts of a tree. "Yes, grandfather," he replied with a touch of misery, "though I think you have more faith in the power of stories than do I."

"I have faith in you, Wolf, and have seen you hold others in your spell with only your words."

"Then I will hope to bring many words home with me."

"See that you do," Wabeno said coolly. "See that you do."

They set off with the sunrise the next morning in four canoes, threshing at the waves along the southern shore of Kitchi Gami. That night they camped in forest of white birch beyond a long stretch of dunes and then paddled on past the painted cliffs to the isle of Kitchi Minissing. For much of the way the waves thundered on the shore and often it rained. But just as often the sun shone and the lake was as placid and smooth as a pond. Within a quarter moon they made the portage at Kiwewina, the long peninsula that jutted into the lake almost all the way to Minong. Thereafter, they paddled hard for the islands to the west, still a long way off.

Paddling the length of Kitchi Gami with only fish and a pemmican of nuts mixed with venison and tallow to eat is no small feat. At times the straining men were chilled half to death by winds out of the north and torrents of rain that could last a full day, filling their canoes to the point of bursting. Often they spent their nights wet to their bones, patching their leaking canoes with pine pitch and cedar roots as the battering waves took their toll. All of them were gaunt with hunger and the ceaseless toil of paddling on, on and on amid the waves, accompanied by the hoarse chant of a singer, urging them forward.

At last they reached the uttermost western shore of Kitchi Gami and it was time to say farewell as they collapsed on the beach and gave thanks. As promised, the warriors of the Ojibwe spent a day in the final portage, carrying Wolf's canoe with its cargo of copper and tobacco down a thin trail in the forest. At the end of the trail they came to a stream, little more than a creek, the way of which was blocked in many places by fallen trees and beaver lodges. Yet this was the way to the Misi Sipi, the grandfather of rivers, and that night Wolf, Red Eagle and the warriors shared a final pipe by their fire and uttered the prayers of parting.

The People of the Pipe

It took three days for Wolf and Red Eagle to make their way up the stream through a cavern of overhanging trees, which loomed in a black tangle of branches above them, blotting out the sun.

The stream seemed to deny any passage, barring the way with dense tangles of twisting cedars and fallen trees beyond count. The current leapt and danced past clawing limbs and submerged trees as if mocking their progress. No sooner would Wolf and Red Eagle climb into their canoe than they would be obliged to leave it again to wrest their way around another pile-up of dead oaks or splintered limbs. Sometimes, they had to empty their canoe of its copper to drag it around a fallen elm or a shattered pine bristling with hundreds of branches combing the stream. Other times they would find themselves sinking up to their knees in black, sucking mud, besieged by clouds of mosquitoes, only to begin the process once again as they struggled on.

"Ah, if misery had a mother, it would be this place," Wolf muttered to himself, oppressed by the darkness of the overhanging trees. He reflected that he had spent as much time wading as he had in paddling.

"What say you, brother?" Red Eagle called from the front of the canoe as they dragged it past yet another barrier. This time it was a beaver dam that eased their misery for a few paddle-strokes while crossing its ponded waters.

"I said we are fortunate to have so many cedars here, for they will help us to mend our canoe," Wolf replied. There was no point in bringing the boy's spirits as low as his own, though in fact it seemed as if Red Eagle did not mind wrestling their way forward. Perhaps the boy thought of it as a game, or was simply eager to take another step closer to home.

But pausing to rest for a moment on a low rise amid the marsh surrounding the dam, they were surprised to encounter a large beaver waddling toward its lodge through the reeds. The beaver looked up, just as surprised to find the two of them sitting there, but only for a moment as Wolf's club came crashing down on its head. That night, after thanking the beaver for the gift of its life, they made a meal of its tail, wrapping the rest of the cooked meat in packets of birch bark for the trip ahead.

Gradually, the creek became a rivulet, widening enough to make the going easier as they skirted the maze of fallen trees. Then at last on their fourth morning they came to a slender river, not much wider than the creek they had finally succeeded in clearing.

That led to a broad lake, rimmed with many villages of the Dakota. They paddled across it by night, observing a galaxy of fires lining the shore.

"Should we not stop?" Red Eagle asked as they paddled in the darkness, lit only by stars.

"Not until we reach your people," Wolf replied.

"These are my people. We are of the same blood."

"Would you have me leave you here? They might hinder us. They might keep you."

Wolf almost wished the boy would say yes, but instead Red Eagle grunted agreement, digging at the water with his paddle. "As you wish, brother. As you wish."

And so they pushed on, over a fearsome portage at the first breath of dawn and along yet another river.

At last they came to a gentle stream flowing south.

"This surely is the Wakpa," Red Eagle said.

The Wakpa? The grandfather of rivers? Wolf's eyes lingered in disbelief on the gently flowing current. The river before them was no wider than the underhand toss of a stone, nothing at all like the stories of the Misi Sipi that he had heard so often around the lodge fires.

"No... This is a child and we seek a giant," he said. "This cannot be the great river, for I have heard that it is as wide as a big lake."

"You are wrong, brother. Even a giant begins as a child, and this one gathers many streams as it travels south. Rest your thoughts, you will see it grow much larger."

Wolf looked doubtful, but gave a shrug. "Even a long story has a small beginning," he agreed.

Though the river was slight, its blockages were easily avoided and they made good time that day under the sun. In less than half a day the width of river doubled, and by the end of the day it had doubled again. The next day it doubled again and again, growing larger as other streams and rivers joined its way south.

The Misi Sipi also grew wilder as it flowed south, passing over many low waterfalls and rapids. "It is the reason we call it Wakpa, the river of the great falls," Anokasan said after they had fought their way through a treacherous stretch of rapids that threatened to rip their canoe in half.

Two days later, they came upon the junction of another river of nearly the same size flowing from the west. By now the Misi Sipi had indeed grown as wide as an inland lake and Wolf had to squint to make out features on its far shore.

"This is the river of my people!" Red Eagle said excitedly. "I know this place, for my people spent a season here, fishing where the two rivers meet." Indeed, there was a tumbledown lodge upon the riverbank where the boy said that he and his family had sheltered.

Ahead, the Misi Sipi grew even larger beyond its meeting with the river flowing from the west. Wolf eyed the way south wistfully, thinking that he would much prefer to paddle on down the fast-running Misi Sipi than struggle against the other river on the way to the Pipestone People. But he had promised Wabeno that he would deliver the boy and was curious to see the quarry that was the source of many legends. Thus, they turned at the bend and pushed their way to the west.

Yet as they paddled, Wolf could not help but wonder how he would be received by Red Eagle's people, they being ancestral enemies of the Ojibwe. And though he had dismissed the threat many times, he wondered if the raiders who had killed the boy's uncle still wandered the forests along the river. He had slept uneasy for the past few nights with the sole weapon of his serrated club by his side.

Then too, now they were passing through territory occupied by the Chaiena, a people who lived where the woodlands of the east met the prairies of the west. Red Eagle claimed that his people were at peace with the Chaiena, but Wolf was wary. Often, he saw smoke rising in thin tendrils through the trees, offering signs of their villages. He steered for the opposite shore as they passed by, waving friendship and good intentions to any who stood watching.

There were so many different peoples in the world, he mused. Surely, there must be villages, tribes and clans beyond count. Truly, the world was filled with wonders.

The going was hard against the current from the west and the boy was of little use, slapping his paddle at the water at the front of the canoe. But by now Wolf was well seasoned from traveling immense distances across the vast lakes of his homeland and his powerful back, shoulders and arms were the match of two strong men put together. He pushed tirelessly upstream, always on the lookout ahead for dugouts blocking the way or men with weapons running along the shore.

But as the boy had predicted, they had nothing to fear as they made their way upriver, and gradually, the villages of the Dakota began to succeed those of the Chaiena. To Wolf's surprise, these were a hodge-podge of bark dwellings interspersed with those fashioned from mounds of earth. Added to these were conical dwellings of tall poles covered with the skins of buffalo and painted with many symbols and pictures.

By now, the forests lining the river had given way to prairie and rolling hills that faded to shades of purple in the sunset. The prairie filled Wolf with an eerie sensation; there was no place to hide in this land without trees.

As with the land of the Chaiena, Wolf kept to the far shore as they passed each village of the Dakota, for who could say how a different clan might receive the boy and a stranger? For his part, Red Eagle scanned each village as they passed, looking for signs of his people.

Two days to the west, the boy's voice rang out from the prow of the canoe.

"There!" he shouted, pointing to a large village ahead that was so crowded with lodges that it threatened to tumble into the river. "There!"

At the side of the river, a group of women looked up from where they were rinsing leather, knee-deep in the current. Beyond them, a troop of dogs ran down to the riverbank, barking in excitement and alarm. A call went up from the women, and as Wolf pushed toward the shore it seemed as if the entire village was pummeling down to the riverbank. A cold knot formed in his stomach; Wabeno-inini had prophesied his safety, but what did the old man know? Even now, men with clubs and spears were pushing their way through the gabbling crowd gathered on the bank.

And then the prow of their canoe touched the shore barely two arm-lengths from those gathered there and the entire crowd went silent as if they had seen a ghost.

And indeed they had, for Anokasan-Duta leapt from the canoe and raised his arms with his thin body clad only in a breechclout and the moccasins of the Ojibwe.

"Brothers, sisters, uncles, aunts!" he cried in a high piping voice. "Take me in your arms! I have returned!"

The crowd parted and a man stepped forward with his lank hair falling loose to his shoulders; he was slight in stature, but lean and hard-muscled. Wolf saw at a glance that it was Red Eagle's father, for they wore the same narrow face. But whereas Red Eagle's face still had a boy's tenderness, his father had a gaze that was stern and hard. The man crept to the boy's side, careful as a panther and knelt down, caressing his face and staring into his eyes in disbelief. "My son, how is this possible?" he said in barely a whisper.

But there was no such reticence with the arrival of the boy's mother. A hubbub arose and a woman burst from the crowd. With a scream of joy she ran to her son and grasped him in her arms, sobbing and laughing as he laughed and jigged in her arms.

Then the whole crowd erupted with ululating cries and laughter, dancing on the bank of the river like a huge bucking animal. And to Wolf's astonishment he was lifted onto the shoulders of a knot of stout men and danced up and down on the muddy shore amid wave after wave of cheers.

That night, Wolf was feted with a feast of buffalo, turkey and turtle as tales were shared around the fire with the whole village looking on. Red Eagle's father said he'd been pursued by their attackers for a day and a night after he had left his son, finally losing them in the forest. Yet it had been another two days before he dared to leave his hiding place, and then he had wandered for half a moon in search of his son. The land in which they had been hunting had lakes beyond number and many looked just the same as the one where he had hidden his son. For many days he had wandered the lake country, risking discovery and death, calling his son's name.

"At last I found my brother's body lying mutilated and dishonored," he said. "I buried him on a hill looking west and then grieved at not finding my son, for I had given him up for dead."

"And who were these men who attacked you?" Wolf asked. "Odugamies?" These, he knew, were the sometime enemies of the Dakotas. They lived to the east along the shore of the great lake, Mishi Gami.

"This I do not know, for when they fell upon us there was no time to look for signs among them," Red Eagle's father replied. "Who knows? The wind blows from many directions, and with it come raiders from unknown lands."

For his part, Red Eagle said that he had been rescued from death by the Ojibwe and treated kindly. He confirmed that Wolf was nothing more than a wandering trader who had shown great courage and strength on the journey home.

"His grandfather told me that he is a fool, and feeble-minded," he vouched with a boy's glibness, "yet I have found him to be a worthy friend."

"Thank you Anokasan-Duta," Wolf replied when it was his turn to speak. Turning, he addressed the assembled elders and the crowd behind them. "Your son had taught me the ways of your people and of your language and I am honored to walk among you. My people have returned him with a gift of our fine copper, wrested from the earth with great difficulty from a great distance. I myself helped to dig some of this from the bosom of Grandmother Earth."

At this there were smiles and murmurs of gratitude all around, yet Wolf noted the face of an old man scowling in the shadows beyond where Red Eagle's mother and father sat. He made out the silvery tips of buffalo horns glinting from the man's headdress by the light of the fire

"And what do you seek of us in return for your gift?" the old man called out in a ragged voice. "You did not bring the boy and gifts of copper such a great distance for nothing."

This Wolf had expected, for a trader did not give his gifts freely. A gift was expected in return, and if the gift was not deemed worthy it could be refused until a finer gift was offered.

But unlike those traders who had experienced many seasons and much guile in the exchange of goods, Wolf was not yet smooth in the ways of the gift-giving and receiving ceremonies.

"I... I seek only your friendship, grandfather," he said awkwardly.

There was a long pause from the shadows beyond the firelight, and Wolf sensed that more was expected of him.

"Who would believe a man who seeks only friendship?" the man called out at last. His voice was raw with scorn.

Wolf settled his pipe in his lap and recovered his wits. "You have seen through me, grandfather," he said carefully. "I am a dog, cowering beneath your gaze. So know this, I have come seeking a great treasure among your people."

"A treasure?"

"Yes, grandfather, I will scratch your back if you will scratch mine. The elders of my people crave the red pipestone that is sacred to all who walk the earth, and it is said that you are its guardians. Consider this: a gift of our copper for a gift of your pipestone."

"Hmph."

This seemed to satisfy all within hearing. But the old man in the shadows shuffled off beyond the firelight, filling Wolf with unease.

He slept beneath the shelter of his overturned canoe that night, as was his custom whenever he traveled. That morning, he awakened to the sight of a pair of tall, fringed moccasins. Squinting up from the shelter of his canoe he beheld the old man from the night before.

The elder had a gray face like dried fish skin, with his eyes sunken deep within his skull. He looked enough like Wabeno-inini, Man of the Dawn Sky, to be his brother, and Wolf knew at once that he was the shaman of Red Eagle's people.

"Come, we will eat together, then smoke," he said.

Wolf roused himself and the two of them sat on a log by the river, sharing a handful of dried buffalo meat that the old man had brought along. It was sweetened with honey and Wolf found it to be quite good. "It is the tongue," the old man said when he asked. "Always tender, always good."

Then, a pipe was produced with a handsome bowl of the red pipestone, bearing a simple design without embellishments. Wolf offered some of his tobacco, brought so far away from the Tionontati, and the old man coughed up a lungful in astonishment at its richness.

Wolf could see that they were off to a good start, yet he was uneasy. Why had the shaman sought him out? He knew soon enough.

"You are no simple trader," the old man said, leveling his gaze upon him.

Wolf resisted the urge to protest, waiting for the shaman to speak further.

"I see something strange about you - there is a spirit about you," the old man continued, gazing above Wolf's head. "I saw it by the fire last night and I see it still. You are not what you appear to be. Your eyes - they are the eyes of a wolf - they are not of any man who walks the earth."

Cold fear gripped Wolf's bones. Had the old man seen through him so easily? Did he think that he was a spy? That could only mean his death.

But then Wolf recalled that Wabeno had not asked him to spy on the Dakota, only to seek their pipestone as a pretense for traveling on down the river. It was enough to make him relax and he mustered a bemused expression as he passed the pipe back to the shaman.

"But grandfather, here you see me, walking the earth and smoking with you," he said in an easy way.

"There is a magic about you, a sorcery," the old man continued, still gazing in bewilderment at whatever it was that he saw hovering around Wolf's body.

Wolf took a chance. "Perhaps it is only a spell of protection cast by my grandfather Wabeno-inini of the Mide-wi-win of my people," he said, adding, "I make no excuse for my eyes. They are what the Great Spirit gave me."

"Wabeno? Even I have heard of him," the old man said with a start. "He lived among the Dakota for a time as a boy."

"Ah, and perhaps he has heard of you?"

"Perhaps. Split Tail, you may call me that, though my true name is a secret, even to my people."

"Know this then. My grandfather's pipe is old and broken. He seeks a new one to travel with him when he walks the star trail and I have come to seek the stone to make it."

This seemed to satisfy Split Tail, though he remained doubtful as to the spell Wolf spoke of, maintaining that there was a strange aura that shimmered about his body in a way that could not be accounted for, certainly not if he was only a simple trader.

As for Wolf, he assumed the old shaman was simply addled by age.

Nonetheless, Split Tail offered to take Wolf to the sacred quarry, which was a day's paddle away, followed by a long walk over the plains. They spent the rest of the day in conversation. Split Tail showed a great deal of interest in the affairs of the Ojibwe shamans and Wolf responded as best he could, professing ignorance of many of their doings. It would not do to have the old man know that he, too, had studied the ways of magic and healing, even though he had fallen short in his studies.

It turned out that Wolf had little to fear of the Dakota who lived close by the prairie, far from the Ojibwe. "Your enemies are the Dakota of the forest," Split Tail explained. "We hear their complaints, but know nothing of your people."

Early on, Split Tail asked if he had heard of the Mandan, who lived far up a river called the Pekitunoui. The river flowed from the northwest and was nearly as big as the Misi Sipi.

"They call themselves the People of the Pheasants, the See-pohs-kah-nu-mah-kah-kee," he said. "They are known as traders throughout the plains which spread from here to a wall of snowy mountains. They trade even as far south as the great salt water."

"They sound like a people without roots."

"No, their roots run deep! They are a people beyond count and have many great towns, filled with lodges made of timber covered with earth."

"No grandfather, I cannot say that I have heard of them, for I am new at trading and this is the furthest I have traveled."

"Well, watch for them and learn, for they are sharp traders. Perhaps someday you will reach their towns with your gifts."

"Perhaps if I grow wings and fly," Wolf said with a faint smile, "for it sounds like a long paddle upriver."

"Ah, know this. If you wander, they will find you!"

Split Tail said the Mandan cultivated great fields of maize, supplementing their crops with trade. They had no need to move in search of game with the seasons, as did the Ojibwe.

All this and more Wolf learned on his trip to the pipestone quarry with Split Tail and a company of young men eager for any adventure. They made their way up the river to the west, after which there was a walk of two days across the plains, with Wolf hobbling along as best he could.

Wolf surveyed the plains which stretched out of sight in every direction. One of the Dakota had told him that it took almost two full moons to cross them, assuming that one could walk a considerable distance each day. Beyond the plains, he was told, stood a wall of mountains, beyond which the sun made its bed each night.

At first, Wolf had the impression that the plains were drear and barren of life, but that quickly changed when he flushed a brace of deer from a thicket along a twisting brook. The plains, in fact, were teeming with deer, bear, elk, buffalo, wolves and panthers doing the endless dance of predators and prey. At times the sky grew black with clouds of birds, which nested in a thundering cacophony in the cottonwoods lining the rivers.

He also learned that the plains, which looked so bleak from a distance, were riven with streams and rivers. When the Dakota sought water, they simply followed the tracks of buffalo, which had dug trails as deep as trenches through the hills and valleys toward their watering holes.

"We know of your big lake, Kitchi Gami, but these plains are far larger," one of the Dakota boasted around the fire one night. "Your lake is but a minnow, and this," he gestured, "is a catfish, which might swallow Kitchi Gami whole."

Wolf gave a polite grunt in reply, but he could not dispute it, for Split Tail had told him that the plains were even greater from north to south, disappearing into troubled lands were few dared to go.

At last they came to the sacred land of the red stone, marked by a long, low cliff that rose from the earth, diving underground again some ways off, as if it were the back of a huge serpent. At the feet of the cliff were signs of many diggings and beyond it the plains opened up in all directions, colored in shades of red, pink, purple and green at the will of the sun.

Like the copper mines of Minong, the quarry was nothing more than a series of trenches dug a man's height into the earth, revealing the sacred

red stone that was easily carved into the pipe heads and calumets that were valued all over the Great Turtle Island.

Wolf was surprised to see the men of several tribes digging at the rock, including a party of Odugamies, who greeted Split Tail and his retinue of young warriors with cheer. "All may dig the stone here, even our enemies," Split Tail replied to his astonishment. "The stone welcomes all who come in peace."

That night they mingled with the Odugamies, sharing a pipe before they turned in and Wolf marveled that the world was even stranger than he had imagined. What would Wabeno and his people think when they learned that he had slept amid the snoring of their mortal enemies?

Toward sundown, Split Tail had produced a large calumet, the pipe of peace. It was strung with bright red cardinal feathers and its stem was wrapped in shell beads from the far-off sea.

"Would you like to hear the story of this place?" he asked those who had joined them. There were perhaps twenty men and women gathered, not counting their children and dogs.

"Yes, grandfather, very much," came the response in murmurs. All had heard the story before, but it was always good to hear it again.

"Then know that once this quarry brought forth the pipes of war," Split Tail began. "For long ago, men believed that the red stone ran with the blood of their enemies.

"But then came a great spirit, who looked upon the men of the earth with sorrow, for shedding blood had never been the purpose of the stone. The spirit sent word to every tribe, bidding them to gather in this place. How the word was sent, I do not know, for it was long before our grandfathers' fathers. Perhaps the birds were the messengers, or perhaps the clouds or the wind, but every nation heeded the call and the wisest among them gathered here. Here! Right where we sit now!"

A thrill ran through the crowd and Wolf felt it as well, tingling through his toes as he imagined the faces of many lands gathered before the cliffs painted black beneath the setting sun.

"Do you see that cliff, brothers? Do you see it sisters?" Split Tail pointed to the highest rim. "It was there that the spirit stood as tall as the mountains, gazing down at the multitude as if from a thundercloud! Some say the spirit appeared as a bird of many colors with piercing eyes. Others say it was a being of light in human form, shining like a rainbow filled with sunlight."

Then, Split Tail leered and posed a question that his listeners had heard many times before.

"Brothers, was the spirit a man?"

"No!"

"Sisters, was the spirit a woman?"

"No!"

"No, the great spirit was not as we are! It was not as the animals, or the plants, or as the water or the earth! It was the spirit of all things! All that we are and all that lives! And it was on that cliff that it broke a spire of pipestone that reached up to the sky. It fashioned the stone with hands that whirled and crushed rock like cyclones! And what did it make brothers? Sisters, what did the spirit make?"

"A pipe!" shouted every voice among them.

"Yes, a pipe." Split Tail paused to draw on the calumet, exhaling a long plume of smoke and nodding eagerly before passing it on. "A pipe as long as three tall pines laid end-to-end; and taking it up, the great spirit smoked as the people stood below him. It breathed the smoke in every direction from whence they had come, north, east, south and west. Then, in a voice that shook the earth like thunder, the spirit told them that this ground was sacred! It told them that the red pipestone was the red of their flesh and could be used only for the cause of peace! No killing must come from the pipes of this quarry, no talk of raiding or taking trophies. Only peace!"

At this Split Tail nodded and those gathered in the circle nodded with him, reflecting on his words. Somewhere in the shadows a baby cried.

"Do you hear that?" Split Tail said. "We are as infants here, we are all children, happy to see one-another. That is the meaning of this place, and that is why no harm can come to any who travel here, for all are welcome."

"But what became of the spirit, grandfather?" a young voice piped from the crowd.

"Ah! At the last breath of the pipe the spirit followed the smoke into the clouds, where it looks down on us even now. It left behind two guardians in the rock to watch over this place. They are the spirits of two women who tend ovens within the stone. Sometimes you can hear them talking as you dig."

It had been a satisfying story and Split Tail had done well in the telling. Many in the crowd averred that they, too, had heard the spirits speaking as they dug, and Wolf was reminded that similar spirits spoke within the mines of Minong.

Thereafter, he spent three days freeing up a section of the soft, red rock and chipping away at its surface. He came away with several large packets of stone wrapped in buckskin, which he dragged back across the plains on a travois of two long poles.

The trip was fruitful in other ways as well, for each night he and Split Tail had shared stories by the fire. The old shaman was astounded by his tale of Paija, the one-legged she-monster that lived in the land of the Cree. In turn, Wolf was surprised to learn that the Dakota had a tale that was similar to the Ojibwe's dragon of the lakes, Misshipeshu, and its eternal battle with the thunderbird, Animiki. Their beast was a horned serpent known as Unktehi, a monster which crawled across the plains, fighting the thunderbird Wakinyan. Like Animiki, the Wakinyan flapped its vast wings to create thunder and cast webs of lightning from its eyes.

Over the space of several days, slowly so as not to arouse suspicion, Wolf guided the stories into those involving animals, hoping to learn something of the sunktanka. Split Tail told him of a boy raised by rabbits who had become a hero among the Dakota, and also of a creature of the forest, which looked something like a man, yet was a giant by comparison and covered with fur.

These too were stories similar to those which Wolf had learned among the Ojibwe and he began to despair of learning about the sunktanka. He was loathe to bring it up directly, thinking that Split Tail would deduce the true purpose of his mission and unmask him as a spy.

But on their final night at the quarry, Wolf had finished his story of the caribou hunt among the Nippissings when Split Tail said that he, too, knew a story of strange animals.

"There is a legend among the people who live far south of here of an animal that came to them from another world," he began. "It is a magical beast with a tail that flows like a woman's hair."

"Magical?"

Split Tail nodded. "Even so. It is called the sunktanka."

"*Ehn?* Is it like the caribou? Does it have antlers"

"No," Split Tail shook his head. "It is only a legend. It was an animal found wandering by the great salt water far to the south. No one had ever seen it before or since. It could run as fast as a deer, yet it was not a deer. Some say that it came from the belly of a giant fish that washed up on the shore of the sea, though others say it was a great swan with white wings. Whether it was a giant bird or a fish, no one can say, but it also disgorged a band of strange men dressed as clowns who were unable to speak the language of those who found them. They stank horribly and were as hairy as bears. They were quickly taken as slaves, and just as quickly died, for the legend says they were a weak and fearful race of men who had no women. Can you imagine?"

"And what of the sunktanka?"

"Ah, some say it lives among the people known as the Adai, who carry it about as they follow the buffalo."

"They carry it?" This did not seem possible, for Wabeno had said the sunktanka was as large as a female elk.

But Split Tail insisted it was so. "It is a sacred animal, carried from place to place. How, I do not know, but I believe that more sunktankas will come in the time of our grandchildren. I have dreamed of it."

"Do these people live among the Mandan?"

Split Tail made a face. "No, they live far to the south, far down the great river and beyond. They wander in search of the buffalo. Who can say where they live?"

Again, those dismal words: who can say? Wabeno's answer for so many things.

"I would like to see this sunktanka. I will look for it in my travels."

"Ah, you might as well try cutting the moon in half with your fingernail," Split Tail replied. "Who can say where the Adai live? Only those living two moons to the south, far from your trail home."

Wolf hesitated to ask Split Tail about the sunktanka's eyes. Wabeno had said they were the color of robins' eggs. But as Split Tail had never seen a caribou, he thought of a way to ask.

"Some of the caribou have eyes that glow as red as the coals of a hot fire," he said, hoping the shaman would not see through the lie. "Does the sunktanka also have strange eyes?"

"This, I do not know, but there was never a mention of it. Its eyes can only be brown or black, for that is the way of all things except you, brother. You with your wolf eyes and your red-eyed caribou."

Split Tail gave him a wry smile and Wolf had the feeling that the old man had seen right through him.

Wolf was footsore when they returned to Red Eagle's village, for he was not used to walking long distances with his bad leg and was grateful to have a few days to rest his sore muscles. In time, he learned that the boy's father was named Lone Dog. He was a dour man of few words. As Wolf had noted on first sight of him, Lone Dog was not given to refinements of his hair, nor did he wear much in the way of ornaments or paint. In that way, he seemed as spare as the plains on which he lived.

Still, Lone Dog invited Wolf to share his lodge, giving him a sleeping place on a low bench along the wall. The lodge was a marvel to Wolf's eyes, being constructed of packed earth over a framework of logs with a smoke hole allowing light from above. But Lone Dog snorted in derision when

Wolf praised him for his abode.

"Brother you are kind, but this is the home of a rabbit compared to the lodges of the Mandans," he said. "They too live in earth lodges, but their homes are as large as caverns build around the trunks of great trees."

"Split Wing has spoken of the Mandans to me, but I have not heard much of their lodges," Wolf said.

"I know of them only in stories," Lone Dog admitted. "But some of their lodges are said to be large enough to hold ceremonies viewed by hundreds. They live in many large towns across the plains along Pekitunoui, the big river to the west."

"And do you see them often?"

"No brother, for they are at war with our western cousins. We do not wish to see them this far east. They are farmers, scratching at the earth for maize, but they have many fierce warriors among them."

Lone Dog had nothing to say of the Mandans beyond this, only that their towns were surrounded by ditches, high walls of earth and tall palisades. Yet over the next few nights he shared the story of his own village as they sat smoking before the fire.

As with the Ojibwe, Wolf learned that Lone Dog's village was occupied only part of the year. Much of his peoples' time was spent roaming the plains in search of *tatanka*, the buffalo.

"Once, we lived in the forest, like your people," he said. "Not long ago! But then we learned to hunt *tatanka* and little by little, we have followed their trail to live among them."

Even so, it was a hard life hunting the herds of buffalo beyond count. Men scouted the plains on foot, running great distances to find the herds and then devising ways to kill them. Their women, children and elders trailed along behind, dragging their tents and belongings on long poles.

"Sometimes we dress in the skins of wolves to crawl among the herds, rising up to kill or frighten them," Lone Dog said. "Then, if we can, we drive them over a cliff, dashing them on the rocks below, or into a river where they are easily killed."

"But rivers and cliffs are not always where men might wish them to be," Wolf noted.

"No, more often, we creep up on the herds on our hands and knees through the tall grass, hoping to bring down the weakest among them. Not all return from the hunt, for the *tatanka* have sharp horns and their bulls are jealous of their mates. There are warriors among them who gore and trample our hunters."

Days later, Wolf made ready to leave. He gave a third of his copper and a packet of his tobacco to Split Tail and Lone Dog, remembering the Oda-wa's advice to save plenty of trade goods for the way ahead.

The village threw a feast in Wolf's honor the night before his departure. A dead buffalo had come floating down the river with its hoofs protruding from the current, and Wolf was told that the bloated carcass was considered a great delicacy. Many said it was a sign of good fortune, having arrived just as Wolf was preparing to depart.

Having little firewood, the women of the village roasted the meat over a fire of buffalo dung, which was not to Wolf's liking. The flaming dung added the faint taste of shit to even fresh meat and he never got used to it. Nor did he care for the rotted meat of the drowned buffalo, which had been rendered to a jellied mush, for who could say how long it had floated in the river? He was served a large scoop of it in the hollowed-out skull of a bear. Somberly, he dabbed at the gray blob with his knife, managing to down a few bites without puking.

"Good," he said solemnly, setting the skull aside after a polite interval, grateful that a dog finished what was half eaten.

"Would you like some more?" Lone Dog's wife asked, eager to share.

"Ah, thank you sister, but I think I will smoke now," he replied, producing his pipe.

After that, there had been dancing, drumming and declarations of eternal friendship with the Ojibwe, although as with all such promises, this was soon forgotten.

By then it was late summer, and soon the air would be growing chill and the leaves turning color. With his canoe loaded with pipestone, dried buffalo and the remains of his copper and tobacco, Wolf waved farewell to the Dakota and turned his prow downstream. The current caught him in its grasp and sped him swiftly along, a strong man paddling fast toward the waters of the Misi Sipi.

The Tiger

Even at a distance it was clear that the wreck of the *Tiger* had been accomplished at the hands of men and not the sea. Only the caravel's mainmast remained and both the forecastle and the afterdeck had been torn away, as had the entire upper half of the ship. The *Tiger* had been beached and lay on its side with the stones of its ballast hauled out and piled by the shore. Two-thirds of it had been shorn away, leaving the hull only the height of a man's head.

"What have you done with my ship?!" Captain Cabeza roared when at last his barge came swirling crazily through the surf to crash on the beach. The raft splintered with the impact, tossing men into the surf as if they were dolls. The warhorse Montoya kicked free, narrowly avoiding a broken leg as it bellied beyond the broken timbers in the waves.

"It was Captain Sincid's doing!" cried Akmed, the shepherd who had lost half of a hand to the slaver's axe. "He is rebuilding the ship."

"Captain Sincid? Where is Mendaña?"

Akmed looked uncertain at this. He shrugged and held out what should have been two hands. "Dead."

"And where is Sincid? Where are the men?" Captain Cabeza glanced wildly about the beach, unable to believe his eyes. First the good fortune of finding his ship and then the fools had taken it upon themselves to destroy it!

"They've gone to trade with the Indios," Akmed said. "They left me here to guard the ship."

Akmed had been left behind with a rusty saber and orders to keep any wandering Indians at bay, although most were back at their town in the parley with Captain Sincid. Yet his worth as a guard was futile once Cabeza's starving men spied an open barrel of salt pork, and also one brimming with fresh-baked biscuits. They swarmed over the barrels, threatening to stave in even more when Cabeza raged among them waving his sword. "Just one, just one!" he cried. "Share out what you have and save the rest for rationing."

Along with the precious supply of food were ten barrels of the gunpowder which had been loaded aboard at Hispaniola. Narváez had been able to carry only a few casks of it on his expedition inland.

After every man had eaten, Cabeza put them to work scraping the rust from their weapons and sharpening them as best they could with stones from the beach. He still had 39 men along with Willow and the dog, Dragón, but all were half dead from months of hunger and disease. Akmed told him that Sincid had a company of 17 well-armed men in good health, thanks to trading with the Indians for their maize.

"What has he been trading?" Cabeza asked.

"Nails, my lord."

"Nails? What could the Indios possibly want with nails?"

"It is the iron, my lord. They have never seen the like of it and they crave it as much as we crave gold."

This and the destruction of the ship remained a mystery for the rest of the day and into the next afternoon. Both the foremast and mizzenmast had been sawed away, leaving only the mainmast. The *Tiger's* sails were lying in disarray on the beach and its ribs stood stark above the deck where the upper part of the hull had been removed.

"What madness is Sincid planning?" Cabeza muttered to himself over the fire that night as he huddled among his men on the beach.

To this, no one responded, not even Akmed. But sitting at Akmed's side with Dragón lying to her left, Willow could not help but believe that he was keeping a secret. He was no longer the cocky bravo she'd known in Morocco, nor even the surly slave she'd encountered again on the shores of Florida. He had grown quiet, apprehensive, and prone to quick starts with darting eyes.

"Woulds't thou speak with me?" she asked quietly.

Akmed gave her a cautious look. "I would gladly lay with thee, princess, but speak? No, not if I wish to keep my tongue."

"And why is that?"

"It is yet to be seen who'll take the upper hand, your lord Cabeza or Captain Sincid, and I've learned that one should not bet against him. He has made friends of the Indios and even now could be coming against us with an army in the hundreds. They call themselves the Mauvilans and have a large town nearby with numbers beyond count."

"A town? Like Sevilla?"

"Nay, not even like our own home of Badis with its walls of stone and mud bricks. They live in houses fashioned of wood with thatched roofs. There are hundreds of them beneath a tall hill crowned by a temple where their priests hold forth. The town itself is surrounded by a wall of sharpened trees. It's a tall palisade that could not withstand a cannon, yet only a fool would attempt to storm it, for there are five thousand of them, at least! They are farmers, with vast fields of a grain they call maize, yet every man among them is a warrior, guarding every kernel of what they grow."

"Why have they not come against you?" she wondered. "You are so few, they could easily take what they want."

Akmed shrugged. "Captain Sincid has bedazzled them with gunpowder, making fireworks to awe them. He set off two bombs on the beach when a thousand of their warriors first came upon us and they ran off as if the lord of thunder himself was among them. They think he is a spirit of the fire."

"A magician."

"Aye, even a sorcerer. But seeing their numbers, Sincid resolved to trade with the Indios, rather than attempting an attack, and praise Allah, that has served us well so far."

Willow thought of the Indians they had encountered in the forests of Florida. At best there had been two-hundred of them quelled by the flaying swords of the conquistadors. But facing a thousand such warriors would mean certain death and she had little faith in the diplomacy of Captain Sincid.

Yet the next day they heard the sound of trumpets and drums in the forest and then the movement of many feet and voices. Willow saw flashes of bright colors through the trees - reds, yellows, blue and white - and then the colors were revealed to be the feathered headpieces of an entourage trailing Sincid and his men through the forest. Behind them, dressed in rough-spun cotton came a long straggle of men, women and children.

The trumpets were revealed to be conch shells, which continued to blare as the serpent of Spaniards and Indians wound its way along the beach to where Captain Cabeza stood waiting, backed by every man at arms who was able to stand. The captain had fury written on his face as if his head might burst from its pressure, but as the crowd drew near, Sincid greeted him like an old friend.

"God's grace it's good to see you captain, for as you can see we need every man we can muster," he cried, backed by hundreds of Indians.

With so many eyes upon him, Cabeza swallowed his rage and beckoned Sincid to join him behind the shelter of the beached ship where a long conversation ensued in low tones.

But as for the Mauvilans, their hubbub died to a murmur as they reached the shore, gaping in awe at the apparition on the beach where Willow and Dragón stood alongside the destrier, Montoya. Slowly, they approached en masse and when they were only a few footsteps away, Willow raised her palm for them to stop. Dragón had begun growling and baring his fangs.

"Hold!" she cried, yet it was all she could do to control him as the Indians pushed closer.

With a whoop, Croen sprang out in front of her, spreading his arms and driving the crowd back before the dog leapt among them. "Get back, ye mad eejits!" he cried. "Get back, fools!"

But the crowd needed no encouragement for by now Dragón was raging at the end of Willow's leash and he was a terrifying sight in the best of circumstances.

"They've never seen the like of a horse before, nor a dog like Dragón, nor even a blackie like thee," Croen said as the crowd retreated. The people stood talking in astonishment among themselves, pointing and gesticulating. One fixed an arrow to his bow, but was dissuaded by an ornately plumed man who was clearly their leader.

"God help them if they killed the captain's horse!" Willow cried, relieved that the crowd had retreated to a safe distance.

"Amen to that. No need to provoke our struttin' rooster," Croen replied in a low growl.

"Truly, the captain would go up like a fire in a hay barn. But think on it: our ship and its hairy men must seem a marvel to these people. That and the horse."

"Aye, it would be like my people seeing an elephant for the first time."

"Are there no elephants in Eire?"

"Nay, nor camels. Nor snakes."

Soon enough, the novelty of the horse, the dog and Willow's dark skin passed and the Indians began laying basket after basket of maize by the shore, after which many took to the water, frolicking in the waves. What a happy people, Willow thought, wishing that she, too, had the courage to venture into the sea.

As for Sincid's men, they seemed anything but comforted to find the ragged remnants of Pánfilo de Narváez's army awaiting them on the beach. Cabeza's men had starved to the point of death, yet they had also been toughened by their long march through Florida and many of their swords were still stained with blood. Willow took satisfaction in knowing that they looked as haggard and dangerous as demons. Sincid's men looked soft by comparison; they had been well fed and it was clear that they were intimate with many of the Indian women, who fawned about them, begging for presents.

The women, of course, did not escape the attention of Cabeza's men, for many of them were beauties to move the heart of a poet with their thick hair streaming over bared breasts and down to their waists. For the first time in months Willow was grateful to have the men's eyes elsewhere, for all this time she had depended on the wrath of Dragón and the captain for protection against them. It was true, many of them thought of her now as a sister, or even a daughter, but men being men, she had never strayed from Dragón's side through all of their troubles.

In time, Sincid and Cabeza emerged from behind the hulk of the *Tiger*. Sincid wore a smile, though his eyes were still cold as a lizard, while Cabeza came forward with a resigned scowl.

Then a strange ceremony ensued as the Indians rushed forward with their baskets of maize and were rewarded in turn with the gift of a single nail, these being spikes as long as a man's ring finger and half as thick.

"What in the hell's privy is this?" muttered a sailor standing alongside Willow and Croen.

"Ah, Sincid has pulled the nails from the upper hull of the ship and is paying for the corn," Croen replied.

"But a nail? A simple nail? Of what use could it be?"

"Perhaps they wish to build a palace."

Then Willow recalled her youth in Azemmour, where iron was a precious thing among the poor.

"I see it now," she said. "These people have no iron, and a spike might serve many purposes. It could be used to cut stone or punch leather. It could even serve as a knife."

"Or a weapon, I suppose. A fine tip for their arrows to pierce a Spaniard's hide."

"More than that, they might think the spikes are magical."

"Certainly," Croen said, nodding. "Like the nails which pinned our Redeemer to the cross. I glean that these are a holy people, despite their appearance! And consider this: a nail has a usefulness, whereas gold is of no use at all except to glimmer. And yet what do we value?"

"Thou art wise, Croen, and if it were in my power I would gift you with a pot of nails to make your fortune."

Croen gave a low laugh. "Yes, princess, I think that would make me king of these Indios."

That evening the Mauvilans prepared a feast, roasting ears of maize in a pit of coals along with a fat stag which had been taken while browsing in their fields. While the soldiers of Spain cavorted with the Indian women and played a rough ball game on the beach, captains Sincid and Cabeza met by a campfire in the woods. Fearing to mingle with the milling conquistadors and Indians, Willow sat in the shadow beyond the fire with Dragón lying by her side.

Captain Cabeza glared at Sincid, looking as if he longed to strangle the slaver. "Tell me again what madness led you to destroy the ship," he said in a low growl.

Sincid smiled in return, but even the red glow of the fire could not conceal the coldness in his eyes.

"As I have struggled to make you understand, sir, I have not destroyed the ship. I have made it equal to our mission."

"Ah, yes. The gold, the riches of Cibola," Cabeza sneered. "And you have found, what? Only the corn of the Indios and the frolics of their women. And now, death on these shores with all of us marooned."

Cabeza spat into the fire, beyond which a tussle had broken out on the beach where a Spaniard had been clubbed in the ball game. "Look at this!"

A mixture of disgust and resignation settled on Sincid's face as he stared at Cabeza. "Captain, you give up too easily, for I have indeed found Cibola, or at least the word of it, and this ship is reborn to take us there."

"Reborn?"

"Aye, as a galley."

"A galley."

"Aye, to take us upriver where there thrives a golden empire, perhaps as rich as that of Peru or the Mexicas. Perhaps even richer," Sincid said, eager now to command Cabeza's interest.

Sincid said that he and Mendaña's squadron had sailed the coast of Florida for two months, seeking signs of the conquistador's expedition or a bay where they might await their return.

"Our pilots were lying fools. They knew nothing of the coast and in time Capitão Mendaña commanded me to sail to Cuba in the brigantine, bringing messages home and seeking supplies. But I did not wish to leave, so I joined the crew of the *Tiger* with a few of my men, not wishing to forsake my share of riches.

"But time passed and still we could not find you, so Mendaña resolved to sail for Cuba while the sea was yet calm enough for sailing. He planned to return with fresh supplies in the spring. Ah, but then we were caught in a gale that blew for three days, tossing us like a wood chip on the waters and one morning we woke to find the fleet gone and the wind blowing hard toward a lee shore."

"And where is Mendaña now?" Cabeza said sharply, cutting Sincid off.

"Gone! Gone in the night with the gale. It was he who took the rudder when our helmsman fell sick. We were sailing under bare poles, being tossed to our graves when I came on deck to find the captain washed overboard. It was only with the greatest difficulty that several of us seized the rudder shaft and held the ship into the wind! But it blew on and on, straight into this bay where at last the angels smiled on us through the storm. God save us, there were no rocks, no reef. Only sand met our keel when at last we were grounded just offshore beyond any hope of freeing the ship."

And then, Sincid said, an army of tattooed and painted warriors beyond count had covered the beach, hooting and yelling at the grounded ship.

"What could we do? We were only a skeleton crew with our brave captain dead and no hope of surviving such a force. As they came wading toward us through the surf I seized on a plan that saved our filthy necks."

Sincid had filled two kettles with gunpowder, lowering them with lit fuses over the side of the ship. Packed loose, the gunpowder went up in towering sheets of flame, thunder and sparks. Just then, his men had fired the culverin into the mass of oncoming warriors. It was a medieval cannon, eight feet long and narrow, firing an iron ball. Culverins had been mounted on many merchant ships in the hope of some slim protection from pirates.

"And did you kill any of them?" Cabeza asked.

"Nay, lord, we fired the cannon with a double shot of powder, yet no ball, hoping only to frighten them," Sincid replied with a look of glee lighting up his face. "And frighten them it did! They ran as if the dogs of hell and all its devils were on their heels!"

After a day spent cowering aboard the grounded ship, Sincid took command and the men began moving supplies onto the beach. It was then that a delegation of Indians arrived, this time bearing gifts.

"I didn't know what to give them in return, but their king espied some scraps of iron that had fallen off a chest and it was clear he thought of it as a great treasure."

"And for this you resolved to tear the ship asunder?"

"Nay lord, nay! It was only when our friendship with the Indios was sealed that I began seeking Cibola by signs. It was then that the vision of the galley came to me."

Sincid had found a patch of ground that was thick with clay, and with many sailors being skilled at carving bone and ivory, he asked the most talented among his crew to craft a city in the clay.

"Some of the men had been with Cortez at Tenochtitlan when the Aztecs fell, and they were eager to share what they knew. Thus, we created a masterpiece in clay, sculpting a city riven with canals and topped by pyramids. And by signs, I made the mayor of the Indios to understand that we sought such a place in the heart of this wretched land."

By now the disgust had melted from Cabeza's face, and sitting in the shadows beyond the dying fire, Willow could see that Sincid had set the hook.

"King? Mayor? Which is he?"

Sincid shrugged. "Who's to say? But he took one look at our model and knew it at once. By signs he told us that there runs a great river not far west of here, and up that river is a city as grand as the one we fashioned in the clay. A Tenochtitlan! A Cuzco! A city as rich as Napoli or Sevilla here in the new land! Captain, we have found it!"

"And gold too?"

"Yes, yes!" Sincid said excitedly. "I showed the king the ringlets of my own ears and he said by signs that there was all the gold we could carry, with a people eager to share it."

Cabeza made a face and frowned. "The Indios of Peru and Mexico were hardly eager to share their riches."

"Ah, but with the gunpowder, lord, they might be convinced to be eager. And God bless us, we have ten barrels of it."

"Yes..."

"And you see now the need for a galley? Only a galley with many oars will make it upriver."

Cabeza's eyes wandered to the wreck of the *Tiger* and it was clear even to Willow that the exposed ribs rising above the hull were meant to be oarlocks. "A caravel is hardly meant to be a galley," he muttered. "This has the look of a clam shell."

"Ah yes, it is fat-bottomed and will handle like a pig, but its belly is wide enough to carry a kingdom in gold."

"And our return?"

Sincid shrugged. "We will row to Cuba, or return here to rebuild the ship."

"And how will we do this when you have given away our nails?"

"With nails of gold, captain. Nails of gold."

The Parting

It was two more weeks before the *Tiger* was ready to sail and Willow spent much of her time cutting the sails of the ship and sewing them into a triangular lateen canvas. Captain Cabeza had argued with Sincid over the wisdom of destroying the square-rigged sails, but the slaver had prevailed.

"Have you ever heard of the feluccas which sail the Nile, captain?" Sincid argued. "They use lateen sails to tack their way upstream. Square sails are useful only for the winds of the open sea."

"And have you sailed the Nile, sir?" Cabeza replied with his usual vein of contempt.

"No, but..."

"Then how can you say that the ship will manage?"

"With forty men at the oars, captain, along with our lateen sail."

At last Cabeza was convinced. Thus, Willow occupied herself under a clump of long-leafed pines just off the beach, cutting and sewing per Sincid's instructions. From time to time her eyes caught those of Philip Garon, who had been posted to guard the beached ship, warding off villagers trying to pry more iron from the hull. The one-legged Frenchman was of little use elsewhere, but instead of watching the ship he spent much of his time glaring in Willow's direction. In his diseased mind he had come to blame Willow for the ravaging of his leg by Dragón, and then the keel-hauling which had shredded him even further.

Once, unable to avoid him on a narrow trail off the beach, he had brushed past and whispered, "You owe me a leg, darling, and I will have one of yours, but not before I make you my beast."

Willow had given him a hard shove in reply, but even with only one leg and a peg to stand on Garon stood as firm as an oak. He had been diminished by his wound, yet was still a huge man and his cow face and thick lips made him seem even larger.

Thus, Willow lived in fear beneath his gaze, knowing that only Dragón stood before her and his grasp, for she suspected there were few among the hard-bitten conquistadors who would come to her aid if he should try raping her. Only the captain, Croen and Akmed.

She had seen little of Croen during their time on the beach, but a friendship blossomed with Akmed, who came to her as a bee seeks a flower. They sat together speaking in Arabic of their lost town and the foibles of their people, and sometimes they prayed together, bowing to the east where Mecca must surely lie, somewhere far beyond the sea.

"Inshallah. It feels good to pray," he said, one day after they had repeated their devotions.

"Yes."

Willow eyed Akmed, whose face was pure with the light of their morning prayer. She had never imagined him to be inclined to pray, and indeed, he had been a shirker back in Badis. But slavery had changed him. Much of the rascal had been drained from Akmed's spirit after Sincid severed his hand and he had been cowed even further during his time as a galley slave under Sincid's whip. In fact, Willow thought, it was a wonder that he lived at all, considering that many weakened men had succumbed to disease in Hispaniola and Cuba.

But Akmed had been spared from starvation and the horrors of the march through Florida and still had the strength Allah gave to all young men. And yet Willow wondered if his transformation was merely a show.

"Why dost thou sit with me when there are so many pretty maidens among the Indios?" she asked one day.

"Making eyes at a pretty woman is a fine thing, yet speaking to one is far better," he replied. "I cannot talk with any of them, and what would we speak of if we could?"

"But they are eager, and thou art handsome." Willow blushed, for it had been a bold thing to say. An admission.

"I desire more than their caresses," he said with a wry smile. "Besides, the Indio women want presents for their favors, and I have none to give. But you... I can give you my words, and yours are like honey to me."

"Thou art a flirt and a romancer," she teased.

"Yes, but it is pleasant to sit and talk, is it not?"

Willow agreed that it was, and though Dragón had growled at first with Akmed's intrusion, he had grown easy with his company. The three of them sat in the sand, enjoying a mild breeze under the sun.

Across the way, Garon flapped his tongue like that of a lizard in their direction.

"I will kill that man," Akmed said coolly.

"Stay away from him. Don't let him spoil our time together." Willow reached out a finger and turned Akmed's chin in her direction. Their eyes met and she knew that she was lost.

And so, it seemed, was Croen.

Two days before the ship was to leave, Croen wandered up the beach with a tall Indian woman by his side. She was much older than the maidens who mingled among the conquistadors and sailors, yet she had a noble bearing, fine looks that had withstood her years, and eyes that sized up Willow at a glance as being no threat.

"I want ye to meet someone," Croen said, sounding a trifle nervous. "This is Nemi. I think her name means some sort of flower or plant. She's a widow, like me."

"Ah, she seems a fine woman," Willow said politely. "Nemi," she addressed the woman, nodding. Nemi nodded in return, a bemused smile crossing her lips. She said a word back to her and Willow somehow knew that she had addressed her as "daughter."

Croen put his arm around her and pulled her giggling shyly to his side. "We're betrothed," he said.

"Betrothed?"

"Aye. I made her to understand my intentions and she agreed. More to that, her family agreed, for no man can be accepted without the consent of the family. Her father's as old as time itself, and Jesus knows I'm an old clam, but he gave his consent."

"No! What will Captain Cabeza say? He will never agree to take her with us."

"Ah, no. Tha's what I came to tell ye. I'm nay goin' with ye."

Willow's head reeled as Croen stared to the sand with Nemi leaning into him. He had spoken once before of running away to join the Indians when they reached the New World, yet she had always assumed it was idle talk. But now it seemed beyond belief that she might lose him on this distant shore.

"Not going with us! But you'll be hung as a deserter, or more likely dragged to the ship in chains, for it's said we'll need every man where we're going."

"Aye, but not an old man. I've already spoken with the captain and he's granted my wish," Croen replied. "I made the case that I'm of little use to his expedition, being one more mouth to feed. He's leaving me here to guard the timbers on the beach, should he and the men come back to rebuild the ship."

"But you'll be alone among these people! They are not our kind."

"Our kind? Murderers dressed in steel and helmets? Ah, the Indios are not a bad sort compared to the lot of us. I find them quite merry and it's pleasant to have Nemi for company. She's already taught me a few words and we've grown cozy, if you catch my meaning. I hope to preach the Gospel to them, once I learn their language. What I remember of it, that is."

"But thou planned to be a prince of Dublin."

Croen gave a snort. "Better to be a fisherman with a good woman and a full belly here than perish as a beggar in the gutters of Dublin, for I doubt the captains will find the gold they seek and my share of it would be feeble at best. His lordship is leaving me the skiff and I told Nemi's father that I have skills as a fish-slayer. Aye, I presented him with a fat tuna for a dowry! Once I give these people something besides corn to eat they'll love me sure enough."

That night, Willow sobbed herself to sleep as she lay in her hammock, stretched between two palms on the beach with Dragón dozing on the sand below her. The thought of losing Croen had torn her heart out by its roots, yet she could not stay behind with him, for the captain had told her that she was needed to command Dragón on the journey ahead.

The next day, Akmed came to sit beside her again as she sat sewing the lateen sail.

"As salaam alaikum," he said, peace be with you.

Willow eyes were solemn and her face tight-lipped as she looked up at him. Without a word, she rose and led him down the beach to the shelter of a windswept thicket of brush commanding a bluff. Then, spreading a length of canvas on the sand beneath the sun, she laid herself down with her heart pounding and her breath growing rapid and shallow. Slowly, she lifted her skirt, caressing her thighs as the hem rose higher.

She took him by the hand, and pulled him to her. Her eyes spoke the words - *take me* - as she arched her back with her hair streaming behind her on the sailcloth. The day was hot and still beneath the blinding sun.

Now was the time, she thought. Now was the time to surrender all that she had been to this new life, this new land. All that she had been was gone forever. There was no going back. The words trembled on her lips and then: "Come lay with me..."

A fire blazed in Akmed's eyes as he dropped his breeches, and glancing up, Willow could see that her lover was more than ready.

The Fisherman's Tale

Many towns came and went along the river as Wolf paddled south, and yet it seemed as if it was a river of ghosts.

Heading south along the Misi Sipi he passed mounds along the river that had been raised long ago by thousands of hands carrying baskets of earth beyond count. Once, these mounds had stood at the center of large towns surrounded by fields of maize, beans, sunflowers, tobacco and squash. The largest towns served trade routes that ran in every direction: from the great lakes of the north, to the plains and mountains of the west, to the farming towns of the east, and down the river to the southern sea.

Several times Wolf stepped from his canoe to wander through the ruins of an abandoned town, finding its avenues, fields, plazas and mounds grown thick with trees and the remnants of homes gone to rot.

Yet in many places, the descendants of the mound builders still lived among the earth pyramids, with hundreds living in villages defended by high palisades. Even so, Wolf suspected that these were a lesser people than their ancestors.

At first he traveled by night along the river, leery of the many tribes that came and went with the current. But curiosity overcame his fears once he discovered that there were many traders paddling up and down the Misi Sipi. He was just one more who could expect a welcome in the river towns, where his cargo of copper and pipestone was eagerly sought. Even his canoe seemed a wonder to those he encountered, for most of the river people traveled in clumsy dugouts and atop barges of timbers lashed together, whereas Wolf's canoe was as sleek as an otter in the muddy current.

By now the Misi Sipi had grown the width of many long bow shots. At times it boiled with a devastating current and rapids that he barely survived. Great trees tumbled like grasping monsters in the current or sprang from the river's depths, their shattered limbs stabbing at his canoe. There were powerful eddies at the bends in the river and whirlpools that threatened to suck him under. Other times, enormous geysers spouted with the eruption of gases from beneath the river bottom. Heavy winds swept up and down the river, swirling the prow of his canoe around as if it were the whirling fan of a maple seed. At times Wolf flailed at the dark water with all his strength, narrowly missing a timber jam or a jumble of barely glimpsed rocks that threatened his death. Often, he ran his canoe aground on sand bars at mid-river and watched as the sky grew dark with migrating birds. Many of the sand bars provided his refuge at night as he slept beneath the shelter of his canoe.

Once, he paddled past two immense figures with hideous faces carved into a cliff overlooking the river. They were of two monstrous beings, neither man nor beast, but perhaps creatures of the underworld which had clawed their way to the surface, only to be locked in stone for many lifetimes. He lowered his head as he paddled beneath their stern gaze, thinking that perhaps they were sentinels, warning of the way ahead. Looking back over his shoulder, it appeared as if the stone faces were watching him.

One day he came to a medium-sized town standing atop a bluff overlooking the river. As with many others, it was defended by a high wall of sharpened pines, beneath which ran a muddy lane down the hill from its heights. An old man stood at the bottom of the lane, casting a net from his perch atop a levy of rocks and Wolf stopped to talk. For once, he did not have to speak in the language of hand signs, for the old man had spent his childhood among the Dakotas. He had been captured as a boy while his people were hunting along the river and had been carried downstream into slavery. In time, he had married into the family of his captors and was now a member of their clan.

Wolf offered to share a pipe in return for one of his fish, and after the gifts were made the two of them sat by the river and talked.

"What came of those who built the mounds?" Wolf asked, pointing across the river where a lone hill rose in a conical shape, crowned by several trees.

"Ah, they are still here," the fisherman said, waving to the town above the river. "They are not what they once were, but they are still here. Some of their towns prospered even into the time of my own grandfather; they still had temples atop their mounds, They still had priests."

"Priests? I do not know this word."

The old man looked at him as if he were a simpleton. "Men who beg the spirits for rain, corn and infants."

"Shamans."

"Yes."

He pointed across the river. "That place over there was once the home of more people than the leaves on a tall tree. It took a full day to walk across their fields."

"If their bellies were full, then why did they leave?"

"Eh, it was not for lack of fertility, for the soil along this river is as rich as Grandmother Earth can make it. But a time came when the maize would not grow. Perhaps it was a time of drought or disease or years of darkness and cold. Perhaps the soil lost its strength. Perhaps it was all of that at once! But there were many mouths to feed with fewer crops each year, and those who lived here lost hope. Their priests and chieftains tried to hold them with threats of force and cruelty. But like a flooding river, a starving people cannot be contained, and there were revolts in towns all along the river. And then..." he raised his hands in resignation, "people left and started over."

He added that when the towns of the mound builders died, so too did their beliefs, along with the practice of piling baskets of earth for year after year on behalf of their priests.

Even the people of the northern lakes had heard of the mound builders, for they were only a few lifetimes in the past and stories of them were still told around the winter fires. The People of the Mounds had traded for copper with the miners of Minong, and also for furs from the Ojibwe. Now, paddling through their lands and walking through their empty villages brought the old stories to life for Wolf, along with a reverence for what had slipped away.

"It is strange to walk in their footsteps," Wolf said after the fisherman had concluded his tale. "Tell me, father, are these places haunted?"

"Eh, yes," the old man grunted, "sorrow visited many of these towns. Those who disturb their graves risk being devoured."

Wolf nodded. This was no surprise, for the world was filled with spirits and ghosts. One could hear them whispering in the night or see their faces drawn in the knots of trees, the pattern of waves, and the flight of clouds.

"Brother, you have seen many things along this river," Wolf said.

"Yes, even ghosts."

"Perhaps you can tell me of an animal I seek."

"Perhaps." The old man hauled in his net, which had rested limp in the water as they spoke, yet now revealed a catfish as long as his arm.

"It is called the sunktanka," Wolf said, repeating the description of the quizzical beast. "It is said to live among a people known as the Adai."

"I have not heard of them, nor of this animal," the old man replied, wrestling with the catfish, which slipped and careened in his hands. "But perhaps you will find what you seek at the Great Mound of the Bird Men."

"The Bird Men," Wolf repeated, searching his memory. Something about them was familiar, yet he could not grasp it. "Are they near?"

The fisherman chuckled. "Yes, very near, yet very far. The Bird Men are long dead, though their Great Mound lives on. Once, long ago, they stood atop their mound dressed in the wings and feathers of eagles, hoping to reach the sky. Yet now all of them lie in their graves, long dead, barely remembered."

"How then may I speak with them?"

"Oh, not them, but you will find the grandsons of their grandsons among those who live in the shadow of the Great Mound. They are a people called the Cahokia and only a small band of them live there. They might know of the Adai and the animal you seek, for once the Great Mound stood over a town of people beyond count. It was the largest town on all of the Misi Sipi and traders traveled there from the ends of the earth to drape their people in gifts."

"Gifts?"

"Yes, of copper, shells, furs, feathers, dyes, pottery and slaves. Anything a people could desire! If anyone will know of your sunktanka, perhaps they will remember."

"Thank you father," Wolf said, presenting a handful of tobacco in gratitude. "You have done me a great favor. Can you tell me where I might find these people?"

The fisherman accepted the gift and smiled. "It is not far, a day's paddle at most," he said. "Soon, you will come to Pekitunoui, the great river of the Mandans, which flows from the west. Beware its violence! You must pass by as far away as possible. Then, look for what appears to be a mountain just beyond the marriage of the rivers. It is the Great Mound and the Cahokia people live in its shadow. Powerful spirits still dwell there. Perhaps they will help you."

"As tall as a mountain? Why was such a thing made?"

The old man chuckled. "Do you see this land, brother? It is low and flat for as far as you can see. This river valley is the same for as far as a bird can fly in three days! In a land without hills, what man does not wish to touch the sky? That is why the mounds were built, brother. Only that."

Wolf camped on a sandbar amid a tangle of driftwood that night. He was grateful for the old man's fish, for his own attempts at fishing had been thwarted by the muddy water of the river. Many times he stood in his canoe, peering into the river with his fishing spear poised to strike, only to find that he could see nothing moving beneath the murk of the Misi Sipi, which ran dark brown, heavy with mud and silt. Yet he knew that the river was filled with delicious catfish bearing long whiskers with which they probed the river bottom, and he resolved to trade some of his goods for a net at the next village he came upon.

The next morning he woke to find himself soaked with the morning dew, and after eating a handful of the dried buffalo that Lone Dog's people had given him, he pushed on with his leathers still wet and chilled.

Wolf had not slept well that night. The immensity of the river only served to make Wabeno's quest seem hopeless and foolish. He felt lost amid its current, as if he were no more than a leaf, and the river seemed to have no end. Those he met in the towns along the way scoffed when he said he hoped to reach the Great Salt Water to the south, claiming that the river ended in a maze of swamps that crawled with monsters, barring the way to the sea. He began to doubt that he would find the Adai people, and as for the sunktanka, perhaps it was only a make-believe beast of the sort that lived in stories meant to amuse children. Wabeno had dreamt of the beast before hearing of it from Red Eagle, but did that make it any more real than the creatures that walked the stars?

So it was with a glum heart that Wolf set off, knowing that each paddle stroke was taking him further from home. At mid-day he heard a roaring ahead and saw a long sandbar jutting almost a third of the way across the river. The sandbar was piled high with driftwood and the trunks of great trees that were strewn with eagles and gulls minding the river. Wolf paddled his canoe to the eastern bank of the Misi Sipi in order to skirt a barrage of whitecaps and watched agog as an island of interwoven tree trunks came swirling out of the mouth of a huge river pouring in from the west. As the island of trees swept past, whirling round in the current, it reminded him of a wolf coughing up the fur ball of a devoured animal. Surely, this was Pekitunoui, the river of the Mandans, of which the old man had spoken.

The Misi Sipi swelled in size yet again with the marriage of the new river and for a time Wolf was swept along by its stampeding current. Soon, he saw a tall, solitary hill, which even from a distance looked as if it had been fashioned by the hands of men. A waterway joined the river, running in the direction of the hill, and to his surprise it looked as if it, too, had been constructed by men. The walls of the stream were dug in an even wedge and lined with stone.

What wonder is this? Wolf thought as he left the river for the man-made stream. He had seen other canals at the ruined towns upriver, yet they had long since been choked with vegetation and he had not understood their purpose. Yet the spring floods of the Misi Sipi had managed to keep this waterway clear except for a welter of willows and reeds breaching the canal in places. Picking his way through, Wolf paddled to a field of maize beneath the vast mound. There were no Bird Men dressed as eagles waiting for him when he arrived, but there was a humble village nestled at the edge of what had once been a plaza large enough to hold tens of thousands of people, and above the village there rose an immense pyramid of earth.

The base of the pyramid was a vast bulwark of slanting earth, so large that a group of children playing on its slope looked as tiny as ants from where Wolf stood. Atop this base rose a somewhat smaller wedge of earth, but the width and height of it was still larger than any mound that Wolf had seen along the river. And atop this wedge stood the rotting posts of huge trees, which had sheltered a temple of the Bird Men's gods many lifetimes ago, yet were now eaten away by ruin.

As the old fisherman had said, the Great Mound did indeed appear as a mountain to Wolf's eyes, and he knew from talking to other river-dwellers that this, too, had been raised by tens of thousands of hands filling one basket at a time through the course of what must have been several lifetimes.

Spying him at a distance, the children began running down the mound in his direction, laughing and crying out as they ran. Hearing the ruckus, a tall man emerged from one of the huts in the village and seeing Wolf, raised his hand in greeting. Soon, Wolf was overwhelmed by children, begging for presents, and it was clear to him that traders were still welcome among the ruins.

The tall man approached and spoke a word of greeting, but Wolf could not understand him, and so they conversed with hand signs. Wolf signed that he had come to trade and the man of the village nodded his assent. Soon enough, Wolf deduced that the stranger was the head man. By signs he asked the name of his people.

"Ca-ho-ki-a," the stranger replied.

Wolf was a guest in the head man's lodge that night. It was a large abode with a tall roof of thatched reeds that sheltered three families and Wolf was impressed with how snug it seemed. He was invited to join in a meal of roasted muskrat, maize and a vegetable called goosefoot, which he had never eaten before.

But he struggled to make himself understood, for there were limits to what sign language could convey and his host was not familiar with some of the hand signals he made. The chieftain had not heard of the Adai people and was mystified by Wolf's pantomime of the sunktanka creature, laughing at his efforts. Frustrated, Wolf drew what he thought the sunktanka might look like in the clay lining the lodge, but this too brought giggles and a mystified gaze, for at best the beast looked like a female elk with the long hair of a woman on its head and tail.

Filled with the same glumness that had overwhelmed him on the river, Wolf slept on one of his host's sleeping mats that night, cheered only by the flirtatious glances of his pretty daughter, who lay on her own mat across the lodge. He considered that it would be a fine thing to invite her outside for a caress under the cover of the night, for by her looks she seemed willing. But he was not yet on easy terms with her father, and suspected that romancing his daughter might be dangerous.

Thus, he fell into an uneasy sleep, plagued with a dream of the sunktanka which looked like an elk, yet was not an elk; which raced like a deer, yet was not a deer; which had the long hair of a woman, yet was not a woman. In his dream the sunktanka sprouted the wings of the Bird Men and flew chattering like a jay over the Misi Sipi, with its eyes as blue as robin eggs.

The next day, Wolf climbed to the top of the Great Mound and sat on the ledge below its ruined temple. Fall was drawing on and with it came cool breezes and the whisper of winter. From what he had been told, he was only halfway down the river and would have to turn back now or spend the winter in the South. It was not an unpleasant thought, for often the north wind Biboon seemed fierce enough to strip a man's flesh from his bones during the long winters on Kitchi Gami. And yet for a change Wolf felt heart-sick for home and the company of friends around the fires of Boweting. He wondered what Sweet Grass was doing, and if she was happy being married. And once again, as he thought so often, he considered the fate of a man condemned to travel, with no woman to call his own.

Having no woman meant that Wolf's leathers were in a wretched state, with no skilled hands to mend them. He had worn the same breechclout since his time with the Tionontati, rinsing it frequently. But now the thin leather was in tatters and he was happy to trade a handful of pipestone for a loin cloth of cotton dyed a handsome red. That, and new doeskin leggins and a stout jerkin. With his heart lifted, he flung his old leathers into the canal, feeling as if he was a new man.

He felt even better the next day when three dugouts made their way up the canal and a company of traders hailed the village. These, he learned, were men of the Mandans.

Better still, the leader of the traders spoke a language similar to that of the Dakotas, and to Wolf's great surprise, the stranger had heard of him.

"I know of you brother!" the trader said, with his eyes widening. "Your name is spoken far up the river."

Buffalo Drum

The trader was a big man around the waist and had a broad face decked in triangular black tattoos which ran from ear to ear across his cheeks. Yet his eyes were set close together and he had a large nose, which gave him a jolly countenance. His manner was just as easy, as was that of the five traders in his group, who laughed and cavorted with the Cahokians as if they were old friends. That night, Wolf learned that their leader's name was Berek Hah Ptemde, Buffalo Drum, and that he and his companions had made this trip several times before. The traders had locks of hair that trailed in braids down to their waists and beyond. Buffalo Drum's hair was threaded with elk teeth and shells and he wore the scalps of two of his enemies among the Crow on the thong around his waist. These, Wolf learned, could be attached to his locks with resin to make his hair even longer when the occasion arose.

Buffalo Drum had spent half a moon traveling down-river from the Mandan homeland with the aim of trading razor-edged obsidian shards for shells, tobacco and other goods from the people of the lower Misi Sipi. The river of the Mandans was almost as wide as the Misi Sipi and Buffalo Drum claimed it was even more dangerous, filled with treacherous rapids, water falls and tangles of fallen timbers. After some difficulty in making himself understood, he told Wolf that he and his companions came from a large town called the Big Two Ditch Place far up the river.

"We call it this because long ago, our grandfathers dug two great ditches around the town as protection from our enemies," he said after a fashion. He added that the town stood on a rise above the dry moats, protected by a stout wall of cottonwood trunks. The perimeter of the wall bristled with the spikes of sharpened trees.

"But why?" Wolf asked, mystified as to why the Mandans would need such defenses.

"Brother, if you have been attacked by warriors beyond count, bearing shields and lances, you would understand why. We have much and the people of the plains have little. When they are hungry, they look in our direction."

Days ago, the traders had encountered Lone Dog's band wandering in search of buffalo on the plains alongside the river.

"Though the Dakota and our people are often enemies, we hailed them with news of a great herd up the river to the west," Buffalo Drum said. "They thanked us most courteously and we passed a meal with them. They said to watch for you, brother! They said you are a crazy man, searching for a deer with a woman's hair that no man has ever seen."

Wolf gave a small laugh. "I am only a trader like you, offering copper, tobacco and pipestone along the river, but my brothers among the Dakota spoke the truth. I am a crazy man and a tale-teller. I have heard of this magical deer and hope to see it. Perhaps someday I will tell stories of it."

"Perhaps even eat it?" Buffalo Drum asked slyly.

"Perhaps. It is a creature called the sunktanka."

"I do not know it." Nor had any in Buffalo Drum's band.

"Ah, perhaps it is only a legend, but it is said to live among a people called the Adai, who carry it with them as they follow the buffalo."

Recognition dawned in Buffalo Drum's eyes. "I know these people! They speak the language of the Caddo and are a small people, not many in number and very poor, with little to trade and less to eat. You would do well to beware them, lest they decide to eat you."

"You jest, brother," Wolf replied.

"Who's to say? They eat cactus in the starving time and pray for buffalo. We have traded among the Caddo people who live by the Great Salt Water and have passed through the lands of the Adai on our way. But that is far down the long trail across the plains, through the lands of the Arikara, the Pawnee and the Wichita. It is far easier to travel on the river, for when we cross the plains we must rely on slaves to carry our goods and it is wearisome to plod along with them."

A long trail across the plains? If that was so, Wolf knew that his mission was over. Walking for more than a few days was not possible with his lame foot.

"But have no worries, brother," Buffalo Drum said, as if sensing his thoughts. "You can journey to the Adai by another path, up the Red River to the south." This, he said, was a large river that joined the Misi Sipi before it reached the swamplands of the sea. "It runs to the west through the lands of the Caddo and the Adai."

"Is the river truly red?"

"No, but the canyons and dusty lands from which is flows are harsh and have been reddened by the sun. You will know the river by its taste, for it is salty."

Wolf could see that Buffalo Drum was missing the little finger on his left hand, and gazing about, he noticed that all of the Mandan traders were missing the same finger. One was missing his pointer finger as well. It was rude to bring up such a thing, but Buffalo Drum was quick to notice his interest and had a fast tongue.

"You wonder at our fingers? Know this, we are all warriors as well as traders and the loss of a finger is expected of every man among us."

Buffalo Drum said that each spring when the willow leaves reached their peak along the river by his town, the Mandans threw a bull dance which lasted four days. "Our hunters dance in the hides and heads of the buffalo in the heart of town so that summer's hunt will be one of plenty," he said. "It is a huge festival, drawing crowds beyond count, with many standing atop the lodges to view the dances, waving flags and streamers. Brother, along with those dressed as buffalo there are eagles and bears dancing to drums that rival thunder. That and a great cloud of dust which can be seen all the way to the far mountains."

"Ah, I wish I could see it!" Wolf imagined standing on an earth lodge, the size of a small hill, watching the dancers whirling below amid a crowd of thousands.

"Perhaps someday you shall. But there is more, much more. Toward the end of the bull dance, a black spirit with a hideous face comes running from the hills waving a war lance and setting all of the women and girls screaming in fright. On his head is the buffalo mask, yet he bares the long teeth of a demon. And around his waist is fastened a buffalo's tail, while before him waves a huge black cock that is as long as my arm!"

"Is he truly a spirit or a demon?" Wolf asked, though he guessed the answer.

"Many think of him as the bull spirit of the buffalo, but truly, he is only a man, painted black in shining bear grease with white stripes zig-zagging his legs. His cock has a red head and is carved of wood. It is held erect with a thong attached to his lance. But he joins in the dance and humps each dancer from behind. Brother, for an entertainment, there is none like it!"

At this, Buffalo Drum gave a hearty chuckle before remembering himself.

"Ah, but it is a sacred ceremony, very serious," he went on. "Then the buffalo spirit flees back across the prairie from which he came, yet this time with every woman and girl chasing him, laughing and screaming as they run. They pelt him with rocks, they whip him and lash him with sticks. It is a merry celebration."

"We too have festivals in my land," Wolf began, hoping to share the celebrations of the Ojibwe and the Odawa. But the Mandan had warmed to his tale and said there was yet much to tell.

"I myself have played the spirit bull and have endured the women's teasing," Buffalo Drum went on. "It is a great honor to bring down the bull for once the great cock is stripped away the woman who claims it is given a fine dress as a gift. In return, she presents the buffalo cock to the elders for the beginning of the *phok-hong* ceremony."

This, it turned out, was an ordeal meant to harden the young men of the Mandan to the extremes of endurance and the torments of excruciating pain. "When a boy is ready to become a man he must enter the great medicine lodge for four days of fasting without food or water..."

Wolf listened to Buffalo Drum's story, with the sack of his stones tightening at the telling. After four days when the young men were comatose from lack of food or water, the priests of the Mandan pinched a knot of muscle in their chests and made an incision with a double-edged obsidian knife, which had been chipped and knocked so as to make the incisions as painful as possible. Then, wooden splints were shoved through the wounds on each side of the chest and attached to long ropes of leather. Other cuts were made in the fleshy parts of the youths' knees and hips with more splints, and to these were tied thongs bearing the heavy skulls of buffalo, elk or bears.

Then, each youth was lifted by the ropes to the rafters of the lodge to hang for more than a man's height above the dirt floor, suspended by the splints through his chest, with the animal skulls dangling below him. None was expected to cry out if he wished to be considered a warrior.

"Ah, but even then it is not over," Buffalo Drum went on. "For then poles are used to spin the men about as they hang, faster and faster, spinning, spinning, spinning until many finally do cry out in their pain, or faint as if dead! Then they are lowered to the floor and the chest splints are removed."

Yet even then the ordeal was not done, for after this the would-be warriors were dragged out into the plaza where thousands stood watching, to be dragged around and around in circles by runners as if on a race track until the splints and thongs holding the skulls from their knees and sides ripped clean through their flesh.

"This you see is not muscle, but mere flesh and skin," Buffalo Drum said, "so there is no great harm to the warrior. If the flesh fails to tear, the youth must wait alone on the prairie until his wound rots away, for the splint cannot be removed by hand."

He added that there was little blood lost in the ceremony, owing to the days of thirst and fasting. Upon the *phok-hong's* completion, most of the new warriors arose as if their ordeal was of little concern and held out their left hand to have their little finger sliced away with an axe. "Those who are especially warlike have the pointer finger removed as well so that only two fingers and a thumb remain on their hands."

"But what good can come of this?" Wolf asked. He had heard of the hand mutilations of the Haudenosaunee, yet that practice of clipping fingers and thumbs was done to humiliate their captives and slaves.

"It is to show that the only fingers they value are the two that are used to fire an arrow."

"That is a fierce tale, brother, but I would not make a good Mandan warrior if that is the way to it," Wolf said, grimacing at the thought. "I am better suited as a trader and a story teller and will remember your words until I lay in my grave. I will tell it around the fires of my own people, though I think they will not believe it."

At this Buffalo Drum laughed. "Truly brother, for if you were a warrior of my people you would have this."

Parting the thongs of his leather jerkin he revealed two jagged and puckered scars riven like lightning bolts across the top of his chest.

The Swamplands

At last the *Tiger* was ready to sail with its hull reduced by two-thirds and its protruding ribs fitted with oarlocks. The oars themselves had been milled by hand from the forest of pines ranging along the shoreline. The pines also provided the rollers atop which the ship was careened from the beach, with every soldier and sailor standing waist-deep in the surf, pulling at a rope.

Captain Sincid had predicted that the newly-wrought galley would handle like a pig, but it performed well enough in the waves, certainly far better than the raft that Captain Cabeza and his men had arrived on. All of the ballast stones had been removed from the hold, which had been dried and tarred with a pitch made of pine sap. Of great surprise was the discovery of a medieval cannon at the bottom of the hold, which had been abandoned there as part of the ballast. It was an ornate and ancient bronze beast, perhaps a century old, colored a blue-green with the passage of time. The signet of the Crown of Castille was stamped on its breach, along with the name of King Joan II el Gran. On its rump lay a sculpted turtle and the legend, *La Tortuga*. As a weapon it was too large to be useful on the open sea, since the recoil of its discharge would kick any ship to splinters, yet Captain Cabeza decided to bring it along in the event that the siege of an Indian city might be necessary. Around it stood the ten barrels of gunpowder shipped from Hispaniola.

More than that, the *Tiger* was well-provisioned with weapons. A score of crossbows packed in whale grease had been found in the ship's hold, along with hundreds of quarrel and tricot bolts. That, and bundles of ten-foot-long pikes and a barrel packed with swords. Best of all, the eyes of Cabeza's musketeers had lit up at the sight of the *Tiger's* arquebus with its supporting pole - a large-bore musket that verged on being a small cannon. Their enthusiasm dimmed, however, on finding only four matchlock muskets in the stores.

Crowded amid the store of weapons, barrels and hundreds of baskets of corn, beans and squash were fifty-eight men, twelve women, the stallion Montoya and the fretting dog, Dragón. Of the women, eleven had been taken from the village, who thought they were going on a romp when they climbed aboard the *Tiger*, not knowing that they would never return home. Soon enough they began keening and crying, gesturing toward their rapidly fleeting homeland, bound for a grim life as slaves of the Spaniards.

The shore was empty of Croen, and Willow thought wistfully that she had barely said goodbye to him. He had seen the women piling aboard the ship and had fled to the forest, fearing the wrath of his new people once the kidnapping had been discovered. He had waved to her from a clump of trees off the beach before disappearing into their darkness.

"Farewell Croen!" she called in vain to the dwindling shore. "Good fortune, prince of Eire!"

The *Tiger* cleared the bay, reaching a calm sea. Willow noted with some satisfaction that the lateen sail she had labored so hard to sew was driving the galley through the waves with not a single man needed to pull its forty oars. West they sped, on to the great river the Indians had spoken of and the rich cities beyond.

She was no longer the meek serving girl of before, as comfortable as a cat in the house of a Moroccan noble. Nor had she grown as rough and coarse as the soldiers who had been her constant companions for months of misery. She was somewhere in between, toughened by her ordeals, yet still remembering how her mother had maintained the grace of a woman even during the famine of Azemmour when they had eaten rats to survive. But there was no denying that she had changed. She had lost the well-rounded breasts that her mother had bequeathed her; her body was lean and hard-muscled now from tramping the jungles of Florida and her will had grown strident, even demanding. To her surprise, she had grown accustomed to ordering the men about as a result of handling Dragón for so long. The men accepted her chiding and commands good-naturedly, for she was their sister now, and like them, a warrior.

Yet an empty space had grown in Willow's heart the further they pushed into the New World. She felt rootless, lost, aching with the need for a home. In a way, Croen had been her home, and now the last of him was falling away at the stern of the ship. Ahead, she was certain, lay only death.

Prior to their departure, Willow had requested an audience with Captain Cabeza, speaking a few words into his ear. He in turn had spoken to Sincid, who now insisted on being called captain. The root of the matter was the Frenchman, Philip Garon, who continued to stare at Willow with his wide eyes and cow face as if he were in fact, a cow, gazing in stupefaction from its pasture. Garon was posted to the stern of the ship and warned to stay away from Willow, whose post was at the bow with Montoya and the dog. He was ordered to keep his distance, but he had been told as much before and had ignored the order. Sometimes, he came drifting her way like a ghost, gazing in stupefaction, as if he had no more sense than a simpleton. Willow had screamed at him on one occasion, threatening to sic Dragón on him, but still he came floating alongside her at odd moments, gimping with his peg leg and its leather truss. She had taken to avoiding his eyes, and yet could sometimes feel them burning in her direction. The man was obsessed with her, and more than once, she itched to seize a crossbow with murder in her heart. If anyone needed killing, she thought, it was Philip Garon.

As for Akmed, he too had changed since the day they'd left Morocco. He had been spared starvation in Florida, having stayed with the ship, and now he was two hands taller since leaving home. He had grown a beard and a mustache and his hair flowed down his back, rendering him even more handsome than the flirt he'd been in Badis. He was truly a man now, Willow thought, remembering how he had rammed her until she gasped for breath. Her mother had told her that the first time would hurt, but instead she had felt a great release, as if the act had driven all the cares and worries flooding from her body, filling her with something like ecstasy. They had been together only once, but Willow yearned to lay with him again.

Alas, there had been no chance for intimacy in the final days leading up to the launch of the ship. At best, she and Akmed had crept a short way down the beach to pray together. The Christian soldiers did not seem to care that two followers of Islam were among them; they had their own ceremony each night on the beach with a priest holding Mass.

It was on one of these occasions that Akmed told her the fate of *Capitão* Mendaña.

"Mendaña avowed that he would take the ship back to Cuba with the fleet, but Sincid kept whining that we should push on along the coast in search of treasure," Akmed said. "He seemed civil enough, but I could see that he was angered by Capitão Mendaña's rebuff. In time, they had some heated words, but Mendaña was firm and the matter seemed settled.

"Then one night the pilot fell ill from the shitting sickness and Capitão Mendaña took a turn at the tiller. I was sleeping on the deck not far from the captain when I heard the thump of Garon's wooden leg. He approached the captain with a tot of brandy. The night was chill and a north wind was blowing. Garon offered the cup, saying it would help to warm him. Certainly, the captain must have had suspicions, but how was he to know that the Frenchman and Sincid were in league against him? He took the cup, giving thanks and after his first sip, Garon slipped a cord over his neck and strangled him as if he was no more than a doll!

"I was about to leap to the captain's aid when Sincid came slithering like a snake in the darkness past where I lay. By the light of the stars I could see that he had a long dagger in his hand. Ah! I did not dare to move then, nor sound the alarm, for he would have skewered me like a pig, I'm sure of it! But in a trice he pierced Capitão Mendaña's belly for good measure and the two of them tossed him into the sea."

"But how did they explain it?" Willow asked. "A man does not simply disappear unless the sea is bucking like a horse."

"When the men awoke it was Sincid at the tiller and he professed ignorance of the captain's disappearance. Then Garon came forward and said he had felt the ship rocking in the night, as if it had struck a sandbar. He said that perhaps the captain fell overboard while taking a piss, though none of the crew believed him, for they loved the captain and knew he was wise to every whisper of the sea. But who among us could deny it in the face of the blackguards' evil looks and the swords at their belts? By then, the ship had turned north, sailing for half the night away from the fleet."

Akmed had kept his secret, not even whispering it among the crew, but Willow lost no time in telling the tale to Captain Cabeza, who only grunted and did not look the least bit surprised. "It is an interesting story and

I thank you for it," he muttered, "but it is the tattling of a galley slave and whether there has been a murder or not, we need the Portuguese where we're going."

"But sir, should you not watch your own back?"

At this Cabeza raised an eyebrow and scoffed. "Captain Sincid knows his place," he said simply.

The *Tiger* sailed along the coast for two days, finding nothing of the great river that the Mauvilans had spoken of. Instead, the coast was honeycombed with swamps and rivulets, yet with currents of fresh water flowing far out to sea. If Croen had been with them, he could have told them that they had encountered a delta, likened to a web of streams through the swamps that made up the outstretched fingers of the Mississippi. But Captain Sincid knew nothing of such things, having sailed only among the ports of the western Mediterranean, while Captain Cabeza was a military man who was ignorant of the sea.

So it was that the galley began a series of forays into the swamps draining into the gulf, hoping to discover the great river leading inland. Time and again the oarsmen put their backs into plowing their way up a likely channel, only to find the way blocked by a sandbar or a barricade of sunken trees. The swamps were filled with a fog of mosquitoes and biting insects. Willow was grateful to have a cotton robe traded from the Indians, which she wrapped around herself until only her eyes peered out upon the storm of bugs. Huge live oaks gathered on the swampy shores, dripping with ghostly, mite-ridden strands of vegetation, as if they were giants bent on grasping the ship in the night and overcoming it with spirits. Owls hooted in the darkness around the stalled galley at night, and often they heard the screams of panthers, the chirping of millions of frogs, and the terrified cries of animals and birds being eaten alive in the eternal torment of predator and prey. By day, alligators, two or three times the length of a man lay in the shallows as the galley swept past, while water moccasins whipsawed through water that was black as the night.

Again and again the *Tiger* pushed up one waterway after another, sometimes grounding in the muddy bottom of the swamp. Then it was all hands on the oars, and ropes tied as pulleys around trees, if any were present, to pull the galley free to seek another channel. What the headman of the Mauvilans had neglected to say was that the great river was easily gained by way of a dugout, which could make its way around sandbars or through tangles of trees and shallow waters. But it was quite another thing to thread a galley the size of the *Tiger* through the capillaries that opened onto the river.

Several times captains Sincid and Cabeza got into roaring arguments as the swamp irritated their tempers beyond control. They fought over whether to push on or whether to return to Cuba or even Mexico, sometimes changing their minds back and forth as if they were whirling cats. Yet each time, it was the lust for gold that won the debate, for as Captain Cabeza noted in his fly-bitten misery, there was nothing for any of them to go back to.

This was especially true for Cabeza, for his share of the expedition was backed by investors at court and if he returned empty-handed he could expect to spend years rotting away in a dungeon. Perhaps even worse was the knowledge that he would be disgraced in the eyes of his peers; pitied and laughed at as his deeds faded to nothing. Gradually, Cabeza grew ever more morose, snappish and lost in dismal thoughts under Sincid's watchful eyes. Captain Sincid had not forgotten the day he had been humbled at the slave dock in Sevilla and with glittering eyes he savored the moment when he would make the captain of the conquistadors beg for mercy.

Then one day after nearly two weeks of probing with the threat of mutiny in the air, the galley pushed its way up an unlikely rivulet to find a wide opening through the trees, beyond which there fluttered a snowfall of white egrets. At first, the crew imagined that they had come upon a lake, but a strong current ran from upstream and around the next bend they found the Mississippi in all its glory, rolling like a galloping horse, almost a kilometer wide.

The exhausted, filthy, bug-ridden men screamed with delight through their tears, huzzahing even louder as a breeze rose from out of the south and the sail was hoisted aloft.

Within a day they began seeing the palm-thatched shanties of fishermen along the river and then small towns, with lines of their residents gaping on the riverbank as the *Tiger* pushed north. Drained by their two weeks aboard the galley, they docked at one of the villages, only to find that its residents had fled to the forest, leaving plentiful supplies of smoked fish behind.

They pushed forward for another two weeks with the same scene repeating over and over again as crowds of villagers gaped from the riverbank only to desert their homes when the ship came to rest. Somehow, word of their approach had traveled up the river, most likely on the tongues of fleet runners. Increasingly, they found only the ruins of burning villages, with all of their inhabitants missing, along with their stores of food.

"They think our ship is some sort of monster," Willow said to Akmed as they swept by yet another smoldering village. "To them it must look like a giant bird or a fish."

"Or a turtle with wings."

"Yes, but only one wing."

"Who can blame them? We must appear as hairy beasts and demons, for they have no hair on their faces and many of them pluck their scalps as well."

"Yes, beasts," she agreed, for she had seen how the Spaniards abused the Indian women aboard the ship, shuddering at their fate as they were raped each night, sometimes within her sight. Once, she had driven away three men attacking a slave who was barely out of her girlhood, but the men simply carried the girl toward the stern of the ship and set on her again.

Early on, the women had cried out piteously to the villagers lining the riverbank, who understood them well enough. They recognized them as captives in the hands of bad men and this, too, was relayed up the river. The women were shushed after that on threat of death, but it was too late to stop word of their terror and abuse.

Nor did the Spaniards know that the Mauvilans had sent runners overland along trails through the forest to tell the tribes along the Misi Sipi of their stolen women. This, and the Mauvilans hoped to keep any future trade with the Spaniards to themselves.

For his part, Captain Cabeza did nothing to stop the debauchery. When Willow begged him to intervene, he shrugged in irritation. "The men must have their pleasures," he mumbled. "What else have they for amusement?"

But even as the villages along the river emptied and burned, still the expedition gathered enough corn to stave off hunger, and often their arrival was so sudden that there were stores of smoked meat and fish to plunder. There were also several fishermen among the conquistadors, and these rigged nets to troll the river and sank hooks in quest of the huge catfish, carp and gars that roamed the dark waters.

Then one day the *Tiger* rounded a great curve in the river and Willow beheld a vast town on the left bank. It was perched on a high bluff, surrounded by a palisade of sharpened pines that ran for half a kilometer atop the hill. Beneath the bluff, a network of canals ran from the river to fields of corn and cotton, stretching out of sight to the flatlands beyond.

"Trouble ahead!"

Akmed was at the bow of the ship, posted to watch for snags, sandbars and the huge rolling logs that tumbled just beneath the surface of the river. He was first to spy what looked like a bad dream.

Dead ahead in the river was a wall of dugouts beyond count, barring the way and bristling with screaming warriors. With a shout from Sincid the galley shipped its oars and coasted to a halt before drifting backwards in the current. Although the flotilla was still half a mile off, a horrible shriek arose from its multitude as the warriors shook their bows and spears, screaming their war cries.

Then, from the town atop the bluff came an answering cry as hundreds of warriors emerged from its gates and began running down the hill. The river had narrowed to a pinch at the bend beneath the town and now its banks were filling with men equipped with long bows within shot of the *Tiger*, should the galley choose to retreat. Even worse, hundreds of warriors were piling into dugouts to attack the ship from the rear.

"What do you think, captain?" Cabeza asked, sidling up to Sincid.

Sincid squinted at the flotilla ahead and then turned to see the dugouts being launched from behind. He frowned as if poring over his accounts. "Who can say? Enough to sink the Catalan navy, at least," he replied. "I would guess three hundred of their boats ahead of us and a thousand men, at least. At best we can ram them, but if they swarm us..." He made a slicing motion with his finger across his throat.

"I have no doubt of it." Cabeza looked down on the faces of his expectant men from his perch at the bow as the oncoming wave of attackers dug at the river with their paddles. With their screams and war cries growing louder with each stroke, he drew his sword and raised it aloft.

"For God, Spain, and to save our skins!" he cried. "Load the culverin and prepare the bombs. Ready the pikes, and throw the women overboard!"

"Overboard?"

"Yes, do it now!"

"Fucking hell!" cried a wide-eyed conquistador at the captain's feet, shaking his head no, yet his comrades needed no further urging to lighten the ship, and every woman of the Mauvilans was flung screaming over the gunwales. They twirled in the wake of the *Tiger*, some dog-paddling for the shore, but most begging the men in the oncoming dugouts to save them. Willow saw one woman go under the brown current, only to be yanked back to the surface by a warrior clutching at her braid.

The flailing women in the water had slowed the onslaught of the dugouts from behind as they were rescued one-by-one, yet ahead the Indians' flotilla was converging in what looked like an impenetrable mass directly in front of the *Tiger*.

Upon the river the first arrows were dappling the water, drawing closer with every breath, and now came a unified chant from the warriors, booming like thunder and accompanied by the sound of drums. *"Hey-oh! Hey-oh! Hey-oh!"*

The men on the *Tiger* were still putting on their protective leathers and chain mail when the first arrows began piercing the deck, and every shield was hoisted overhead to make a turtle of the ship. Several of the musketeers worked in a frenzy loading the culverin and preparing the bombs, scooping black powder into canvas sacks with fuses dipped in turpentine. By now the ship's store of pikes had been passed out and shoved halfway through the oarlocks, ready to plunge at the attackers. Between the oars and the ten-foot pikes, the *Tiger* bristled as if it were a porcupine.

"But what of the city?" Sincid cried, nodding his head to the bluff. "Surely, there must be gold there!"

"We are sixty men against thousands," Cabeza said, not bothering to turn around. An arrow glanced off the dragon of his steel breastplate, knocking him back a step, yet unharmed.

"But Cortez..."

Cabeza turned on him with a wry smile. "You were not with us in the heart of Florida, captain, to witness the sky turning black with arrows. What you see is a city of farmers. There may be a small sprinkling of gold there, but it is the cities of pyramids that drip with treasure. The chronicles of Spain tell as much. Pyramids, captain, pyramids!"

"But..."

"But ours is a greater need at present, for by the time the hourglass is a quarter gone, the Indios will be firing twenty-thousand arrows on our heads. Have you seen a black rain, captain? Have you seen men pierced with a dozen such bolts?"

Captain Cabeza needed to speak no further for Sincid's eyes went wide in fright as an arrow zipped past his neck. He screamed for the culverin to be loaded, but this was already well underway, with a trail of gunpowder slopped at its breach at the bottom of the deck. Hurriedly, Sincid called for more bombs of powder to be packed into baskets.

"*Hey-oh! Hey-oh! Hey-oh!*"

Now the arrows were dappling the river with the oncoming force of a fall rain. Gradually, they gathered in a storm as the river began to boil with the hail of arrows. Ahead and behind the chant of the warriors grew louder and inexorably closer and it seemed to Willow that their attackers would be clambering over the sides of the galley at any moment.

"*Hey-oh! Hey-oh! Hey-oh!*" The thundering chant echoed over the water both from ahead and behind.

But if Captain Cabeza had learned one thing in the swamps and forests of Florida it was the need for protection from the arrows and slings of the Indians. Every man had been ordered to fashion a shield during their time on the beach, and now some hoisted the shells of sea turtles over their heads. Others held up rough panels of pine hewed from the forest. As for Montoya, Captain Cabeza eased his horse to its knees and then to its side, commanding his soldiers to fold the spare sailcloth several times over its body. Willow cowered beneath her own shield with Dragón, begging the dog to lie still while she soothed the frightened horse.

Even so, the ship was at the mercy of the oncoming warriors, for the forty men at the oars were of no use at all in returning fire, and they huddled clumsily beneath the shields balanced on their backs, with the butt-ends of their pikes lying in their laps. Only eighteen men had their hands free for fighting, yet these were equipped with deadly crossbows, matchlocks and Spanish steel.

"Hey-oh! Hey-oh! Hey-oh!"

And then, with the men holding their shields above themselves and the heads of the rowers, the command was given to ram the roaring mass of Indians ahead.

"Pull you devils!" Sincid screamed beneath the cover of an old shield that had been left behind. "Pull or we fry in their kettles tonight!"

And pull they did, with the power of forty oars driving the galley straight into the swirling mass of dugouts and screaming warriors, some of whom clawed at the side of the ship, only to be slashed away with the flailing swords of the conquistadors. By now the sky had indeed turned black with arrows which fell as if in a thunderstorm on the *Tiger*, and many got through, striking the screaming men onboard. But many of Cabeza's men still had their light armor of heavy cotton and leather jerkins studded with metal plates, and though there were grunts and screams among them, few seemed to have been hurt in the onslaught.

Still, the horde came on with little but the flashing swords and pikes to stop them. As many as two thousand warriors were on the water now, surrounding the ship and pressing in from all sides as if a swarm of ants overwhelming an upturned beetle.

Then, as if in a dream, a tall warrior came dancing over the river, skipping from one dugout to another like a god with wings on his feet. Nearly naked except for his swirling tattoos, he had ringlets of brightly-colored feathers circling his elbows and ankles and his head had been plucked clean, save for a long braid that sprang from atop his skull. All eyes turned to him as if he were a dancer in a ballet, yet one bearing a club as long as his arm. With a final leap, he sprang to the rail of the *Tiger*, clutching at the rigging. Shrieking, he raised an arm high overhead and sent his war club slashing down, crushing a rower's head.

A great cheer rose up from the armada of warriors as their hero stood on the rail of the *Tiger*, clinging to a rope and waving his club serrated with shards of onyx. He turned in exultation, urging his followers over the side of the ship, but the cry died on his lips as he was stabbed in the groin from below with the thrust of a pike's steel point. He fell headlong into the galley and lay on its deck, snarling and writhing as his life was hacked away by the Spaniards' steel blades.

"Up! Up and over the side!" Sincid cried, with his eyes gleaming with malice.

But the men needed no urging and three of them lifted the lifeless warrior and flung his body high over the gunwale where it flew topsy-turvy before careening into the dugouts below. The warrior's head hit a prow, while his hips collided with another dugout, capsizing both.

Clearly, the warrior had been a man of some importance, because for a moment a hush fell over the battle, followed by a deafening groan and then a roar as the warriors seemed to go mad. Hands clawed at the galley from all sides, only to be hacked away by the swords of the panting men on deck. The muddy water of the river was filled with severed limbs and the bodies of bleeding warriors and drowning men; yet on they came with men leaping to their feet in the dugouts, scrambling over each-others' bodies to climb up the hull, which rose only six feet above the waterline. Men leapt over the backs and shoulders of other men, clawing at the sides of the ship, only to tumble into the water to be replaced by other men as the dugouts piled prow-upon-stern against one-another in an immense raft. Above her, Willow screamed as three men climbed over the railing where she lay, and no longer able or willing to contain him, she unleashed Dragón who leapt up in a fury, slashing at a warrior as the others recoiled in horror.

But by now more warriors were clawing their way through the swords over the side of the galley and its forward momentum had been lost, with all of its oars in a tangle. Two of the Spaniards were dragged from the ship into the writhing mass below, never to be seen again. The *Tiger* had rammed a score of dugouts, but there were too many and dozens of warriors had seized the oars, stalling the ship.

It was then that the culverin spoke.

Cabeza's musketeer had endured a devil of a time lighting the gun. His slow match had been extinguished by an unlucky splash from one of oars when ramming speed had been ordered. It had taken many long minutes to retrieve another kettle of coals from the bombardiers across the deck, which was crowded with men churning beneath their shields amid the haphazard jumble of supplies. Even then the touch-hole had been soaked and a musketeer struggled desperately to dry it with a length of twisted cotton, cursing in a fever as the arrows fell all around him. It was only when the ship seemed in danger of being swamped that the double-shotted cannon spoke at last, blasting a hail of stones from its mouth directly into the mass of dugouts ahead.

BAAAAAAAAM!

The cannon blast had been the signal for the bombardiers, who lit their fuses and flung the flaming bags of black powder into the dugouts alongside the ship. Bewildered, the warriors had flailed at the bombs, but only for a moment as the sound like all of the thunder in creation broke in a black cloud among them.

Instantly, the sunlit day turned to pitch night as an immense fog of black powder smoke spread in all directions on the river. The culverin had done little damage, since being eight feet long it was meant to fire a ball at an enemy ship, its gauge being too narrow for the kind of grapeshot and shrapnel used on a battlefield.

But it was the 30-foot tongue of flame from the culverin's maw that did the trick, along with a double load of gunpowder that threatened to blow the gun to pieces. That, and ten of Sincid's bombs had exploded aboard the dugouts, sending billows of sparks and black smoke churning among the warriors, some of who were horribly burned or blown to pieces.

Aboard the *Tiger*, every man froze in the darkness, gagging on the smoke as the world seemed to fall away, revealing hell itself. Instead of war cries now there came the screams of dying men and the choking of those who could barely breathe in the stinging smoke. But even then the battle was not over, for the spilled powder on the *Tiger's* deck had ignited, and now a tall plume of fire rose above the ship near where Willow lay cowering with Montoya. To those looking on from the waterline, it looked as if a monster was moving on the water through the roiling smoke, breathing fire as it pushed through a maze of bodies and overturned dugouts.

"God's balls! Get that fire out!" Cabeza screamed as the ship pushed forward. The men were once again at the oars, plowing awkwardly through the mass of dugouts, many of which had been overturned. Pikes and shattered oars stabbed at the swamp of dugouts as the Spaniards frantically attempted to push their way through the melee.

To the rear, the warriors had regrouped and were paddling in their wake, but at last the *Tiger* reached open water and it was no contest now as the ship surged forward. A bucket line had been formed of every man not at the oars and the fire at the front of the ship was soon quelled. By some miracle of a western breeze, the flames had never reached the remaining barrels of gunpowder.

At the back of the ship, a wounded man cried out piteously for his mother, and everywhere there were groans and cries of pain as the men dealt with arrow nicks and piercings.

Behind them, the Indians gradually fell away, crying triumphantly in their wake. They had defeated a dragon filled with demons and the tale would be told around their fires for a lifetime, or at least until the men of other dragons fell upon them, bringing swords and disease.

Willow found one of the feathered arm bands of the tall warrior on the deck as the galley sped away. If she had known the birds of this new land she would have recognized the brightly-colored tufts of a bluebird, cardinal, scarlet tanager, canary, and perhaps even those of a macaw, traded at an immense distance from the tribes far to the South. She picked it up, thinking to keep it, but then considered that it had brought no luck to the fallen warrior and she threw it overboard. She watched as the feathered band swirled gaily on the muddy water of the river before disappearing in the galley's wake.

The conquistadors took stock of their casualties, adding two men lost over the side of the ship to the butcher's bill. The skull of the brained rower had swelled to the size of pumpkin; he died in Willow's arms. The man who had called out for his mother choked off his cries and died with his face awash with blood. Captain Cabeza's fair-haired lover took an arrow in his left eye, and though he lived, he would never be considered a pretty boy again. Another man took a shaft through a shoulder joint, while a fourth had a horrible gash across his throat, as if it had been slit. But both survived their wounds and the next day a Mass was held aboard ship to thank Almighty God for their deliverance.

The ship limped on for two days upriver, with all aboard taking a turn at the oars through the night, spelled by all aboard the ship, even Willow. Those not manning the oars were set to bailing the bottom of the galley; the exploding gunpowder had burned a hole partway through the hull and the pine pitch they'd used to seal the *Tiger* had only hastened its destruction. Yet they could not stop, for who knew if the warriors were pursuing them? And soon enough, both Cabeza and Sincid realized that neither could they go on, for who knew what hostile tribes might await them ahead?

At last they grounded the galley on a sand bar to make repairs and the exhausted men piled out of the ship and collapsed in the mud, praying to whatever gods they knew to save their skins.

It was mid-December and the gales out of the north had grown stronger, cutting like knives through their tattered clothing of wet cotton. Men were sent to the forest along the riverbank with orders to cut oak for the ship's repair, but the oak was as tough as iron and it took several days to hew planks of it into a shape suitable for the *Tiger's* repair.

For once, Cabeza and Sincid agreed that they could not go on. The attack on the river had dispirited the men; they had expected to find the treasures of Peru only a short way up the river and had instead found a wall of screaming warriors. Several among them had been with Cortez only a few years earlier for the attack on Tenochtitlan, but that had been accomplished with the help of smallpox and an army of tens of thousands of Indian vassals who hated their Aztec overlords. But on this heartless river it was clear that there would be no Indian allies.

"We're in no shape to attack a city the size of the Aztecs if we find it anytime soon," said one of the veterans of Cortez's campaign in a fireside council. "We barely survived a town of farmers!"

To this there was a chorus of agreement, and even Captain Cabeza had to admit that his men needed rest and regrouping.

Thus, a decision was made to send men along the riverbanks in search of a suitable place to build a fort to live out the winter. While the rest of them shivered on the sandbar, sheltering against the rain in the lee of the galley, companies of men bristling with swords, pikes and crossbows were sent upriver in search of a likely fortification. Days later, they returned with news that a village had been found on a hill overlooking the river with broad fields all around its base. The villagers had fled at the sight of the Spaniards, but their stores of maize had been left behind and these were now being guarded by a nervous band of six conquistadors who awaited the arrival of their mates to ensure their survival. Within an hour the *Tiger* had been manhandled off the sandbar and pointed north. For the first time ever, the men at the oars were grateful for the exertion and the heat it brought to their soaking bones.

On Christmas Day, 1528, the *Tiger* coursed alongside a levee of stones jutting into the current beneath the village and its jubilant guards. Captain Cabeza leapt down from the galley with his sword drawn and commanded all to kneel by the river. Then, with the flag of Habsburg Spain unfurled and with their sole priest making signs over the men with his swinging rosary, Captain Cabeza claimed all of the land from the river to far beyond the horizon for King Charles V.

The Red River

Wolf was anxious to leave, but Buffalo Drum's tale of the Mandan warriors had reminded him that he was a collector of stories as well as a *gi-imaabi* and that Wabeno-inini had charged him with learning as much as he could about the tribes along the Misi Sipi. Wolf could not imagine what the Man of the Dawn Sky would make of the Mandans, but he decided to linger among the Cahokians until he had learned something of the Bird Men.

"I know little of them, but the headman knows their story" Buffalo Drum said. "Perhaps if you gift him with some pipestone he will speak."

The head man's name was Three Quails, the same tall man with the pretty daughter who had given Wolf a sleeping bench in his lodge. Buffalo Drum spoke to him, half in sign language, while Wolf held out his gift. Three Quails shot a suspicious glance at Wolf, but accepted the pipestone and shrugged his assent. He muttered a few words and motioned them to follow.

"There are ghosts," Buffalo Drum said cryptically.

Three Quails led them along a trail overgrown with brush and small trees to an area of many low mounds. Wolf could see that some effort had been made through the years to clear the area, but the earth was winning the struggle, slowly covering the mounds with vegetation. At the far end of the clearing there stood a low mound that had been half devoured by a flood the prior spring, and drawing closer, Wolf could see that it contained a grave.

"A Bird Man," he said.

Buffalo Drum nodded. "You see his wings? His beak?"

"Yes. Somewhere he still flies."

Lying in the open grave was a skeleton with the bones of its hands clasped over its chest. Its clothing had long since rotted away, but thousands of shell beads lay among the bones and beneath the skeleton's ribs where they had been sewn into a burial shroud. Wolf made out the pattern of wings fashioned from shells glimmering in the mud, and also a beak slanting sideways, all half buried or barely glimpsed in the damp earth. A long tail of purple and white shell beads extended beneath the skeleton's legs.

"A hawk man," Wolf said with some satisfaction. Before him lay a treasure beyond imagination. It looked as if there were as many shell beads cloaking the corpse as there were stars in the sky, enough to bedazzle every woman of the Anishinaabek... yet all untouchable. As with the Mandans and the people of Cahokia, Wolf would never dream of scooping the beads of a dead man, for the ghoul would certainly return for them if they were stolen.

"The people here call him the Falcon," Buffalo Drum said. "Three Quails took a great risk bringing you here, for the Falcon has many slaves and some say he still flies by night."

Wolf had already noted the slaves, for all around the beaded skeleton lay the yellowed, decaying bones of many others, some missing heads or hands, others laying in rows, the bones of their feet protruding from the yet-uncovered earth. Skeletal hands appeared to be grasping for the sky, as if they belonged to those who had been buried alive. The ground was still soaked from where it had been washed away by the river and soon, Wolf suspected, all of the dead would be revealed before slowly melting away through the wear of the seasons and the mining of insects.

Three Quails had remained hidden behind a clump of trees at the far end of the clearing so as not to be noticed by the dead. Wolf could not blame him, for he could feel the quavering of their spirits calling from the mound and billowing through the trees. The dead had been disturbed by the wearing of the river and had awakened, confused and angry. It was an eerie place, and shaking off their whispers, he was glad to leave them behind.

"The river tickles their bones. They are not yet at rest," he said as he and Buffalo Drum made their way back to the village.

"Hah! Only the old buzzard!" Buffalo Drum replied. "What sort of fools would join him in his lodge of dirt?"

"Only those who had no choice."

Later, Three Quails told them that other mounds had been opened by the flooding river, revealing hundreds of skeletons buried with their chieftains and priests, the victims of ancient beliefs that were now forgotten.

"Perhaps this is why this place was lost," Wolf said. "Perhaps the people rebelled against the sacrifice of their children."

"Ah, perhaps it was simply filth and disease," Buffalo Drum said, "for can you imagine this place filled with more people than there are stones in the river? Imagine the shit, brother! Where would they put it all?"

Wolf had no idea, but was grateful to have visited the grave of the Falcon, though he had resisted listening to its spirits. Perhaps Wabeno would make some sense of it when they sat together over their pipes someday, though somehow Wolf doubted it.

That night, Wolf presented Three Quails with a copper amulet to thank him for his hospitality. It was a polished disc that shone like the setting sun over the Misi Sipi. "If you polish it with river sand you can keep it bright, otherwise it will turn brown," he said.

The next day after being pounded half senseless by the Mandans with the back slaps and shoulder bumps of farewell he exchanged good luck charms with the traders and set off down the canal to the Misi Sipi. No one could tell him how far the Red River lay, only that it was a long way, perhaps even the length of a full moon paddling to the south. Once again, Wolf wondered what Wabeno had been thinking when he tasked him with this mission. The old man could not have known how far away the land of the sunktanka was or surely he would not have sent him on such a long journey. He might as well be paddling into the afterlife, he thought glumly.

But Wolf was hardly inclined to turn back now. With winter dawning upon him, he was grateful to be heading south.

How was he to know that he was only halfway down the Great River? Few along its banks knew that it had begun as a humble stream far to the north and just as few seemed to know how far it ran to the south. Smoking his pipe by the fire at night, Wolf mused that the Misi Sipi ran the length of half the world or more.

Days passed into weeks as he pushed on down the river, passing many towns and villages. He soon learned that countless people lived along its banks among the tribes of the Choctaw, Tensas, Quinippissa, Arkansas, Tensas, Natchez, Chicakasas, Coroas, Oumas and more. Often, Wolf was warned of the tribes further south on the river, but he soon deduced that these were simply ancestral enemies, which were disparaged as having evil intentions.

Mostly, he was welcomed at every village he came upon, for who doesn't love a trader? Some of the towns were the walled capitals of tribes that held sway over many villages. But these were not just along the Misi Sipi, for Wolf soon learned that there were many such towns lying up the rivers he passed. Once, on a whim, he took a turn up a river to the west to visit the capital of the Casqui people, trading pipestone on its quay before strolling its avenues amid hundreds of lodges with thatched roofs. It, too, had a tall pyramid crowned by a temple, which had been piled high through the effort of thousands of hands.

A flock of ducks tethered with a long cord waddled down a hard-packed passage between a row of lodges, driven by a boy carrying a wand. Wolf looked on dumbstruck, for such a thing was unknown in the north. Walking in the direction from which the flock had come, he came upon a market unlike anything he had seen before, with stalls covered with thatch in a long row beneath the pyramid mound. The meat of turtles, dogs and deer hung from poles alongside that of ducks and fish and there were vendors trading feathers, shells, jewelry, baskets, ceramics, carvings and many odd things. Wolf had never seen the like of it and he gaped as a line of slaves passed by, carrying baskets of corn on their backs, tethered with straps around their heads. A fat man wearing a white cotton robe and a tall crown of feathers gave him a bemused look and huffed his way up the pyramid, disappearing into the temple at its peak.

But it was the women who commanded Wolf's attention, for there were many beauties among them, elaborately coiffed and swathed in cotton skirts, feathered earrings and necklaces of shells. Some had tattoos swirling around their breasts, while others had babies slung from their shoulders as they worked. Their eyes were darkened and alluring, either with paint or tattoos, he could not say. A group of women his own age cast appraising eyes upon him, clucking their approval and Wolf blushed in response, for the maidens of the Ojibwe would never be so bold. Somehow, the women of the Casqui made him feel small, as if they were privy to secrets that he would never glimpse or understand.

Although Wolf didn't understand the language of the Casqui people, by signs he was given to understand that the town stood at the heart of twenty villages of farmers, who tilled fields of cotton, maize, beans, sunflowers, tobacco and squash. Scratching at the dirt with a stone hoe was not the life that he would choose, but he noted wistfully that the farmers along the Misi Sipi were plump compared to those of the starvation-plagued Ojibwe, who got by on fish and game.

At first, his arrival had aroused suspicion among the Casqui, who had been at war with a neighboring tribe since the days of their grandfathers' grandfathers. A company of tattooed warriors had come down to the river to question him when he landed, and by signs and a display of his cargo he had convinced them that he was only a trader. This was aided by a gift of tobacco to each warrior, who accepted it with nonchalance, for there was already tobacco of better quality to smoke in their land.

But it wasn't long before it dawned on him that every tribe along the Misi Sipi likely had its foes. This was made even clearer one morning when he awoke to find that he had camped in a battlefield on arriving the night before. Not far from the shelter of his overturned canoe he found the scattered remains of severed limbs, torsos pecked by birds and gnawed by animals, and a carpet of broken arrows. The rotting heads of three warriors were impaled waist-high atop sticks jammed in the earth. They grimaced through sightless eyes, their scalps chopped away with flint knives. Wolf sat on a fallen tree among them, calmly chewing a breakfast of corn porridge which Three Quails had provided in a gourd.

"Thank the Great Spirit you do not have this to eat," he said, addressing the dead men. "It needs a taste of honey or salt."

But if the heads of the dead warriors had anything to say on the matter, they kept it to themselves, and Wolf was soon back in his canoe, more cautious now. He began avoiding villages, skirting them on the far side of the river. Once, he was chased by men paddling hard in six dugouts, but they were no match for his fleet canoe and he easily outdistanced them, mocking them in a loud voice as he paddled. Where once he had felt as strong as two men, now he felt as strong as three from the endless days of pushing his canoe ever south.

Then one day, three-quarters of a moon south of the Great Mound, he came upon a broad river flowing from the west into the Misi Sipi. He paddled a short way up its current and dipped his palm into the water, bringing it to his lips. As Buffalo Drum had said, the river had the faint taste of brine. Wolf breathed a prayer and scattered two fingers of tobacco on the water in thanks. At last, the Red River.

He paddled for days to the west and gradually the land grew drier and redder as the Mandans had predicted. The forest dwindled, giving way to brush lands and then prairie. Further west lay red, rolling hills, while on the north side of the river the plains opened up in a sea of grass.

Here and there, Wolf stopped to trade, learning that he was among the Caddo people, whose confederacy included many clans ranging far upriver. No one had heard of the sunktanka, but that was no surprise, as Wolf knew it was the name given to the creature by the Dakota. Still, his efforts to describe the beast by sign language produced only puzzled looks. There was no such animal roaming the prairie, though Wolf had the impression that some had heard mention of it. Mostly, the river-dwellers looked at him as if he were a crazy man, and why shouldn't they? He was far from home, coming from a place no one had ever heard of, nor could imagine.

At a small village he was offered a meal of corn soup, laden with shreds of prairie dog meat.

Thank you, Wolf signed as he ate, rubbing his stomach to show that the meal had been pleasing. He offered a handful of tobacco in gratitude, but this was met with a grin and refusal by the elder who had welcomed him.

We have much tobacco already - no need, the elder said by hand signals.

"Are you Adai?" Wolf spoke.

"Adai?" The elder shook his head, no. *That way*, he signed, pointing upriver.

How far?

Long way – a poor people in a bad land. No rain, no corn. Always hungry!

Again, as always, a long way. But still, Wolf was heartened that someone at last had heard of the Adai and he resolved to push on. He would reveal the mystery of the sunktanka one way or the other. Surely they would know if the beast was real or simply a myth.

At first, he passed many villages along the Red River and was astounded by their lodges, which towered in conical shapes fashioned from woven grasses. Gradually, the villages grew smaller, poorer, and drought-stricken. Several times, knots of villagers looked up to watch him pass, offering no signs of greeting, and Wolf suspected that traders were few in this land where there was little to offer in return.

At night he camped on the north side of the river where the plains began, scraping a stick of hardwood against the groove of his fire plank until a curl of smoke rose from its tinder. A low fire and a fish to roast over its coals were his only comforts as the stars rose above the plains, flooding the sky with their pale light. Out of the darkness came the yip of coyotes and the howling of wolves as they called to their mates. Wolf thought wistfully that even his namesakes had lovers, while he was the lone wolf among them. He felt utterly lost as the people along the river grew more suspicious of a wandering stranger and the country grew dryer and more hostile.

He was sick for home. By now, the Ojibwe would have traveled to their winter hunting grounds and would be snug as wrens in their lodges, buried in snow. They would be listening to other storytellers by the fire at night, nestled in the bosom of family and friends. But for Wolf there were only the chill stars for company, and the howling in the night.

One night he stayed awake until almost dawn, watching the stars as they slowly wheeled through the sky. From time to time, a star zipped through the darkness, signifying a soul who had come back to walk the earth again. Wolf knew that the falling stars were the souls of those who had done great deeds and had more deeds before them.

Then one morning, nearly the length of a full moon up the Red River, he awoke to find himself surrounded by six warriors, all of them naked except for scraps of leather strung over their genitals. He attempted a few words in the tongue of the Dakota, but this seemed to anger them, and by signs he endeavored to make them understand that he was not their enemy. An in-between man, barely out of his boyhood, took his lance and drove it through the bottom of Wolf's precious canoe, which had been double-hulled with birch by the most skilled canoe-builders among all of the Anishinaabek. One of the warriors groaned at the damage, for the canoe was clearly a thing of value, but the damage was begun and the others joined in, punching holes in the birch bark with their spears and clubs. The in-between man leapt into the air and came crashing down on its midsection, bouncing off its surface in a backflip that landed him with a loud thump on his back. He lay in the dirt groaning with the wind knocked out of him.

Wolf scrambled to his feet, betraying no emotion as his beloved canoe was smashed to pieces. It had been his home on the water for more than two seasons since leaving Boweting, and he resisted the tears welling in his eyes. Yet even as he stood among his raging captors he remembered that the spirits had never meant for him to be a warrior and there was little hope of resisting. Wabeno's words arose in his thoughts, "your stories will protect you."

Ah, but how to share his stories with a people he could not speak to? There was only one word they might understand.

"Are you Adai?"

By now the in-between man, perhaps only fourteen winters old, had risen to his feet and dusted himself off. He made motions to stab at Wolf with his spear, but was shoved roughly aside by a man who appeared to be their leader. He was a thin man, but well-muscled and as lean as a hank of leather.

"Adai," he answered with a nod. He leaned over and studied the markings on Wolf's club and then gazed at the patterns of his moccasins.

"Ojibwe," Wolf answered, making signs that he was a trader. "Ojibwe."

But there was no glimmer of understanding in the lean man's gaze. Instead, he produced a length of hide rope, slipping a noose around Wolf's neck. The last of Wolf's trade goods were gathered up, the precious pipe stone and a few scraps of copper. At best he had been lucky to seize his pipe and the pouch holding his tobacco, tucking them into his belt. The in-between man attempted to seize his pipe, but this was too much to bear and Wolf swatted him away with a hard slap across his face, not caring if he was beaten.

"No touch!" he shouted loudly, and his meaning was plain enough.

But the warriors only chided the youth and laughed, for a man's pipe must be respected.

Wolf had told many stories around his home fires of captives who were led shitting and crying in fright in just such a situation, but again Wabeno's words came to him, along with a calmness that he could not explain. At the least, he had found the Adai and perhaps soon, the sunktanka.

The warriors' village lay just around the next bend in the river at the end of a pathway that crossed a low hill of red sand. There were perhaps thirty grass huts shaped like stubby pine cones, beyond which were some parched fields of maize. Past the fields lay a chaparral, dense with brush and cacti. To the north, on the other side of the river, the vast plains opened up, disappearing to low red hills in the distance.

With a whoop the warriors announced their approach, and every soul in the village ran forth to meet them at the heels of a score of barking dogs. The villagers jigged and gabbled about him, with some of the young ones rushing in to slap at his sides. Wolf shuffled forward with his gimp leg and raised his hands in what he hoped was a sign of peace.

But the villagers would have none of it and after they had talked stridently among themselves he was dismayed to see the women rushing to their lodges, tearing sticks and branches bearing thorns from the walls. It was clear they meant to make sport of him and he prepared to bleed.

Yet there was a trick he had learned from his uncles among the Good Hearts and now he almost grinned at the thought of it. Almost, for the failure of it could mean his death.

He would summon Paija, the she-monster of the Cree. The hairy creature with the single leg that descended from her huge belly; a gobbler of human souls.

The women and children had gathered in a twin row at the heart of the village, eagerly hefting sticks, clubs and thorny branches. Wolf could see that he was meant to be the entertainment of the season, perhaps the entire year, and he prepared himself. A chant arose from the crowd, which he took to mean, "run, run, run!" Excitement lit up every face as the crowd leaned in on the pathway with upraised arms.

Then the noose was lifted from his neck, and he was shoved roughly forward. But rather than dashing through the gauntlet as the villagers expected, he lifted his gimp left foot to his right knee, standing on one leg.

Ancient Wabeno, perhaps, would have known a spell to make himself appear as the horrid Paija to the villagers, but Wolf reckoned he might do almost as well with the theatrics taught to him by his uncles among the shamans.

Somberly, he gazed upon his would-be tormentors as they stood shuffling in anticipation.

"Paija," he called out to them, low and menacing, lifting his hands in claws and contorting his mouth. Then, in a booming voice, *"Paija!"*

Slowly he extended his leg, and then reaching forward, still balanced on his right leg, he gave his left foot a hard twist into what should have been its normal position. The result was a loud *crack!* that gave those standing nearby a shiver. Instantly, to the crowd's disbelieving eyes, his clubbed foot snapped back to the same lame place it had occupied since he was a babe.

But the horrible bone-breaking sound of his obstinate foot had been heard by all and the entire crowd gave a horrified gasp. Wolf twisted his foot again, and once again there came an excruciating *crack!* as his foot twisted into place and then snapped back to its lame position. Wolf noted with satisfaction that some in the crowd had a sickened look on their faces, while others were plainly terrified by what they had witnessed. Then, he flared his strange gray eyes, bared his teeth, and made the sign of claws with his fingers, pointing to his lame foot and snarling. The meaning was clear enough - a demon dwelled there!

But he was not done with them yet, for as the crowd shrank before him, he lifted his lame foot crossways to his knee and rolled his eyes up into his head in a way that was hideous to behold. Then, raising his arms high overhead, he took three leaps toward the crowd on his right leg, flaring his eyes wide open and howling like a wolf.

Brothers, sisters, know this: Wolf had spent many seasons perfecting the cry of the wolves to serve as part of his storytelling. Many times he had delighted crowds of hundreds of the Anishinaabek with a long, wavering howl, which he could deliver at an unearthly volume. Now, the gaping crowd of villagers stood frozen and trembling before him and with a beast-ly snarl he rolled his eyes back up into his head and hopped three more leaps on one leg into their midst, throwing his head back and howling even louder. Ah, that horrible, lingering howl! It washed over those gathered before him, who stared back in terror. Then, throwing his eyes open and baring his teeth, he held out his arms, curling his fingers into claws.

It was enough. A scream went up as the women and children fled the plaza in terror. Looking over his shoulder, Wolf could see that even the warriors had scrambled back, uncertain as to what they should do. But their leader looked at him and snickered with the trace of a smile on his face, as if to say it had been a good trick.

Wolf nodded in return, grateful that his back had not been festooned with arrows in the wake of his magic-making. The old medicine-maker of the village had joined the leader, whispering in his ear, and now they stood looking gravely in his direction.

What to do? With a snarl and a lurch here and there to frighten any re-maining tormentors, Wolf strolled deeper into the village, hoping to learn more of his captors.

He didn't know what to make of the Adai. He had imagined that the guardians of the sunktanka would be a grand people, perhaps as great as those of the Bird Men with their tall pyramid of earth. Yet these farmers were a lowly bunch and it seemed unlikely that this would be the home of such a creature. There was nothing in the village that looked like a deer, yet was not a deer. There was no creature with the hair of a woman on its head, nor on its tail. There was nothing much at all except for some drying racks and clay pits where the villagers stored their food. A few fine pots perhaps, and some looms where cotton was being rendered into cloth, but...

Rounding a corner he spied a low platform at the end of a line of huts, and sitting in the shade beneath the platform was a woman who appeared to be sewing. Drawing closer, he saw that she was strangely dressed, unlike any of the women of the Adai, and her hair fell in ringlets as black and bright as the silver reflected from a raven's wing. But it was her skin that was the most striking; it was almost as dark as the Misi Sipi, yet as smooth and rich as that of a mink. For a moment their eyes locked and he thought that she was the strangest woman he had ever seen. She gazed up at him with green eyes flecked with motes of gold and nodded gravely, as if she had been expecting him.

And there, lying atop the wooden platform above her head in a scatter of dusty bones bleached by the sun, was all that was left of the sunktanka.

Death in the Forest

Willow had watched the newcomer's pantomime from the far end of the village and had laughed when the crowd ran screaming in terror at what looked like the antics of a clown.

The man had a limp, much like that of her father, whose leg had gone dead from a paralyzing disease. She felt a vague sense of satisfaction as he made his way to where she sat sewing beneath the altar of the Adai. She did not know why the Adai insisted on her sitting there for part of each day, except that perhaps it had something to do with her jade-colored eyes and her dark skin, which had been the subject of many caresses. That, and the skeleton of the horse which lay on the old blanket above her head. She guessed it was a sort of altar.

The newcomer was not a tall man, but he was powerfully built with a broad, flat chest and muscular shoulders. His eyes were a beautiful gray, their irises rimmed with gold, and they seemed kind, wise. She decided that he was quite a handsome man, only a little older than herself.

"As-salam alaykom," she said in Arabic in the vain hope that he might know her language.

To her surprise, the stranger responded as if he knew exactly what she had said, offering a greeting in return, though she could not make out the words. Then, he pointed to the bones on the bier above her head. "Sunktanka," he said.

"Yes, truly, sunktanka," she replied, offering a smile. "Whatever thou wish, wanderer."

He did not understand what she said, but his eyes had lit up and he smiled at the word, sunktanka. Clearly, he meant the skeleton of the horse, which the villagers seemed to revere.

She was also sure that the stranger was destined as a slave, if not a sacrifice. Like herself, he'd been led to the village with a rawhide cord around his neck.

Willow had been a slave of the Adai for nearly two months now after being captured by a band of their hunters near the fort of the Spaniards. Now, she was hundreds of miles west of the *Tiger* and its men, contemplating a dreary fate in this land of red dust.

After the *Tiger* had landed on Christmas day, the Indians of the village had gradually emerged from the forest, timid at first, but encouraged by overtures of friendship from the conquistadors. It was Montoya that brought them forth; they had never seen anything like him and the horse appeared to be a magical creature, especially after they saw Captain Cabeza riding him through their fields.

Soon enough they found themselves enslaved and put to hard labor. Three of their men had resisted, but by signs and the wielding of an axe, Captain Cabeza told them that he would have their hands cut off if they resisted.

"Aye, it's the way we treated shirkers among the Taino people in the West Indies," Willow heard one of the conquistadors say. "Hundreds of them! They fell in line quick enough, though it was a gruesome business."

The villagers needed no more convincing. They were set to digging a ditch around the village perimeter and carrying felled trees from the forest to build a wall, sinking the base of the trees into the earth. Those who tarried were whipped.

Willow had been shocked beyond words by growing brutality; it was as if the last candle of civilization had been snuffed as the Spaniards descended into darkness and debauchery, chasing down terrified women and threatening any who resisted. More than ever she missed Croen and the chance to speak with him.

She was even afraid to speak of it with Akmed, for he of course, had lost his own hand to Sincid's axe. Often in the voyage up the river she had seen Akmed caressing what was left of his cloven hand, and if he spoke of it at all, it was only to repeat his vow to murder Sincid when the chance arose.

There was also the looming threat of Philip Garon, who seemed intent on lurking close enough to fill her with anxiety. For months she had slept alongside Dragón for warmth as well as protection, but her sleep had grown restless and she found herself waking many times during the night, listening for sounds of the Frenchman creeping her way. There was a brook near the village where Willow went to bathe, and twice she saw Garon peeping at her from a distance. Dragón had seen him as well and she had run naked from the water to restrain him. She had not forgotten the Frenchman's vow to make her his beast, but as long as she had the war dog by her side, there was no way that he could seize her.

Soon enough, most of the villagers escaped to the forest, and from time to time the warriors of other bands appeared beyond the perimeter of the rising fort, firing a few desultory arrows in its direction. The remaining villagers were evicted from their huts and left to sleep outside amid the winter rains, sheltered only by one of the spare sails from the galley, which were spread to make an open-sided tent. Yet in twos and threes, the villagers began disappearing into the night, sneaking past the dozing guards.

Several times captains Sincid and Cabeza had met with the village elders, chattering on about gold, waving trinkets of it before their eyes, and sculpting pyramids of clay in the village square. The old ones seemed mystified as to what the bearded demons were seeking, but conceded that yes, there were many old mounds along the river, leaving out that most were no higher than a man's head. How were they to know that the feverish captains meant high pyramids with their childish models of clay? As with the Mauvilans, the elders of the village agreed to anything the white devils asked in the hope that they would soon disappear.

Paradoxically, Willow felt less safe as the fort grew around her. The men had made a brothel of one of the Indians' lodges and a line of them waited outside each night as the terrified women of the village were led inside. Some of them had looked to her in the hope of rescue, for she was clearly untouchable, but what could she do? Once, she made a weak appeal to them as Christians and had been laughed at and threatened with rape herself.

"Do not become devils!" she had cried, attempting to snatch three frightened women from their grasp. "Remember that you are honorable men!"

But the men were no longer honorable, and in fact, never had been. One of the taller of them stamped at her and seized a woman's wrist, dancing back with a curse when Dragón leapt forward with bared teeth.

In the past, she had relied on the protection of Captain Cabeza, but he had grown increasingly strange, muttering and mumbling to himself and looking through her when she came to beg on behalf of the Indian women.

"Captain, please, the men are abusing the women in a way that is intolerable in the eyes of your god," she said.

"God? We are beyond the eyes of God."

"But surely your Jesus would condemn the treatment of the women."

Cabeza gave her a dull look and she could see that he didn't care.

"Women? These women of the Indios? Desist," he said, raising a hand. "I have a disease and no other concerns. The men can do as they wish."

"A disease? In your stomach, sir?"

"Yes, in my belly as well as my brain. It is an illness that has sickened me to my core," he breathed. "An illness that only gold can cure."

Turning, he had walked away, muttering "only gold" over his shoulder.

But that was not Willow's only concern.

Sincid and Cabeza had become like two roosters, circling each other for dominance. Their sparring had begun turning the men against one-another with jibes and accusations. There could only be one leader of the expedition, and now the captains spoke with an iron frost to each other, not bothering to conceal their loathing. The infection of their hatred had spread among the men, who took sides as the captains pecked at one-another.

Those in Sincid's camp remarked that he was a bold man for taking the ship into the heart of the New World in search of treasure, rather than returning to poverty and despair in Cuba. Only Sincid had the skills and daring required of their mission. In their eyes Captain Cabeza was a weakling, a fancy man of the degenerate Spanish court who would get them all killed.

But those who followed Cabeza held that he was the less treacherous of the two and less reckless. They muttered that Sincid was illegitimate, a filthy Portuguese pirate who would stab them all in their backs when the treasure was won. His evil ways would get them all killed... With both the captains and their men spiraling into anarchy, Willow had never felt so vulnerable.

One day, the two had gone spitting mad over a small slight. Sincid had leaned over and seized Cabeza's fork from his dish to spear a piece of duck from the cook pot and Cabeza's eyes had flared in disbelief. The silver fork was an heirloom, one of the few things he had left in the world.

Captain Cabeza stared at the fork in Sincid's hand and looked as if he would gag. "Why you ignorant fool! Greasy pirate! How dare you?"

Startled, Sincid had recoiled, then with a sneering look of condescension he had tossed the precious fork into the coals of the fire pit.

Cabeza scrambled for the fork, poking with his knife among the coals, but in an instant he realized that he had done wrong; he should have demanded its return from Sincid's own hand. Instead he had made himself look weak, even craven before the men. His face lit with the fury of a bonfire.

Sincid glared at him contemptuously from the other side of the cook fire, as if daring him to act. And Cabeza did. Scooping a handful of ashes and cinders, he flung the flaming mass into Sincid's face.

It was only the intercession of the men that prevented blood from being shed, and as it was, Cabeza suffered painful burns on his right hand, while Sincid had received a flaming cinder in his left eye, which remained red for a week.

"Why doesn't the captain kill the slaver?" Willow wondered as she and Akmed looked on. "He has far more men and could have him gutted and hung at his leisure."

"Yes, but who among us would pilot the ship?" Akmed replied. "Do you know how to sail? Nor do I. Sincid knows the ways of a ship, and even more, he knows the mysteries of the sea. He is the only one among us! We may yet find treasure, but without the Portuguese we'll never see Cuba again."

"There is still Croen," she reminded. "He knows how to sail and could surely find his way to Cuba."

"Truly, but Croen is two hundred leagues behind us now, hidden beyond the swamp barring our way to the sea. He may be a card in Cabeza's deck, but in the meantime, the captain has no choice but to keep Sincid alive. For all we know, Croen is dead by now."

With Croen gone, Willow's only companion was Akmed. He was busy slaving with the villagers most of the time, tasked with carrying trees for the palisade from the forest in a human centipede that groaned beneath the weight of the tall trunks. But the two of them still found time to pray together and speak, and even to make love in a forest glade down the hill from the fort. Twice they had joined together since their first coupling on the beach.

Even so, Willow's feelings for Akmed were uncertain. Once, she had seen him in line at the brothel and it had filled her with rage. Was there no hope for her? Were all men so unjust? She thought of her father... he had been honest and kind. What would he think of the man who clenched his daughter?

It was also true that the rogue of Badis still lurked in Akmed. On their last time together he had manhandled her to the ground and had forced himself on her in a way that filled her with alarm, cuffing her when she protested. He had apologized after a fashion, yet with a smirk on his face.

"Thou art learning the bad ways of the men," she accused. "Remember to be gentle or..."

"Yes princess, I will do better," he said, interrupting, though his eyes glittered with amusement. "But remember thou art not the only plum on the tree."

How quickly a man could change, she thought. Weeks before, Akmed had eschewed the company of the Indian maidens, making her feel special with his yearning to talk of their homeland, yet now he seemed infected with the brutality of the men.

"Thou make'st me low," she said miserably.

"We are all low now," he said, hitching his breeches. He left her sitting on a fallen tree in the woods.

How was Willow to know there were eyes watching from afar?

Three weeks after they had landed, the fort was well underway, with its defensive ditch and palisade gradually encircling the village. An abatis of hundreds of sharpened stakes bristled outward between the ditch and the palisade of pines. The men had driven the villagers to the brink of death, working to exhaustion themselves. The ancient cannon found among the *Tiger's* ballast had been lifted from the bottom of the ship by means of a tripod of timbers, then dragged up the hill to the fort on pine rollers. Cabeza had installed it in a bastion constructed of stone overlooking the river. If the Indians from down river attempted an attack, *La Tortuga* would be there to answer them.

Willow was put to work with the Indian women, harvesting what was left of the maize in their fields. She was also tasked with fashioning rope from a field of hemp; Cabeza reasoned that extra rope might come in handy when they departed in the spring.

It was toward evening one day that she wandered down the gully to the brook where she bathed. Her hands ached from stripping the hemp to dry it for cordage and she was looking forward to a last dip in the brook before the season grew too cold to bathe. Dragón gamboled back and forth on the trail in a playful mood.

She had reached a small hill above the brook when Dragón spied a deer and took off running after it, huffing low and growling in excitement. The dog flew over the hill on the deer's heels, which leaped as if on springs through the forest.

"Dragón!" she hissed after him, not daring to shout. But there was no way the dog could hear her, and after a moment she heard it yelp.

"Dragón!" With her heart pounding she ran up the trail, rounding the hilltop. Before her, the trail snaked down into the gully, which lay in shadow now with the sun going down. At the bottom of the hill she could hear the dog whimpering, then growling and snapping. There came a liquid cough, followed by a loud thunk and another yelp. Then silence.

Willow froze, as stock-still as the deer staring at her through the trees on the far hill. Abruptly, it flicked its tail and leapt into the forest.

"Dragón?" she called, not daring to move. Yet what choice did she have? The war dog was her only champion among the crew spiraling into savagery. But more than that, she loved him as she had loved the lion, Aslan. Loved him as much as any woman loves a child. There was no way she could leave him now, not after he had saved her so many times.

Silently, Willow crept forward, peering into the gully for any sign of movement. She glimpsed something black amid the grass beside the brook at the bottom of the hill and gasped, knowing it must be Dragón lying there. She turned to run and then with her heart rising in her throat, forced herself to turn back again. She stumbled forward down the hill, sobbing, wanting to scream... Too late, she glimpsed the edge of a brown tunic as she passed a broad oak tree.

"Hello sweetie." It was the Frenchman, Garon, hidden behind the tree. He seized her by her hair and pulled her twisting and clawing to within inches of his face. "I've come to get what's owed."

Twisting away and struggling with all her strength against the arms gripping her shoulder, Willow glanced toward the brook where Dragón lay. The dog was lying there with its eyes open and its tongue lolling from its mouth; the bolt of a crossbow was buried in his ribs, with another jutting from his chest.

"Dragón!" she cried, knowing it was hopeless.

Garon jerked her face back his way and his wide eyes loomed before her, making it seem as if his flat stare filled the whole world. She gagged on his breath and squirmed as he pulled her forward, kissing her cheek and whispering in her ear.

"Oh princess, did you know? I've been here every day, waiting for you, waiting for my chance. I planned to take your leg, as you've taken mine, but seeing as your beast is now barking in hell I suppose the debt is half paid."

"Stinking pig! Let me go!" She twisted in his grasp, but he gripped her as if she was nothing more than a doll.

"You should have taken my coin, sweet, when you had the chance," he went on as if he hadn't heard her. "Now there's a price to pay and I swear I'll wring it from you, but it will go hard on you darling, I promise you that."

Garon paused to take a breath, relishing the moment. She squirmed in his grasp and he slapped her hard across the face.

"Did that hurt?" he went on. "No, for what could you know of pain? How could you know the pain I've felt? D'you know what it means to have your leg cruelly carved away and to hump around on a post of wood like a puppet? No, I suppose not, but know this: I've not had a moment's peace since the barber's saw bit my flesh in Hispaniola. It aches, it gnaws at me. I cannot sleep, cannot think of anything but the pain of it. Many times I've been tempted to bleed myself to salvation with my own hand to still the pain! The endless pain! Only one thing has kept me alive and that was the thought of thee, child. The thought of making you pay for my ruin. Do you see this awful peg on which I limp? Do you see it? Can you imagine what such a peg might do to a woman? The pain of it..."

Garon breathed heavily, searching her face for signs of terror, his eyes dancing with glee. Willow quivered like a rabbit, but said nothing, trying to think of how she might reach the dagger on its thong beneath her dress. Only Akmed had ever known of it; her father's gift had been her secret all along. She had never forgotten his words to keep it by her side; the slim blade lay beside her even when she bathed naked in a stream.

Garon held her in an iron grip with the spent crossbow at his feet. Her only hope was to reach her knife with the faint chance of stabbing him in the neck. Or, as Father had once instructed, in the eye.

"Do you mean to strip me then, ugly toad?" she said, taunting him in the hope that he would take the bait. Her anger over Dragón had overcome her fear and she managed to spit in his face, kicking for his groin. Perhaps he would release her long enough for her to grasp the knife beneath her dress. Perhaps in the moment that he lifted her hem she'd be able to seize the dagger from its sheath...

But there was to be no unveiling, nor any chance. Instead, Garon lifted her as if she were a toy. Turning, he dashed her head against the trunk of the tree before throwing her to the ground.

A light exploded in Willow's brain as the back of her head hit the tree and moments later she found herself in a daze, lying on her stomach on the ground with Garon lifting her dress from behind. She was barely conscious, limp as a dead fish, being pulled up on her knees from behind with no chance of reaching her dagger and defending herself. Her stomach lurched and she gagged, flooding with sick resignation as she struggled to crawl from his grasp.

But then in her daze she saw grim faces above her and the lean, half-naked bodies of men melting from the forest.

One of them clubbed Garon hard behind the ear with a serrated club and he tumbled over sideways with his face blanching white with shock. In an instant, the side of his head turned from pink to red and began oozing blood down his chest. Just as quickly, four hard men were on him, sitting on his chest and roughly binding his hands and feet. They stood him against the tree and bound him to its trunk.

There were six of them, wearing little but paint and tattoos. To Willow they looked like demons from a black dream, but they ignored her and stepped to where Garon's crossbow lay, studying it with interest.

Garon's mouth had been stuffed with moss and leaves and now his eyes darted about in fright as he struggled to scream. The warriors tossed the crossbow aside and took to examining his wooden leg and the bucket which held it strapped to his stump. One of them produced a long knife, which looked as if it had been chipped from black glass, and cut the leather strap binding the bucket and its peg to Garon's waist. The warrior examined it closely, recoiling from the stench of the leather sheath at the bottom of the bucket, before probing the stump of Garon's leg with the knife. He screamed at its touch, then gagged as the moss clogged his throat.

"Thou were ever an unlucky man when you chose to molest me!" Willow cried from where she sprawled on the ground. "Know this, dung, Dragón awaits you in hell when these devils have had their way with you!"

But Garon had no time to digest her words, for the leader of his tormentors had lowered the Frenchman's breeches, spreading his thighs and slapping the underside of his testicles with the flat side of the long knife. Garon's eyes bulged in terror as they whispered mocking words into his ears. Willow could see what was coming and turned away, clapping her hands over the sides of her head. Even so, she could hear Garon screaming and choking through his gag as the obsidian knife went to work on him, and then the sound of him being clubbed to death with his oaken leg. She heard murmurs of approval over her shoulder as the dead man's face was methodically carved away.

The deed done, two of them dragged Willow to her feet and pushed her deeper into the forest where the whitetail deer had stood, while two others grasped Dragón's legs and dragged him along behind them.

Soon, they came to a clearing where Willow found a rough camp of nearly thirty of the escaped villagers who glared at her with murder in their eyes. Only the intercession of two women saved her, and she recognized them as being among those whom she had tried to protect from the Spaniards.

By now the sun was setting, yet the warrior who had wielded the knife gave orders to leave. Although Willow could not understand his words, she sensed that he feared pursuit by Cabeza's men once Garon's body was discovered. No one complained; indeed they seemed eager to go. They picked up what few things they had and set out in single-file toward the north with three warriors ahead and three behind.

Along with them came the body of Dragón, slung upside down on a pole carried between two men. All night they walked a trail that was silver in the moonlight; it was not hard to follow, the sky was bright with stars and the moon was nearly full.

Morning came and with it the throng of her captors collapsed in exhaustion. A fire was made and Willow watched dumbly as the body of Dragón was dismembered and roasted over a spit. She was not offered any of the meat, nor did she want any. At her feet lay Dragón's head, kicked into the coals for roasting.

The trail carried on to the north, reaching another river three days later, which Willow suspected flowed into the Mississippi. Indeed, the trail was a shortcut between the two rivers and the hunters had been intent on visiting their distant kin when they had come upon the Spaniards.

One by one, they had found their kinsmen shivering with hunger and fright in the forest surrounding the village and had gathered them in a place of safety. It was they who had stood in the forest beyond the fort, observing the Spaniards and their slaves at work. It was they who had fired their arrows, testing the Spaniards' defenses. The hunters had plotted their vengeance, waiting for one of the demons to stray from the fort. They had been tracking a whitetail when they discovered Garon lurking behind a huge oak and had watched as he killed the dog and tormented Willow by the brook. Now, the chieftain named Black Knife led the way with Garon's dank blond scalp dangling from his waist.

Willow was delirious from exhaustion for days after her capture. The refugees had been granted a brief rest when the dog had been devoured, but at best she'd had an hour's fitful sleep. Nor was she used to walking so far after weeks on the ship. She stumbled on footsore and exhausted, eating only a palmful of parched corn each day.

At times she wept for Dragón. In her homeland, dogs were filthy, snarling nuisances, good only for cleaning the gutters, but she had grown to love Dragón and her chest ached with his loss. She sobbed as she slouched along, stilling only when she was cuffed by a warrior.

Late on the third day of their march they came to a village where several of their party were met with great joy. In time Willow would learn that these were members of the same clan. All along the river were villages united by the ties of kinship, and in twos and threes, members of their group were left to their relatives. There at last she received a bowl of cornmeal mush and a meaty bone which had not yet been drained of its marrow.

Willow lost count of the days as they followed the path along the river to the west. Villages came and went and each time their people flocked to see her, remarking on the ringlets of her hair and the darkness of her skin. Even in Sevilla she had been considered exotic, but here the daughter of an Arab Bedouin and a negress out of Timbuktu was beyond comprehension.

It wasn't long before the forest faded into a sea of brush and then grasslands which spread to the far horizon. The villages changed with the terrain, for their conical houses were made of woven grass and reeds, shaped much like the bee hives on Abu bin Nisar's estate. In some of the larger villages there were lodges big enough to shelter thirty people.

To her relief she was not raped, for unlike the Spaniards and the Portuguese, the Indian men who held her captive seemed disinclined to think of such a thing. Later she learned that rape was considered beneath their dignity. Several times she tried speaking with her captors, making signs that she was hungry or thirsty and they gave her bemused looks, beckoning her to speak with the women instead. These she approached with trepidation, expecting to be shunned or reviled; to her relief she was treated kindly, as if she were a sister.

At last there came a day when there were only two of the villagers left in their company along with the six hunters. They had been walking for more than two weeks along the riverbank and Willow had long since given up any hope of being rescued by Captain Cabeza and his men. If anything they would be buttoned up and quaking in their rough fort after finding Garon's mutilated corpse. But what kind of life awaited her? Each village had grown poorer and more dismal as they journeyed up the river, with the country growing dryer, parched and red. Hills of red sand rolled on the horizon while the brush alongside the trail was thick with thorns and cactus. Once, they came across a snake lying in the middle of the trail which was as long as a tall man and as thick as a tall man's arm. The snake had a diamond pattern to its skin and a strange rattle on its tail, which buzzed a warning. The warriors had gazed upon it impassively for some time, not bothering to disturb its progress as it slithered into the brush.

At last they came to Black Knife's village and a joyful celebration at the hunters' return. They had taken three deer and a bear along the way and Willow had been tasked with carrying the gutted body of a young doe slung over her shoulders. She tossed it on the pile of carcasses at the center of the village, grateful to be free of its musky odor and the ache in her shoulders. Then, as was the habit of every village she had passed, she stood inspection for the gleeful villagers. The women of the village swarmed around her, fingering her curls and caressing her skin with wondering eyes. An old woman kneaded her breasts and smiled, nodding as she gazed into Willow's eyes. Another woman attempted to pry open her mouth to inspect her teeth, prompting Willow to give her an outraged shove. Only then did Willow understand and she uttered a loud laugh and a curse, prompting the women to step back in surprise.

"Thou think me a camel!" she cried. "I am no more than a prize camel at my father's corral in Azemmour!"

The village women didn't understand what Willow said, but they nodded in agreement. "Camel?" one of them said.

"Safasaf," she replied - Willow - pointing to her chest. "My name is Safasaf."

"Sa-fa-saf." Her name was repeated in Arabic along with words of welcome. Although she was weary to the point of tears and filthy from her long march, Willow offered a smile and bowed low before them. She had learned long ago at her mother's market stall that it was wise to make a good first impression.

Then, with something approaching the feeling of a ceremony, the women had led her to a low wooden platform at the far end of the village, atop which she found the skeleton of a small horse. The skull had been painted red and festooned with beads made from shells and seeds. Willow had the eerie feeling that the horse's skull was grinning at her, as if to say, you are mine now.

That afternoon the women dressed the game, putting Willow to work scraping bits of tissue off the bloody hides. Most of the meat was hung to dry in the sun out of reach of the village dogs, but one of the deer and much of the bear was roasted and Willow thought she would swoon at the delicious scent of the cooking meat. She'd had been given mostly corn and prairie turnips to eat on the long walk to the village and now she was filled with an animal craving for meat.

This was served on a wooden platter with everyone in the village reaching in to grab a share, with the dogs of the village crowding close behind them, leaping and whining as bits of gristle and bones sucked of their marrow were tossed their way.

What a feast! Willow's face was still greasy with bear fat when the last sliver of meat disappeared, only to be pulled to her feet as the sound of drumming broke out. Her stomach heaved - it had been so long since it had been full - yet she held herself together, joining a long line of excited women. Then to her surprise, every woman in the village began to dance and sing in a line that circled around the gathering place, with children flocking around them or joining in the procession. Around them, the men clapped and stamped before beginning their own dance. The male and female voices merged and Willow's heart lifted. She had no choice but to join the dance, and though she felt awkward with the unfamiliar steps, it felt good to be back in the company of women again. What would old Abu bin Nisar think of her now? What would Mother and Father say? They would surely be scandalized, but perhaps they would also smile.

But if Willow thought she was to be pampered in the village of Black Knife as if she were a prize camel, she was mistaken. The next day she was put to work harvesting maize in the field beyond the village, and thereafter commanded to dig for roots in the brush alongside the field. There was firewood to collect and cotton to twist into thread. She was given a place to sleep in the lodge of a family that had recently lost an old woman to tumors, directed to lie on the dead woman's bench and its worn buffalo hide.

It wasn't long before Willow reflected that her life as a slave had spiraled a downward course; first as the serving girl of Abu bin Nisar, then a captive of the Spaniards, and now this, grubbing for roots and maize among the drought-stricken fields of a people she came to know as the Adai. What had she done to provoke the wrath of Allah? What sort of life could she have along this dismal river?

But then came the stranger with the crippled foot and the strange gray eyes rimmed with gold, almost like those of her fierce, beloved father. In time she came to understand that his name was Animi-ma'lingan, He Who Outruns the Wolves. But to Willow, he was known simply as Wolf.

Prickly Pear

To Wolf's dismay there were no dugouts in Black Knife's village and the forest had long since melted away, leaving only the plains to the north and a dense chaparral of brush to the south for as far as an eagle could see. Without a way to paddle down the river there would be no chance to escape, for Wolf knew that even if he attempted to run early in the night, his pursuers would quickly catch him within a day. And then there would be punishment.

By signs he attempted to make his captors understand that he was a fisherman as well as a trader. Perhaps if he could lash a couple of logs together under the pretense of fishing, he could float away. But to his surprise, the people of the plains ate fish only as a last resort to starvation, and there were few logs in the village to speak of, these being precious, having been dragged a great distance from the forest far down river. As a last hope, Wolf resolved to swim across the river and hide in the brush on the other side until his captors gave up looking for him. He doubted that any of the Adai could swim, and most likely they would not think to look for him there. But this too would be risky, for the river was not deep where it passed the village; it was perhaps chest-high and could be waded.

Then too, there was the sunktanka. Wabeno had instructed him to bring the beast home, if he could, and its painted skull would surely be prized as a great treasure by his uncles among the shamans. It would be a shame to come so far and not seize it.

Last of all, there was the woman with the dark skin and the green eyes circled in the color of the sun. Something in his chest had twinged at the first sight of her and somehow, he imagined, she had something to do with the mystery of the sunktanka.

He was put to women's work on the morning after his capture, gathering the winter harvest of maize and grubbing for roots alongside the strange woman, with no ceremony or pretense of adoption. Wolf knew readily enough that he had the status of a slave among his captors, for though he had scared some of them into shitting themselves in the whipping ceremony, the head man known as Black Knife had looked upon his performance as being more comical than that of sorcery. His command was the only thing that kept Wolf's back from being riddled with arrows when he had rolled his eyes and hopped on one foot, uttering his ghastly howl.

Lodgings were scarce in the village. Nor did any of the villagers care to invite a man with the eyes of a wolf into their homes. Instead, Wolf was directed to sleep beneath the platform that held the skull of the sunktanka. Thankfully, he was given permission to cover its sides with bundles of brush. This offered scant protection from the cold winds and freezing temperatures of the plains as the winter rolled on, but Wolf was granted an old buffalo robe to roll up in at night. He took to wearing the tattered robe to the fields and was grateful for its warmth, for even though he prided himself as being of the hardy Ojibwe, no man could survive the icy fingers of winter without protection, not even this far south.

The length of a full moon passed, yet Wolf made little progress in learning the Caddo language of the Adai, who disdained his company, even though he tried by signs to make them understand that he had many stories to share. What people did not wish to hear stories through the dull passing of winter? he wondered, for his tales had been in high demand in many lodges of the Ojibwe. Nor had there been any ceremony of adoption into the tribe; he was simply a slave, treated neither harshly nor well, simply with indifference.

Yet, little by little, he learned a few words, along with the name of their village; it was the Place of the Red Sand.

The woman with the dark skin was also a mystery. There were no markings upon her or her clothing to indicate what tribe or clan she might be from, and she wore sandals instead of moccasins, the beadwork of which might offer a clue. Wolf knew enough of the tongues of the Haudenosaunee and the Dakota and had even learned a few words of the Caddo people, yet she knew none of these. He sensed by the weight and tone of her words that she was attempting to speak two different languages to him, but both were utterly unfamiliar. To his surprise, she seemed to know nothing of sign language; when he attempted to speak to her with the motion of his hands, she gave him a blank look in response.

Still, she gave a merry laugh when he gazed back in puzzlement at her words and his heart warmed. He noted with some amusement that she scorned the stoop labor of the women in the tribe. It was as if she thought the work was beneath her and she was frequently threatened with a stick. Once, she caught him smiling at her after she'd been beaten, and she had smiled in return.

One day, the two of them were directed into the brush lands in search of prickly pear fruit. These were the deep red fruits which grew on the pads of the cactus and were best taken during the heat of the summer when they were juicy and sweet. Yet it was a hungrier winter than most in the Red Sand Place, and the cacti growing some distance away had not been harvested. Although the fruit was spiny with thorns and had long since shriveled, they were commanded to gather as many baskets of it as possible, along with the slimmer and more tender pads of the cacti, which might be roasted and eaten.

That afternoon, the two of them found themselves in a clearing some distance from the other pickers, and though Wolf was loathe to share his name with a stranger, it seemed as good a way to start as any. He sat back on his haunches, pointed to his chest, and gave the low musical howl of a wolf.

The woman looked at him gravely and nodded. "*Lobo*," she said pointing at his chest, Wolf.

"Animi-ma'lingan," he replied, before realizing that his full name might be too much for her to understand. "Ma'lingan... *Lobo*," he added, making signs with his hands to indicate that both meant Wolf.

Then, to his surprise, the woman pulled a shining object from the folds of her tunic where it lay strung on a cord. She blew a few notes on it and he realized it was some kind of flute. To his even greater surprise, she began to sing in a soft voice that shivered him down to his toes.

> "I am a lonely wolf in the forest,
> At night I sing my lonely song,
> For my lost love,
> The mate that I love,
> Now he's gone,
> And I'm alone.
>
>
> And I sing oooo, oooo-ooo, oooo-ooo, ooo-ooo-ooo-ooo."

The woman finished her song, smiling in satisfaction. "Ma'lingan!' she repeated with a smile, and he knew well enough what she had been singing about. But that was not all, for there was a narrow brook nearby, hidden and almost choked with brush except for a few trees straggling along its bank, and by signs she directed him to follow her.

At the edge of the brook stood a small tree with its long leaves falling in sweeping tendrils. She picked up one of its fronds and pointed to her chest.

"Safasaf," she said. Willow.

Wolf nodded gravely and repeated her name. In his own language, willow was *oziisigobimizh*, but he understood her well enough. After that, they sat cross-legged a few feet apart and played the naming game, repeating each other's words in kind. Sun, earth, face, eyes, grass, sky... Wolf had a quick ear with languages; his memory was part of his gift as a storyteller, and now he savored every word from Willow's lips.

For her part, Willow had been eyeing Wolf for some time. She sensed a cagey intelligence within him and unlike the Adai men, he was easy with his smiles. That, and his eyes were uncannily like those of her father. There was also a Bedouin toughness about him... She suspected that he would not remain a captive of the Adai for long.

As for herself, a more dismal fate awaited, for one day Black Knife had brought his son to the lodge where she slept, calling for her to come forth. The chief's son was barely out of his boyhood, perhaps fourteen or fifteen years old, with spots still on his face, yet by signs she was given to understand that they were to be married.

A filthy word arose on Willow's lips when comprehension rippled through her - one that was used only by the coarsest of men among the conquistadors. Married to this cretin!? The boy looked at her insolently under his father's solemn gaze and Willow had shook her head, no, and frowned in refusal. But if the head man and his son cared for her feelings, they did not show it. Black Knife had nodded as his son stood smirking by his side and then the two of them turned and walked away.

Married? But when? How? The weeks had passed and there had been no ceremony, but Black Knife's son had come creeping around her lodge to peer at her. Sometimes she could hear him whispering through its matted wall at night, as if urging her to come out.

Now, she sat in the sun with Wolf, using sand to rub away the spines of the prickly pear fruit. She knew that it must be February or March by now, yet it was an unusually warm day. The fleeting thought of Ramadan crossed her mind and she realized that it had been more than a year since she had observed the month-long fast required of all the Faithful. But who knew when such a fast might occur in this strange land? Nor had she bowed to Mecca in all the time since she'd been captured. What was the use? Allah had forsaken her.

But across from her Wolf repeated another of her words in their learning game. "Sand," she said in Spanish, letting a handful run through her fingers. "Sand," he repeated, smiling.

Yes, sand, she thought, running through my fingers like my fate.

The Wedding

The village had planned on two ceremonies that spring, the first of which was endured by Willow.

Black Knife's ancient mother had come calling, shriveled and dry as a corn husk with age. With some difficulty she gave Willow to understand that her grandson's name was Root. Then the old woman had pointed to the morning sky where the faint moon could be seen, hanging a little more than halfway full. By signs, Willow understood that she was to be wed when the moon was full.

The next morning she had crept away from the task of digging prairie turnips, and after climbing the low hill on the path alongside the river she had run for her life as if all the demon *shaytans* of her father's tales were on her heels. All day she ran along the twisting trail along the river, hoping to get as far as possible before she was discovered missing. That night, she had hidden in a thicket, shivering at the sound of animals and birds rustling in the brush around her. Sleep was impossible and she rose with the frost-covered dawn and ran again, skirting a small village and its barking dogs.

But the dogs were her doom, for the village men soon caught her and Black Knife and his men arrived later that day. With them came Root, out of breath and angry at the treachery of his betrothed.

Wolf had heard the ruckus in the village and noted with some satisfaction that Willow had fled. It would be a good test to see if escape was possible. But he wasn't surprised when she was returned the next day, as angry as a spitting wildcat, and he resolved to take her with him if he could find a way to escape.

Then came the day when Willow was married. She had been draped in a long gown fashioned of shells which Root's mother and grandmother had worn on their own nuptials.

"You sit, you sit," Root's mother said with a stern face, pointing to the place next to her son.

Willow scowled and sat next to Root, looking neither right nor left during the meager feast which followed. Then came dancing and drumming, and a few words from the old shaman of the village.

Then came the thing she feared most. Root's mother hovered over her with bright eyes and a grin filled with ragged teeth. "You come now, you come!"

Root's mother and his sisters dragged her up from where she sat, pushing her along to a small hut at the edge of the village where she was expected to do the wedding deed with her new husband. Willow squirmed and cursed the whole way, uttering the most horrid oaths of the conquistadors - words that would never have crossed her lips in the span of a lifetime, yet now she no longer cared.

Even so, having been forewarned of the wedding, she had taken steps to ensure that her new husband was both satisfied, yet denied.

When she was still a girl, about to be sold north as a servant to Abu bin Nisar, her mother had sent her to talk with a coarse, older woman with unruly hair, a hard face and dark, appraising eyes. The woman was well known as a midwife in their quarter of the city, but had lurid knowledge of other things as well, and they had a long talk about the secrets of lovemaking that only women knew. Willow knew about the "unspeakable act" of course, having observed the rutting of camels, horses and donkeys. Yet the woman known as Sheka had been shockingly frank about the finer points of the act and many other things having to do with men and their crude desires. One of these had been how to escape the embrace of a man, particularly that of a young man. Willow's young ears had burned at Sheka's instruction; the awful thing she spoke of had seemed both strange and unlikely at the time, yet now she resolved to give it a try.

The hut to which she had been led was low and only a few steps wide. Beyond its walls, Willow could hear the villagers gathered as she and Root were ushered inside. She thought of Sheka's advice, imagining that the task before her could be no worse than pulling burrs from around a sheep's filthy bunghole, or at least she hoped not.

Prior to the wedding ceremony, she had secreted a small gourd of bear grease in her dress. Now, Root put his hands on her hips, murmuring his desire. But she pushed him away and uttered a sharp command:

"Strip!"

By signs he understood her meaning well enough, and in a moment her boy husband had dropped his breechclout and stood naked and erect before her.

Willow had raised her left finger solemnly to her lips, shushing him and smiling lasciviously, as if he was in for the time of his life. Root stood gasping in the dim light of the lodge with his legs shaking in anticipation. Outside, she heard the murmuring crowd, and she gave a small cry as if in the throes of the wedding act.

She gazed into Root's eyes, whispering the unclean words of seduction that Sheka had told her, hoping that Allah was not listening.

Then, with her right hand dripping with warm bear grease, she had reached for his cock. It quivered in her grasp, and with only three languid strokes of its shaft, Root gave out a cry of ecstasy as his jism shot forth against the walls of the lodge.

"Ah! Aaah!" he cried, doubling over. To this, Willow added her own voice, crying, "Aaah!" loud enough for all outside to hear.

A dab of Root's spunk had soiled Willow's hand and with a grave sense of ceremony she wiped her palm down the length of his chest as if this was the proper way of pleasing a newly-wed husband. For his part, Root seemed happy enough, for he was nowhere close to being a full-grown man and had been quite nervous as they had entered the wedding lodge. Yet now he was pleased to hear the cheers outside, for the villagers had heard him cry out and knew that the deed was done. He laid himself down, preparing to nap.

"I have milked thee like a goat, fool, and that is all you will ever have of me," Willow said grimly as he closed his eyes, though she knew that in time Root would demand more of her. How easy it would be to cut his throat, she thought. But she was no murderer and he was just an ignorant boy.

Yet she had a reprieve, for it was March, and thus, not the lovemaking season. As with most peoples of the Great Turtle Island, the Adai were careful to avoid lovemaking in the spring so as not to have a babe born during the winter when there were difficulties enough without the addition of a newborn. Root's wedding had been the exception, but for now, Willow slept with the women in Black Knife's cramped lodge, while her husband slept with the men as was proper. Once more he approached her in the brush lands when the chance arose, again receiving the hand of refusal. Yet again, Root seemed happy with the outcome, as if it were the natural course of things between a husband and wife. Still, Willow dreaded the day when she would have no choice but to bend for him, and then no choice but to bear Root's children. He had none of his father's gravity and was still a boy in every way, inept, insolent, and without promise.

Wolf had observed Willow's marriage glumly, wondering when her belly would swell. Another woman, gone! And this was one that he yearned for... A plan of escape had begun to take shape in his mind as he lay on his pallet of straw at night and it no longer included Willow, for how could he steal another man's wife? It would be hard enough to escape on his own, especially if he took the sunktanka with him.

The animal, he gradually learned, had been found wandering the prairie, and unlike a deer it had waited patiently until a band of Adai hunters had approached it. They had quickly killed and eaten the strange beast, finding its meat to be stringy and tough. It was only after they had bleached and stripped its skeleton atop a hill of red ants that they had learned that it had escaped from the belly of a great fish, or perhaps a sea bird, which had washed up on the shores of the Great Salt Water to the south. Its companions had been a clan of hairy-faced men who had died one-by-one after their enslavement by a tribe of the Caddo living along the coast.

Hearing the tale, the Adai had begun to regret the death of the strange beast and had resolved to let it live on at the center of their village. Its skeleton was now borne aloft with them on a platform when they forayed out in search of the buffalo, and indeed, it had brought them a great deal of good luck in the hunt. Kinsmen from up and down the river came to view the sunktanka's bones, and it was the one great thing that the Red Sand Place was known for.

Wolf knew that it would be risky stealing such a treasure and that every village along the river would be watching for him. But he was bold enough to think that it could be done. In fact, he smiled at the challenge, imagining the chagrin of his captors once they discovered it gone. Yet he knew their vengeance would be excruciating if they caught him.

It had been a difficult winter, colder than most, and the prior year's harvest had been diminished by drought. The cache of maize, beans, sunflowers and other crops had dwindled to dust and the villagers were reduced to eating the woody pads of prickly pear and what roots they could scrounge from the brush. Occasionally, the hunters brought in rabbits, badgers, deer and prairie dogs, but their catch was meager at best.

Wolf had watched the last of the corn disappear, kernel by kernel, until even a handful was denied him. He was told to forage as best he could. Several times he vouched his skill at fishing, but the people of the Red Sand Place thought of fish as trash, barely fit to eat. Constructing a weir of sticks in the river, he managed to catch a few catfish, wrapping them in leaves and roasting them over coals. Yet, except for Willow, the people of the village grimaced at the bewhiskered fish and declined his offer to share. Instead, the Adai staked their hopes on the coming of the buffalo.

"Soon the buffalo come," Black Knife said to him one evening, turning up his nose at Wolf's catfish.

"I have not seen them," Wolf gestured to the empty plains across the river. "All winter, nothing. What if they do not come?"

"You help bring them," Black Knife said with a grimace before walking away. Wolf had no doubt as to what his cryptic words meant. It hastened his plans for escape.

The river had risen considerably as spring drew on, flowing faster, deeper and colder than when Wolf arrived. No one among the Adai could wade it now, yet he was sure that he would be able to swim to the other side if the chill did not kill him first. All of the Ojibwe knew the danger of cold water, for a swamped canoe could mean a quick death to those who could not wade to shore in time once the ice melted on the northern lakes. But Wolf was less sure that he'd be able to manage the current while hampered by the skull of the sunktanka and a part of him nagged to steal Willow away. He might be able to swim the river, but he doubted the woman could make it. By signs she had told him that she could not swim.

He had noticed early on that she had no affection for Root, barely hiding her contempt. Once, Root had raised a stick to her, but had been cowed by the murder in her eyes and had turned away, laughing as if the beating that he threatened was merely a joke. Mostly, he stayed away, joining the hunters for several days at a time. Thus, Wolf found time to sit and learn more of the language she called Espanól.

Yet he still knew only a few words and thus there were many things he could not ask her. What was her clan? Where were her people? Why was she so dark; had she been burned by the sun? At best she was able to explain by signs and a few words that she had come from down the river. Once, he had attempted to question her about the sunktanka and she had nodded vigorously, answering yes, and drawing the shape of the creature with her arms.

"Are your people of the sunktanka?" he asked, for these words were easy enough to express.

"Yes," she said. "*Caballo*." Horse.

"*Caballo*," he repeated.

"*Caballista?*" she asked, raising her eyebrows and pointing to his chest.

Wolf sensed that she was teasing, but he had no way of knowing what a horseman was, never having seen or heard of such a thing.

"Do you mean I am horse too? I do not understand."

"*El caballo es Montoya*," she said gravely.

"Montoya?" The horse was Montoya... what could that mean? Perhaps, he thought, Montoya was a sign of sorcery or magic.

"Montoya is magic?" He waved his hands in the air to signify invisible forces.

"No, Montoya is horse. Name of horse. Wolf, you. Montoya, horse."

"Ah."

"I was keeper of Montoya, and a dog, Dragón, and had a friend, Croen, yet they are lost to me now," she said sadly, doubting that Wolf could understand her.

And yet somehow he did, for he clasped his hands together in fists and clutched them to his chest. "Lost," he said somberly. "Dragón, Croen, Montoya. Lost."

"Yes."

And so their word game continued, with many misunderstandings and false starts. But Wolf looked forward to speaking with Willow each day, sneaking away with her as best he could while foraging amid the brushy chaparral. He looked for a sign that she would have him, hoping that she would let him steal her away, yet though her eyes lit up at his approach, she remained guarded, even distant.

As for Willow, her heart had begun to yearn for Wolf, who seemed both kind and a fellow conspirator. Yet, she had long since learned to hide her feelings behind a wall of bravado and indifference. If he only knew how tender she was inside... Yet a woman of the Faithful did not encourage a man unduly; this too her mother had taught her. Thus, she did her best to show Wolf that she was chaste and pure, despite the marriage she considered a sham. She also felt deeply confused, for what possible good could come of romancing a fellow slave? She knew what Black Knife had done to Garon, and if she wasn't careful, great harm might also come to Wolf. As it was, the village women had seen them talking together several times and were gossiping among themselves. She saw the gleam of their accusing eyes and knew it would go hard on Wolf if their tongues kept wagging. No, she thought, it was best to keep her feelings for him at arm's length, if only for his own protection.

Spring drew on with the bright promise of the sun mocking the starving villagers. With its warmth came the tender green of new life among the shoots of maize, yet also the knowledge that its harvest was still months away. A band of hunters was dispatched into the brushlands in search of buffalo, only to return a week later close to death from starvation themselves. The plains across the river remained empty as desolation descended on the village.

Black Knife himself went on a three-day fast on a bald hill not far from the village, shivering in the wind and rain as he appealed to the spirits to bring on the herds. Nothing came of it. A buffalo dance was held with everyone in the village joining in, yet again there came no sign. Then the old medicine-maker of the village sang himself sick over the course of two days. Nothing.

All of these things came and went in Wolf's understanding, and when at last the warriors of the village presented him with a loop around his neck, the ends of which were tied to the legs of two guards at night, he knew what was coming.

"They mean to kill you," Willow said, bringing a gourd of water to where he sat imprisoned beneath the sunktanka's bier.

Wolf nodded and smiled, yes. But he had not yet been painted and knew there would be a ceremony before he was sacrificed. The ceremony was sure to come, for what was the life of a slave when it might yield the return of the buffalo or the rains that nurtured the maize? At the least, he would be one less mouth to feed.

"Come with me," he said, gazing into her eyes.

Willow was startled. "What? How?"

"Tomorrow night." He raised a finger straight up, signifying mid-night. "When all sleep."

At the thought of escape a surge of blood rushed to her head and for a moment she felt as if she might faint. Go with this man? "Yes, I will try. But how?"

"You will see."

Wolf had spent the winter anticipating his death. No one had adopted him to replace a lost brother or son, nor did his lowly status as a slave seem likely to continue for long. He had heard of the rituals of other tribes, particularly those of the corn-planters, and had suspected for some time that the villagers meant to shed his blood in the spring, if only in the hope of bringing rain and a bountiful maize crop. Now, his fate seemed even more certain with the plains being empty of buffalo.

Thus, within a moon of his capture he had gathered several handfuls of spoiled plums which had fallen unnoticed into the grass beneath a tree by the river. These he had mashed to a pulp and mixed with a small amount of water in a gourd. He had sealed the gourd with a corn cob.

Long ago, in the time of their grandfathers' grandfathers, the shamans of the Ojibwe had noticed the strange effect of rotting fruit on birds and small animals. Pigeons were observed flapping helplessly on the ground under trees after gorging on fermented fruit, while woodchucks and the like were rendered so senseless that they could be scooped up by hand. There was a powerful medicine in the spoiled fruit that had been added to the herb craft of the Mide-wi-win.

Although he had been a poor student of other practices, Wolf was thankful that he had taken an interest in the medicine of herbs, roots and healing barks during the time with his uncles. Thus, he had concocted a potion of plum juice in his gourd, adding the shriveled fruits of the prickly pear and sweetening it with honey. At first it had smelled foul and he almost tossed it to the dogs, but gradually, after sifting away the pulp and adding more honey, he found that the potion had cleared to a thin syrup and could be tasted without grimacing. From time to time he took a small sip, noting with satisfaction that the drink quickly made him feel drowsy and strange. It had sweetened and seemed pleasant enough, though he considered it a poison.

But there was something more. During his time with the Tobacco People of the Tionontati, he had been introduced to a plant which created a pleasant euphoria when it was smoked. Some collapsed in giggles and laughter with its effects; others fell into a slack-jawed reverie. It was not a plant that did well in the chilly land of Kitchi Gami, but while combing the brush for prickly pear, Wolf had found a tall bush of it, planted, perhaps by a passing bird. This too he prepared, drying the buds of the herb as the Tionontati had instructed.

But all his plans and preparations would have been in vain were it not for the women of the Adai.

At the first hint of spring the women of the village had begun constructing several strange contraptions. At first, Wolf imagined them to be small shelters, as they were made of a half circle of supple branches, bowed into ribs. These were covered with tanned buffalo hides.

"What are you making?" he asked.

One of the women looked up and made the sign of horns, then cast a leaf on the water. "Bull boat," she said, gesturing to the far shore. "For the hunters."

Wolf had snorted at the thought of it, thinking of his fine canoe lying shattered just over the hill. By comparison, the bull boats were like nut shells. The women were preparing three of the skin boats, each no wider than the length of a man in diameter. The boats were meant to ferry the village men across the river so that they might hunt on the distant plains.

Yet in an instant he had grasped his salvation.

That night, two guards watched over Wolf, who was bound to them by the noose around his neck. Both were barely men, yet easily capable of running him down. Wolf gave no thought of trying to overwhelm them; instead, he produced his red stone pipe and invited them to smoke the last of his tobacco, procured so long ago from the Tionontati. It was a much finer tobacco than the young warriors were used to, and after some hesitation, they joined him in smoking.

"You will have this pipe when I have gone," he said agreeably after a few puffs on its stem.

"Why should we not take it now?" the more arrogant of the two asked.

Wolf made a face. "That would bring a curse on your head brother. Do not test the spirits until the time of your gift is at hand."

Then he pretended to take a drink from the gourd he had prepared, smacking his lips and uttering a sigh of satisfaction.

"What is that?" his other guard asked.

"Oh, it is only a bit of water, sweetened with honey and plums," he replied. "You would not like it."

His guards frowned but said nothing as the pipe passed around again. Wolf feigned taking another drink from the gourd, humming to himself.

"Give us a taste," the arrogant one said at last.

Wolf gave a wide yawn, tamping the spent ash from his pipe. "Tomorrow, brother, tomorrow," he said. "We will drink it to celebrate my passing."

Then, before the guards could demand more of him, he drew back into his rough shelter and curled up as if to sleep, leaving them shivering and mystified outside.

Morning came and Wolf was not permitted to leave the village. He spent the day sitting in the shadows beneath the skeleton of the sunktanka, watching the women preparing the paint to be used on the morrow. It was a red land and his captors prepared to send him to the spirit world painted a bright vermilion. As for his sacrifice, he had no idea. By fire? By the obsidian knife of the head man? If he escaped, perhaps the villagers would find another to sacrifice.

He thought ruefully that he had learned enough of their language to speak a few words, but never enough to tell the stories which Wabeno had said would protect him. Perhaps Wabeno was unaware of how many tongues were spoken in the world, for Wolf had already collected several.

Down by the river a group of women were admiring their handiwork as they took a bull boat for a short spin along its bank, laughing in delight. Wolf marked the best of the three boats, casting about for something which might be used as a paddle. He saw Willow standing among them and she nodded as he caught her eye.

Tonight or never, he thought. It must be tonight.

At dusk his guards came to him, seeming nervous, perhaps thinking that if Wolf intended to bolt it would be on their watch, for this was to be his last night on earth.

But Wolf greeted them as if they were old friends, offering them the last of his dried catfish. This, of course, they declined and he sat happily munching as their empty stomachs grumbled with hunger. Neither had eaten that day, and had consumed only a trace of maize the day before.

"Are you hungry, brothers?" he said at last. "Let us smoke, then, for all know that tobacco kills the hunger."

Once again, Wolf produced the handsome red stone pipe which had been given to him by the shaman Split Tail the prior summer. It was simply carved, without embellishments or symbols, but it had a tall bowl that tapered down to its stem. Wolf had packed most of the pipe with the herb of the euphoria plant. He filled the top of it with tobacco.

Darkness crept slowly on. It had been a warm day and both of his guards were already drowsy from the effects of starvation. "I do not care to smoke tonight," said the younger of the two, making as if to go to sleep.

"Ah, you are only hungry, brother," Wolf said. "Come, take the pipe. It will revive you and fill your stomach." He lifted a cinder to the pipe bowl, breathing in the tobacco. Half-reluctant, the younger guard took a pull.

The pipe went round the circle several times as the sun took its last look over the horizon.

"Your pipe has a strange taste today," said the older guard.

"I have saved the best of my tobacco for last," Wolf replied. He had feigned smoking the pipe by inhaling the layer of tobacco at its rim, and yet he could feel a trace of its euphoria creeping his way.

The pipe went around again and again as the guards savored its flavor.

"It is good!" the younger guard giggled. He began playing at the cord which ran from his ankle to the noose around Wolf's neck.

"It is powerful," the other agreed, weaving on his haunches with a foolish look on his face, "but it has made me even hungrier."

"We must smoke another pipe to lessen your hunger," Wolf said, reaching for more of the euphoria plant. To his mild surprise the younger guard renewed his giggling, as if the thought of smoking another bowl was the funniest thing he had ever heard.

"No... thirsty," the other said in a daze, waving a hand languidly. "Your tobacco has turned my mouth to cotton."

The words were barely out of his mouth when he began to chuckle and then jigged up and down on his haunches, laughing at the absurdity of it. "My mouth is cotton!" he exclaimed.

Truly, Wolf thought, bringing forth the gourd and pretending to take a long drink of it. He wiped a trickle of the potion from his chin and uttered a loud "aaah!" of satisfaction.

"Brothers, I fear this will be too sweet for you," he said, "for it is mixed with honey and the juice of plums."

"I like honey!" the young guard said with a broad grin on his face.

"Gimme," the older demanded.

But Wolf held back, clutching the gourd to his chest. "Brothers, I must warn you, this will make you strong with a woman. Strong as a rutting bull!"

"How do you mean, brother?" the older asked, his eyes narrowing.

Wolf made the sex sign, poking the circle of his thumb and finger on his left hand back and forth with the pointer finger of his other hand and nodding solemnly. "Like this, brothers, like this."

Only his skill as a storyteller kept Wolf from laughing at his own words. He had said as much to credulous listeners in the past as a joke, bidding them to drink from a gourd full of piss to a great deal of hilarity after one among them was foolish enough to take a sip. Now, he could not resist embellishing the claim.

"Many women have swooned in the arms of a man who drinks this," he said gravely as the two sat slack-jawed before him. "For it is a sweet drink, brothers, and it sweetens a man's stones. I myself have had three women at once after drinking this, and even then I ached for more. And brothers, know this," he added in a low voice. "The women ached for me."

No more encouragement was needed. The younger of the two seized the gourd from Wolf's hands and took a long swallow, gasping at its taste, while his partner seized it just as quickly, taking two long gulps.

"It is sweet, as you say, but it burns," the older guard said, grimacing.

"Ah, you must not drink too much, for that is the fire that will burn in your stones," Wolf cautioned. "You will be lusting for half a moon, at least."

This only served to make his guards drink even more, and soon they had gulped down the entire gourd. They began to sway, with their eyes closing, and the arrogant one sang a few snatches of song, slurring his words.

"You have tricked us," he said drowsily after a time, weaving with his eyes half shut.

"No brother, you have tricked me."

"Unh?" The guard was weaving harder now with his head spinning. Abruptly, he collapsed on his side, chuckling at the strangeness of it. He made a lazy circling motion with his hand and pointed to his head, offering Wolf a stupefied grin.

"Shhh, brother, you are only sleepy, as am I," Wolf replied, yawning. "Oh brothers, I am tired," he murmured in a soft voice. "Sleepy, I feel sleepy... I can barely keep my eyes open... I am going to sleep now. Sleep like a baby..."

But there was no need to say more, for both of his guards had collapsed with their heads on their chests with the empty gourd between them. It was as if they were dead, though Wolf knew they were simply lying at the depth of a slumber unlike anything they had ever known. He slipped a fine obsidian knife from the older guard's sheath and cut the cord around his neck, tying a short length of it around the ankles of each of the sleeping men.

"Amuse yourselves, brothers," he whispered as he tied the knots. "Amuse yourselves."

Across the way he saw a shadow moving at the mouth of Black Knife's lodge and after a moment, Willow stood before him.

"What did you do?" she asked, gazing at the sleeping guards.

"Ojibwe magic," he replied in his own tongue, not knowing the words in Spanish.

Willow nodded nonetheless. At her side she carried a small bag of maize which she had hidden away. It was barely two handfuls, only enough to last a day.

"Let's go," she said, agitated. Root's grandmother had stirred when she had risen, and Willow had given the excuse that she felt sick and needed to purge her bowels. But the old woman would surely sound the alarm if she didn't return soon. Willow grappled for words, not knowing enough of them to explain the need to hurry.

But Wolf understood her agitation well enough, and putting a finger to his lips, he reached to the top of the platform and seized the shell-covered skull of the sunktanka. Willow gave him a questioning look, but said nothing as they made their way down to the riverbank.

That day at Wolf's instruction, she had wandered over to the ruins of his canoe and found its paddle lying in the brush by the river. It had taken Wolf a long time to make her understand what he sought, drawing pictures in the sand and pointing over the hill beyond the village. But now the paddle lay hidden a short way from the village and Willow ran for it as Wolf pushed two of the precious bull boats into the current where they twirled atop the water, spinning toward the far side of the river. He was close behind them, dragging the best of the three bull boats through the water along the riverbank.

They had traveled only a short way around the bend beyond the village when the alarm was sounded. Over the hill a dog began to bark, and then another. And then there came a man's questioning voice, sounding deep and low in the night, followed by the shrill voice of Root's grandmother. Dimly, they heard muttering as someone came upon the sleeping guards and then cries of rage as the two leapt to their tangled feet and promptly fell on their faces. But it was too late, for Wolf and Willow were already out of sight of the village with their bull boat spinning in the current. Wolf flailed at the water with his paddle; the round boat seemed to have a mind of its own, wandering wherever the river took it.

"It is like chasing a rabbit," he said in frustration.

At this Willow gave a tinkling laugh, for somehow she had understood. The boat of buffalo hide spun along like a bubble, or perhaps a magical carpet out of one of her father's fairy tales, and what lay ahead seemed as uncertain as what lay behind. Yet a feeling of exhilaration swept through her as if she might go skipping among the stars: for the first time since her childhood she felt truly free.

Wolf and Willow

It wasn't long before Wolf and Willow learned that a bull boat was not meant for a lengthy trip down-river. Morning came and cold water was sloshing over their ankles at the bottom of the boat, which sagged like an udder in the river. Wolf pushed into a quiet nook on the northern riverbank, well beyond the villages they had passed in the night. Together, they heaved the bull boat over, with its bottom facing the sun.

"We must let it dry for the day," Willow said by signs and what few words they shared.

"We will travel by night, sleep by day," Wolf agreed.

To what end? she wondered, a troubled look crossing her face.

"Do not worry, I will take you to your people," Wolf said, guessing her thoughts.

But at this, Willow gave a bitter laugh and said nothing, leaving him to wonder. Surely, her mother and father would be waiting for her, along with all the kinsfolk of her clan. Surely, she must miss them.

Willow had told him there was a long trail connecting the Red River with the Misi Sipi, but he knew almost nothing about her people except for some bad things that Black Knife had told him.

Black Knife had said that Willow's people were demons who came from the belly of a river monster. Wolf suspected that this was simply a large canoe, like that of the Odawa. He had seen cottonwood dugouts carrying as many as twenty men among the Caddo people on the Misi Sipi. He doubted that Willow's people could have a craft larger than these. As for being demons, he had heard many tribes along the river bad-mouthing their neighbors.

Surely there would be a great celebration at Willow's return, he thought. Although he expected no reward, he could not resist the fantasy of carrying her away if she would have him, for his heart had gushed open and he could barely look at her without it surging in his chest.

They had eaten their small supply of corn in the night and now he could hear Willow's stomach rumbling.

"Are you hungry?"

"Sir, you are very polite to ask, but yes, I am very hungry," she replied.

"Soon," he smiled, making a tiny sign with his fingers.

The inlet was a good place to build a fish weir, but spying an overhanging tree, Wolf had a better idea.

"Willow," he said, pointing.

"Yes, a willow tree. Do you mean for us to eat it?"

Wolf laughed and cut an armful of supple branches with the knife he had taken from the drugged guard. He fashioned them into a conical shape the length of his leg, using strips of willow bark to tie the end. Then, after weaving a hoop of branches around the open end, he wove a small opening, with a crown of sticks pointing inward.

Willow sat and marveled without a clue as to what Wolf was doing. She watched the powerful muscles of his back working beneath his skin as he bent over the emerging basket. From time to time he looked over his shoulder and flashed his white teeth in a smile, nodding happily. It had been a long time since she'd seen a man smile in a way that was not evil - not since Croen left - and this man seemed so gentle compared to the rough band of soldiers and sailors who'd been her companions for over a year. She was shocked at how quickly he'd picked up Spanish; by contrast, she knew only a few words of the tongue he called Anishinaabemowin. His eyes were intelligent and daring, and unlike almost every other man she'd met during her long ordeal, she did not feel uneasy with him. If anything, she felt a melting sensation when she looked into his strange gray eyes. Despite all their hardships, somehow he made her laugh.

At last the trap was finished, looking like a conical basket to Willow's eyes. Wolf held it up with a satisfied look. "Good."

He waded a short way into the river and pushed the basket into the water, securing it to the sandy bottom with several large rocks. Then he waded amid the reeds lining the bank and reached into the water, bringing up a crayfish.

"Bait," he said, crushing the wriggling crustacean in his hand.

Willow grimaced, but she understood well enough. Wolf waded back to his trap and gingerly placed the oozing body of the crayfish within.

"We sleep," he said, gesturing to the overturned bull boat.

Sleep? Willow tensed. Was she to sleep beside a man she barely knew? She liked Wolf well enough, but this was not proper. Still, she was faint with exhaustion from being up all night and could see the haggard look on Wolf's face as he tipped the bull boat a little to the side, spreading his buffalo robe on the sand beneath it. He motioned for her to crawl in, raising the obsidian knife and uttering a word she did not understand. "Defend."

Willow shrank back with alarm written on her face. But Wolf's own face filled with consternation as he realized she had not understood him. By signs, he indicated that he would sleep at the entrance of their cupped shelter to defend them against any intruders. He held up his hands at the end of his pantomime and smiled.

"Ah, defend," Willow said, *"proteccion."*

"Si, proteccion," he repeated. "Me, you, together, safe."

Again he beckoned her to climb beneath the shelter of the boat and this time she acquiesced, with Wolf climbing in behind her. They lay together in the darkness of the bull boat, with water dripping on them from time to time.

"Is good, yes?" Wolf asked. He had a reassuring smile on his face in the dim light of the boat and again his teeth flashed in the dusk.

"Yes, it is much good," she said, barely able to keep her eyes open. "Good to escape the bad people."

"Not bad people, just hungry."

"Ah." They were lying so close that she could smell his body, a blend of wood smoke, perspiration and vitality, not unpleasant. She wondered if he would take her now. He was far stronger; he could do as he wished and she was too tired to resist...

Wolf gazed at Willow's sleeping face with satisfaction. If only she knew that molesting her was something he could not imagine, for lovemaking was freely given among his people and not coerced. He had intended only to make her feel safe by lying next to her.

Carefully, he rolled back into the sunlight outside the boat and crept amid the brush at the top of a bluff overlooking the river. For a long time he stood hidden amid the saplings and trees, gazing up and down the river for any sign of movement. The villages, he knew, were all on the southern side of the river, but Black Knife's warriors could run along the river trail as fast as he and Willow could float and there would be other bull boats at the villages along the way. Far down river, where the forest began, there would be dugouts.

But the nook in the river was well-sheltered and a good place to hide, with the underside of the bull boat blending into its surroundings. Nor could Wolf see any trail along the north bank of the river. If there were men searching for them, they would have to claw their way through heavy brush filled with thorns and cactus.

Long after Willow had gone to sleep, Wolf returned to the shelter, being careful not to push against her. Even then, his heart kept beating like that of a captured rabbit as he listened for signs of movement along the bluff. He listened for a long time, thinking that sleep would never come, even though his body cried out for rest.

Late in the day, Wolf awakened to find Willow clambering over his chest.

"Pee," she whispered. She'd waited an hour or two for him to wake up and could no longer hold it. All day she had lain snuggled against him, with half of the buffalo hide wrapped about them as a blanket.

Wolf nodded and watched as she crept beneath the shelter of the bull boat. He listened as intently as a bird in its nest; there were no voices outside, nor the tread of Black Knife's warriors. Perhaps they had not been followed, for starving men could not afford to lose what faint energy they had left by chasing two escaped slaves. They would need all of their strength to pursue the buffalo, if the herds could be found. Perhaps they were even happy to be rid of them.

With rising spirits, Wolf emerged from their shelter to find Willow grinning over her shoulder down by the river. There were two fish in the trap and these were soon gutted and prepared for eating.

"But we have no fire," she said wistfully, gazing at the raw fish.

Wolf gave her an amused look and held up his blade. "I have a knife," he said, as if the matter was resolved.

And so it was, for he headed into a grove of cottonwoods along the river bank, returning with a length of dead branch that was split down the middle. Cracking the branch in two, he braced a length of it on the ground with his foot and dug a groove down its length with his knife. Then, taking a stick of hardwood, he began scraping back and forth along the length of the groove, at the base of which he had placed a small pile of woody fluff.

Willow watched in amazement as Wolf scraped at the grooved wood as fast as his arms would allow. Once again she marveled at the muscles of his arms and back, flexing furiously as he coaxed heat from the wood. Soon, she saw a wisp of smoke rising from the tinder. Wolf gathered it in his hands and blew forth a flame.

He placed the palmful of flaming tinder beneath a pile of twigs and looked on with satisfaction at the growing cook fire.

"Truly, thou art a magician!" Willow said.

He in turn, was mystified by the amazement in her eyes, for surely the woman had witnessed the building of a fire before. Yet it seemed not so, and with the blaze growing bright between them, he held up the split branch and beckoned her to touch.

Willow solemnly fingered the wood, noting that its groove was still quite hot. The fires in the village had been kept alive by replenishment of their coals each morning, and she had never seen one started.

Sundown drew on and she felt much renewed by the meal, which Wolf had filled out by roasting the roots of a water plant. By now their boat was dry, with its skin stretched taut again by the sun, yet it would still be an hour or two until it would be dark enough to brave the river.

"Thank you," she said.

"Thank you," Wolf said in return, nodding with a pleasant smile. There were so many things he wished to tell her, and to ask.

"The men," she made a stabbing motion as if with a spear. "They come?"

Wolf shrugged, pointing to the brush and then the river. "Much trouble for them. Little trouble for us."

She knew so little about him. "Where are you from?"

He pointed to the north. "Far that way. Far to place of big water."

He spread his hands and then pantomimed with his palm over his eyes as if looking at a great distance. "Kitchi Gami, big water."

At this Willow gave a tinkling laugh and Wolf grinned in response.

"Ah, so thou must come from an ocean far to the north," she said. "That must mean that we are on an island after all, though surely one as large as Spain, at least."

Wolf nodded agreeably, though he had no idea as to what she had said.

Satisfied that she had learned something, Willow was eager to play the word game again. It was exhausting and made her head hurt, and she had to repeat the Anishinaabemowin words many times, while Wolf seemed to pick up Spanish much faster. Yet gradually, they were able to speak in small sentences, building on their talks in the village. Now, with a long trip down the river before them, they would have time for learning much more.

Darkness came and they tumbled the bull boat back in the water. Wolf had fashioned a paddle for her and together they kept the boat as close to the north side of the river as possible as they drifted downstream. At times they practiced speaking as the night wore on before drifting off to their own thoughts. Deep into the night, Willow pulled her pipes from her tunic and played some low tunes, singing the songs she had learned as a child. The Arabic was nothing like the Spanish that Wolf had heard, but he loved the sound of her voice, and hummed along as best he could. There was no one along the southern bank of the river to hear them, and no one able to give chase if they did. Once again, they drew into a cut in the river as the dawn came on and once again they laid the fish trap.

The days passed by and again there was a fire, and sometimes a fish, and sometimes not. Each day, as the upturned boat dried anew in the sun they slept beneath its shelter, wrapped in the buffalo robe. Sometimes Willow awoke to find herself clutching Wolf's body as a child hugs her doll, as if he might drive away all the feelings of terror that lived within her. She could smell his hair, feel the strength of his arms, and she marveled that despite her clasp, Wolf never made a play for her, though it was obvious that he desired her when she climbed over him in the morning.

Five days of this crept by and still the river rolled on as if it would never end. The words poured between them and they smiled back and forth, laughing and singing as the bull boat floated like a bubble in the night. There seemed to be nothing grim in the man, and this, too, seemed a marvel to her. The fish, the fire, sleep, talk - each day seemed much the same on the lazy river, yet gradually there arose a longing for more.

Willow had never been truly devout, yet she knew that her transgression with Akmed had been a sin in the eyes of Allah. What would the Supreme Being think if she sinned again? Yet for a long time now she had felt that she was far from the eyes of God in this strange land, and perhaps those of the Archangel Gabriel as well, who wrote the doings and fate of all humankind in his great book. A passion for Wolf had blossomed in her heart and she had begun to yearn for his caress. Yet, it was only proper that they should be wed in order to consummate her feelings. But how? The priest of the Spaniards would refuse to marry them unless they were baptized as Christians, and that was impossible. Her conversion would dishonor her father and mother, lost to her though they were. Yet her peril and their escape from the village had only sharpened her feelings, making them grow faster and wilder than might be wise. This, too, she knew, yet what profit was there in caution when she had finally found a man who was tender, strong and kind?

On the sixth day Willow could barely sleep as she tossed in the humid warmth of the sun beating on the steaming boat. Her body was filled with an aching she could barely resist and late in the day, as she once again clambered over Wolf's sleeping body, she paused above him, feeling the stiffness between his legs as she smiled down upon him. His eyes opened wide, gazing into hers, pleading for more, and she felt as if she might drift down into their depths, not caring if she ever returned. She rocked on top of him playfully and he groaned, grasping her hips. Carefully, she lifted her tunic and lowered herself down, fumbling with his loincloth and rubbing her bare skin against the heat of his body. Soon, they abandoned their clothing amid the close heat, rocking into each other, feeling rapturous as they gazed into each other's eyes. It was a long time before they left the shelter of the boat.

And so they were lovers now, and Wolf had never felt so happy. And yet he was troubled, for what would Willow's father think of him? And what could he offer to prove he was worthy to be his son, now that his trade goods were gone? A man did not just marry a woman; their families were joined as well. At best, he would have to sneak away with her like a thief, and this was not honorable.

But as the days passed and it became easier to speak, his ears were filled with a tale that seemed stranger than any he had ever told around a fire back home.

From what he could understand, the place where Willow had been captured by the Adai was not truly her home, nor were its people of her clan.

"My mother and father live far beyond the Great Salt Water to the east," she said when he asked of them. "They live in a land called Africa."

From what Wolf could gather, Willow's father kept a herd of animals that were as big as the moose, yet were not moose. Nor were they the same as the sunktanka, but had long, gangly necks, spindly legs and a large hump for a back. This, and her parents lived in a large town by the salt water in a land that was as dry as the Red Sand Place of the Adai.

There were many things that Willow told him that he did not understand. She had said that her father kept his animals behind a barricade of wood, yet Wolf had never heard of anyone keeping moose, bison or caribou in such a fashion. How could it be possible?

He was also surprised to learn that he would not be meeting Willow's father and mother.

"Why are you not with them?"

"I was sold when I was a child," she replied, trying to make Wolf understand what the word sold meant, for it seemed to have no meaning in his world. "It is like being traded. I was traded so I would not starve."

Gradually, Wolf came to understand that Willow had been a slave of the men in the big canoe that had brought her over Zhewitaganibi, the salt water. But, he reasoned, such a canoe could not hold more than twenty men, even if it was larger than those of the Odawa. Yet Willow had counted on her fingers and toes three times, indicating that there were perhaps sixty of them. He doubted that any dugout could be that large. How had they arrived, and how had such a small force taken a large town of the Caddo people? It remained a mystery. Despite Willow's repeated warnings, he was eager to see their canoe and the strange men for himself, if only from a distance.

But far more tantalizing, Willow had told him that the men called Spaniards had a living sunktanka with them, the thing she called a *caballo* - a horse.

Early on she had questioned him about the skull of the horse, which lay in the seepage at the bottom of their boat. Most of its red paint had washed away and its web of shells and beadwork was torn and scattered.

"I was sent to find it," he said. "A people called the Dakota call it the sunktanka."

"But why did you come such a great distance?" she asked, for Wolf had told her he had traveled many cycles of the moon from his home in the north.

Wolf struggled for the words in Spanish, speaking somewhat and telling the rest in the language of signs. "My teacher is Wabeno, the Man of the Dawn Sky," he said at last. "He is a master of medicine and can talk to the spirits. He saw the sunktanka in a dream and sent me to find it."

Willow smiled at this. "Would you like to see a living horse?"

"Yes."

"There is but one in all this land."

"I will bring it home to Wabeno."

"This is not possible."

"Why?"

"It belongs to the Spaniards. They will never give it up. They will kill you if you try."

"Other men try to kill me already," he said earnestly. "You say they are bad men? I will steal it from them."

But Wolf's threat to steal the horse was without conviction, for what man could steal a deer, an elk or a moose? Willow tried to explain that in her land many animals had been tamed and were led about or kept in corrals, but it was difficult for Wolf to imagine such a thing. What did tamed mean? At best, he recalled the flock of ducks that had been shuttled from the market in the town of the Casqui people. He still thought of the Spaniard's horse as being a sort of deer, and its capture seemed unlikely, for according to the legends the sunktanka could run very fast and far and Wolf could barely run at all with his clubbed foot.

Still, it was worth considering, for Wabeno would not have sent him on such a mission unless he had been given a vision of its success.

The villages along the river grew more numerous as the prairie fell away and the forest began. Now, there were a few villages on the north shore as well and they began to see dugouts. Still, they kept on floating down the river at night and sleeping by day as the bull boat dried in the sun. Privately, Wolf did not think the boat would last much longer, for the buffalo hide was beginning to wear at its ribs. Even a small leak would sink them, for they had no way to patch it.

Then one afternoon they awoke to the sound of rustling outside the shelter of the boat and Wolf peered out to see the legs of three warriors standing outside. One of them stooped low and grinned.

They were three men of the Caddo, the same age as himself. He crawled out of the overturned boat and they gave him a bemused look as he greeted them.

Their's was a slightly different dialect than the Adai, yet they understood one-another well enough and it was clear that they meant no harm. Soon, Willow crept out from under the boat as well and they looked at her with awe, for her dark skin, green eyes and ringlets were unlike that of any woman they had ever seen.

"Brother, is she your wife?" the tallest of the three asked.

"Yes, brother," Wolf lied, for it wouldn't do to have the strangers think otherwise.

"You are as strange as she," the warrior noted.

"Yes, we are like wolves of the same pack. We are of the Ojibwe people, far to the north."

None of the three had ever heard of the Ojibwe and Wolf invited them to join him in a pipe. "I would tell you more of my people and the wonders up the river."

This, all agreed, was a fine thing, and the warriors produced the body of a young doe from their dugout. Wolf made a fire and they talked while the meat cooked on a spit of green wood over the flames.

"At last, something besides fish!" Willow exclaimed.

"Yes, these are good men and mean us no harm," Wolf replied.

But he could hardly tell them the truth of the escape from their kinsmen far up the river, so Wolf wove a tale which they could easily believe.

"I am a trader a long way from home," he said. "We were traveling up the Red River with pipestone, copper and tobacco when bad men set upon us. They robbed us and took our canoe, leaving us this shabby boat of skin."

"Surely, these were not men of the Caddo?" said one of the three, his eyes narrowing.

"No, brother. I think they must have been your enemies, the Dakota. You should watch for them and take care they do not creep up on you."

The three looked at one-another, frowning. The Dakota lived far to the north beyond the Pawnee and Arikara, yet there were raids from time-to-time.

"Is it possible these men were demons?" the tall one spoke again.

"What do you mean, brother?"

"We are leaving our dugout here to walk the pathway to the Great River," he replied. "Men have been summoned from all the lands of the Caddo to attack a nest of demons that have taken a village of our kin. We are gathering warriors beyond count, as many as there are stones in the river."

"Demons?"

"That is what we have been told. They are as cold and cruel as demons, though they are only men with strange clothes and hairy faces."

"Then they are shadow men, the kind of men my people call *wdjibbon*," Wolf said with certainty. "They are not demons, but nor are they fully human. They are men who have surrendered to evil."

"Yes, brother, evil men, and we mean to rid the earth of them."

"When will you attack?"

"On the night of the half moon."

The plan was to engulf the Spaniard's fort with a storm of fire arrows. The logs of the palisade might not burn, but the grass lodges within surely would. A mass attack from all sides would follow amid the smoke.

"But won't your own people die in the attack?" Wolf asked, for he had been told that the villagers were held captive each night in the fort.

"No, brother. Our people have whispered to them of the plan as they labor in the fields. They have been told to flee when the moon is half full."

It seemed a good plan, and Wolf wished them well, thinking ruefully that the sunktanka would most likely be slaughtered.

It was still early evening when the warriors took their leave, paddling for the south bank of the river where the overland path to the Misi Sipi began. The river had grown wide here, yet Wolf could see there were the tracks of many dugouts in the sand on the far side where the boats had been dragged ashore and hidden in the brush. While he and Willow had slept their days away, the river had filled with warriors rushing to the long path and the rendezvous with the Spaniard's fort.

"There lies our way forward," he said as the warriors reached the opposite shore.

That night, they paddled their skin boat across the river and dragged it up the far bank. To Wolf's delight there were many dugouts hidden beneath the brush along the riverbank with no one standing guard. He selected one that was long and narrow, knowing that it would travel faster in the water, and then piled his fish trap and the battered skull of the sunktanka in the middle of the boat. Willow seized a paddle, and as they set out, she marveled at how much faster the dugout moved than their bull boat. Several times the dugout wavered in the water and she feared it would tip over, yet Wolf quickly seemed to grasp its nature and after a time, so did she.

"It is only a day now to the Misi Sipi," Wolf called out to her, for he had seen the broad pathway on his trip up the Red River earlier that winter. But how far down the Misi Sipi would the Spaniard's fort lie? If the Caddo warriors were traveling a short cut through the forest, then surely he and Willow would not beat them by way of the river.

Yet the river felt good beneath Wolf's paddle, and few men could match him for speed and strength. He put his back into it and they sped downstream, to what end he couldn't imagine.

Mutiny

The Red River broadened and surged as it hit the Misi Sipi, colliding with the great muddy river in a torrent that sent Wolf and Willow spinning sideways in its flood. The dugout tipped and Wolf thought that they would surely capsize, but he ruddered hard with all his strength at the stern, righting the boat a half-breath before it keeled over. He paddled as if his life depended on it, cutting through the white-capped current to a sandbar.

The final stretch to the south down the Misi Sipi had the feeling of a race as Wolf paddled almost sick with exhaustion in the hope of reaching the Spaniards before the Caddo attacked. Several times Willow warned him that they must approach the Spaniards with caution, yet he had not listened. How bad could her people be when Willow was so tender? His desire to see the living sunktanka overwhelmed his good sense and he pushed on, as heedless as a child. When at last they spied the palisade of the fort on a bluff over the river, Wolf had been shocked beyond words by a sight on the riverbank.

It was a creature unlike anything he had ever seen: half man and half she-elk, walking slowly along the riverbank. The creature was caparisoned with ribbons of yellow and red, with white plumes adorning its two heads.

Willow had never told him that men rode on the backs of horses. She had simply assumed that he would know as much. It took only a few moments for Wolf to realize that the horse and its rider were not a single animal, but he shook his head at the apparition and could not resist drawing closer. At last he had found the sunktanka! As the legends had said, it was like a deer, but not a deer; with a woman's hair on both its head and its tail. The man on its back wore a jerkin that glimmered in the sun, making him shine like a spirit of the sky, and as Wabeno had seen in his dream, the sunktanka's eyes were rimmed as blue as robins' eggs around its pupils.

Just as astounding was the Spaniard's canoe, drawn up alongside the riverbank. It was colossal compared to even the largest canoes of the Odawa and had what looked like a tall tree sheared of its branches growing in its midst. Wolf was agog at the sight of it; clearly it could hold one hundred men or more.

"No, not yet!" Willow cried from the bow of the dugout, as they sped forward, but Wolf impulsively dug his paddle for the shore and leapt to the riverbank, startling the horse and its rider.

The rider looked down at Wolf, stricken with fear and hammered the flanks of the horse with his heels, dashing away as his men came running.

"He only wants to see the horse!" Willow called after him, but Captain Cabeza had rounded a pathway leading up the bluff to the fort and was well past hearing. He sped up the hill astride the warhorse Montoya, looking as thin and gray as a wraith in the distance.

Four men surrounded Wolf with drawn swords, which he recognized easily enough as weapons. He raised his hands in surrender and they eyed Willow quizzically.

"Look here, the blackie's back!" the leader of the guard cried. She recognized him as a man named Pedro, with whom she had clowned with good-naturedly from time to time. "Where's the dog?"

"Dead many months now, sir," she said meekly. "Eaten by those who held me captive all this time. This man saved me and I pray you to treat him kindly."

"Well he's not one of ours," Pedro said. "Lucky he didn't get a sword up his ass, the way he jumped out at the captain."

"He was only enchanted by the horse."

"I don't imagine the captain will be enchanted with him, then. He's not the man you remember."

"What do you mean sir?"

"I mean that mutiny has worn his nerves raw, my lady."

"Mutiny?"

"Aye, Captain Sincid's in chains now, and he's had a taste of the red iron too. His men have been put down, but the captain fears traitors behind every tree and privy. You might best have stayed away."

Wolf listened intently, understanding little of what was said. Willow continued talking for some time, looking both heartened and worried by turns.

"What's he looking at?" the Spaniard said abruptly, pointing at Wolf.

"I imagine he thinks you rather strange, sir," Willow replied. "He has never seen mustachios on a man, nor a beard, much less those as red as yours."

Wolf nodded, hoping to appear pleasant, but the captain of the guard gave him a troubled look and spoke off to the side to Willow. "Sorry, love, but you'll have to see their highnesses."

"Who?"

"It's our own little inquisition. Evil bastards, I'm afraid."

With that, they were led up the hill to the fort to determine their fate.

That afternoon they were hustled before a court of two officers and the sole priest of the expedition, the same three who had sat in judgment of the mutineers. Captain Bartolomeu Sincid sat manacled on the ground before them. At first Willow mistook him for a heap of rags, but then he lifted his head and glared at her. His arms and hands had been horribly seared with red hot nails to force the names of his co-conspirators, and now whatever humanity was left in him had been seared away as well.

The court was conducted in the great lodge of the village, which was large enough to accommodate a crowd of more than thirty. Sitting in the darkness beyond the judges was Captain Cabeza, who said not a word during the proceedings.

Cabeza had the look of a cadaver and Willow barely recognized him. It was as if he had caved in upon himself; his eyes were sunken and his skin seemed gray and ghostly. He appeared to have aged twenty years, with nothing left of the strutting commander she had met in the slave market of Sevilla. He looked like a beggar, shrunken within a rich man's rags.

But worse than that, he seemed to look right through her, as if they had never met.

As for Captain Sincid, he had not changed a lick. He was still a disagreeable scarecrow with a mop of frizzy hair and black eyes like that of a hunting lizard. Sincid's eyes gave no hint of fear as he sat brooding on the ground; they reflected only spite and anger. His wounds pulsed red and angry across his arms and hands.

Sincid and Cabeza had jabbed at one-another all winter as hunger, anarchy and despair descended on the expedition. The enslaved villagers had continued to flee as the winter wore on and too late, the Spaniards realized that they were gleaning the fields at night, taking the last of the maize with them. The village caches had been less than a quarter full when the *Tiger* had arrived, and now the maize pits were down to their last kernels. Nets had been laid in the river and it was only the daily catch that kept the Spaniards from starvation. No one knew what the few remaining villagers ate.

Gradually, Captain Cabeza fell almost mute, as if his mind had journeyed to some far-off world. As the winter wore on and their hunger increased, Sincid began seducing Cabeza's men with promises of gold and food, to be plundered from villages up the river. Without any leader to rudder them, many seemed willing to turn in Sincid's direction. But only if Cabeza was dead.

Gathered in council, a handful of men had agreed to Sincid's mutiny.

"Our success depends on a single thrust of a blade as the captain lies sleeping," Sincid told them. "I will ease him into the next world as gently as one might bleed a pig."

Three nights ago, he had crept into Cabeza's lodge, unaware that - stricken with anxiety - the captain slept in his chain mail and his *cuerra* of thick leather, studded with bronze plates. Sincid had screamed in triumph as he buried his dagger in the captain's chest in the darkness of the lodge, yet the blade was stymied by one of the *cuerra's* plates. The captain had taken a bad scrape with the deflected blade and he awakened with a roar, rousing the guard who had been dozing at the doorway.

Thus, the mutiny was shattered as confessions were tortured from Sincid and his men. And then Willow and Wolf had arrived.

Wolf's appearance at court never came. He was separated from Willow at the entrance to the lodge and hustled into a cage of stout logs that was crowded with prisoners.

"I will speak for us!" Willow called back, certain of success.

But to her surprise, the judges were anything but welcoming.

"You tell us there is an attack brewing," the chief among them said after she had repeated her tale of abduction and rescue.

"Yes, lord, I am given to understand that there could be a thousand warriors. Perhaps even more."

"But it was this man of the Indios who told you thus."

"I have no reason to doubt him," she replied. "I saw him speaking to those who were gathering."

"And why should we believe this savage?"

"If you wish to keep your testicles and the hair atop your head sir, you will believe him."

"Still your filthy mouth! Have you taken this man to your bed?" the priest asked abruptly. He had a supercilious face and the air of a know-it-all. "Tell us, have you been a bad woman, a harlot? A traitor to those who love you?"

Willow gave him a look of disbelief. "Did you not hear me, sir? We are all in mortal danger!"

Sincid saw his chance in Willow's warning.

"She speaks the truth!" he cried from where he crouched on the dirt floor of the lodge. "Her man is my ambassador among the Indios. As the woman claims, I have a thousand men waiting in the forest, and woe to those who do me harm!"

"What? Liar!" Willow cried. "There is an army raised against you, but it has nothing to do with this pirate, nor with the man who rescued me!"

But Willow's tale had given Sincid a glimmer of hope and the judges wavered between certainty and disbelief as he embroidered his lie. Slowly, he turned their heads. After all, Sincid was a captain of men - or had been

- while Willow was a mere dog-handler, a Mohammedan, a slave and a woman.

"My lords, many times I have met with the man she calls Wolf in the forest and he has whipped up an army against you!" Sincid railed. "Release me if you would save your skins!"

Again and again Willow denounced him, yet Sincid always seemed to have an answer, conjuring monstrous forces at his command in the forest, and little by little, the judges told Willow to be still as the slaver mesmerized them with his lies.

The judges wavered, but it was the priest who turned the screw in Sincid's favor. "Are we to believe this woman who has been lying in sin with a heathen creature from the forest? Magistrates! She has been months among the Indios, perhaps plotting against us! Bear in mind, she is no Christian!"

The priest stood, glaring at Willow and pointing an accusing finger. He was the same pest who had harried her like a horsefly all he way across the Atlantic, insisting that she convert to his faith. She had rebuffed him at every turn, and now he had his revenge. She shrank back, remembering the burning figures on the wharf at Sevilla; they, too, had been accused by just such a priest.

"No! Fool! Listen..." But she choked off as the priest leered as if he were a fox with a mouse in its teeth.

But there was something more than that.

"I have not forgotten what you owe me," Sincid whispered to her as the judges conferred. "You and your shit-born captain denied me a silk purse of gold in Spain and now I will have payment, if only to savor your misery. I saw what you did to the wretch Garon, and his vengeance speaks through me."

Willow was speechless at this, nor was she given a chance to speak further. She was held blameless in the plot but all three judges agreed that Wolf must die. If he was the go-between for an army of Indians as Sincid claimed, he would best be executed; and if he was innocent, then his life would be no loss to the Spaniards.

The Turtle and the Snake

Their brother did not die easy.

Six of the mutineers had been led up the stone steps where the Spaniards stood waiting in the blistering heat, the air wavering in a curtain above the mud-brown river. One of them was a young Caddo man of the village who had been recruited into their plot, hoping it would rid his people of the invaders. The seventh man was Wolf.

Wolf was as sure as he had ever been that his captors were *wdjibbon*, the shadow men without color whom his uncles among the shamans had told of long ago around some forgotten fire.

Now, the villagers stood watching, as did the pirate Bartolomeu Sincid, who was chained to a post and stood cursing and snarling at the men standing in a circle around him.

The Caddo man was the first to go. The thing around his neck was neither a necklace nor leather, nor a rope of braided bark, but a noose of metal unlike anything his people had ever known; it was unfathomably strong, yet bound together and released by a metal twig no bigger than an arrowhead used for birding.

Their brother had been strapped chest-up to the demons' hollow log, which was as hard as stone and made of the same strange metal as the noose. It lay tarnished as green as a frog in a crib of oak, pointing to the impossibly wide river, which lay sullen and steaming in the sun.

The bronze log was *La Tortuga*, a short and squat medieval cannon, designed for lobbing red-hot cannon balls over the walls of fortified towns back in Europe. Now, it served as an altar on which to punish the mutineers.

Nothing made sense; for the villagers it was as if they were drifting through a dream filled with improbable things. Prior to the arrival of the *wdjibbon*, none had ever seen bronze before, nor iron, a cannon, manacles, collars, swords, keys, or even steps.

Yet it was clear that the shadow men were bent on amusing themselves. They clustered around the captives, bearing a thicket of lances and their strange long knives which glimmered in the sun.

Their brother was an in-between man, not yet 16 years, but he knew what was coming. Piss ran down his leg as he began his death song in a high piping voice. Hovering over him, one of the *wdjibbon* with a shaved head and dressed in a brown cloak made signs over his chest and muttered words which the villagers took as a sacrifice to the sun. All understood that the pale-faced man was a witch of some sort, a sorcerer.

A man could die a worse death, for the sun was the giver of life to whom all men across the Great Turtle Island prayed as it departed the world each evening. To give one's life to the sun meant a chance to live again in the spirit land.

The victim's mother burst from the crowd and ran to where her son was tied, only to be dragged away screaming and pulling at her hair as she was restrained by a group of women. Then the villagers watched in silence for the blow to come, either with a axe or one of the long knives. But it was not to be.

Instead, one of the *wdjibbon* came forth with a cup of smoking embers. Their leader gave the nod and the fire-bearer lit a flame with a handful of brush and dabbed at the *Tortuga's* cotton fuse.

A thin spout of flame burst from the touch-hole at the base of the cannon below their brother's feet and then came a deafening crash as a tongue of fire shot over the river, louder than any thunderclap that any of them had ever heard. The *Tortuga* juddered and bucked in its restraints like an angry beast, yet even so, all heard the crack of their brother's head as his skull bounced off the surface of the metal. Almost immediately, blood began to pool from his ears, dripping to the stones below.

The bound mutineers waiting in line gave a collective gasp and some fell to their knees, raising their arms with their hands clasped together and begging for mercy. Yet from the Spaniards came only feral laughter and cold smiles.

But though he was bleeding from his ears, the youth had not died. With his skin beginning to fry from the heat of the smoldering metal, he sang his last words in a cracking voice.

> "I am here, then I am gone,
> Only the earth and sky
> last forever.
> Now I join them,
> Mother, father,
> Now I join them.
> Now I live forever."

With a sign from the leader of the Spaniards, their brother was lifted from the transport of his death and tossed over the rim of the bastion to the mud of the riverbank below.

The next among them was a one-eyed sailor named Pike, who'd served as one of Captain Sincid's lieutenants in planning the mutiny. He was a scrawny, small man with a permanent scowl on his face, yet now his one eye cast about as if he were a dog about to be gelded and the men holding his arms had to drag him cursing and screaming to his doom. He was strapped to the opening at the end of the cannon and blown in two, his upper torso, arms and head flying over the wall as his legs dropped to the ground with his intestines twining beneath the cannon's maw. A great hurrah! went up among the Spaniards at the spectacle. The third was a grizzled conquistador, forced to lay belly-down on what was now glowing a dull red. He shot off its surface as quick as a frog from a fire, screaming a war cry, only to be pierced in three places by the long knives of those he had once called brothers. He disappeared over the wall with the others.

One-by-one the mutineers died as Sincid raged and then fell silent. Off to the side, Willow noticed that the last of them was one of the pirates who had attempted to rape her on the day she had been kidnapped in Morocco. His wide-eyed face was contorted in a lunatic grin and a stream of pleas flowed from his lips in Portuguese as he begged for forgiveness, but he too was blown to bits with the remains of his head, neck and a shoulder flopping down the hill.

Then it was Animi-ma'lingan's turn. He Who Outruns the Wolves.

Wolf was given time for contemplation as several villagers were commanded to clean the mess beneath the cannon. Above him, he saw the pale moon floating, barely visible in the morning sky. He noted wistfully that it was the day of the half moon and tonight's attack would come too late to save him. By now, the warriors of the Caddo would be within hearing of the Spaniard's fire-log. What would they make of it? Silently, he gazed upon his captors, composing his death song.

"Where is your magic now, shaman?" Willow's voice came from over his shoulder with a note of hysteria. "If ever there was a time, you must use it now!"

Wolf had told her of his studies among the shamans after reaching the Misi Sipi, but she had misunderstood him, for the medicine-makers were only men, not gods, and he was not much of a magician to begin with.

He turned and offered her a thin smile, hoping that she would not see the fear in his eyes. "See me now and remember. Death does not own me yet."

But Wolf was not so certain of his words and Willow was even less so. She had been commanded to step away and was peering from the crowd with her face drenched in tears.

The men who had bound Wolf had been a ragged bunch, their chests covered in jerkins of boiled leather and their legs sheathed in a parti-colored cloth unknown to the Anishinaabek. They had the smell of fish guts about them and their faces were rimmed with thick matts of hair, as if they were not men, but bears. Some had no hair atop their heads, looking as if they had been scalped, yet showing no wounds.

Their skin had been burned a golden brown by the sun, and yet when they stripped, their bodies were as white as the bellies of fish. Some of them had eyes as dark as cherries, almost as dark as those of the Ojibwe, yet others had hair the color of sand and eyes as blue as the sky.

The mopping done, the war chief of the *wdjibbon* motioned Wolf forward. Unlike his unkempt men, his hair was smoothly groomed and he wore a breastplate not of bone, but of the same metal that fashioned the long knives. It glimmered a dull gray like the surface of Kitchi Gami, now many moons to the north. The chief of the *wdjibbon* was addressed as His Excellency, but behind his back his men had begun calling him *El Serpiente*, the snake.

Captain Cabeza had been shaved for the occasion and had downed a gourd filled with the last of the *Tiger's* brandy. He had rallied somewhat upon seeing Sincid and the mutineers chained to a stake alongside the cannon. Emerging from his lodge to oversee the punishment, he had heard Willow's pleas from the crowd. But the war dog Dragón was dead now and she was no longer of any use to him. She had barely escaped being sentenced to death herself.

Captain Cabeza stared at Wolf and noted his clubbed foot. He had seen others among the Indios who lived with their wounds: broken arms that had been poorly set and jagged scars taken in battle which had not been sewn. He had heard Willow vouch for the man at the court judging the mutineers. What could she see in the man? He was an Indio, a godless heathen.

"Which will it be, creature? A ride on the turtle or a look down its mouth?" He expected no answer, for none among the captives could possibly know the language of Castile. But gesturing with his hand, he offered a choice.

Yet now, the many days of trading words with Willow came to Wolf's aid. He searched his memory for a story which might save him, finding none except the truth.

"Soy un comerciante como usted," he said at last in perfect Spanish. "I have come to trade for your horse."

Captain Cabeza recoiled as if he had been struck and Wolf noted with satisfaction that the warriors of the shadow men murmured in surprise. None of them had ever met anyone in the New World who spoke their language. The witch in the brown robe crossed himself, touching his head, his heart and both shoulders.

"A trader? It speaks," Cabeza said at last. "What is your name, creature?"

"Creature? What is this?" Wolf glared back at him. Though he had learned a great deal during his time on the river with Willow, her way of speaking was still strange to him. Nor was he inclined to reveal his name to the white demons who held him. No man gave up his name to a stranger, lest it be shouted in the forest to malevolent spirits.

"Your name, villain." Cabeza placed a hand on the hilt of his sword.

"No name for you," Wolf said coolly, lifting his upraised palms to signify he meant no harm. "I not hurt you big man. No fear me."

Again, Cabeza looked as if he had been struck, rearing back. "What? Fear you?"

"His name is Wolf," Willow piped behind him, striding forward. "He is a great chief among his people and you would do well to spare him."

Wolf grimaced; he understood the word, chief, and he was no headman, nor could he ever be one. At best, he was a minor shaman who had failed every test of the Mide-wi-win. They had despaired of him, casting him into the guise of a trader to serve as their spy on this wretched trip. What tales he could tell them now! But his uncles among the shamans were far away on the cold shores of Kitchi Gami, further than a man could walk in the length of four moons.

It would not do for the shadow men to think of him as a chieftain, for who knew what tortures they might inflict on such a prize?

"I am no chief," he shook his head. "Trader."

"Then where are your goods, trader? And how do you imagine you would take my horse?"

Cabeza had seen the skull of the horse taken from the dugout in which Wolf and Willow had arrived. It had provoked a long conversation with the judges of the court, and indeed, had helped to revive him from his torpor. Somewhere, they reasoned, there must have been other Spanish travelers, murdered perhaps by the man with the strange eyes. That and Sincid's lies had marked Wolf for death.

"All taken by the Adai," Wolf replied. "Lost."

"Adai."

"A people who live far away." Wolf beckoned to the west.

"And so I take it you meant to steal my horse and all I have left in this wretched land," Cabeza said with a cheerless smile.

Wolf understood only that the captain had said something about stealing his horse. There was no way he could deny it and for once in his life, no story arose in his thoughts which might serve to rescue him.

By now the sun had risen straight overhead and Wolf could see rivers of sweat trickling from the metal bonnet worn by the chief of the *wdjibbon*. Unwilling to seek the shade before the eyes of his men, Cabeza's patience had come to an end.

"If you have nothing to give then we will send you to your ancestors," he said, motioning Wolf toward the cannon. "Which will it be, a ride on the turtle's back or death at its mouth?"

So now the time had truly come. Wolf turned his gaze to Willow, a woman who meant more to him than he knew how to express. Her cheeks ran with tears. He nodded solemnly in farewell as the Spaniards hustled him forward.

It would only do to face the sun as he died, so that he might offer himself to the Master of Life, who must surely be gazing upon them even now.

"Feed me to your monster's mouth," he said in Anishinaabemowin, nodding to the cannon's black maw.

As he expected, the leader of the shadow men gave a sly smile and motioned instead for him to be strapped by his back to the top of the cannon.

La Tortuga was the length of a man, yet the ancient cannon seemed as broad and squat as its turtle namesake. Although it no longer glowed red it was still hot enough to singe Wolf's hair, raising a stink that made him gag. He lifted his head from its surface to keep his scalp from frying. He squirmed at the heat radiating across his back, but the thickness of his leather jerkin kept his skin from blistering.

His thoughts scrambled for the words of the devils who held him. Their language seemed even more important now than the song he would sing upon his death. Yet again, no words would come.

"Tell me, are you a demon or something worse?" he spoke in his own language, staring at Cabeza with contempt.

The captain shrugged and motioned the fire-bearer forward.

Against all reason, Wolf found himself smiling. The sun, which had seemed so fierce moments ago now seemed comfortably warm, and even the cannon had cooled. It was time to compose his death song telling of his deeds, those he had loved and the marvels he had seen in his short life, but again, the words wouldn't come. Animi-ma'lingan, the man nicknamed Wolf by his friends and family felt strangely ambivalent. How could a young man think of death when life beckoned him on? He felt, rather than heard, a rustle among the shadow men and a breeze threading his way amid their ranks. Two of the soldiers jerked sideways in alarm, as if a ghost had passed between them. Then the heat of the sun and the warmth of the cannon itself fled the scene, replaced by a chill; perhaps it was only the vain hope of a condemned man but He Who Outruns the Wolves was as sure as he had ever been that a spirit of great power walked among them.

Time froze as the fire-bearer and his cup of red embers moved at the crawl of a snail toward the touch-hole that would send him to the spirit land. A branch was lit and down it came, as slow as the winter was long. The flaming branch was only a hand's length from the powder at the touch hole when Wolf wrestled one last time at his bonds, his efforts revealing the necklace beneath his jerkin.

The motion revealed the faintest flicker in the noonday sun as the light struck the cowrie shell and silver amulet draped on a leather thong over his chest. Too late, the captain of the *wdjibbon* had turned his gaze to the river. It was the fire-bearer himself who stilled his hand.

"My lord, there is something you must see," he said

The Vision

Wolf heard voices around him, but it was a long time before he spoke.

For the space of a single breath he had glimpsed a face in the sky above him. It was neither man, nor woman, neither young nor old, but a face of dazzling beauty peering faint and half-seen amid the wispy clouds. He was overcome with the feeling that beyond the face lay the tide of all things living and dead, gathered in a weave of creation beyond his understanding. He was sure that the smile had the power to bend fate, and it had filled him with a deep longing to follow.

Gradually, he became aware of the hubbub around him. Hands were shaking him; his necklace was being fingered...

"Wolf! Wolf!" He heard Willow calling, and then her face was overhead, pleading and oily with tears. "Wolf! Can you hear me?"

He offered a wan smile. "I am here."

"I thought you had died! You were so still..."

"Yes. Perhaps." He was still savoring the vision, in no mood to talk as the Spaniards jostled around him.

"You have cheated death!"

"No one cheats death," he said somberly, still feeling dazed. Then, thinking of the vision, he added in Anishinaabemowin, "But sometimes death can be persuaded."

The thong had been snapped from his neck and was being examined closely by Cabeza, along with several of his lieutenants.

Abruptly, the captain came forward and held the amulet before his eyes. It was the silver fish which the miner Winter Mink had given him so long ago among the copper pits of Minong.

"This is silver!" he said, as if it was an accusation.

Wolf said nothing, still thinking of the vision and wondering what it meant. Yet now he knew why no story had come to save him, for clearly he was meant to be an actor in his own tale.

The shadow men's priest came and spoke into the captain's ear, crossing himself as he spoke.

Cabeza was thunderstruck as the priest filled his ears.

"A fish! This is the symbol of the Christ our Savior, the fisher of souls!" he cried. "The bishops! The bishops of Cibola! Where did you find this?"

A loud murmur of excitement ran through the Spaniards gathered at Cabeza's back. "A fish! The bishops! Proof!"

Again, Wolf said nothing, but gazed at Cabeza with irritation, still bound to the cannon. He had long since learned the word, fish, but the rest of what the Spaniards said meant nothing.

"Fish, yes. Catch many fish. Trade," he said at last, nodding to his ropes.

Cabeza understood him well enough. "Untie him," he commanded.

Suddenly, Willow found herself redeemed in the eyes of the captain. She was brought forward to serve as interpreter. Wolf was helped down from atop the cannon and he stretched. It had not been a comfortable berth.

Then, taking off his moccasins, he sat cross-legged on the earth atop the bluff and bade the others to join him for a parlay.

Captain Cabeza balked at this. "Am I to sit in the dirt?"

"It is the habit of the Indios," Willow spoke into Cabeza's ear. "They have no chairs."

"Sit!" Wolf commanded, gesturing angrily at the ground.

The captain cursed, but had a length of cloth brought forward and settled awkwardly on the ground, ordering his lieutenants to do the same. Willow sat alongside Wolf, whose face betrayed no emotion. He sensed that he had something to trade now, but wasn't quite sure what it was. It dawned on him that the Spaniards wanted something more than fish. It could only be the amulet... perhaps they believed it contained a magic beyond his understanding.

Slowly, and with much back-and-forth with the Spaniard's priest, Willow told him that the fish of his amulet was the symbol of a great spirit named Jesus.

"They believe that the shamans of their god live somewhere in this land," she said. "They are known as the bishops of Cibola."

Cibola meant nothing to Wolf, but he nodded gravely at her words as if he was well aware of the place and the men called bishops.

"Shamans," he said. "I understand you."

"Tell us where you found this," Cabeza asked again.

Wolf held out his hand. The silver amulet did not mean much to him, but the single cowrie shell on the thong had been given to him by Wabeno-inini as a sign of his membership in the Mide-wi-win and he was loathe to give it up.

With a nod, Cabeza handed the thong to one of his men, who carried it to Wolf's side.

Tying it once again around his neck, he spoke. "Far to the north."

"Is silver mined there?"

It took some time for Willow to explain the word mined, but at last Wolf understood and nodded, yes. He did not have the words to convey that small traces of silver had been found in the rock alongside its cousin, copper, but it was true that it had come from the same pits.

"And is there gold in the north?" Cabeza leaned in, his eyes intent on Wolf's answer.

Gold? This was another unfamiliar word.

"It is a bright metal that shines like the sun," Willow said.

Ah, now he understood. When copper was polished, well before it turned brown or green, it shone a bit like the sun, only redder.

"It is like the sun," he conceded. "But like at sundown."

"Ah, so it is red gold," Cabeza said with satisfaction lighting up his face. Around him, the faces of the conquistadors brightened as they murmured amongst themselves.

"Yes, red gold," Wolf replied, eager to please, thinking once again that the Spaniards spoke of copper. Actual gold was unknown to him.

"And is there much of it? Is there much gold?"

Wolf thought of the copper pits of the Minong, which had been worked since the time of his grandfathers' grandfathers, going back to the days of the Old Ones. Surely there was a great deal of the metal the Spaniards sought in the ground. He looked up to find Captain Cabeza leaning toward him with begging eyes, as expectant as a hungry dog.

"Yes," he said agreeably, stifling an impulse to laugh. "Much gold!"

"And is there a city in this place? A city with pyramids?"

Wolf gave a questioning look. "A city is a large town," Willow told him. "A pyramid is a tall hill, only made by the hands of men."

Ah, the place of the Bird Men, he thought. They wish to see the great mounds along the river.

"Yes, I know of such a place," Wolf said, spreading his hands to the sky to indicate the vast size of the Great Mound above the village of the Cahokians.

Confident in his growing language skills, Wolf assumed that pyramid was another name for the mounds along the river.

"There are many pyramids to the north," he said, delighted to see the amazed expressions on the faces of the Spaniards. Still, he wondered, what could the Spaniards care for the simple mounds along the river? There were none among them like that of the Cahokians.

But Cabeza and the men gathered in a circle around him gaped in astonishment. A new Peru had been found! Perhaps another Tenochtitlan with cities of towering pyramids and chambers filled with gold!

"Treasure. Are you sure he speaks of treasure?" Cabeza demanded of Willow.

It took a long time for Willow to convey the meaning of treasure to Wolf, but at last he understood. Something of great value to many people... That could only mean something like the countless shells adorning the corpse of the Bird Man in the shadow of the Great Mound. That was a treasure that any might covet, and yet it was cursed, for no sane person would disturb a grave.

Curse. This too was a word that was hard to explain, but he worked it out with Willow.

"A bad thing. The wrath of ghosts and evil spirits."

At last she turned to Captain Cabeza. "Yes, he says there is a great treasure at the place of the pyramid, but those who disturb it will be cursed," she said. "I think he speaks of demons and ghosts, but it is hard to make out."

"Cursed?" Cabeza scoffed. "A superstition of the Indios. Atahualpa also claimed that the treasure of the Incas was cursed before he was strangled by Pizarro. It was he that was cursed!"

"I do not know Atahualpa, my lord, but he insists that the treasure is cursed," Willow said, nodding to Wolf. "It is guarded by a ghost. I'm sure that's what he means."

"You are all cursed," Wolf said with a low laugh as he followed their exchange.

"What?"

"The warriors gather and tonight is the half moon," he said, pointing to the sky. "Tonight they attack."

Once again, he had Cabeza's attention in the palm of his hand.

"How many are against us?"

Wolf lifted a hand and swept a finger in an arc across the forest beyond the fort and the village. "As many as the leaves on the trees."

This, he did not truly know, but it was a way of indicating thousands, and he was sure that he and Willow would not survive the attack, despite the Spaniards' defenses. Their fire-log faced the river and would do them no good except to frighten the attackers for a short time. There were also still gaps in the palisade where the wall had not been completed. Once the raiders' fire arrows fell from the night sky, the village of grass huts would become an inferno, an oven.

It didn't take long for Captain Cabeza to understand as much.

That night there was a firestorm on the bluff above the river as a shower of flaming arrows fell upon the lodges within the fort. From a distance, the village appeared as if it were a volcano roaring on the heights above the river, with its flames rising hundreds of feet into the night sky. A trail of sparks rose and fell, winking amid the stars, and over the river came the roar of the fire as it devoured the village. Amid the roar came the thundering chants and war cries of the Caddo warriors.

Far up the river, Wolf and Willow stood at the bow of the *Tiger* as forty oars flashed over the water, digging and pulling in the darkness as the galley sped north. Distantly, they could hear the echoing war cries of thousands of warriors descending on the empty village. More warriors, perhaps, than there were leaves on the trees.

The Treasure, At Last

To Wolf's eyes, the Spaniard's galley was a wonder beyond compare. When the wind blew from the east, west or south, its red triangular sail was raised and the *Tiger* zig-zagged from one bank of the river to the other, tacking north against the current. When there was no wind, or worse, when the wind was out of the north, the rowers were put to work, heaving with what little strength remained to them.

Starvation began taking its toll on the ragged company. In the rush to abandon the village, Cabeza's men had been able to round up just three baskets of maize, not enough to last more than a day.

Yet they soon discovered more villages lining the river, which had all been forewarned of the demons downstream. Captain Cabeza set his men to raiding, and when the *Tiger* coursed up on an unsuspecting village like a dragon out of a nightmare, its people would flee to the forest, leaving easy pickings for the men waving swords and pikes. Village after village was stripped of its caches of food as the galley pushed north.

Wolf watched the raids glumly. They passed the mouth of the Red River, and beyond this, he knew, the towns would grow larger and more numerous. Perhaps the Casqui people would learn of their approach and swarm over them in the night.

This had been a concern for Captain Cabeza as well, and each night he sought out a sandbar or a small island in the river upon which to beach the *Tiger*. The river was treacherous enough by day, but impossible to navigate by night, for there were often the trunks of huge trees tumbling downstream in the current and jagged branches of trees just beneath the surface of the water, along with whirlpools, eddies and unexpected rapids. Sometimes huge fonts of water would bellow from the river's depths as the gases buried beneath its muck exploded skyward.

One night, the boat was roused by the screams and curses of Captain Sincid, who had been chained to the mast. By the light of the moon they found the night watchman, Akmed, pissing on the bound man's face.

"I'll kill you! I swear it, I'll never forget!" Sincid raged, his face and beard soaked with Akmed's salty urine.

Captain Cabeza nearly did the deed for him, but all aboard knew the reason that Akmed had only half of a left hand, and who among them would not seek revenge for such a thing? This, and they could hardly afford to lose a man, should the need arise to storm a city the likes of Cuzco or Tenochtitlan. By now, Cabeza had a force of less than forty men; several had died of dysentery over the winter, slowly bleeding to death from their bowels. The giant Garon was dead, and two others had been picked off by arrows from the forest. Then too, the man who had taken an arrow in his shoulder at the battle on the river months before had died of his infected wound.

Thus, Akmed got off with a warning.

"Do that again and you'll sleep at the bottom of the river," Cabeza promised.

But that was hardly enough to satisfy Sincid, who vowed that he would sail them all to hell instead of Cuba if and when the gold was found unless Akmed was punished. So it was that Akmed was stripped naked the next day and bound to the mast, with Sincid himself allowed to give him twenty lashes with a makeshift whip. Indeed, Sincid made it to twenty-eight in a blind fury before his hand was stilled, and spent the rest of the day, chained once again and glaring at all who met his eye.

This too, Wolf observed with something approaching wonder, for no warrior among any tribe would permit such a thing, nor would any war chief be permitted to impose such brutality.

Willow had been ordered to tend to Akmed's bleeding back, and their reunion had been awkward.

"Thou art the plaything of the Indio now," he glowered.

"Keep still," she replied, dabbing at his wounds with a poultice of sooth-ing plants which Wolf had prepared, along with some bark to chew, "and do not think ill of him, for he has given this for you to chew. He says it will ease your pain."

They had grounded on an island mid-river and Wolf had stripped the bark of a young tree, which he knew to be useful in damping one's pain. He had also collected a gourd of water from a spring, instructing Willow to use it to cleanse Akmed's wounds with it, rather than the muddy water of the river.

"Chew this shit?" Akmed looked at the proffered bark, sweating tears of pain as Willow dabbed at his back.

"He is a physician in his country and says it will help."

"I have seen you making eyes at him."

Willow gave no reply. She had avoided any display of affection around Wolf, knowing that the men would not approve. Yet Akmed had kept a hawk eye on her since her return and had guessed that she was Wolf's woman now. She had avoided his gaze, much less his embrace, and that made her all the more desirable, and the pain of losing her more acute.

As for herself, Willow wondered where the sweet youth she had prayed with had gone off to, for now Akmed seemed a snarling, hectoring nag. He was fond of bragging that he had been a favorite among the Indian maid-ens, even though they had no choice but to suffer his embraces.

"You belong to me," he persisted. "I swear to Allah I will have him killed."

"You disgust me," she said, throwing down the poultice, which was pink with his blood. "Chew the bark as I've told you or soak in your pain."

And so the *Tiger* crept on as the days passed by. Garlands of flowering trees blossomed along the riverbank as spring erupted in its glory. Over-head, flocks of birds darkened the sky as they migrated north with the season. Within a week Cabeza's men had gathered enough maize, beans and sunflower seeds from villages along the river to last them for a time, and the captain took to skirting the larger towns, piloting the *Tiger* along the far side of the river past them. Fleets of dugouts and rafts dogged them as they passed, with hundreds eyeing the strange craft and its occupants.

Wolf quickly tired of the captain's nagging.

"How far is the city of the pyramids?" he asked again and again.

"Far," Wolf responded cryptically. This was true, for a lumbering galleon converted to a galley was no stallion of the waves and the *Tiger* plodded slowly at best. As Captain Sincid had predicted some time ago, the ship handled like a pig amid the currents of the river, sometimes veering sideways despite the efforts of the man at the rudder. Wolf mused that he had traveled three times as fast down the river in his canoe as the *Tiger* could manage while pushing against its current.

"Half a moon or more," he said on the fourth time Cabeza summoned him.

"Half a moon? What is this?"

"He means two weeks, captain," Willow said.

"And what of Cibola? Have you heard of Cibola and its bishops?"

Wolf gave him a weary look in response, not understanding what the captain meant.

"He means a place of shamans," Willow said.

"Yes, there were many shamans there, but they are long dead," Wolf replied, thinking of the Bird Men and their temples.

"But is there much gold?" Cabeza pushed. "Enough to fill our ship?"

Wolf hesitated, knowing that the captain craved the shining metal above all else. He had seen a scattering of copper among the people of the Cahokia, hammered into spearheads, amulets, earrings and more. But these were things which had been traded to the mound builders long ago and the Cahokians had only a few items from the long-dead past.

"Perhaps," he lied. "Go and see."

Captain Cabeza had cursed, but there was nothing to be done for it and Wolf, in turn, was mystified. Several times they had passed by towns where mounds had been built along the river, yet the Spaniards never bothered to stop. Were these not the pyramids that they sought? They had described hills made by men! Yet they passed by as if they had not even seen the low-lying mounds along the river. He decided it must be only the Great Mound of the Bird Men that would please them.

But why? And why did they lust so for copper? It was a useful enough metal, but nothing as helpful as the Spaniards' iron or steel. Nor had he come to understand that copper was not the gold that the Spaniards wished to find. Copper was the only metal that Wolf knew that could shine like the sun and he continued to think of it as the metal the Spaniards called oro, gold.

"They have a disease that can only be cured with gold," Willow said simply when he asked her. "But once they find it they will grow even sicker, as if they are insane."

Wolf was more than willing to believe that the Spaniards had a sickness, for between the glowering looks of Akmed, the hateful stares of Sincid and the gloom of the despairing men they had no more spirit than a band of ghosts. Still, on they pushed, and it was as if he could read their thoughts.

Gold. He suspected that they would find little of it at the Great Mound. As for reaching the mines of the Ojibwe at the isle of Minong, there was no chance that they'd be able to portage their huge canoe to the great lakes of the north. They'd have to abandon it, and once in the forest they would be easily picked off by warriors hidden among the trees.

But this Wolf kept to himself.

Willow was once again charged with the care of Montoya and Wolf spent a great deal of time admiring the horse. He was astonished to find that he was able to caress the horse, for such a thing would have been impossible with a deer.

"Its eyes show wisdom," he remarked of Montoya's strange blue eyes, which rimmed its pupils in a tight circle.

"Nay, he is what a friend called an eejit," Willow replied, brushing the horse's back with a comb she had made of straw. "It means a fool."

"He is no fool. He is wise in his own way, as are all animals."

"I suppose. He has made it this far, so perhaps he is not an eejit."

Ah, but how far would she go, and to what end? she wondered. From time to time her gaze caught that of Wolf's and she saw longing there, feeling a pang in her own heart in return. They had been lovers, but could they be something more? Perhaps she could make a life with this man in the New World, as Croen had done with the woman of the Mauvilans. Perhaps not...

As for himself, Wolf would have long since slipped over the side of the ship and swum to shore if it had not been for Willow. He was resolved to steal her away at any cost. She, and the horse, Montoya.

Two weeks dragged on as the *Tiger* made its way slowly up the river. Captain Sincid had to be gagged for raving like a madman and exhorting the men to mutiny from where he sat chained to the mast. Only the fact that Sincid would be needed to sail the ship back to Cuba kept Captain Cabeza from cutting out his tongue.

But Sincid's words had found their mark and there were mutterings once again among the men that perhaps it would be best to cut their losses and flee for their lives. For how could they hope to overcome a golden city of thousands of Indians with such a small force? Several times Captain Cabeza took pains to remind them that they still had eight barrels of gunpowder along with the culverin and an arquebus. "These alone will frighten any city into submission."

Truly? When Cabeza spoke, the men eyed him and then the barrels and the guns, which were puny, almost nothing at all compared to the armaments they had witnessed in Europe. Could eight barrels of gunpowder truly topple a kingdom, perhaps even an empire? Only Captain Cabeza seemed certain that it was so.

Then one day they rounded a bend in the river and through the trees Wolf saw a familiar sight, the Great Mound of the Cahokians. "There!" he pointed.

Captain Cabeza squinted to the east, shading his eyes from the sun. What he had expected to find was an elegant pyramid of stone painted in many colors rising above a city of tens of thousands. Instead, he saw a tall hill covered with trees and brush with a few awe-struck natives standing open-mouthed on the riverbank. Still, he could make out the squared-off corners of the Great Mound, indicating that it was indeed an earthen pyramid. In the distance, he spied a pathway to the top, where even now a number of Indians stood gazing down on the *Tiger*.

"Crossbows and armor all around, and load the arquebus," Cabeza growled as the *Tiger* grounded by the riverbank.

The arquebus was a heavy musket, about four feet long, mounted on an oak staff to bear its weight. Cabeza's arquebus had been made in Holland, featuring the latest advancements in firearms. It was a matchlock outfitted with a small metal wheel behind its priming pan that bore a fuse of hemp, which could be lit at both ends. If one end of the fuse was extinguished, the matchlock wheel could be turned so that the other end could ignite the powder in the priming pan to fire the gun.

The arquebus had been used to great effect in conquering both the Aztecs and the Incas and now Cabeza deemed it prudent to bring it ashore.

But as it happened, the gun was not needed, for as Wolf remembered, the Cahokians were few in number and most of them scattered at the conquistadors' approach. A few of the braver among them emerged from the forest to gaze in wonder at the ship, and also at Montoya, who gamboled in the overgrown plaza, eager to be free of confinement. By signs Wolf made them to understand that they must not kill what they took to be a strange sort of deer.

Captain Cabeza frowned upon the humble lodges of the village, constructed with reeds tied in bundles. Dimly he made out the shapes of dozens of low mounds, but all were overgrown with brush and trees. His men stood silently behind him, some cursing under their breath.

"This place is as old as the Bible," he muttered. "Surely, its time was hundreds of years ago."

"It was two hundred years ago at least, my lord," Willow spoke up. "Wolf says a great people lived here in the time of his grandfathers' grandfathers, which is his way of marking time."

Cabeza grunted, and led his men forward to where the pathway led to the top of the Great Mound. The pyramid was one hundred feet tall and covered fourteen acres, every inch of which had been laden one basket of dirt at a time by those who lived hundreds of years ago in the city at its base. It was a hard climb and the day was hot and humid. When the long straggle of men reached the top they stood panting with exertion before the ruins of a huge ancient temple. There to meet them stood Three Quails, the headman of the Cahokians, along with several of the village elders.

"Sunktanka," he said to Wolf, indicating the horse far below. It was one of the few words he recalled from Wolf's visit in the fall.

Yes, I have found it, Wolf replied in sign language, but beware these men. Tell your people to hide their food and flee to the forest. Give no sign that you understand.

"What are you telling him?" Cabeza demanded.

"Only that you are friends who hunger for gold," Wolf replied.

Three Quails offered a grave nod, giving no sign of alarm as he held out a bundle of tobacco in greeting. Cabeza bowed in return and then stepped forward to examine the amulet dangling by a cord from the headman's neck. Three Quails had kept the disc polished as Wolf had instructed and now it glimmered a dull orange in the morning sun.

"Gold," Wolf called from over Cabeza's shoulder.

The captain turned with a look on his face, as if he had just been goosed. "This is copper," he said.

"Gold," Wolf repeated knowingly. For was this not the bright-as-the-sun metal the Spaniards sought?

For the first time it occurred to Cabeza that Wolf had no idea as to what gold was, and dread swept through him at the thought that perhaps there was no gold to be found anywhere along the river, not even in this ancient city.

"Jesus save us all," he said softly, extending his right hand where the golden heirloom ring of his forefathers lived on his ring finger. He waved his ring before Wolf's eyes. "This is gold. This!"

Wolf had seen the ring many times, but had assumed it was another form of copper. "Gold," he pointed to the ring, then to the disc hanging from Three Quails' neck. "Same."

"No Wolf, it is not the same," Willow said quietly, steering him away from the captain, whose face was blanching white with disbelief.

"What is it captain?" one of the men spoke up from behind. "You mean there's nothin' here?"

Only the grumbling and angry frowns of the soldiers kept Wolf from being executed on the spot, for suddenly Cabeza realized that he was at the knife's edge of having his men turn against him. He had to keep them busy.

"Dig here!" he roared, waving his sword in a broad sweep. "Beneath the temple, dig it up!"

All that was left of the temple were dozens of broken and rotting trunks of great trees which had supported its roof nearly two centuries ago. Its outline was more than one hundred feet long and almost fifty feet wide. On his prior visit, Three Quails had told Wolf that in the time of his ancestors, the temple had stood almost as tall as it was wide. "As high as a tree, rising up to the home of the birds."

There was nothing to indicate any treasure hidden in the earth beneath the ruins, but the Spaniards dug in a fury just the same. Easing away, Three Quails fled to the village below, taking the elders with him. Wolf's gray eyes pooled with satisfaction as he watched the villagers fleeing far below. There would be no harm done to them by the Spaniards.

The digging continued for three days beneath the humid sun. At sundown on the third evening, with a hole dug deeper than a grave and the entire floor of the temple excavated, the exhausted, filthy men collapsed in the agony of revelation. There was no gold to be had atop the Great Mound.

"You promised us silver, gold, treasure!" Cabeza raged at Wolf, who had been ordered to dig along with the Spaniards.

"There is treasure here," Wolf replied. "Not gold, but treasure."

"Where?"

Wolf pointed to the south, where lay the burial mounds of the Bird Men. "There, but you must not touch."

"What do you mean?" The captain's face had grown haggard. "God's mercy, I'm being eaten from the inside out by this dithering! Tell me, damn you!"

"There are ghosts among the bones of the Bird Men," Wolf explained. He had anticipated this moment and had spent some time with Willow working out the words, pantomiming the vision of a ghost.

"So these are graves?"

Wolf nodded.

"Great men, buried with their riches? Pharaohs?"

"Pharaohs?"

"Kings, rulers, potentates..." Cabeza sputtered.

"He means chieftains," Willow said.

"Yes, but you cannot touch. The treasure is cursed! There are spirits there, many spirits, and they are angry."

A knowing smile melted the strain from Cabeza's face. "Ghosts and curses be damned. Show us the way."

Wolf responded with a grim look as if to say it was the captain's funeral, but he was more than happy to leave the work of digging up the temple floor, and turning, he headed down the Great Mound as Cabeza assembled his men.

Down the slope and through the trees lay the grave of the Falcon, washed open by the wayward river. The grave was much as Wolf had left it the prior fall; if anything, more shell beads had been exposed, glistening in the morning's rain.

Wolf marched to the grave with Cabeza and his men at his heels. "Here," he said, pointing. Before them lay the treasure of thousands of shell beads which had been woven into a burial shroud for the grave's long-dead occupant. As Wolf had noted the prior fall, the beads were treasure enough to delight every woman among all the clans of the Anishinaabek and more.

But then to his utter shock, Captain Cabeza gave the command.

"Start digging!"

Half a dozen men bulled into the grave as if they were pigs at a trough, digging at the muck which cradled the skeleton of a man who might once have been a chieftain or priest commanding tens of thousands. Within minutes they had hacked the skeleton from the earth, trampling the thicket of bones of those who had joined the corpse in the afterlife. There were perhaps twenty thousand beads in the grave, yet these were scattered as if they were of no more consequence than feed scattered to chickens.

Through it all, Wolf stood gaping with dread. The conquistadors were up to their hips in the yellowed ribs, thigh bones and skulls of the grave before he was able to speak.

"You have ruined it!" he cried.

"What do you mean, ruined it?" Cabeza replied, for even he had taken a turn digging, while other men attacked the burial mounds nearby.

"The treasure. Can you not see?" Wolf scooped a handful of the precious shell beads from the mud. "The shells!"

The Ring and the Tiger

Once again there had been a misunderstanding and once again Wolf's life was suspended by a hair.

By the look on Captain Cabeza's face Wolf knew that he must think of a story that might save him, and quickly, but for the moment he was too confounded to think. The Spaniards had asked him for gold and treasure and he had delivered both! Yet they had desecrated the grave and scattered the shells without a thought as to their value. Now, the beadwork of shells beyond count was trampled into the muck around the open grave. The bones of the dead were scattered everywhere and he could almost see their angry spirits quavering over the desecration.

Captain Cabeza's eyes pulsed as if they might spin in their hollows.

"Shells?" he cried, "these stinking shells?" He kicked at the dirt and around him his men looked up, questioning.

"Ghosts! Can't you see?" Wolf replied, pointing to the scattered skulls, femurs and ribs, for now it was not just the curse of the corpse that would follow them, but the spirits of all of the slaves and virgins that had been sacrificed along with him. He could see their dark forms moving and muttering behind the men, lurking over their shoulders. Could the Spaniards not see?

"These shells? These stinking shells?" Cabeza repeated, as if he could not believe his own ears. He clutched his temples and closed his eyes in anguish. "Hang this fool from the nearest tree!" he cried.

Four men sprang forward, grasping Wolf by his arms, preparing to drag him away.

Willow gave Wolf a look, but it was clear that he was too befuddled to speak. "Tell them something!" she hissed.

But he looked back at her as if he'd been struck dumb. He tore away from his captors and collapsed on the ground, clutching his head.

It was then that she decided to offer a story of her own making, if only to cool the captain's temper.

"Captain, you cannot blame him," she said, "for these shells are a great treasure among his people. Gold is of no value to them, but these shells come from the sea, which is far away, and they find them useful as ornaments and for trade. To them they are much the same as gold."

"We expected gold, pearls, silver," Cabeza said coldly, looking up through tearing eyes. "Yet your pet has made fools of us."

"But it was merely a misunderstanding, a problem of speaking. Perhaps he can yet lead us to what you seek. Have you never heard of the 'Ring and the Tiger'?"

"What?"

Cabeza's men gave him a questioning look. A rope had been fetched, but Willow held a hand aloft, signaling them to hold. Stupefied, they obeyed, but only for a moment. "Do you still want him to swing, Captain?" one of the men grasping Wolf spoke up.

The captain frowned at Willow but seemed to have cooled a degree. "The ring and the tiger," he repeated, "what of it?"

Willow searched his eyes, a pinched look of concern on her face. She angled closer to Wolf, standing between him and the captain.

"It is a story of misplaced things, my lord. Shall I tell it to you?"

Cabeza nodded wearily and his men lowered their swords at Wolf, who sat in the mud, scowling at the mistreatment of the grave. He muttered an apology to the spirits of the scattered bones, seeking forgiveness. But his words went unnoticed as Willow began her tale.

"Once there was a proud young queen of the Parsis in Babylon who was as mighty as any king; mightier even than Alexander," Willow began. "Her army could fill a plain stretching to the horizon. She had an army of two hundred thousand men and a personal guard of five thousand amazon warriors.

"Amazons," Cabeza said dully, looking pitiful and sick as he sat in the mud by the open pit with his knees spread wide.

"Yes, lord, and she had battalions of war elephants and twenty thousand horsemen. That, and war machines such as scorpions, siege towers and catapults that had toppled castles in three-score lands. And as you can imagine, she was as beautiful as any man could desire."

"Was there ever any other sort of queen?"

"This I do not know, captain. But I do know that she was richer than Solomon. She had treasures worthy of a dragon's hoard; vaults filled with emeralds, diamonds and rubies. She ate off golden plates - nay, she had a thousand golden plates, along with silver cups filled with wine at her galas attended by the vassals of many lands. Even her privy was fashioned of solid gold."

At this, Captain Cabeza snorted with a cheerless smile. "A golden privy. And I suppose that she shat bricks of gold too?"

"This I do not know, sir, but it is well known that the lady emptied her bowels into a golden bucket beneath a golden chair."

"Continue."

"But among all her treasures, the queen valued a simple golden ring above all else. It was a ring without ornamentation, engraving or any gemstone. It was a simple golden band of the sort a woman of a lowly household might wear, humble, thin and plain."

"And was this a magic ring, I suppose?"

"No sir, not magic, but cursed. There was nothing special about the ring at all, except that it had been a gift from the queen's great grandmother when she had been a child of ten years old. And the queen had ordered her necromancer to put a curse on the ring, should anyone steal it."

"I don't catch the meaning of this."

"Why sir, only that a treasure is in the eye of its beholder, as is the case with these humble shells your men have trampled. But that is hardly the end of the tale."

"Ah"

"One day, while the queen was holding an audience with emissaries from Cathay, the ring was swept into a dustbin by a housekeeping slave. You see, the ring had rolled off the stand where the queen kept it and was swept up and tossed out with the palace trash.

"The queen's wrath was like that of a gryphon, a hydra or a jinn! She assumed that her ring had been stolen by her slaves and had every eunuch and serving girl among them tortured. Yet all were blameless and professed their innocence, and no matter how cruelly she pressed them, the ring was never found."

"So where was it then?" Cabeza asked, irritated. It had not escaped him that Wolf was much the same as the innocents who had been tortured in Willow's story.

"Why, it was in the refuse heap behind the palace, along with the dinner bones, tattered rags and the cast-offs of a rich woman who had everything, except for the thing that she desired the most. And one day a poor rag-picker spied it at the very bottom of a pile of rotting filth, glimmering in the aftermath of a spring rain.

"As you can imagine, even a simple golden band was a great treasure to the lowly rag-picker, who was among the lowest of the low. He exulted among his friends and family, for even though the ring's worth was less than a grain of sand compared to the queen's hoard, still it was enough to feed a family of rag-pickers for a year."

By now all of Cabeza's men were gathered around Willow, their eyes wide and shushing for silence as the fate of the golden ring unspooled. They were men from the gutters and the dusty farms of Spain and it as not hard for them to imagine themselves in the rag-picker's shoes, assuming he had any.

"And so the poor man set out to exchange the ring for a purse of silver coins, but his lips were too loose and the ring was cursed, and ere he could reach the shop of a goldsmith, robbers set upon him and stole it, for they had heard news of it in town. But even then the ring's journey was not done, for the chief of the robbers gave it to his wife as a gift.

"Both the chief and his wife were as evil and low as the sewers of Babylon, robbing and murdering people in the hills or taking them for slaves. The robber's wife was a wicked old thing; sometimes she would stew the bones of those her husband killed and feed the gruel to their slaves."

"Truly?"

"Yes, lord. And know this: the robber's wife had little concern for her new bauble, for it was but one tarnished ring among the twenty that she wore on her fingers. If only she had known that the Queen of Babylon would have ransomed it for a room filled with gold!"

"If only," the captain said miserably, clutching a handful of mud and shells before tossing it aside.

"Years passed by and the queen grew old and frail. Her only happiness lay in her daughter, who had been born shortly after the precious ring disappeared. Even though she had riches, slaves and soldiers beyond compare, still, her daughter was the only joy in her life. Is it not always so, my lord?"

"I suppose." Cabeza tapped the point of his sword impatiently on the ground between his legs.

"Ah, but the robber's wife was even older than the queen, with a heart so black and hard that it was incapable of breaking. Yet one day while she and her husband's band of brigands were roaming the hills in search of a caravan to plunder, she came upon a tiger prowling just outside her tent and was eaten, ring and all. The ring had finally wrought its curse."

"A tiger, you say?"

"Yes lord, she was devoured in three or four mouthfuls, I imagine, but not before suffering the most exquisite terror and pain! There were many such beasts roaming the wilderness outside of Babylon. It says so in your Bible."

This, Willow did not know, but since she was making the story up as it came to her, it seemed like a worthy detail.

Captain Cabeza was impressed by the revelation, however, and seemed to have forgotten about stretching Wolf's neck as he bade Willow to continue.

"As it happened, the queen had no son, so her daughter was trained in the arts of war and the hunt. She became a great warrior at the head of her mother's army."

"An amazon princess, I suppose."

"Yes, sir, and one of the things she loved most was hunting - riding over the hills with her bow and spear. Then one day as it happened, she and her retinue were chasing a boar in the forest when a tiger attacked, clawing at her stallion. Her horse was much like your Montoya, I imagine."

"Ah."

"Yes, and the warrior princess did not flinch or quail. She thrust her spear straight through the tiger's heart, and what do you imagine they found when the beast was skinned and gutted?"

"The golden ring," Cabeza said dully.

"Yes, lord, and the dutiful daughter returned it to her mother, who was overjoyed to see it again, making all right in the realm."

Cabeza sighed at the conclusion and spat off to the side.

"That is a preposterous story," he said at last, and at least one of his men agreed, for there had been a groan from among those who stood listening, "but it is well told and I do believe you could sweep the stars from the sky with such ilk if you found a broom long enough to reach them. But tell me, what am I to draw from it?"

"Why sir, only that the humblest of things can be a treasure to both the mighty and the meek, and that sometimes riches may be found where we least expect them."

Cabeza shook his head as if trying to clear it. "And will you vouch that your man Wolf will pull a golden ring from a tiger's ass?"

"We might ask him."

By now Cabeza's anger had cooled, and though Wolf felt that his own fate was still in question, Willow's story had given him time to think of a ruse which might foil his captors. A return to Kitchi Gami and the home of the Anishinaabek was unthinkable, but just ahead lay the mouth of another great river leading to a land filled with warriors beyond count - men willing to torture themselves with rites of unspeakable pain to prove their valor. Surely they would prove the Spaniards' undoing.

Much that Willow had said made no sense to him. Was she speaking of the ship when the old woman was eaten? She spoke of a tiger... but how could a ship eat a woman? And what was a queen? What was a ring? These were words he had not yet learned. But noticing that the captain was referring to him, he spoke up.

"There is another way," he said. "A place of treasure."

"Like this place?" Cabeza asked, his eyes cold and hopeless.

"No, a big place with many people, many towns. The land of traders."

"Traders."

Wolf nodded, thinking of Buffalo Drum's story of his home, the Big Two Ditch Place, a large town of earthen homes encircled by two ditches and a wall of cottonwood trunks, behind which gathered hundreds of hardened warriors. Warriors who would burn the Spaniards to cinders.

"Many traders, many towns," he said.

"And are there pyramids and gold? We must have gold, not this..." Cabeza swept his hand over the desecrated grave, "this trash."

By now Wolf was well aware that gold was poetry to the Spaniards' ears; they were mad for it, lusting as a gaunt wolf pack goes mad for the scent of a wounded moose. He sensed that in their blind lust they would believe a lie that would not fool a child. But he also knew there was no silver or gold among the Mandans, else Buffalo Drum and his men would have worn ornaments of it. Yet the Spaniards' desire would lead them into a snare fit for a rabbit.

Still, it would not do to make the trap too obvious. Wolf thought of the pit mines of Minong and the red pipestone quarry of the Dakota, where things of great value lay beneath the earth. Perhaps the Spaniards also knew of such pits...

"There are no pyramids," he said vehemently.

"But is there silver? Is there gold? Is there a metal like that of my ring?"

Wolf frowned. "Yes, but you would not want it."

"What? Why?"

"It must be dug from the earth." He raised a hand in resignation. "It is under the ground. Our people do not care for it."

"You do not care?"

"Why should we dig for metal when there are shells of great value?" Wolf said scornfully.

"Dig? Do you mean a mine?" Captain Cabeza's eyes widened.

"What is mine?"

Captain Cabeza made digging signs with his hands, and then paddled sideways as if he were a mole, crawling underground. Wolf suppressed a laugh, but could not help a twinkle in his eyes. He looked to Willow for confirmation of the word and she nodded.

"Yes, a mine," he said. "The earth is filled with gold. It lives alongside the silver. There are rivers of silver and gold in the earth in the land of the traders."

"And where might this be?"

"North," Wolf pointed. "To Pekitunoui, the way to the Mandans. Some call it the Missouri, the River of Log Canoes."

The Way to the Mandans

And so began another long haul to the northwest along the river that met the Misi Sipi just beyond the ruins of the Great Mound.

"You have sent them chasing a chicken," Willow said as they stood at the stern of the *Tiger* with Montoya.

"What is chicken?"

"It is a bird like a goose or a duck. It is very hard to catch with your bare hands."

"Yes, they chase a duck, but soon we will leave, if you wish," Wolf replied.

"Where will we go?"

"I will make us a canoe and take you to your mother and father. I will take you home to your people."

Willow gave a husky laugh. "That is kind of you, but we could never reach them, for it is a journey of many months down the river and across the ocean."

This, Wolf knew, but courtesy demanded the offer, and now the alternative trembled on his lips.

"Then you will come to my people," he said shyly. It was as much a question as a proposal.

Willow gazed into his eyes, thinking that they were as bold as Wolf's namesake. What to make of him? They were already lovers and she doubted she'd ever see home again. At best she might have the life of a slave among the Spaniards if she stayed with Cabeza and his men. That fate could only lead to horror. But what kind of life would she have among Wolf's people? Wolf had said it would be cold there in the winter and had spoken of snow, a thing she had heard of, yet never experienced. Snow! The thought of it filled her with wonder that she might see it... and what was a little cold? Had she not shivered beneath her thin blanket back in Morocco? But how could she make a life among a people so different from her own? It was possible only if her love for Wolf could sustain her.

There was no other choice.

"Yes, I will come with you," she replied gravely. "But how? When?"

Wolf looked to the dwindling trees along with river and the distant plains, calculating their chances.

"Soon. In two days, maybe. We will look for signs in the clouds and wind."

"Walking? Across these plains?"

"We will take the horse with us."

Willow scoffed at this. "They will chase us down."

"We will ride it, like the captain." Wolf had observed Cabeza riding Montoya at their stops along the river, taking care to consider how it might be done. Ahead, he knew, lay the empty plains where they might easily slip away if he could manage to guide the horse. If they could get even a bow shot away from the Spaniards they could easily outrun them. Then they would be free to head north to where Lone Dog's people lived. And then, somehow, he would bring both Willow and the sunktanka home to

Boweting and the heartland of the Ojibwe.

"And have you ever ridden a horse before?" she asked lightly.

"No. You must guide him." He remembered her tales of riding great beasts in her homeland. Willow had said they were twice the size of Montoya.

"I have ridden camels, but never a horse."

"Can you do it?"

Willow's brow furrowed. How hard could it be? Montoya knew her better than his own mother. "Yes," she replied. "I can ride us both away. But how will we steal him?"

It would be easy, he thought. They would lead Montoya a short way from where the conquistadors camped for the night on the pretense of feeding the horse and then ride away.

"You will see!" he smiled, catching the skepticism in Willow's eyes.

"Yes, brave prince, I will see when I see."

The thought of stealing the Spaniards' horse filled Wolf with both dread and desire. What if the horse refused to accept them on its back? What if it refused to move? He could only imagine the worst if Cabeza's men caught him in the act of stealing the stallion.

The River of the Mandans was even wilder than the Misi Sipi, jammed with pile-ups of trees and riven with rapids and small waterfalls. Now, the hemp ropes that had been fashioned months before came in handy as Cabeza's men dragged the *Tiger* through one set of rapids after another by edging it along the bank of the river. The cursing of the men outweighed their anticipation, for although Wolf had assured them that the gold mines of a people known as the Mandans lay somewhere up the river, he had not divulged how far that might be and gave only vague answers when asked.

"Far," he said.

But Wolf did indeed know how far, for Buffalo Drum had told him that he and his traders had spent the length of half a moon paddling down the river, so at best Wolf imagined it would take the *Tiger* three moons pushing upstream against the current, even with every man at the oars.

But that was the least of it, for there were fewer and fewer villages along the river as the land gave way to the arid plains. The Spaniards' supply of stolen corn was diminishing rapidly, yet there were few villages to raid, and these had scant stores of maize. For who would grow crops in such a land when there were buffalo to pursue? Yet although the plains teemed with elk, antelope, buffalo, quail and deer, the conquistadors were not adept as hunters. Cabeza's crossbowmen had been trained for mass attacks against armored horsemen and infantry firing the heavy bolts of quarrels and tri-bladed bodkins. These were useful for piercing armor, yet the men were utterly lost when it came to bringing down an antelope. Hunting on the plains required the skills of concealment or of men working together to drive game over a cliff or into a river.

Thus, the *Tiger* bore an increasingly hungry crew, with its fate growing dimmer with every stroke of its oars.

Chained to the mast by an iron collar around his neck, Captain Sincid had all but given up speaking and sat glowering in his filth, surrounded by a galaxy of flies. In the weeks since his imprisonment, he had grown docile, despite his hateful stares, giving the impression that he had dwindled to the state of a feeble-minded madman. Some of the coarser men had taken to calling him Sea Bitch, throwing him half-eaten cobs of corn as his meal and taunting him with barks, snarls and yelps as if he were a cowering dog.

Chief among them was Akmed who never passed by without an insult or a taunt. In his hometown of Badis, a dog had been the lowliest of beasts, a garbage eater not much higher in the scale of things than a rat, and now Akmed delighted in tormenting the fly-bitten pirate, spitting on him when he was sure that Captain Cabeza wasn't looking. It was as if Akmed had become a scorpion, eager to sting and lash, again and again at the man who had taken his hand.

Some weeks before, Wolf had warned Akmed not to tease a snake they had found hissing by the side of the river, yet Akmed had always been a reckless sort, and had not listened. The rattler had whipped away in a fury, but not before lashing out in a whip-crack, its fangs barely missing Akmed's leg. Akmed had drawn back, somber-eyed, but Wolf sensed that he had not learned his lesson.

As for Captain Sincid, he no longer seemed to recognize Akmed, other than as one of his tormentors in general. He bore up under the spitting and curses, whining and shrinking away from all who came near. As the days wore on, Sincid was given leave to remain with his hands free, for it was tiresome to keep shackling and unshackling him for the business of eating, pissing and emptying his bowels. He had become to all appearances a cringing, sniveling dog, caved in upon himself and of no threat to anyone. Only an iron chain around his neck bound him to the mast.

But at odd moments, Willow caught the gleam in Sincid's gaze as he looked upon his tormentors with a lizard's calculating eye. Perhaps it was a woman's intuition, but she imagined that the Sea Bitch was only biding his time.

And so it was, for one day when the *Tiger* had beached on a sand bar and all of the men were off the ship praying at Mass with the lone priest,

Akmed had taken the opportunity to poke at Sincid with a stick, jabbering taunts in his ear beneath the afternoon sun. Sincid had gibbered in fright, shaking his head in alarm and cowering like a monkey.

This had goaded Akmed even closer and his eyes shone with delight as he leered over the cowering slaver. He gave Sincid a swat with his stick and was rewarded with a mewling cry, which filled him with glee.

For a few moments at least, Akmed had the Sea Bitch in his power and his head swam with delight.

"Come on filthy dog, whine for me, grovel," he said as he jabbed at Sincid. "Thou stinking Sea Bitch, thou cur! You'll never be free and someday I will piss on you as you lay in your grave, dong-sucking filthy pig..."

Akmed had always prided himself on his cursing and now words fell from his lips as if a waterfall. "Son of a donkey and a whore! Lady-man! Puke!..." He switched back and forth at Sincid's face with his stick.

"No, no.. please no!" Indeed, Sincid was groveling now, crying piteously and holding his arms up against the sting of Akmed's stick.

"Beg for me, insect! Know your place! Leech! Man-whore! Your mother was a snake and your father a worm!"

The bully in Akmed had replaced his last shred of humanity, and it was as a bully that he was doomed. The iron chain binding Captain Sincid to the mast was only three feet long, but his arms gave him another two and he had long since calculated the ring of death around him. Cowering against the mast in apparent terror and begging as if for his life, he tempted Akmed a half-step closer.

"No, no, no," he quavered like a child. "No hurt, no spit. No, please, master, please..." Sincid cowered beneath an upraised arm, seemingly beaten, raw and helpless below Akmed's shadow.

Only another half step remained, and Akmed took it with his hand raised to deliver a stinging slap. But the blow never came, for Sincid gazed over his tormenter's shoulder and pointed in alarm. Akmed turned to look and the Sea Bitch struck as quick as a snake. Grasping the chain behind his neck with both hands, he reared up and lashed out, encircling Akmed with his legs. As quick as a spider snares a fly, he drew him to the trap of his wiry arms.

Willow and Wolf were on the sandbar with Cabeza and his men when they heard a scream from the ship, then a gurgling cry that was cut off sharply as Captain Sincid crushed Akmed's larynx with both hands around his throat. It took some moments for the men to clamber back over the side of the ship, but once aboard they saw a sight that was a step beyond horror: Captain Sincid was kneeling on Akmed's chest, pinning him to the deck, and in his hand he held a bloody wooden spoon.

"There now pretty boy, who's the dog now?" he whispered over Akmed's prostate body. "Who is the bitch now?"

Sincid was dragged off Akmed and slammed against the mast as his prey writhed on the deck. Willow retched at the gore at the bottom of the ship where Akmed's eyes lay, torn out by their roots.

"God, Jesus save us!" Captain Cabeza cried, looking stricken to his bones as Sincid glowered in a heap on the deck only a toss away from Akmed's writhing body. Both of Sincid's hands were drenched with Akmed's blood, and with a snicker, he took to licking them.

As for Akmed, he was ruined, but not dead. He twisted in agony on the deck, unable to speak, clasping his hands to his bleeding face and gagging in horror.

"Finish him," Cabeza ordered in disgust. "He is of no more use to us."

The men gave a questioning look but understood well enough. A small conference was held amongst them and a delegate came forward bearing a sword, the point of which he settled on Akmed's ribs, just where it might pierce his heart and send him to peace.

Yet by then the men had received time to think on the matter.

"But he can still pull an oar, sir," one spoke up as the executioner paused.

"God damn us all!" Cabeza cried, but it was true; even blind and speechless Akmed could still be of use at the oars, for what was he, after all, but a galley slave? And so he was spared, for now.

Once again it was Wolf who ministered to his wounds. He had taken care to collect whatever medicinal herbs he could find as the *Tiger* made its way up the river, and now he made a moist poultice to pack into Akmed's empty sockets. He also made a tea of the bark which relieved pain.

"It is willow, like you," he said as Willow watched his ministrations. "It helps with pain."

"Are there many such plants here?"

"Yes, there are many," he nodded, though he did not know the words in Spanish to describe them. Sumac root for toothache, blackberry root for a sore throat, green cranberries to counteract poisons, burning sage for purification... Wolf sang a few words over Akmed's prostrate form, hoping they would help. The air seemed to hum around him.

"Thou art a saint," Willow said, nuzzling against him. She no longer cared if the men of the expedition noticed her affection, and Cabeza had made it clear that no one should harm Wolf. Just as Captain Sincid was their only hope of crossing the sea back to Cuba, Wolf was their key to finding the riches of the Mandans.

"Saint?"

"It is a good shaman, the best of all shamans."

Wolf laughed at this, caressing Akmed's forehead with another soothing poultice as his patient lay propped up and groaning against the hull of the ship. "I am only a small shaman," he said, "my uncles are the great ones. They are the Good Hearts."

"Then they must be angels."

"Sometimes harsh old men with big noses," Wolf said with a grimace. "Saints, angels, I don't know these things."

Nor did he care, for he did not consider himself adept at medicine. At best he was able to offer Akmed some simple remedies from his knowledge of herb craft.

"He will die soon."

"From his wounds?"

"His spirit. Gone."

This proved true enough, for a day later when Akmed was recovered enough to return to his oar, he trembled and sobbed at the task with a sincerity that Captain Sincid had only pretended. For his part, Sincid jeered at the mast, spitting and cursing until he was gagged once again. But if anyone dared to look his way, they caught his black eyes questing back and forth like those of a reptile, waiting for the chance to strike again.

And so the *Tiger* pressed on with a shaken and unhappy crew, constrained from mutiny only by the fact that they were now more than a thousand miles into the heart of an unknown land with no hope of surviving should they flee. But, Willow wondered, how long could they go on without food? Every man aboard the ship wondered the same and each day the portion of corn in their wooden bowls grew smaller as Captain Cabeza ordered the ration cut again and again.

Several times they saw tattooed men paddling heavily-laden dugouts downstream. But the river was broad and those paddling with the current had the advantage of speed. They scuttled away like water bugs, despite the halloos coming from the ship.

"Who are they? Are they the Mandans?" Captain Cabeza asked.

"Yes, they are the People of the Pheasants," Wolf said. "They are See-pohs-kah-nu-mah-kah-kee, the Mandans,"

He pointed out the long braids of the fleeing paddlers, wondering if Buffalo Drum was among them.

The slow crawl up the Missouri settled into a routine of rowing hard against the current and lining the ship around its rapids. Often, they contended with the summer winds, which swirled in all directions. Sometimes the wind blew with the power of a gale behind the ship, so strong that a man could barely stand against it. Then the *Tiger* flew up river with only half its sail raised, with the canvas in danger of splitting. Other times the wind blew in a fury against them and they were obliged to wait it out, with even thirty oars being useless against its power.

Buffalo Drum had told Wolf that there were ferocious storms out on the plains, with black twisters that rose to the clouds, drilling across the land and carrying everything in their path into the sky. At other times the plains were covered with lightning and thunder, stabbing at the earth and turning night to day.

"I would like to see these things," Wolf had said at the time, and now as they pushed into the heart of the plains he wished to see them even more, but except for an occasional far-off storm, he was disappointed.

Then one day they saw a line of red dust rising on the horizon, and rounding a bend in the river they came upon a procession making its way across the plain. As the *Tiger* drew closer, they observed hundreds of men, women, children and dogs, straggling in a long line to the west. Many were busy pulling a brace of long poles from which their baggage was strung. Much of the dust was raised by the travois poles, which dug at the earth as they were dragged forward.

"They are buffalo hunters," Wolf told Captain Cabeza. "They follow the herds, taking the meat."

"Meat sounds sweeter than gold to me now," Cabeza muttered. "Do they have meat?"

"No. Only after the hunt," Wolf said, but he had hesitated a moment before answering.

"Liar," Cabeza said dryly. "Surely they have a bounty of it."

Ahead, the procession halted at the sight of the *Tiger*, its red sail and the centipede of its oars. As with all others who had seen it, the ship was like a vision from a dream.

Across the plain, a handful of hunters came loping in their direction. They wore their hair in long braids and were almost naked.

"Prepare the culverin," Cabeza spoke over his shoulder to the musketeer. Turning, he spoken quietly to his men, "Everyone to arms, but keep them down."

The men coming toward them were far leaner than those who farmed the rich soil of the Misi Sipi. They had rarely tasted corn, and sweet foods other than honey were unknown to them. To Wolf's eyes they were as lean and hard-muscled as his brothers among the Ojibwe - men who lived on lean meat, wild rice, nuts and roots. Their bodies were taut and weathered by the eternal wind and sun of the plains.

They stopped a bow-shot away and crept forward in a half circle, squinting into the sun at the *Tiger* and its crew.

"Wolf!"

Wolf gaped in recognition. To his surprise, Anokasan-Duta - the boy named Red Eagle - stood at the head of the hunters along with his father, Lone Dog.

"You have found the sunktanka!" Red Eagle called out, oblivious to the bearded Spaniards, who had unsheathed their swords beneath the gunwales and were appraising the odds. Almost a year had passed since Wolf had seen him and he seemed no longer a boy. He had grown a hand taller and his body was ribboned with hard muscle. His eyes shone brightly, betraying no fear, and he ran out ahead of the hunters, eager to greet his old friend, even as his father cried out for him to stop.

Wolf struggled to remember the Sioux tongue as Red Eagle ran towards him. *"Beware, these bad men will do you harm!"* he called out as best he could. *"They hold me prisoner!"*

But Lone Dog's hunters hardly needed a warning, for even as Wolf cried out the conquistadors began swarming over the side of the ship, and with a thunderclap the culverin spoke, belching a tongue of flame over their heads. The cannon had been loaded with a rounded ball of chipped limestone which skipped once, twice, and then just a hands-breadth over a travois being pulled by two women.

"Run!" Wolf cried in the Sioux tongue as Lone Dog stared back in amazement, and had it not been for his son, perhaps he and his hunters would have stood there and died. But on the heels of the cannon blast had come a barrage of crossbow bolts and Red Eagle had cried out as one pierced his thigh. He looked down in disbelief at the bolt driven into his leg and then at the oncoming Spaniards. Then, collapsing, he stumbled and fell to the dust with his hands clutching at the bolt.

There was a moment of shock and disbelief, with several of the hunters scrambling to unleash arrows of their own at the conquistadors. Although Lone Dog was of medium stature and as lean as a blade, he tossed his son over his shoulder and ran as if he were no heavier than a pheasant, half dragging him across the plain.

It would have been a massacre had it not been for the meat. Almost all of Lone Dog's warriors were out on the hunt, while he and a token few had stayed behind to guard the procession. The women dropped their loads and ran, hustling their children and the elders before them as the Spaniards raced across the plain. The men stopped at the abandoned stores, pillaging the dried buffalo meat, the taking of which had required weeks of pursuit in the heat of the summer.

Wolf looked on futilely as the Spaniards plundered the procession, thinking that now would be a good time to flee. But Montoya was still aboard the ship and was not easily off-loaded, and so too was Captain Cabeza.

"You tried to warn them," Cabeza said.

"They are friends and you were foolish to attack," Wolf replied. "Trade! You should have traded!"

But trading had never crossed the captain's mind during all the time he had crossed this ill-starred land and now he gave Wolf a quizzical look in response.

"God has given us steel and gunpowder and the power of heaven to take what we wish," he said coldly, though he knew his words would mean little to Wolf. "God and our king commands us to glory and a greater purpose than you can understand. These people have been sent to serve our needs."

Wolf said nothing, but his thoughts boiled with anger. Looking over the plain, he saw Lone Dog and his people disappearing over a low hill. The captain was a fool to think there were so few men among them. Soon enough, they would regroup and a hunt of a different sort would begin.

Ahead lay only the bare plains, rolling in an undulating blanket to the far horizon with many twists in the river, which was fraught with rapids and tangles of sunken trees. It would be slow going at best, he thought, and Lone Dog would have little trouble finding them.

The Hunted

The men of the *Tiger* were a good deal jollier after their stomachs were filled close to bursting with the plundered meat, and for the first time in weeks their spirits lifted. As for the threat of the Dakota, they had seen only a small number of men attending a large number of women and children. The glow of a distant fire burned miles away over the horizon and the guard was doubled that night, but none among them felt any sense of danger.

How were they to know that beyond the hills Lone Dog had gathered his hunters in council? Now, more than two hundred warriors from his band and that of two others sat huddled around a fire of dried buffalo dung, debating the best way to attack the hair-faced demons. The Dakota knew every twist in the river ahead, and every place where it narrowed. The blast of the culverin had shaken them, but they noted that it had thrown only a single stone, causing no harm, and the plains were often filled with lightning and thunder that was far more frightening. The shaman, Split Tail, promised that he would summon spirits to protect them from the fire log, if only they would avoid its mouth.

Thus, several days passed by as the *Tiger* pushed on to the northwest along the Missouri. Guards were doubled at times when they had to drag the ship along the shore past rapids, but no painted warriors appeared from the bluffs over the river and none were seen on the prairie.

"We have lost them. They have fled," Willow said to Wolf on the third afternoon as she scanned the plains.

"They are only waiting," he replied. He had seen birds rising from behind the low hills along the river and once, several antelope skipped from the shelter of cottonwoods lining a stream. At times he saw rustling in the tall grass along the river. Could the Spaniards not see? It was plain that they were being hunted.

But with their bellies filled with meat the subject once again turned to the mines of silver and gold which surely lay ahead. Wolf found himself inventing ever more elaborate lies as Captain Cabeza pestered him for details. Soon, the earthen homes of the Mandans grew in the captain's mind to be the estates of lordly traders living in what must be a city of tens of thousands.

"And how far is it?" the captain wondered over and over, as if he were a child on a trip to the fair.

"Not far now. Soon we will see the fires of the Mandans," Wolf said, though he knew that their home must lie the length of two more moons upriver, as far away as a falcon could fly over the course of many days. Soon, he thought, he and Willow must make their stab at freedom, for the captain could not be fooled forever.

Then on the fifth day after plundering Lone Dog's band the *Tiger* struck a jagged, submerged branch which pierced the hull. The ship was grounded on a mud flat and emptied of half its stores to make repairs.

The flat where they had grounded was a miserable, stinking stretch of ankle-deep mud, swarming with flies and mosquitoes. Captain Cabeza had wrinkled his nose, ordering his men to make camp on a low bluff over the river, setting a guard of two men at either end of the ship below. Still chained to the mast, Captain Sincid made a third man on the ship, and slumped over his oar in utter misery, the blind Arab shepherd, Akmed, made a fourth.

Pulling an oar for days on end beneath the blazing sun of the plains had been agony enough, but now the pain of his empty eye sockets and crushed larynx was beyond endurance. Death, sweet death was all that Akmed could hope for as he broiled at his bench.

Akmed had thought a good deal about his plight since his blinding almost two weeks before, and had rediscovered his faith in Allah, the Deliverer of Fate. In the quiet of the night Allah had spoken to him of a plan that even a blind man might carry out if he moved with stealth. Especially a blind man who wielded a dagger.

He had also remembered a story, and now it grew fond in his thoughts. When Akmed had turned fourteen, his father had sat with him to explain the fate of every man who served Mohammed and the Faithful. He had been told that when he died, he would be greeted by seventy of the fairest maidens ever encountered by any man, and that the best qualities of each woman would be distilled into a single bride of dazzling beauty, who would serve any need that he could imagine.

The bride floated before his sightless eyes as he rowed, beckoning him to her spectral arms. She was his only balm against the curtain of pain and his torture at the bench.

Now, Akmed hungered for death and the woman his father had promised him, thinking it might be especially so, considering what he planned for the Christian infidels. Surely, a martyr would be rewarded in Paradise.

Akmed knew that small lanterns with a low flame burned at either end of the ship where the guards stood watch at night. He had filled them with oil himself before his blinding. He also knew from his own time at watch that the guards often dozed off, falling asleep as the hours crept past midnight when nothing was heard on the river except for the croaking of frogs and the hoot of night birds.

Thus, he slumped over his oar, pretending to sleep at his station as he had done for several days now, listening in the stillness over the river. Hours passed and from the both ends of the ship there came a soft snoring. Quietly, he slipped from his bench and crawled along the bottom of the hull, making his way through the barrels and baskets remaining on board. Quiet as a snake he made his way, slipping noiselessly forward in the darkness, crawling over the ribs of the ship, heedless of the bumps and scrapes to his shins. He paused by the sleeping guard, listening as his snores continued in ragged bliss. Then, searching for the heat of the lantern on its hook above the bow of the ship, he cursed under his breath as its sides seared his fingers. Gingerly, he reached around for its handle, lifting it with the faintest tinkle from its hook. Undisturbed, the guard slept on.

Then it was back again, creeping along the belly of the *Tiger* with the lantern held before him, moving ever so slowly as to make no sound, nor to drop the flame. Agonizingly slow, but so necessary for his plan to succeed. Akmed's free arm ached as if it were on fire as he strove to keep the lantern aloft while crawling across the soaked and splintered deck, snaking his way around the *Tiger's* cargo. He stopped for a time, breathing hard and begging for strength in a whispered prayer. He was only halfway to his destination, with all odds against him. Yet still the guards snored on and the frogs croaked on the river. It was surely a sign that Allah was with him.

At last he came to the stout vessel which would carry him off to Paradise. Placing the lantern atop the barrel, he began digging at a seam with his dagger.

Only six feet away, Captain Sincid was awakened by the light and a faint scratching, thinking at first that he was dreaming or that the dawn had come too soon. But then he saw the crescent of Akmed's sightless face illuminated by the lamp light and began to scream through his gag, pounding his feet against the deck.

But it was too late, for Akmed had released a trickle of gunpowder from the barrel and that was all he needed to send his tormenter plummeting to hell. He stripped the bandage from his head and grinned as he raised his ghastly face to Captain Sincid, the empty sockets of his eyes yawning as dark and deep as caverns in the red light of the lamp. With a deep-throated chuckle he unsheathed the lantern and touched the flame to the gunpowder, willing himself to Allah.

The camp above the ship awoke to an earthquake as the barrel released a jet of sparks and fire in a blaze spurting higher than the mast before it blew in a massive fireball. A shower of splinters and flames rained over the river as barrel after barrel blew with chest-pounding explosions, blossoming in a blinding fire. In seconds the hull was shot through in a thousand places, red as an iron forge amid the black smoke smothering the ship until the *Tiger* was engulfed in a sheet of flame from one end to the other.

Wolf leapt from a dream to a wall of light, thinking that the thunder and lightning of great storms had finally descended on the plains. Yet looking down the bluff above the river he saw a sheet of fire rising to the stars, with the men of the camp standing stark in its light, gazing in horror at the burning ship.

"The ship!" Willow screamed in his ear, clutching him fiercely with all her strength. "Our poor ship!"

Silently, they watched as one barrel after another exploded in a deafening blast. Words failed them, for even shouting could barely be heard above the fire storm. The *Tiger's* mast was a pillar of fire, and chained to it was the burning corpse of Captain Sincid. As for Akmed, only charred bits of him were found the next day, scattered here and there along the riverbank.

Far out on the plains, Lone Dog and his men gazed in awe as multi-colored ribbons of flame rose in a fireball to the stars, thinking it was the magic of the hair-faced demons at work. Only later that day did they discover that the Spaniards' ship had been burned to the level of the mud flat in a charred wreck.

All was lost. Captain Cabeza knew it and the men knew it as well. That morning they picked their way along the river, seeking whatever supplies they might find tossed as far as half a mile away by the exploding powder kegs. A council was held that night and for once Cabeza let the men speak their minds as if they had indeed become a *democracia*. The debate over what to do carried on until almost dawn, but at last a plan was agreed upon. They would march upon the great town of the Mandans and if they could not take it, they would at least seize the dugouts they had seen going down the river. Then they would make their way back to the gulf in search of Croen and the Mauvilans in order to build a new ship.

It was a mad plan, but there could be no other, for they were stranded on the featureless plains with no hope of escape except on foot. This, and Wolf had assured them that the Mandans were not far off. Not far at all.

A sliver of good fortune remained to the Spaniards in that they had emptied the ship of some of its stores in order to repair its pierced hull. Now, the men took to fashioning the same sort of travois that they had seen the Dakota using to drag their belongings over the plains. The Dakota had used slender pine lodge poles taken from the distant forests, but the Spaniards managed to fashion their own poles from spindly cottonwoods growing along the river. They were poor substitutes, but there was no other choice. Packed on their travois were stores of dried meat, their shields, weapons, and a small keg of gunpowder which had been off loaded from the ship before it blew. A tent was fashioned from the heavy spare sail which had been lugged ashore before the explosion, but this offered scant shelter in the days ahead and tended to collapse in a wind.

Wolf had observed the shields being piled onto a travois. They included a mix of heavy oaken wheels, leather-bound hoops and the turtle shells gathered along the sea coast. With some pride, Willow showed him the light, leather-clad shield with its four-pointed star that Croen had secured for her.

"You must wear this on your back," he said.

"What? Why?"

"Soon the arrows will fly."

As he had predicted, an arrow flew from the concealment of tall grasses that afternoon, piercing one of the conquistadors through the neck. Cabeza's men rushed into the grassland, finding nothing as their comrade bled to death.

Later that day, several men remarked on some wolves that were seen looking their way from a hill not far from the river. These, Wolf knew, were Lone Dog's men cloaked in pelts. Could the Spaniards not see? He kept the knowledge to himself, knowing that the Dakota were scouting them and testing their defenses.

Willow had been told enough of the world to know that mass attacks by vast armies were common in Europe and Africa, owing to the slim value of a soldier's life. Thousands could die at the whim of an emperor or a king. Yet Wolf assured her that the Dakota would not risk the life of a single man.

"They will kill us one at a time until there are too few to fight," he said. "They will hide and strike, again and again."

"They will not attack all at once?"

"No, for if a warrior dies, who will care for his wife and children? Who will care for his old ones, or the family of a brother who has died?"

As Wolf predicted, Lone Dog took care not to lose a single warrior as his war party shadowed and stung, retreating silently into the tall grasses of the plains. The Dakota chieftain could not forgive or forget, for beyond the hills his son lay in a fever from his wound, and the women and children of his band went hungry for lack of the food stolen by the Spaniards.

Soon, Cabeza and his men saw the silhouettes of emboldened warriors shadowing them on the hills paralleling the river as they dragged their possessions along. Lone Dog's warriors had probed their weakness and now they strove to frighten them. The conquistadors heard their howls and screams in the night, sometimes so close that it seemed they were only a few steps away. Increasingly, there were arrows winging from the tall grasses and over the crest of hills. Cabeza ordered an end to fires at night, which had served to make his men better targets.

Wolf prayed that Lone Dog would spare him and Willow, hoping that the chieftain had heard his words of warning days before. He wondered why the Dakota had made no attempt to slay the warhorse Montoya, which was the biggest target among them. Each day, Captain Cabeza mounted the horse and swept the plains around his plodding men. Although he was dressed in chain mail and a steel doublet which would turn any arrow, the horse had no such protection and Wolf reasoned that Lone Dog must be thinking of it as a prize, if only to be eaten.

Captain Cabeza was tattered, yet still handsomely turned out with the clothing and armor he had carried from Spain; yet by now his men wore a mash-up of filthy, torn rags from home along with cotton and leather garb stolen from native peoples. They were anything but a uniformed force, and gazing from the shelter of a hill, Lone Dog and his carefully groomed and painted warriors thought of them as laughable. To their eyes the conquistadors looked like a company of madmen, or perhaps hair-faced clowns. But Lone Dog had seen what their crossbows could do and noted the long knives of their swords and pikes.

"We can take them now! They are sick and wounded!" one of his young warriors cried that afternoon. The call was taken up by many others, eager for glory.

"They are blind to us!" cried another. "We can spring at them from the tall grass as they drag along."

"Don't push me, brothers. I have a plan," Lone Dog replied, pointing to a cloud of dust on the eastern horizon. "Look to the herd! First we hunt to feed our women and children, then we will strike."

The Spaniards pushed on for three more days along the river through the fly-strewn, windy plains. Captain Cabeza grew increasingly anxious, almost hysterical with desire for the great towns of the Mandans to reveal themselves. Yet Wolf knew that these were like the distant mirages on the plains and would never be reached. It was all he could do to keep the captain at bay.

Willow was also anxious.

"When will we leave?" she asked as they lingered in the shade of some cottonwoods by a brook.

Wolf considered. By now the plains were broad around them, running featureless to the distant horizon on both sides of the river except for the low rolling hills. He had not yet found a chance to steal Montoya away from the Spaniards, but Cabeza was at a breaking point.

"Tomorrow night," he said. "We will creep past the guards and take the horse."

"But they will catch us," she cautioned. "Who among us is sleeping?"

Truly, now, every man among the conquistadors slept with one eye open. Cabeza had placed four men on guard each night and this time there was no nodding off. Every man among them shivered with fear in the darkness, awakening at the sounds of a rustling grouse or the yip of a coyote. The guards were wide-eyed with terror throughout the night, for two had been found on succeeding mornings, dead at their posts with bloody heads.

"I will think of something," Wolf replied. But what? The puzzle before him wasn't like escaping from the oafs of the Adai. At best he could untether the horse in the darkness and then make a dash in the night with Willow at his side. Yet even though the moon was barely a quarter full, the stars blanketing the plains were so brilliant that one could see anyone moving in the darkness. It was a risky plan which might easily fail, with the Spaniards alert to every rustle in the night.

But Wolf's plan never came to pass, for on the next day, Lone Dog struck.

Captain Cabeza had ridden his horse to a hill overlooking the plains, and spying a distant line of foliage along the Missouri, he had divined a short-cut between a long looping stretch of the river. It would save them more than ten miles of struggling along the riverbank.

That morning Cabeza's men had set out in a confident mood. The grass was knee-high here, with no place for their pursuers to hide, and the footing was easier than usual.

Not so for Wolf, whose clubbed foot had always made walking difficult, and he was self-conscious about his limp as he hobbled along.

"Rest your mind," Willow said, sensing his discomfort. "My father had a bad leg and we loved him just the same."

"But I am not your father," Wolf scowled and limped on, cursing his infirmity. His bad leg had made him the man he was - a shaman, a storyteller and a spy - but it was of little use on a long march, or as a fighter if the need arose.

All was peaceful out on the plains, except for the endless buzzing of the flies. Cabeza's men had no problem dragging their supplies along, with a man toting a pole on either side of their travois. By mid-day they had made it halfway to the next bend in the river.

Yet that afternoon there came a sound like distant thunder accompanied by a huge dust cloud on the eastern horizon. The line of thirty-four conquistadors stopped in their tracks and looked to the east.

It was as if the earth itself was moving in their direction, not with the speed of the wind, yet steadily in a brown mass that filled half the eastern horizon.

"An earthquake," one of the men muttered, crossing himself. "I have seen it in Córdoba. The earth ripples as if it were the sea."

"Nay, fool," another replied. "The earth was never known to roll like that."

When the apparition was a mile out, it revealed itself as a vast herd, stampeding their way with no chance of shelter or protection.

None of the Spaniards had ever seen a buffalo herd before, nor had they ever imagined a stampede, racing toward them on tens of thousands of cloven hooves. For a time they stood and watched, having little notion of the oncoming danger. But gradually as the herd drew near, they saw the milling, bucking bison careening forward in the thousands; it was a wall of muscle, horns and hooves bearing down on them with no chance of escape.

Suddenly aware, a cry rose up in every throat as the roar of the stampeding herd reached their ears.

"Form up a phalanx and load the arquebus!" Captain Cabeza cried as the tramp of hooves rose like oncoming thunder. "And place all of the baggage before us!"

The men scrambled to obey, and with bristling swords and pikes they formed an arrowhead formation in the mold of the ancient Spartans, at the point of which stood their lone musketeer with the arquebus mounted on its oaken staff.

The gun began firing when the herd was less than a quarter-mile off, the thunder of thousands of hooves blending with the bark of the weapon.

"Fire again, damn you! As fast as you can!" Cabeza roared over his shoulder.

But the musketeer barely needed urging. With two men assisting with powder, tamp and ball, he had loaded again almost before the words left Cabeza's lips. For once, the match fuse was as dry as the sun could make it and its ember ignited a plume in the priming pan, sending another ball into the herd.

Yet on and on the herd came churning and bellowing, with a huge black bull heaving in the lead. Far behind them in the dust beyond the pounding hooves were Lone Dog's men, driving the frightened herd forward in a sweeping mass that ranged half a mile wide.

Once, twice, three times more the arquebus spoke, casting a thin sheet of flame and a blast that went almost unnoticed as the earth began to shake and the air was rent with the huffing and bawling of the herd. At best the gun took half a minute to load, prime and fire, and the frightened musketeer and his men fumbled at their task as those behind them crossed themselves and braced for certain death.

Then, with the earth shaking and a sound like ten thousand drums, the lead bull came charging forward, only a hundred footsteps away with thousands of snorting, huffing bison milling together and following its lead. Its black horns gleamed in the sun, and behind it came an ocean of buffalo, each as large as four men and crowned by horns capable of cleaving a man in two.

"Fire!"

The final blast struck the oncoming bull square in its chest. It bellowed, stumbled and fell, opening a river of tumbling bison that flowed on either side of the phalanx. Then the Spaniards launched their own attack, stabbing at the passing animals with their pikes and halberds and firing their crossbows into their ranks. The buffalo kicked, bellowed and fell as the great herd swept past, engulfing the Spaniards in a choking cloud of dust.

But nothing was finished, for out of the brown dust-cloud dozens of warriors emerged like ghosts from a nightmare, stabbing with their spears, firing arrows and clubbing at the Spaniards who had turned to the buffalo. In a thunderclap they struck and were gone, almost before the Spaniards knew that they had fallen among them. Caked with dust and with the sound of the herd still ringing in their ears, the Spaniards looked around them. Six men lay dead on the plain, with not a single one of them killed in the stampede.

Blood on the Plains

Now a cold dread descended on the men and they took to arguing as to the way forward. Few wished to carry on, for if a small band of the Dakota could harry them so, what could they expect of the Mandans? Captain Cabeza had woven a tale of an empire of great cities out on the high plains to spur his men on with dreams of gold and riches, but now his fairy tale seemed more cautionary than wise, for what could twenty-eight men do against an empire?

Cabeza could see murder in the eyes of his men, yet still he urged them on.

"Perhaps we will find Christians there and the descendants of the bishops of Cibola," he said, none too convincingly.

"God damn the bishops and may He damn Cibola! We haven't seen any Christians yet, captain," said Bartolomeu, a one-armed trouble-maker who was one of the more rebellious men. "Surely there would be signs of the Cross somewhere along this river by now, and Christians too among the Indios if the bishops came this way. It's been nothing but the devil's land for us. God help us!"

This met with general agreement, for it was well known that Christians planted crosses atop the highest hills wherever they settled, and not a single one had been sighted in the New World.

But Cabeza persisted.

"Remember then that these people are renowned as traders. You have seen for yourselves how the people of this land covet our iron; we will offer them trade!"

"What? With the bare bits we've got left?" Bartolomeu replied. "What will we gain by being stripped naked?"

Cabeza smiled at this. "These bare bits as you call them can be traded for the Indios' gold. All of your helmets, shields and armor, traded for gold! That, and we will trade for boats and clothing, with the promise to return with more."

"What? Trading all the way from Spain?"

"Nay, only Cuba. These people value iron as we do gold and silver. Can't you see? We will come to them as merchants bearing treasures beyond belief, and God willing, return as rich men."

"But how will we survive the trip back down the river without weapons?"

Captain Cabeza smiled at this, having an answer for everything. "We will make crossbows with the help of the Mandans and tip them with golden bolts."

At this, there came a general groan.

"Oh, Jesus! God has damned us all!" one of the men cried, tossing his helmet to the ground. He stomped off to sit on a tussock, weeping into his hands.

It was a sketchy plan, but faced with the thought of walking fifteen hundred miles back down the rivers to the sea or going forward in the hope of trading their iron gradually turned the tide of opinion. Even Bartolomeu was convinced at the sense of it, though grimly. "Dead men might walk one way as well as another," he grumbled.

And so they resolved to continue, cutting across the plains wherever they could to shorten the way along the serpentine curves of the river. But first came burials and butchery.

The six men killed by Lone Dog's warriors were buried beneath the turf of the prairie in a single grave topped by a cairn of severed buffalo heads for lack of gravestones. Then the men set about butchering the buffalo that had fallen among them, slicing away tongues, livers and thick steaks to be packed for the journey ahead.

"At least we will not go hungry," Willow said as she helped Wolf butcher the huge bull that had led the stampede. For the first time in her journey and all her travails her father's dagger was proving useful.

"It's the hide we want," Wolf replied, working with the obsidian knife taken from the Adai.

"This thing? It's huge, and it stinks!"

"Yes." But he offered no explanation as their skinning progressed amid a welter of flies. His knife was sharper than the Spaniards' steel and he didn't bother to cut far into the bull's legs. When at last they scraped the hide from the bull's pale flesh they had what was known among his people as a green hide, bloody and moist on the inside, as yet unworked or tanned.

"There is no way we can tan it," Willow said. "Will it not stiffen?"

"Yes, but not yet," Wolf said, rolling the hide into a tight cylinder and placing it atop the travois that he and Willow pulled.

Willow could not imagine what Wolf meant to do with the bull's hide, which was heavy enough to make their burden much more difficult as they crossed the plains. But Wolf offered no further explanation and she accepted it with a shrug. At least they would have something to sleep on that night.

Cabeza's men made it to the bend in the river the next day without any more sign of Lone Dog's warriors. Once again, they looked out, sighting a line of tall cottonwoods winding along the river in the distance, and it was resolved to cross the plains to reach the next bend.

That night, Wolf awakened to find the wind whispering from the east, confirming his suspicions. There was no chance of escape with Willow and the horse; the men slept in what was almost a heap now with their backs to one-another along with four men standing watch. He had to hope that his new plan would save them.

They got a late start the next morning, tending to the wounds of several men who had been injured by the stampeding buffalo and the Dakota's attack. Cabeza also bade his men to gorge on the meat, as there would be no stopping while they crossed the plains. Setting out, they found that the grass was almost waist high, and the going more difficult. By late afternoon they had made only seven miles, with the bend in the river still five miles in the distance. A decision was made to make camp atop a low hill, which might be easily defended.

Still the wind continued to blow from the east, gaining strength with no sign of ceasing. Wolf led Willow to the lee of the hill beyond the safety of the camp.

"We will sleep here tonight," he said. "Let us gather straw for our bedding."

After days of sleeping on hard ground Willow needed little convincing. The tall grass was very dry and easily gathered. Soon, she and Wolf had swept a wide circle below the crown of the hill, piling the straw up for a bed of hay.

"Will we sleep on the robe? she asked. The heavy hide was still rolled up on their travois.

"No, it is still wet."

Before she could question him further, a voice rang down from above. "So you sleep with the wolf tonight, eh darkie?" one of the conquistadors called out, mocking her. "Don't you fear the creepers in the night?"

"He will protect me," she called back. "See to your own skin."

But the men were too tired and thirsty to care if Willow had strayed from their company and they sat staring listlessly at the horizon with each man considering his fate. Night fell, and with it came the snores and mutters of the sleeping men.

"Will we flee now?" Willow asked as she clung to Wolf's side.

"Not yet," for he knew what was coming.

Deep in the night, almost at dawn, the guards noticed a red glow on the eastern horizon. At first they thought it was the sunrise as the sky grew cardinal-red for a mile or more across the plains. But then came tongues of fire licking at the sky in the distance.

"Up! Up!"

Cabeza's men scrambled to their feet, gaping at the oncoming blaze.

"It is only some grass burning," one of them muttered.

Only some grass, and for a time they stood watching as children might enjoy a puppet show. But the fire swept forward at a frightening speed and by the time it was only a mile away the men realized that its flames were billowing sixty feet or more into the sky. The grassy plain had received no rain in weeks, and now it burned as if a furnace.

"*Run!*"

With the fire came the sliver of dawn, brightening the burning plain. The sun rose harsh and hot, as if it was urging the flames on.

And so the race began with Cabeza's men scrambling for their lives in the hope of reaching the distant river. All of their weapons along with the meat and their travois were left behind as they pummeled down the hill and across the plain, with the crackling flames growing louder behind them.

Willow turned to flee, but Wolf seized her wrist. "Not us. We cannot outrun the fire."

"What then?"

"Dig more straw," he said, smiling.

By now they could hear the fire roaring as it came on, with the sky churning black with smoke above the flames. The sun had risen sharp and bright on the horizon, and it seemed as if it commanded the flames forward on a grim mission to cleanse the earth of the conquistadors.

At last Willow understood what Wolf intended to do, and they tore at the straw in a widening circle on the lee of the hill until they reached its crown. There she beheld a scene from hell itself as half the world seemed ablaze with the oncoming wall of fire. By now, the fleeing conquistadors were almost a mile to the west, and in moments, she knew, the flames would sweep over the hill and bear down upon them.

"Your circle will not save us!" she cried above the roar. It was louder even than the stampeding herd - as loud as the fire which had consumed the *Tiger*.

"No, something else," Wolf answered, shouting above the roar.

"What? How?" she screamed.

"Ojibwe magic."

He stood at the crest of the hill, awestruck by the curtain of fire, yet knowing somehow that he could not die. A protective spell came to him from Wabeno-inini, the Man of the Dawn Sky, and now he shouted the ancient words passed down from the Old Ones, or perhaps from the spirits themselves. Although he did not know their meaning, nor even the language from which they were drawn, he spoke the words to the flames, which had reached the base of the hill and were racing up the slope. And though the fire was still a bow-shot away, he was almost flattened by the oncoming heat. The fire was such a clear, searing yellow that the intensity of the color itself was horrifying, as if it were a towering spirit, a being from a world of flame. For a moment, Wolf felt that he was staring into the heart of the sun itself.

The fire reared up as if to seize him and then, grasping Willow's hand, he turned and ran.

Long after, Wolf was uncertain as to whether he had seen the oncoming fire parting as it swept up the hill, or if he had only imagined it. Nor was Wabeno ever able to tell him the meaning of the ancient incantation, only that it was to be used at times when life hung by a hair.

Perhaps it was the wheeling birds of the plains who had told Wolf of Lone Dog's plan, or perhaps he had simply considered what he would do as the grass along their march grew taller and dryer, but there was a reason he had skinned and packed the hide of the huge bull along with them. Now the hide was still green, moist and thick, and as the towering flames raced over the top of the hill he wrapped himself and Willow within its protection at the center of the circle of grass which they had plucked clean down to its roots.

Willow screamed in his ear and struggled in fright as a roar like that of a hurricane swept over them, but he clutched her with all of his strength, offering soothing words in the damp darkness of the thick hide. Then, when it seemed as if their last breath would be stolen from their lungs in a furnace of heat, the fire went galloping past them down the hill, roaring like a raging beast.

Oh, and it is true that the Spaniards made it another mile toward the river, gasping their lungs out with the effort, but the safety of the water was yet three miles off when the flames caught them. Only Captain Cabeza stood a chance as he rode Montoya for the last time away from the wall of fire. He never heard the screams of his men above the roar of the flames, nor saw them burn as candles on the prairie.

But later that day, Wolf and Willow found the captain's charred body by the river, riddled with arrows. His helmet was gone along with his hair, and laying only a stone's throw away was the smoldering corpse of the warhorse Montoya.

"A fitting death," Wolf remarked grimly. He and Willow had made their way past the burnt flesh of the men lying helter-skelter across the plains to where Lone Dog and his warriors stood waiting by the river.

"Brother, are we still friends?" he asked as he and Willow made their way through a throng of more than two hundred men painted red and black for war. Willow trembled at his side, wide-eyed at the grim faces appraising them, some with arrows nocked, others toying with trophies taken from the Spaniards.

Lone Dog squinted and gave him a harsh look, fingering a Spanish blade, as if he meant to bury it in Wolf's neck. He gave a fearsome scowl, raising the blade overhead.

Wolf braced for the blow, but Lone Dog stuck out his tongue and laughed. "Of course we are friends!" he cried. "Brother, I see you have found your dream. The sunktanka - it is better than you said, or at least, it was."

To Wolf's relief, Lone Dog had heard his shouted warning when his hunters had encountered the Spaniards. He had sent a dozen runners to ignite the fires on the plain far to the east, waiting with the mass of his warriors by the river where he knew the hair-faces would be driven. Not all were happy in his camp, for the fire had done the killing for them, and the young men, especially, had hungered for the kill.

But there was a great victory dance and celebration that night as Lone Dog's people filed in from the south. Lying on a travois among them was Red Eagle. His fever had broken and Wolf and Split Tail assessed his wounds, both agreeing that he would live with a fine scar to recall his first battle. Split Tail had staunched the bleeding with a poultice of spider web and then cauterized the wound with a burning sprig of yarrow. Wolf had suggested stitching the wound with a strand of bison sinew, rather than packing it with eagle down, and although Red Eagle gritted his teeth in agony with tears streaming from his eyes as the deed was done, the three of them shared a pipe thereafter and agreed that the healing had been a fine success.

"Brother, you are welcome in our lodges," Lone Dog told him the next day after Wolf had begged off following the Dakota across the plains in pursuit of the buffalo. "Our village is only one hand to the east of the northern star."

He stretched out his arm and held up his palm so that Wolf might know the direction by doing the same at night. "It is seven day's walk, maybe more for you, bad foot."

Lone Dog grinned at this riposte and Wolf grimaced good-naturedly in response. But it was a good plan, for he doubted that he and Willow could make it home before the chill winds and rains of fall began sweeping over Kitchi Gami.

"We will stay with you for the winter, brother, if you agree, and I will fill your bellies with fish from the river," Wolf said.

Now it was Lone Dog's turn to grimace. "Fish... eh."

Up the hill from the river, Wolf could see coyotes, wolves and buzzards working at the bodies of the dead conquistadors out on the plain.

"Do you wish to have their iron?" he asked, but to this Lone Dog gave a quizzical look, requiring an explanation. "It is their metal, like copper, only stronger."

Lone Dog made a face and raised Captain Cabeza's sword to the sky. It flashed blue-gray in the sun, a blade of exquisite Toledo steel.

"We have taken their long knives," he said, waving the sword in a lazy circle, "but the rest belongs to the spirits."

"They are cursed," Wolf said, telling him how the Spaniards had desecrated the grave of the Bird Man.

Lone Dog shrugged. "All weapons are cursed."

The hunters left by mid-day, leaving the women to pack up and follow the trail of the buffalo herd, which could be easily tracked to the west along the river. Wolf and Willow said their goodbyes to the Dakotas, promising to meet again at Lone Dog's village by the river.

But it was the length of a full moon before they started north, for there was yet one thing to do.

Searching the plains, Wolf found a charred axe beneath the half-eaten corpse of one of the sailors. Willow cried out in disgust at what he intended to do with it, but he had laughed at her distress, telling her to sit by the river as he worked. Then, with some effort, he had chopped Montoya's head from its body and skinned it. Ruefully, he cast the eyes away; they had lost their robin-blue color and now appeared a furry gray, not worth keeping.

Wolf found a quiet pool by the side of the river and placed the head waist-deep in its depths, weighing it down with rocks. It took some two weeks for the fish and crawfish to do their work, but after a time Wolf took their leavings and placed the well-rotted head atop a large red ant hill.

While the skull was slowly revealed, he and Willow spent their days exploring along the river and hunting what game they could find. None of the Spaniard's crossbows had survived the fire, but Red Eagle had left them with his bow and more than twenty arrows, saying they would be of little use to him while he mended. One day they crept up on a family of elk watering by a brook and brought down a young buck.

Willow was as happy as she'd been since leaving Morocco, and yet there were mornings when she woke up torn between two worlds. Her love for Wolf had grown stronger, and yet she wondered, who was this man? He said that his people lived what must be hundreds of leagues to the north. Surely, he must be a person of some importance to make such a journey, yet whenever she asked, Wolf had told her he was nothing but a simple trader and a story teller. A fool.

"You are no fool. I don't know what you are... You are a mystery to me," she said, gazing into their cook fire. They had roasted a joint of the elk and sat talking by the lean-to of their camp.

Wolf turned the spit over the coals and considered. "You, too, are a mystery," he replied, "but a good one, and pleasant to gaze upon."

"Yes, it was fate that brought us together, but what now?" she answered with a frown. "I do not know what fate has for me."

"What is fate?" It was a word he had not yet learned.

"It is... I think the spirits," she said, not knowing what else to say.

"Then the spirits are wise!" he laughed. "Don't be sad, I will take you to meet my people and my mother. You will be accepted as a sister and a daughter. You will be treated with great kindness."

Willow smiled at the thought, knowing that a mother did not always treat her son's woman with kindness. And yet, she thought of her own mother, whom she had not seen for many years, nor ever would again. Nor had she ever thought of herself as a sister in the household of Abu bin Nisar, where there had been only two old women for company. It would be good to have a mother again; it would be good to have sisters.

Still, she thought long and hard about what to say next, eyeing Wolf with uncertainty by the fire.

"I would give your mother a gift," she said at last.

"Yes?"

"And one for you also."

"You are my gift," he said smiling.

"Yes, but my gift is a part of me... and a part of you."

Realization dawned in Wolf's eyes and then a flood of tears.

"A child," he said somberly.

"Yes."

He gave Willow a crooked smile and a long, dreamy look and then leapt to his feet. "A great warrior!" he exclaimed, uttering a war cry and dancing a jig.

"Oh, thou art indeed a fool!" she said, laughing. "Yes, a child, but I think it may not be a warrior. Perhaps we will have a princess."

He spun around and gaped at her before the fire. "I do not know this word."

"You will come spring."

Homecoming

And so it was that their daughter was born that spring in Lone Dog's village on the edge of the plains. It had been a pleasant winter, for Lone Dog's hunters had caught up with the buffalo herd and had made up for the meat lost to the conquistadors.

Willow was dressed in skins now; her sailcloth dress had tattered away to nothing, and eager to preserve her modesty, the women of the Dakota had made her a fine tunic of buffalo hide, dyed a bone-gray. She cringed at first with the heft and animal texture of her new garments, but the leather was supple and warm and a defense against the prairie winds. She lined her skirt with a scrim of shells and was pleased to see Wolf's eyes light with approval when she twirled in a pirouette before him. And slipping into her new dress, a peace settled on Willow; for the first time she felt that she was becoming one with Wolf's people.

Red Eagle had made a good recovery, for the Spaniards' crossbow bolt had gone clean through his thigh and there had been no need to prise its barbed head from his flesh. The mending had gone well, particularly as he had been ministered to by a lovely young maiden from a distant clan who was visiting her mother's village that winter. Willow smiled at the sight of them, for though Red Eagle was still an in-between man, she could see that the two were deeply in love. They were never apart, and already there was talk in the camp that they would someday be married, though Red Eagle could scarcely be fifteen summers of age, if that.

True to his word, Wolf had provided a great deal of fish from the river by the village and had spent the winter months fashioning the ribs of a new canoe. He spent a long time searching the distant forest for a birch tree big enough to provide a fitting skin, and it was the Moon of the Crusted Snow before he found it. Then, his obsidian knife served him once again as he stripped the great tree of its bark, sewing it with cedar roots and rawhide thongs to the framework of his new canoe.

As the winter wore on, Wolf spent many nights over the fires of the Dakotas, regaling them with his stories as Willow looked on, not understanding a word he said in Sioux, yet spellbound just the same. He and the shaman Split Tail had also worked on the skull of the sunktanka, staining it red with ochre and then lining it with a jagged lightning design in charcoal.

"It is good," Wolf said, admiring their handiwork. "My grandfather Wabeno will be pleased."

But it was Wolf's daughter who lit a fire in his heart, striking him as far more worthy than a son. She glowed like a dark cherry, a handsome mix of Willow's dusky skin and his own redness, and her eyes were a blend of their own, light gray with flecks of green.

"She is like a cherry," he said, watching the babe nurse at Willow's breast.

"Yes, she is my little cherry flower. She is the flower of my heart."

By now, Wolf knew that when Willow spoke of her heart, she considered it the source of tender feelings and not the source of valor, or simply the wellspring of life.

"I think you have named her," he said gravely.

Willow looked up at him and felt a flood of happiness flowing through her like nothing she had ever felt in all her life. For a moment the world went spinning with a joy that sent her thoughts tumbling in ecstasy as the babe gurgled at her breast.

And so, Willow and Wolf's babe came to be known as Cherry Heart Flower, and the whole village claimed her as a daughter, hoping that she might be an eternal bond of peace between the Dakotas who lived where the forest met the plains and the Ojibwe of the far north.

And so it was, until the end of time.

That spring, Willow, Wolf and Cherry Heart Flower set off down the river while the snow was still in patches along the bank. Willow had reveled in the snow, yet only because Wolf had seen her well-clad in warm furs and a thick buffalo robe.

"My father would have loved this," she said as they coursed down the river to the Misi Sipi. "He had the heart of a wanderer and would have been dazzled by your forests."

"Perhaps your father sees you now, if he has joined the spirits," Wolf called from the back of the canoe.

"Perhaps." But Willow did not think so, for her father's life had been that of the desert, its mountains, camels and dusty cities of mud bricks. In her mind's eye she could see him, still alive and standing on the walls of Azemmour, watching for her across its dusty plains.

Spring had blossomed into summer by the time they reached the homeland of the Ojibwe at Boweting. Wolf had told Willow of Kitchi Gami, and she had expected it to be a salt sea like that of the Mediterranean, perhaps with familiar cities along its shore. Yet to her surprise, the great inland sea of the Ojibwe was that of sweet fresh water, and instead of the filthy cities of Morocco and Spain, they passed a small village or two each day and were hailed from the shore. At times Wolf stopped for an earnest conversation, and though Willow's ear was still new to Anishinaabemowin, gradually, she began to understand and speak her own words of greeting.

Then one day after another long portage and two weeks of steady paddling, the end of the lake came in view, and with it a river striped white with foaming rapids.

And there on the eastern shore, Willow saw a village running out of sight along with riverbank, and a multitude of thousands gathered to greet them.

"Home!" Wolf cried, digging in the water with all his strength.

They reached the shore with a great shout rising from the crowd and then a trilling and singing as hundreds of dancing, singing people rushed waist-deep into the water to greet them. For a moment, Willow feared that the tumult around their canoe would tip them over, but a score of hands gripped its gunwales on either side and sped them ashore.

"Is this the welcome of a simple trader?" she called out, straining to be heard above the crowd.

"They know me as a story teller," Wolf replied, but he could not help smiling as if his face would split. "Word of us has traveled with the birds and the fish."

"But you told me that no one knew! You said your journey was sworn to secrecy."

"Ah yes, only the shamans of the Good Hearts knew, but they are all old men and chatter like squirrels," he said with a knowing laugh. "What is the word? Gossip? They chattered until everyone knew."

Momentarily, Wolf disappeared under a hail of back-slaps and hugs as old friends swarmed over him. To Willow's ire, several were attractive young women who drenched him in joyful tears and hugs that seemed a trifle too long.

Yet she had little time to think on this, for the crowd parted at the sound of drums and flutes and down to the river came a procession of a dozen stern-faced old men who looked like anything but gossips. To Willow's eyes, they looked like ramshackle ghouls sprung from a graveyard. All of them tottered with walking staffs and were bedecked with feathers and necklaces of bones or the claws of animals. One peered through the sockets of a human skull, split in two and tied in a mask over his face, with a ruff of porcupine quills crowning his head that flailed backwards as he walked. Another was cloaked in the head of a bear over his blackened face, with its paws drawn over his shoulders. Others had bones, shells and the skulls of small animals woven into their hair, and chains of leg bones and ribs rattling down their torsos. All looked ancient, sinister, and faintly comical.

But at their head stood a wizened man with a face like a turtle who looked far older - as old as the boulders lining the river. He was wearing a black cloak of raven feathers and a necklace of bear claws. Atop his head sat a crown of antlers, set into a beaded leather cap. And although he was stooped and shrunken with age, Willow could see that he was still taut with muscle beneath his cloak, as if his face had aged terribly, but not his body. His withered cheeks were zig-zagged with the faded black lines of ancient tattoos.

There was nothing comical in the old man's appearance; in fact, Willow felt a stabbing sensation at the sight of him and the feeling that the ground might disappear beneath her feet.

Wolf stepped up the shore, bidding Willow to follow him with their babe. He kneeled in the mud at the base of the old man's feet and bowing deep, held out the painted skull of the warhorse Montoya.

"Wabeno-inini, I have returned."

The old man placed his hand on Wolf's head and raised his eyes to the sky, speaking some words in a hoarse voice that Willow could not make out. Then, giving barely a glance at the elaborately painted skull of the horse, he took a step forward and gazed at Willow and Cherry Heart Flower with an intensity unlike anything she had ever known. For a moment, she felt as if she might be struck by lightning.

Something about the old man made Willow feel as if she was cartwheeling, and for one terrible moment, she thought that he might shiver her heart in two with nothing but a single word. Yet then, a smile blossomed on his wrinkled face and it was as if she was bathed in light.

"Welcome, daughter," he said in a voice like a laughing stream, and this time she had no trouble understanding the words.

Then the whole crowd erupted in cheers as Wolf and Willow were led to the Great Lodge where a feast had been prepared. It was a long night, with dancing, drumming and singing until dawn, and Willow cuddled her baby beneath her robe where it slept, nestled in the warmth of her body.

Many times that evening, Wolf was asked about the strange skull and the meaning of it, and where he had been for so long. But he replied only that it was an odd sort of elk found among the Dakotas where the forest met the plains, and that he had spent his whole time among the People of the Red Pipestone. This, Wabeno and the shamans heard with approval, knowing that Animi-ma'lingan, He Who Outruns the Wolves, would tell them the true story of his travels on the morrow.

Late that night, Wolf and Willow were led to a small lodge and told that it was a gift, built by the apprentice shamans. Soon enough, Willow learned that it was not far from the lodge of Wabeno and his old woman, and once again it dawned on her that Wolf was a man of some importance. Surely, he commanded the respect of the shamans. Though what was the meaning of the horse's skull? Many times she had asked him, and even Wolf did not seem to know.

They slept through much of the day, and that afternoon Wolf was summoned to the Great Lodge.

There was no sweat lodge this time and to Wolf's surprise, no ceremony or gathering of his uncles. Only Wabeno met him and they sat on a bench of oak branches and pine boughs outside the lodge, looking over the river at the bottom of the hill.

They sat there until the early evening as Wolf unraveled his tale of the Pipestone People, the Misi Sipi, the grave of the Bird Man, the *Tiger* and the conquistadors. Only once did Wabeno interrupt him to ask about the poisons he had used to overcome his guards among the Adai, nodding with approval as Wolf described their preparation.

"There is so much more to tell, grandfather," Wolf said at last, knowing he would have to repeat it all for a council of the shamans.

"You have done well, Wolf," Wabeno began, passing the pipe. Wolf had carved a handsome calumet of red pipestone for Wabeno during his time at Lone Dog's village. Now, the old man drew on his new pipe with satisfaction.

"The tobacco is good, eh?"

"Yes grandfather," Wolf replied, "and the sunktanka? Are you pleased?"

The skull of the horse lay at Wabeno's feet, and plans had been made to hang it in a place of honor at the entrance of the Great Lodge.

"The sunktanka? Yes, it is a fine thing," Wabeno said agreeably. "Truly, I never expected you to find it."

"No?"

"No," Wabeno said with a wave. "You might as well have searched for the creature with one leg, or the great beaver who appears as an island, or the thunderbird that storms through the sky. These are things beyond our grasp."

"But you knew of the sunktanka."

Wabeno chuckled and drew again on his pipe, his cheeks crinkling at the thought of it. "As much as anything."

For a moment Wolf's head reeled, and it dawned on him that Wabeno had cast him into the story of a fool's quest, much as he might tell himself around the fires of his people.

"But why?" he said, anger stabbing at him. "Why did you send me on such a journey if you didn't believe in the thing I have laid at your feet?"

Wabeno gave him a grave look. "The sunktanka? It is a fine thing, but it is not for us. It belongs to another place and another people. We will honor its spirit, and in time, your story will be told and honored too.

"But it was the woman I sent you to find, Animi-ma'lingan," he went on, leaning forward with upraised eyes. "It was your woman. I saw that you were lonely and sent you to discover your fate. I sent you to find her."

"Willow?"

"It is so," Wabeno nodded. "Every man needs a mate, and you had none. I could feel your spirit crying out, your need was so strong, yet I began to suspect that you would find none among the Anishinaabek to suit you. You are a mystery, Wolf, and I could see that you needed a woman who is just the same. You are a strange man. You need a strange woman."

Wolf's head whirled, giddy at the notion that Wabeno had sent him to the edge of the world on such a quest.

"*Ehn*, perhaps I am strange, as you say, and she is unlike any woman who walks the earth. But grandfather, how did you know of her? And why, when there are women everywhere?"

"Did you find one among our people?"

"No," Wolf said reluctantly.

"Did you find one among the Nippissings or the Cree?"

"No."

"Perhaps among the Minong?"

"There were few women there."

"Among the Tionontati then."

Wolf thought of the woman of the Tobacco People who wished to be his wife. Now he could not even remember her name.

"No."

"No. Here, there was no one for you, but you had a longing," Wabeno said, spreading his empty palms and gazing upon them as if in dismay. "I saw that your spirit was starving and that you needed a wife more than an old man needs this skull. Truly, I did not know where you would find her, but I had dreamed of the sunktanka and knew from Anokasan-Duta's story that it lived far to the south, perhaps even to the Great Salt Water. There would be many women along the way and I knew you would find one to suit you. You would find a peculiar woman, like you."

Wabeno drew on his pipe and exhaled with satisfaction. "Truly, I thought you would find a woman among the Pipestone People and return to us many moons ago," he went on. "I did not think you would journey so far."

"You sent me chasing a goose, a ghost!"

For a moment Wabeno looked stricken with guilt, but then he smiled, and again came his musical laugh like that of a flowing stream. "But it is good now, yes? You have a good woman now and you have made her even better with her babe."

Something broke inside of Wolf and laughter poured from him like a river from a broken dam. He had spent more than a year away and his life had hung by a hair many times, yet as Wabeno said, he had been blessed by his journey.

"Grandfather, you are a prophet," he said when he was able to speak again. It had been a good trick, though part of him wanted to wring the old man's neck

"Yes, I suppose so," Wabeno said, gazing at his feet. "I prayed that you would return. I sent the birds to watch for you, and the wind."

Truly, the wind and the birds had not been much help, Wolf thought, but he kept this to himself. And it was true, if he had not embarked on Wabeno's mad quest, he would not have met Willow. Tenderness fingered at his chest at the thought of it, and he smiled.

Life did not come easy for Willow among the Odawa and Ojibwe. She was welcomed as a sister and a daughter among them, and in time she met Wolf's mother, who still lived on the isle of Manitowaaling. The old woman's eyes had lit up at the sight of her and Cherry Heart Flower, and Willow thought that she had never seen a person transported with such happiness. Soon they had bonds as tight as the weave of any basket.

Yet Willow was a child of Africa and the desert, and the spirit of those lands was woven into her body and soul. She had never imagined such winters, with the snow sometimes piling up higher than her head and the icy fingers of the north wind Biboon stretching for nearly a third of each year. She had thought she knew what it was to be cold, but the chills of a winter night in Morocco were nothing like that of the winds shrieking over Kitchi Gami, which seemed fierce enough to tear the bark off of trees. She was grateful beyond tears for the thick fur of the bear cloak that Wolf's mother had fashioned for her.

Gradually, however, she learned the ways of her new people and mastered their language. First came the genders: how to say I, you, we, they, us, applying the words to the manner of speaking. Then came the words of many things, which she found harder to remember. And yet, with the mastery of words, Willow found her calling.

One winter night, as they sat before a longhouse fire attended by a crowd of twenty or so, Wolf told a story of a panther he had seen stalking a man along the banks of the Misi Sipi. Something in Wolf's story touched a long-buried memory in Willow's thoughts.

"Once I was the mother of a panther, though we called it a lion," she spoke on an impulse at the end of the Wolf's story. "His name was Aslan, and I raised him from a cub."

Before the spellbound crowd she told of how her father had brought the lion cub to her and how she had reared in it a city of high white walls filled with more people than there were leaves on the trees. A lion, she explained, was a fierce creature that could grow to three times the size of a panther, with fangs as long as knives and a crown of fur around its face. There were many questions. What was a palace? What was a city? Where was Aslan now? How had he not devoured her? The story continued until the lodge fire had dwindled to ashes, yet it was only the beginning.

So began Willow's place as a storyteller among Wolf's people and over many nights across many fires she spoke of elephants, camels and ships taller than the pines, which swarmed with madmen who hungered for a metal the color of the sun. She spoke of pyramids and black kingdoms and the mud walls of Timbuktu. She told of her father's trip to Mecca, and how he drank the blood of his camel when lost in the Sahara. There were tales of Croen, Akmed, Sincid, Cabeza and even simple stories of sheep and chickens. She spoke of the deeds of old Abu bin Nisar to fulfill her promise, given so long ago. Much of this made little sense to her listeners, but they begged for her stories just the same, especially about the war dog Dragón and the horse Montoya, and in time Willow became even more popular than Wolf as a teller of tales. One night, it came to her that she had become like the princess Scheherazade, weaving 1,001 stories to please her listeners at a place unimaginably far from her birth.

Yet Willow never grew accustomed to the cold, which gripped the shores of Kitchi Gami each winter like the hand of death itself, and after a single year Wolf took mercy on her. They began spending their winters among the Tobacco People of the Tionontati at the southern end of Tima Gami, the Lake of the Wendats. It was chilly there, and it often snowed, but the north wind and the cold was far less severe than on Manitowaaling.

Each fall as winter approached, she, Wolf and Cherry Heart Flower made their way south with a canoe filled with trade goods, accompanied by an escort of warriors. Willow never knew that Wolf's real place among the Tionontati was to serve as a *giimaabi*, the eyes and ears of the Ojibwe shamans in their vigilance against the neighboring Haudenosaunee, for this was a secret that he shared with no one, not even his wife.

There were times, however, when Wolf came from a meeting with Wabeno and the shamans only to announce that he was off on another trading mission. Then, Willow set to wondering. Often he was gone for a season or two, but once there was a time when he left for a full year, returning with a long gash across his chest. No matter how hard she pressed him, Wolf would not say where he had been, or what he had done, telling her only that the shamans had sworn him to secrecy.

"You are something more than a simple trader," she said accusingly, as she appraised the ragged tracing, which had not yet healed.

"Yes," he said, with tears streaking his face, "I am yours, and I have missed you more than the sun could miss the sky."

The Beginning and the End

The years passed on as one season melted into another, with a thousand tales told by then. One day, while gathering reeds along an inland lake, Willow gazed upon her reflection in a sunlit pool and saw with a shock that she had grown old. Curiously, Wolf seemed to have aged little through the years, and as for the old man, Wabeno, he looked to be far beyond one hundred winters, yet was still as spry as the day Willow had met him. When Willow questioned him on this, Wolf looked stricken and said that he did not know, for he too had seen his reflection in a pool of water and was disturbed by what he saw. The shamans had begun calling him Old Man as an honorific, yet his ageless face only filled him with fear.

Cherry Heart Flower had grown to be a fine young woman, with piercing gray eyes and skin as supple and rich as that of a mink. Fifteen summers had passed and it was time for her to wed. Yet, although many fine young men courted her, begging for her hand, Wolf approved of none of them, and Willow told her to wait, always to wait.

Then one day while attending the summer festival at Boweting, Wolf and Willow heard a great hubbub down the hill from where they sat sharing a pipe.

"The Dakota are coming! The Dakota!" came a cry from down below.

Strolling down the pathway to the river they saw that it was indeed a delegation of the Dakota, and not the trouble-makers of the tribe who lived in the forest bordering the Ojibwe. It was the Dakota who lived where the forest met the plains, the People of the Red Pipestone. And to their great surprise, stepping from the lead canoe was Anokasan-Duta, Red Eagle, solemnly holding the calumet of peace before him.

Red Eagle was now a man of thirty summers and the lost boy that Wolf remembered had assumed the thoughtful air of a diplomat. He had replaced his father, Lone Dog, as chieftain of his band and was still grieving at his loss. Lone Dog had passed the prior year after being gored by a veering bull in the buffalo hunt.

"You still bear the scar," Wolf said after they embraced.

"Yes, it is all that is left of the evil-ones," Red Eagle replied, gazing at the puckered wound on his thigh.

For a time they spoke of those long-ago days and Red Eagle produced the sword which his father had left him. "We have used it to butcher our meat on the hunt," he said as it lay on the sand, glimmering between them.

Wolf fingered the blade, which had grown dull and pitted through the years. "I remember this very well," he said, "for several times the leader of the *wdjibbon* planned to run me through with it."

But Red Eagle had brought more than an old sword and a peace pipe on the long journey from west of the Misi Sipi. That night after he and his nervous entourage of warriors had been feasted and allayed of their fears with the passing of a pipe, he introduced his son, Secachapa.

"His name means Dead Beaver in the tongue of the Dakota," Wolf explained to Willow when she asked.

It was impolite to ask how Secachapa had been named, but later Wolf learned that Lone Dog had trapped a beaver on the morning of his grandson's birth, and it had been seen as a fortunate sign as they dined on its tail that night.

Secachapa had a merry yet mischievous look to his eyes which reminded Willow of Akmed, the bad boy of Badis. He was only a little younger than Cherry Heart Flower and was surely the son of the beautiful maiden who had nursed Red Eagle so many years ago. It did not escape Willow that when Secachapa's eyes met those of her daughter's they had flickered with something resembling lightning. As for Cherry Heart Flower, she had demurely looked away, only to cast her eyes back his way a moment later with the beginning of a smile. Willow could not deny that Secachapa was an exceptionally handsome young man, and by that evening there was a tension between him and her daughter that was as taut as a fully-drawn bowstring. Soon enough, they excused themselves to sit in the shadows beyond the fire.

"I have taught him some words of your language," Red Eagle said, "though he is a poor student."

"I think he will try harder now," Wolf said dryly.

They sat for a time smoking, and Wolf sensed what was coming.

"We have come to ask for your daughter, if she will have him," Red Eagle said at last, nodding to the darkness where Secachapa and Cherry Heart Flower sat conversing for the most part in the language of signs.

Wolf chuckled at this. "Young brother, this is not for me to say, now or ever. Your son may win the favor of my daughter, but he must also win the favor of my wife."

And so the campaign began, as Willow was plied with gifts and entreaties. Each time she said no through her tears, but gradually she was worn down and overwhelmed as Secachapa and Cherry Heart Flower became inseparable lovers. With her heart breaking, Willow recalled how she, too, had been torn from her mother and cast into the wide world, where by the greatest good fortune she had met a man who had made her whole with his love. How could she deny her daughter the same?

Even so, she was heartbroken.

"We have only her, and if she leaves, what will become of us? What will remain?" she spoke one night, sobbing as she and Wolf sat watching the river flowing silver in the moonlight down the hill from their lodge.

"It is the way of all things, and we will have to bear it."

"But why?"

"We are all just leaves in the wind," he replied. "We grow from the same tree, so close together as family and friends, but there comes a time when we are plucked away. The wind takes us and blows where it will, just as it took you and me."

"But the wind is not always kind," she replied, thinking of the fate of the men who lay scattered across the sea, along the great river and upon the plains.

"You and I made it kinder. We made it bend."

"Yes, through our love," she said, feeling a little more hopeful.

And so a decision was made that Secachapa and Cherry Heart Blossom would be wed. But Willow begged her new son to live among the Ojibwe for a year before taking his bride home to his people. At Red Eagle's prompting, Secachapa agreed.

As a wedding gift, Willow gave her daughter the dagger which her own father had given her so many years ago, making her promise to keep it always by her side, even when she bathed. Willow had kept it just so through all her travels, never drawing blood with it. Nor had it ever been stropped, yet it was still almost as sharp as Wolf's obsidian knife. Its blade was of high carbon steel, forged in the West African trading town of Tadmekka, while its sheath and handle were of solid gold, mined in the Kingdom of Benin. An inscription was engraved upon the sheath, and though Willow could not read Arabic, she knew what it said, for it was the first tenet of Islam: *Lā 'Ilāhā 'Illā Allah*, There is no god but Allah.

"It was to be my dowry," she said, explaining the meaning of the inscription. "And now it is yours."

A year passed and to Willow's relief, her daughter did not leave, for during the winter after their wedding, Cherry Heart Flower gave birth to a son. He was burnished a high red umber like his mother and his eyes gleamed with a touch of his father's mischief. The babe kicked and squealed in his cradle-board, as if he could not wait to run wild over the earth. Yet, if that was his wish, he was disappointed, for a decision was made to remain another year among the Ojibwe.

Then it was as if the heavens themselves had exploded in Willow's heart with a fate she had never dreamed of. "I am a grandmother now," she said, gazing upon the wrinkled face clutched to her daughter's breast.

A grandmother! And when Cherry Heart Flower would let her, Willow rocked the babe on her lap and sang the old songs of her childhood, hoping that somehow, against all reason, he would remember her voice. One night she had a dream that more grandchildren lay slumbering, waiting to be born, and her heart leapt with joy at the thought of their coming.

But then at last, as is the way of brightly colored leaves dropping from a tree, there came a parting and a flood of tears.

A gleaming white canoe was prepared, built by the clan of the finest craftsmen in all the lands of the Anishinaabek. It was filled with gifts and provisions and showered with many spells of protection by Wabeno-inini himself. A company of eight warriors carried the canoe down to the shore of Boweting to the same place where Willow and Wolf had landed seventeen years before. A solemn band of drummers walked in their wake, followed by a procession of hundreds.

Willow and Wolf stood by the shore of Kitchi Gami, waving their farewells to loved-ones they might never see again. Far to the west beyond the Misi Sipi, the People of the Red Pipestone would be waiting to welcome Cherry Heart Flower and her son into their fold, but that did not lessen the pain of their leaving. Willow clutched at Wolf's waist, squeezing with all her strength and howling her anguish as they slipped away. And far across the waves to the west, the last trace of the white canoe bearing Secachapa, her daughter and her grandson winked in the sunlight a final time as it vanished on the horizon.

The End

Afterword

The 1528 expedition of Pánfilo de Narváez was a disaster from start to finish. Plagued by hurricanes, desertion, Indian attacks, sickness and starvation, the remnants of the expedition washed up in Matagorda Bay, Texas. Narváez was last seen spinning into the darkness in a storm on his ramshackle raft, howling into the wind. The 100 or so survivors were enslaved or killed along the desolate Texas coastline by Indians who were enraged by the Spaniards' degeneration into cannibalism. Of the 500-some men and women who set foot in Florida in 1527, only four survived after wandering for eight years across the American Southwest. They made their way through the territories of many tribes by purporting to be holy men and healers.

One of the survivors was Estevanico Azemmouri, the black slave of a Spanish noble who accompanied the expedition. As with my heroine, Willow, Estevanico was from the drought-stricken city of Azemmour in Morocco. Like Willow, he was lost and then found in a new land.

As for Wolf's beginnings, Boweting was an ancient, decentralized community at what is now the St. Mary's River at Sault Ste. Marie, straddling the U.S. and Canadian border. As noted in *The Wolf and The Willow*, Ojibwe and Odawa communities were seasonal in nature, ranging for as much as 30 miles along the waterways of the Mackinac Straits with the intention of securing enough fish to make it through the region's harsh winter. With the arrival of the French voyageurs, some of these communities took to farming in order to trade for the white mans' goods.

The Jesuit fathers of New France preached a sermon to some 2,000 Indians gathered at Boweting for the fishing season in the early 1647, and this was after smallpox had decimated the neighboring tribe of the Wendats. In *The Wolf and The Willow* and *Windigo Moon*, I've surmised that there were likely far more Native peoples gathered along these northern waterways prior to the arrival of white invaders and the devastating diseases they brought with them. Almost certainly, these gatherings would have been a time for the festivals, sporting events and matchmaking described in my books.

One can still visit the Pipestone Quarry of the Dakota Sioux in south-western Minnesota and hear the story of the Master of Life, Kitchi Manito, calling for all Native peoples to live in peace. In other tellings, most notably *The Song of Hiawatha*, the Great Spirit is described as being male in gender, sounding suspiciously like a male sky god in the Western tradition, or the invention of Christian missionaries to coax Native peoples into a belief in monotheism. Thus, I've rendered the Great Spirit as being neither man or woman, plant or animal, earth or water, but the sum of all things.

Wolf's journey down the Mississippi takes him through the remnants of the Mound Builder civilization, which dwindled into obscurity around 1200 for reasons that remain unknown. A lesser civilization of "chiefdoms" similar to city-states arose following the disappearance of the Mound Builders, with a capital at the heart of many outlying villages. At the time of *The Wolf and The Willow*, there was a thriving Indian civilization throughout the Mississippi River Valley and the Southeast, with hundreds of fortified farming towns.

Today, it is possible to visit many ancient mound sites, which are spread throughout the Mississippi River Valley and the American South. The ruins of Cahokia, in particular, are well worth visiting and lie just east of St. Louis. There, one can wander to the top of the Great Mound and marvel at the achievement of piling millions of baskets of earth, one-by-one, in the hope of touching the sky.

The incursions of Spanish conquistadors such as Hernan de Soto, coming on the heels of the Narváez expedition began a rampage of disease, enslavement and anarchy that weakened or destroyed many of the chiefdoms that came after the Mound Builders, making them easy prey for the white settlers and soldiers who followed. The fight for survival against this tide of doom continues in *Windigo Moon*.

As for the outrageous story of torture and mutilation as a rite of manhood told by the Mandan trader, Buffalo Drum, that spectacle was witnessed by the artist George Caitlin in the 1830s, among others. One can only shiver at the thought of what it took to earn one's status as a man among these renowned traders of the Great Plains.

The Story Continues in

WINDIGO MOON

By Robert Downes

From Blank Slate Press
an imprint of Amphorae Publishing Group

Summer, 1588 - The Raid

While picking berries with her sister-wives in a glade east of the village, the girl from the north country fell into a dream of revenge.

Ashagi savored what she would do to her husband, Kesamna'ista, if the chance arose. Just before dawn, she would lift the nutting stone and hammer old Snail Eye's brains out as he lay snoring in the lodge. She would mash them like a woman pounded squash while her husband kicked his life away.

But what then? She would run and her sister-wives would wake screaming. And then old Saya'hupahu would demand that she be put to the slow fire. As the chief's first wife, that would be Red Bird's right, for Ashagi was nothing but a captive and a slave and Kesamna'ista nothing but her master.

As she picked, thoughts of her mother and father arose in her mind and then drifted away, mere wisps of cloud she could no longer fully grasp. She remembered the raid on her own faraway village two years before. She remembered how her family had trembled in their lodge in the chill darkness before dawn when the dogs had begun howling outside, their voices intermingled with that of a wailing baby and the cries of the marauding Dakota.

The enemy had come running from the gray mantle of the forest like ghosts gliding through the fog...

Our sequel begins more than 400 years ago with an attack on a remote Ojibwe village by the aged war chief Secacha-pa, seeking revenge for the theft of his daughter, Bapakine.

But that's only the beginning of this saga which weaves a tale of 31 years in the life of an Ojibwe couple, well before the arrival of white traders and missionaries on the shores of Lake Superior.

At the heart of the story is a blood feud between two rival warriors over the love of Ashagi, a strong-willed woman of great beauty and greater determination. This, amid the struggles of an Ojibwe clan on the cusp of great change -- warring tribes, diseases from far-off invaders, and the onset of the Little Ice Age, which bedeviled the northern hemisphere of the world and its peoples. *Windigo Moon* is set 60 years after the events of *The Wolf and The Willow* and reintroduces the shaman, spy and trader, Animi-ma'lingan, He Who Outruns the Wolves.

Available in bookstores and online.

About the Author

The author of eight books, Robert Downes is a journalist of more than 30 years standing. A veteran cyclist and global backpacker, he and his wife Jeannette live in northern Lower Michigan when they are not traveling. www.robertdownes.com

Printed in the USA
CPSIA information can be obtained
at www.ICGtesting.com
LVHW042332060624
782564LV00030B/467